BABYLON SOUTH

On Monday, March 28, 1966 Sir Walter Springfellow, head of the Australian Security Intelligence Organization, left his home in Sydney to return to Melbourne. He got out of the car, walked into the airport terminal and disappeared. No body was ever found, and the case remained unsolved for twenty-one years.

As a young policeman Scobie Malone investigated the disappearance. Years later some bones are found up in the hills which are presumed to be Sir Walter's, and Detective Inspector Scobie Malone finds himself back on the case. His first task is to break the news to Venetia Springfellow, Sir Walter's glamorous widow, whose ruthless ambition has made of the Springfellow Corporation a hugely successful company.

Then comes news that there has been another death in the family, and one of the Springfellows is to be charged with murder. Police Commissioner John Leeds turns out to have every reason for taking a close interest in the case; but emotional involvement results in his putting unfair pressure on Scobie Malone. Always a straight cop and a decent man, Malone finds his divided loyalties extremely troubling.

Well told, gripping and shrewdly observed, *Babylon South* neatly dovetails two murder mysteries over a twenty-year period. It follows two previous Malone novels, *Dragons at the Party* and *Now and Then, Amen*, in which Cleary, using his detective as a camera eye, looks at life in Australia's largest city in the 1980s. *Babylon South* shows yet again the wit, the mastery of plot and suspense and the subtle characterization for which Jon Cleary is admired.

by the same author

YOU CAN'T SEE ROUND CORNERS
THE LONG SHADOW
JUST LET ME BE
THE SUNDOWNERS
THE CLIMATE OF COURAGE
JUSTIN BAYARD
THE GREEN HELMET
BACK OF SUNSET
NORTH FROM THURSDAY
THE COUNTRY OF MARRIAGE
FORESTS OF THE NIGHT
A FLIGHT OF CHARIOTS
THE FALL OF AN EAGLE
THE PULSE OF DANGER
THE HIGH COMMISSIONER
THE LONG PURSUIT
SEASON OF DOUBT
REMEMBER JACK HOXIE
HELGA'S WEB
MASK OF THE ANDES
MAN'S ESTATE
RANSOM
PETER'S PENCE
THE SAFE HOUSE
A SOUND OF LIGHTNING
HIGH ROAD TO CHINA
VORTEX
THE BEAUFORT SISTERS
A VERY PRIVATE WAR
GOLDEN SABRE
THE FARAWAY DRUMS
SPEARFIELD'S DAUGHTER
THE PHOENIX TREE
THE CITY OF FADING LIGHT
DRAGONS AT THE PARTY
NOW AND THEN, AMEN

JON CLEARY

BABYLON SOUTH

Gllss3ddd
F

COLLINS
8 Grafton Street, London W1
1989

William Collins Sons & Co. Ltd
London · Glasgow · Sydney · Auckland
Toronto · Johannesburg

C115559999
F. LG

First published 1989
Copyright © Sundowner Productions Pty Ltd 1989

BRITISH LIBRARY CATALOGUING IN PUBLICATION DATA

Cleary, Jon, *1917–*
Babylon south.
I. Title
823 (F)

ISBN 0 00 223534 X

Photoset in Linotron Times Roman at
The Spartan Press Ltd,
Lymington, Hants

Printed and bound in Great Britain by
William Collins Sons & Co. Ltd, Glasgow

FOR CATE

Prologue

On Monday March 28, 1966, Sir Walter Springfellow, Director-General of the Australian Security Intelligence Organization, left his home in Mosman in the city of Sydney to return to Melbourne and the then headquarters of ASIO. An ex-Justice of the Supreme Court of New South Wales, he had been Director-General of Security for only a year. It was his habit to fly up from Melbourne each Friday evening, spend the weekend with his wife and return to Melbourne on the 8 a.m. Monday flight of TAA. A Commonwealth car picked him up at his home this Monday morning, as it usually did, and delivered him to Kingsford Smith Airport at Mascot at 7.45. He got out of the car, said his usual courteous thank you to the driver, walked into the terminal and was never heard of again.

It had been a stormy weekend, though not, according to his wife, in the Springfellow home. A huge storm had blown up along the New South Wales coast and there had been considerable damage north of Sydney; the sea had been such that big swells had rolled into Sydney Harbour and for the first time surfies had ridden their boards down Middle Harbour. The storm, however, had not got beyond the Blue Mountains fifty miles west of the city and out on the plains there were cloudless skies and one of the worst droughts in twenty years. Down in Melbourne there had been an ugly demonstration against the sending of draftees to Vietnam and the Prime Minister, Harold Holt, had suffered a barrage of eggs and tomatoes, something a little softer than the draftees would have to face. The report on the demonstration and photographs of the egg and tomato bombardiers were waiting on the Director-General's desk for him. He would have smiled at such criminal acts, but only to himself.

He was fifty years old, handsome, came of a wealthy established family and had made a considerable reputation as a Queen's Counsel before being appointed a judge five years before. His appointment as Director-General had been welcomed by both major political parties, but the public were not invited to comment: national security was thought, in those days, too esoteric for public intelligence to comprehend. Sir Walter, who had been knighted just before his appointment, was considered by his own organization to have no enemies except, of course, the hundreds of criminals he had prosecuted or sentenced and the countless foreigners, traitors and activists his organization was seeking.

He had been married for two years to a beautiful wife, twenty-five years his junior, and it seemed that he lived in the best of all possible worlds. Though, naturally, he did not boast of that during his five days a week in Melbourne, a city which thought *it* was the best of all possible worlds.

'We were perfectly happy,' said Lady Springfellow. 'He must have been kidnapped or something. I just can't believe what's happened. When he took this job he warned me there might sometimes be trouble. But this . . . !'

The Commonwealth Police, who were in charge of airport security, had called in the New South Wales Police after consultation with ASIO. Scobie Malone was then a 21-year-old constable on temporary duty with the Missing Persons Bureau. Sergeant Harry Danforth, who couldn't trace a missing bull in a cattle chute, was in charge of the Bureau, but his men found that no handicap; a lazy man, he left them to their instinctive guesses and hunches. Missing persons usually leave fewer clues than murderers and the police assigned to trace them more often than not have to rely on guesswork. There were dozens of hunches as to the reason for the disappearance of Sir Walter Springfellow, but none of them led anywhere.

'It is some activist group,' said one of the two men ASIO had sent up from Melbourne. They were ex-Army Intelligence, middle-aged and military, and it was obvious they didn't have much time for the two younger men, recent university graduates, who represented ASIO's Sydney office. From where they sat the earth was flat, easily interpreted. 'We'll get some outlandish demand pretty soon.'

The Commonwealth Police inspector shrugged. He, too, was middle-aged, with a countryman's face, gullied and sun-blotched. He had transferred from a bush division of one of the State forces and sometimes he longed for those other, placid days. 'Could be. But three days have gone by and there's been nothing. They usually try to grab their publicity while everything's still on the front page. They're like politicians.' All the older men nodded: they had a common disrespect for politicians. Only Malone, who had never met one, kept his head still. 'What's your opinion on this, Bill?'

Senior Detective-Sergeant Zanuch, of the NSW Police Special Branch, had been seconded to this case by one of the Assistant Commissioners. Ordinary voters who disappeared could be left to a lazy sergeant and a few junior constables in Missing Persons; a senior public servant, a knight and an ex-judge at that, had to be given better treatment. Zanuch, the best-dressed man in the room by far, shot his cuffs, a sartorial trick none of the others, especially Malone, would ever master. 'Will our intelligence system suffer if we, h'm, don't get him back?'

The four ASIO men looked at each other, none of them wanting to be responsible for *that* sort of intelligence. At last the senior man from Melbourne said, 'We haven't even entertained that possibility.'

Malone sensed that Zanuch was less than impressed by that answer; he got the feeling that the ASIO men, especially the two from Melbourne, resented having to call in outsiders. It was their job to find spies and now they couldn't find even their own boss.

9

Zanuch's voice was suddenly a little sour: 'I take it you've seen Lady Springfellow? Good. But I think Constable Malone and I will go over and have a word with her. We can't rule out the possibility of personal problems.'

'The Director-General?' said one of the ex-military men, a happily married man whose wife knew when to stand to attention. 'Ridiculous!'

Malone wanted to ask why it should be ridiculous, but he was too junior and, anyhow, what did he know about life and marriage? At that time he was on a merry-go-round with three different girls, jumping on and off to run for his life before one of them could tempt him into a commitment. The two men from Melbourne, as if reading the question in his mind, glowered at him. The two university men from Sydney knew enough about life not to argue with the men from headquarters, especially ex-military types.

'Do you vet each other's personal relationships?' said Zanuch.

Again all four ASIO men looked at each other, then the senior man answered, 'That's classified.'

'Of course,' said Zanuch, but frowned when Malone made the mistake of smiling. 'Well, we'll go over and see what Lady Springfellow has to say.'

'We'll come with you,' said the senior man from headquarters.

'No,' said Zanuch. 'Our investigations are always classified.'

He and Malone drove over to Mosman, with Malone at the wheel. 'Do you know this part of the world, Constable?'

Malone had never met Zanuch before today; but he had been warned of the senior man's regard for rank. He was known to be ambitious and had used the heads of junior men as stepping stones on his way up. His one handicap, in the police force of those days, was that he was totally honest, a character fault that didn't endear him to certain of his seniors.

10

'No, Sarge, I come from the south side of the harbour. I've played cricket at Mosman Oval, but that's all. I was born in Erskineville and so far I've only worked at Newtown and in the Bureau.' Even in his own ears it all at once sounded as if he came from Central Africa or some other remote region.

'You'll notice the difference here in Mosman. They invented respectability – they think they have the copyright on it. The Springfellows more than any of them.' Then he looked sideways at Malone. 'If you're going to work with me, Constable, could you smarten yourself up a little? Where did you get that bloody awful tie?'

'My mother. She's Irish, she thinks green goes with anything.'

'That's not just green, it's bilious. I'm sure your mother is a wonderful old biddy, but she's colour blind.'

So was Malone, or almost; but he was not blind to snobbery. Zanuch was out to impress whoever lay ahead of them. As the unmarked police car turned into the short dead-end street, Zanuch looked out at the sign. 'Springfellow Avenue. That's something, to have your own street.'

'My mum tells me there's a Malone Street in Dublin.'

Zanuch wasn't impressed. He was scanning the imposing houses on either side of them. It was not a policeman's look; it was that of a social climber. Anyone who lived hereabouts would be in his good books.

'Do you come from this side, Sarge?' Malone said innocently as they got out of the car.

Zanuch gave him a look that should have reduced him to a cadet. 'No,' he said shortly and Malone wondered if he, too, came from Central Africa or its equivalent.

The Springfellow house and grounds were the most imposing in the street. The housekeeper who opened the big front door was just as impressive. Starched and polished, she carried herself with all the confidence of someone who knew that, below her, all the voters, including policemen, ran down to the bottom of the heap.

11

'I shall see if Lady Springfellow will see you.' She went away as if to consult with the Queen of Australia.

But Zanuch was still impressed. 'You can now see how the other half lives, Constable. It may give you some ambition.'

'On my pay?' But he had the sense to grin as he said it and Zanuch, after a moment, found a smile that didn't hurt him too much.

The housekeeper came back and ushered them into the house. Malone, in those days, had little sense of surroundings. Erskineville, where he had grown up, with its tenement terraces and small factories, had never been a major subscription area for *House and Garden*. Now, as the starched Grenadier Guard took them towards the back of the house, he was aware only that this was a large place with large rooms where shadows and dark panelling seemed to dominate. But the young woman who came into the big drawing-room suggested all lightness and brightness, even though she was not smiling.

'I'm Lady Springfellow,' she said, then gestured at the slightly older woman of darker mood who had followed her into the room. 'This is my husband's sister, Miss Emma Springfellow.'

Zanuch introduced himself and then, as an afterthought, Malone. He shot his cuffs and was all police department charm, something Malone had never experienced before. '. . . If you could just dig into your memory, Lady Springfellow, give us some hint that your husband may have let drop in the past week or two, something that was worrying him . . .'

Venetia Springfellow shook her golden head. She was Venetia Magee to a million television viewers; but that was another territory, there she was another person. Malone had seen her occasionally on television, but he was not enthusiastic about daytime TV, unless it was a cricket telecast, and hers was a midday chat show. She was undeniably good-looking, but it seemed to him that she had looked better on TV. Still, with the simple candid curiosity of the young, he wondered what a good sort like her had seen in a man twenty-five years her senior.

'Nothing, he told me nothing about ASIO business.' She had a throaty voice that was not quite natural; the vowels had been worked on, were plummy ripe. 'His only regret was that we were separated for five days each week, he with his job in Melbourne and I with mine in Sydney. But we were going to change that – we were going to live in Melbourne when I had my baby.' For the first time Malone noticed the swelling under the well-cut silk suit with its long jacket.

'You didn't tell me – ' said Emma Springfellow; then stopped. She could have been a beautiful woman if she had had more vanity; beside the beautifully groomed Venetia she looked like someone who never glanced in a mirror. 'But then . . .'

'But what?' said Zanuch.

'Nothing.' She seemed to hesitate for a moment, then was steelily at ease.

'Do you live here, Miss Springfellow?'

'No. I used to, until my brother married.' She had half-turned away, as if she were trying to distance herself from her sister-in-law. 'I live across the street with my brother Edwin and his wife. This house used to be the family home.'

It still was, to her; but she had been exiled.

There was an awkward moment of frozen silence. Then Zanuch turned back to Venetia Springfellow. 'I apologize for asking this – but was there any disagreement between you and your husband? Could he have just gone away for a few days to think over something that had happened between you?'

Her gaze was steady, she looked unoffended by the question. 'No. We have never had a cross word in all the time we've been married.'

Zanuch looked at Emma Springfellow. She had been gazing out the window, as if she no longer had any interest in what was being said. She seemed to start when she became aware that Zanuch was waiting for her to comment. 'Am I supposed to say something? To contradict my sister-in-law?'

'Not at all,' said Zanuch. 'Did he have any disagreement with you? Or any other member of the family? You have only the one other brother, haven't you?'

'Yes. No, we had no disagreement. We were always a very close family.' But her tone said that no longer held true. Malone saw Venetia flinch and he sensed that the gap between the two women was much wider than the four or five feet of carpet that separated them. Emma said, 'You're wasting your time, Sergeant, with that line.'

'We have to try every line,' said Zanuch. Malone had the feeling that he was now less impressed with Mosman. 'I'm sure your brother, running ASIO, would appreciate that.'

'I'm sure he would,' said Venetia Springfellow, not looking at her sister-in-law.

'Did your husband draw any money out of his bank account?' Malone was learning from Zanuch: the senior man knew how to change his line abruptly.

'Not that I know of. We're not the sort who have joint accounts.' There was just a note of snobbery in the answer: Venetia Springfellow, or Magee, wherever she had come from, had also learned.

'Where did Sir Walter bank?'

'The Bank of New South Wales. Their head office.'

'Were you the last to speak to him, other than the driver who took him to the airport?'

'I think so. No –' She hesitated.

'Go on,' said Zanuch carefully.

Venetia glanced at Emma. 'I was at the front door – my sister-in-law ran across the street to say something to my husband.'

Zanuch waited for Emma Springfellow to volunteer something. Malone, callow in the ways of woman against woman, yet knew that he and Zanuch were on the outskirts of a female war. On the beat, as a probationary constable in Newtown, he had seen women fight like men, with fists, or anyway claws, and language that had had a nice medieval ring to it. This, however, was different, somehow more

14

deadly. Knives would be used here, with good manners and kid gloves and decorous malice.

'It was private,' Emma said at last. 'Nothing important.'

'Nothing that would have upset him?'

'I told you – it was unimportant.'

The two policemen stayed only another few minutes, getting nowhere. Venetia Springfellow took them to the front door, thanking them for coming; she could have been ushering out two guests from her chat show. 'Do call me, Sergeant, if you have any more questions. We want my husband back home as soon as possible . . .' Then she glanced over her shoulder at Emma standing in the shadows of the big hallway like a bit-part player whom the cameraman had missed. 'All the family does.'

In the car as they drove away Zanuch said, 'Well, what do you think?'

'If I was the Director-General, I'd have run away from the sister, not the wife.'

'Don't put that opinion in the running sheet. No, I don't think this is a domestic.' Domestic situations were the bane of a cop's life. You might fight with your own wife, but that was no training for interfering in a battle between another warring couple; nine times out of ten both husband and wife told you to go to hell and mind your own business. Except, of course, in Mosman, where the domestic battles would always be fought in whispers and the police would never be called. 'ASIO are probably right, it's some activist group. If it is, that'll be a Commonwealth job, we'll let them worry about it. Keep an eye on it and let me know what you're up to. Check Sir Walter's account at his bank. I'll tell Sergeant Danforth you're to be kept on it for a month.'

'I'm taking a week's leave this Friday, Sarge. I'm going to Hong Kong to play cricket.' That past summer he had played his first season in the State team. 'Australia's most promising fast bowler', a cricket writer had called him after Malone had bought him three beers. 'The Department thinks it's good PR, a cop who's a State fast bowler.'

15

'What would they think if he was a slow bowler?' Zanuch's Latvian parents had brought him to Australia when he was one year old; thirty-four years later there were still certain Australian customs he didn't understand or want to. Sometimes the original white Australians were as puzzling and annoying as the more original Aborigines. 'Have you got your priorities right? We're supposed to be looking for the country's top spy, for Chrissakes!'

Malone said meekly, 'I'll check the bank account.'

Which he did, that afternoon. No money had been drawn from Sir Walter Springfellow's account. 'But I believe he had – has – an account with our Melbourne main branch,' said the bank's manager.

Malone called Melbourne. There was some hesitation at the other end, then the manager there said, 'I'm sorry, officer, we can't give out that information. I suggest you contact ASIO.'

Malone hung up, sat frowning till Sergeant Danforth came lumbering across the room towards him. 'What's the matter, son?'

Malone explained the unexpected blank wall he had run into. 'Do I call ASIO or pass it on to Sergeant Zanuch to handle?'

Danforth dropped heavily into a chair; he had never been known to remain standing for longer than ten seconds. He was a tall, heavily built man, old-fashioned in dress, haircut and manner; he looked like someone who had been left over from the 1940s and wished he were still back in those days. He was only fifteen or so years older than Malone, but two generations could have separated them. 'Ring ASIO. If you don't get anywhere with them, let it slide. We won't wanna get ourselves caught up in any politics.' That was laziness, not wisdom, speaking. 'You know what politics is like, son.'

At that stage of his career Malone knew nothing about politics; but he was prepared to take Danforth's advice. He rang Melbourne and after some interruptions and hesitations was put through to the Deputy Director-General. 'Ah yes,

Constable – Malone, is it? Yes, we have asked the bank to put a stop on any enquiries about Sir Walter's personal affairs. We have looked into it and there is nothing there.'

'Then why stop any enquiries, sir?' Malone was on his way to making his later fame, the asking of undiplomatic questions of higher authority.

'I'm afraid that's classified, constable. Good day.'

The phone went dead in Malone's ear. He hung up and looked at Danforth, still lolling in the chair opposite him. 'They told us to get lost, Sarge.'

'You see, son? Politics.'

So Malone went to Hong Kong to play cricket in front of the English expatriates who murmured 'Good shot!' and 'Well caught, sir!' while the other 99 per cent of the colony shuffled by and inscrutably scrutinized the white flannelled fools who played this foolish game while the end of the world, 1997, was only thirty-one years away. Malone, who took fourteen wickets in the two matches played and, every decent fast bowler's dream, retired two batsmen hurt, was as short-sighted and oblivious as any of the other fools. They all had their priorities right.

When he came back Sir Walter Springfellow was still missing and ASIO and the Commonwealth Police had taken the case unto themselves. Detective-Sergeant Zanuch had gone from Special Branch to the Fraud Squad and Malone himself was transferred from Missing Persons to the Pillage Squad on the wharves.

On Sunday July 17, four months after her father had disappeared, Justine Springfellow was born. By then the file on Sir Walter Springfellow had been put away in the back of a Missing Persons cabinet drawer and Sergeant Danforth, soon to be told to get to his feet and join the Vice Squad, conveniently forgot about it.

Sir Walter's disappearance would remain a mystery for another twenty-one years.

17

ONE

1

By sheer coincidence, without which no successful policeman could function, Detective-Inspector Scobie Malone
was, indirectly, working for Venetia Springfellow when the
skeleton of a middle-aged man was found in some scrub in
the mountains west of Sydney.

'Up near Blackheath. I thought you might like to talk to
the lady,' said Sergeant Russ Clements, calling from Homicide. 'It looks as if it might be her late hubby, Sir Walter.
They tell me she's out there at the studio.'

'Are they sure it's him?'

'Pretty sure. The upper and lower jaws are missing, so they
can't check on the teeth. It looks as if the whole lower part of
the face was blasted away.'

'How did we get into it?' Meaning Homicide.

'There's no weapon, no gun, nothing. The detectives up at
Blackheath have ruled out suicide – for the moment,
anyway. Unless someone found the body, didn't report it but
pinched the gun.'

'What's the identification then?'

'There's a signet ring on one of the fingers – it has his
initials on it. There's also a briefcase with his initials on it.'

'Anything in the briefcase?'

'Empty. That's why the Blackheath boys think it's murder
– if someone had stolen the gun, supposing he'd suicided,
they'd have taken the ring and the briefcase, too. It's him, all
right. You want to prepare her for the bad news? They'll

come out later to tell her officially, get her to identify the ring and the briefcase.'

'Are we on the job – officially?'

'Yep. I just came back from my broker's and there was the docket on your desk.'

'From your *who*?'

'My stockbroker.'

'What happened to your bookie?'

'I'll tell you later. You gunna tell her?'

Malone hesitated. He hated that part of police work, the bringing of bad news to a family. Certainly the Springfellow family had had twenty-one years to prepare itself; it must by now have given up hope that Walter Springfellow was still alive. Nonetheless, someone had to tell the widow and, for better or worse, he was the man on the spot.

'Righto, I'll tell her. Can you come out and pick me up?'

'What about *Woolloomooloo Vice*?' It was their private joke.

'You wouldn't believe what they're shooting today. The actor playing you wears a gold bracelet and suede shoes.'

'I'll sue 'em.'

Malone hung up and smiled at the assistant floor manager who had brought him to the phone. She was a jeans-clad wind-up doll, one year out of film school, bursting with self-importance and programmed to talk only in jargon. She was always explaining to Malone how the *dynamics* of a scene worked. She was intrigued at the dynamics of Malone's call. 'A homicide, Scobie? A real one?'

He nodded. 'A real one, Debby. Where will I find Lady Springfellow?'

'Holy shit, Lady Springfellow! Is she involved?'

'Imagine the dynamics of that, eh?'

He grinned at her and went back on the set to tell the director he would not be available for the rest of the day. He welcomed the escape, even if he could have done with better circumstances; he could not remember disliking an assignment more than this one. *Sydney Beat*, an Australian–

20

American co-production, was a thirteen-part series and he was supposed to spend one day each week with the production as technical adviser. This was the third week and so far it had all been purgatory.

Simon Twitchell, the director, was another film-school graduate; he had majored in temperament. 'Oh God, what is it this time? You're always pissing off when we need you – '

Malone wanted to king-hit him, but Twitchell was small and dainty and Malone didn't want to break him in half like a cheesestick. He also had in mind that, though *Sydney Beat* was supposed to be a police series, the crew and the cast, all at least ten to twenty years younger than Malone, had no time for real cops, the fuzz and the pigs. Sovfilm, making a John Wayne movie, would have been more respectful.

'I was pissed off the day I walked in here,' said Malone keeping his temper.

Then Gus Leroy, the producer, came out of the shadows and into the lights. He was a short, round man who always dressed in black and whose moods and humour could be the same colour. 'What the fuck's the matter this time?' All his aggression, like Twitchell's, was in his language; they would leave bigger men to do their fighting for them. 'You're always fucking nit-picking. What's wrong this time?'

'You mean with the production?' All at once Malone saw the opportunity to escape from this farce for good. 'It'll never get the ratings. Every crim in the country will laugh their heads off – they'll think it's the *Benny Hill Show*. I have to go and see Lady Springfellow. Hooroo, in case I don't come back.'

He walked across the set, watched by the crew and cast. The set was a permanent one, the apartment of the series' hero, a detective-sergeant. Malone had criticized it, saying its luxury would embarrass even the Commissioner, but Leroy had told him they hadn't engaged him as a design consultant. He, an American, knew what American audiences liked and this series was aimed at the American market. Malone walked past a backdrop of Sydney Harbour, a panorama only a millionaire could afford, and out of the sound stage. As the heavy sound-proof door wheezed to behind him, it sounded like an amplification of his own sigh of relief. He would be hauled over the coals tomorrow at Police Headquarters, but that was something he could weather. He had gone in one step from being an adviser to being a critic and he felt the smug satisfaction that is endemic to all critics, even amateurs.

It took him several minutes to get to see Lady Spring-fellow; it seemed that she had more minders than the Prime Minister. Perhaps the richest woman in the land was entitled to them; there was no reason why rich women should be more accessible than rich men. All at once he longed for a call to go and interview someone out amongst the battlers in the western suburbs, someone alone and without minders. But not to give him or her bad news.

'Lady Springfellow says what is it about?' The last line of defence was an Asian secretary, a beautiful Singapore-Chinese with her blue-black hair cut in a Twenties bob and her demeanour just as severe. Malone could see her guarding the Forbidden City in old Peking with a two-edged sword and no compunction about chopping off a head or two.

'I'll tell her when I see her,' he said evenly.

The secretary stared at him, looking him up and down in sections. She saw a tall, well-built man in his early forties, who was not handsome but might be distinguished-looking in his old age, long-jawed and blue-eyed and with a wide good-humoured mouth that, she guessed correctly, could be mean and determined when obstacles were put in his way.

'I'll see what she says to that.' In her Oriental way she could be just as stubborn. But when she came back from the inner office she produced an unexpected smile, though it might have been malicious. 'Watch your step, Inspector.'

'Oh, I always do that,' he said, but there were some in the Department, including the Commissioner, who would have disputed that.

22

Malone had been told that the Channel 15 network was being done over in its new owner's image. The previous colour scheme of the network, from ashtrays to screen logo, had been bright blue and orange, a combination that had brought on a generational bout of conjunctivitis known to ophthalmologists from Perth to Cairns as 'Channel 15 eye'. The new owner had insisted on muted pink and grey, a choice that had viewers, on tuning into the new network logo, fiddling with their controls. The natives liked *colour*, otherwise what was the point of owning a colour set? Even Bill Cosby had a purple tinge on Australian screens.

The chief executive's office was pink and grey; so was the chief executive, Roger Dircks, who sat in a chair at one side. The owner herself sat behind the big modern desk; reigning queens do not squat on their own footstools. She was dressed in pink slacks and shirt, grey calf-length boots and had a pink and grey silk scarf tied round her shoulders. A pink cashmere cardigan was draped over the chair behind her.

'So you're the estimable Inspector Malone?' He had never been called estimable before, not even by the better educated, unembittered crims. 'What do you think of our series?'

He thought he had better get that out of the way at once. 'I have an eight-year-old daughter – she'll love it.'

'It's not being made for eight-year-olds.' The throaty voice suddenly turned chilly, an icy wind over the rocks. 'What's wrong with it?'

'Lady Springfellow, that's not why I'm here. It's something more important – and I think it will upset you.'

Venetia went stiff without moving. He had not seen her in person since that visit to her home in Mosman long ago and he was surprised how little she seemed to have changed. True, there were signs of age, but she had lasted remarkably well. Her skin and jawline had kept their own suspension, there had been no need for lifting, and her blonde hair was still thick and lustrous. Even her mouth had somehow missed that thinning of the lips that comes to ageing women, as if

23

pursing them at the misdeeds of men has worn away their youthful fullness. But then rumour said that Venetia Spring-fellow had never tired of men and was careless of their misdeeds, except in business. She was regal amongst her commoner lovers. Money and power turn a beautiful woman into a fantasy.

'Upset me, Inspector? Then it must be something dread-ful.'

Malone told her, as gently as he could. 'They're certain it's your husband.'

Venetia blinked; but there was no sign of tears. She looked at Roger Dircks, who moved his small mouth as if he were trying to find words to fit it. He was a tall, plump man in his early fifties, with a smooth pink face under a pelt of grey hair that lay on his small head like a bathing-cap. He was dressed in a grey wool suit with a pink shirt and a grey silk tie. Malone, in his polyester blue, felt like an ink-blot on a pale watercolour.

Dircks stood up, moved towards Venetia, then stopped. One did not lay a hand on the Queen Bee, even in sympathy; she was to be touched only by invitation. At last he said, 'This is God-awful, Venetia! It's the last thing you want –'

'Of course it's the last thing I want,' she said coldly. 'You have a talent for the *bon mot*, Roger.'

Malone had an abrupt feeling of *déjà vu*; the last time he had met Venetia Springfellow there had been animosity between her and someone else – had it been her sister-in-law? He wasn't sure; he had forgotten the case till he had come here to the studio and learned that Lady Springfellow was the new boss.

'Do I have to – to identify him, Inspector?'

'No, I think you can be spared that. There's only a skeleton.' She winced a little, as if she found it hard to believe that that was all that was left of a loved one. 'But they'll ask you to identify the ring and the briefcase.'

She said nothing for a while, looking at him and through him. Then she frowned, her gaze focusing. 'I have a memory for faces and names. Haven't I seen you before somewhere?'

24

'Years ago. I came with Sergeant Zanuch to interview you when your husband first disappeared. He's an Assistant Commissioner now.'

She nodded, looked abstracted again. Malone studied her while he waited for her to make the next move. She had come a long way from Venetia Magee, the midday TV hostess of the Sixties; he had never known where she had stood in the ratings, but it had been reasonably high. Her biggest cachet was that she had married into the Springfellow family; old money had meant more then than it did now. Now, of course, she had *new* money, her own, trainloads of it. He could only guess at what she owned, maybe even a major part of the country. She was the only woman amongst the nation's twenty richest voters, a rose amongst some very prickly males who, it seemed, were always photographed looking sideways, as if they expected her to sneak up in ambush on them. It was said that if she wore her success lightly, others wore it heavily. She was a boss to be feared.

She said, 'Did he die – naturally? Or suicide or what?'

'They think it was murder.' He didn't want to describe the state of the dead man's skull. The bereaved should be left with proper memories.

'Murdered?' She frowned again and suddenly, just for a moment, seemed to age.

Then the door opened and a young girl stood there. 'Mother – oh, I'm sorry. I didn't know you –'

'Come in, darling.' Venetia had recovered, the lines disappearing from her face. 'This is Inspector Malone – he's just brought me some bad news. This is my daughter Justine.'

Venetia and Justine: whatever happened to good old names like Dot and Shirl? The daughter had a resemblance to her mother, though she was more beautiful, her features more perfect; she had dark hair, instead of her mother's blonde, but it was cut in the same full style. She was dressed as stylishly as Venetia, though not in pink and grey. She was in a blue silk suit and Malone didn't feel quite so much of a

25

blot. She had all the looks, but there was something missing: her mother's shadow dimmed the edges of her.

'Bad news? What bad news?'

'They have found your father's – skeleton.' The image was still troubling her. A collection of old bones: could one have once loved that? 'Somewhere up in the Blue Mountains.'

'Blackheath,' said Malone.

Justine sat down in one of the grey chairs. Dircks moved to her and put his hand on her shoulder; she was touchable, her mother's daughter but not yet the boss. 'It's dreadful, love. You don't need such a shock –' Then he looked at Venetia, knowing he had said the wrong thing again. His shallowness had less depth than one would have thought. He had risen to this position as chief executive only because he was a survivor; he had no talent, managerial or creative, but that often wasn't necessary in the entertainment business. Selling oneself was as important as selling air-time and up till now he had sold himself well. 'I'll get your driver to take you both home –'

'No,' said Venetia. 'We'll finish our business first. After – what? – twenty-one years, another half-hour . . . When will you bring the ring and the briefcase, Inspector, for me to identify?'

'The Scientific men will bring that, I guess.'

'Was there nothing else? His clothes?'

'They didn't mention any. Can you remember what he was wearing when he disappeared?'

She shook her head. 'Of course not. All those years ago? There would have been a label in them – he had everything made at Cutlers – he prided himself on the way he dressed.'

'I'll see they bring everything to you that they've found. I have to go up to Blackheath now.'

'To the scene of the crime?' said Dircks, once more saying the wrong thing.

'Crime?' Justine spoke for the first time since she had sat down. She had just been presented with the discovery of the skeleton of the father she had never known. All her life she had felt a sense of loss at never knowing him and often, even these days, she sat in front of the photograph of him in the Springfellow drawing-room and wondered how much she would have loved the rather stern-looking, handsome man who had sired her. She had dreamed as a child, as a schoolgirl, even now as a young woman, that he was still alive, that some day he would come out of the past, like a figure in a mirage, and into their lives again. It gave her a shock and a terrible sense of final loss to learn that only his bones were left. 'What crime?'

Venetia looked at Malone: there were certain things a mother should not have to tell her daughter. He caught her unspoken plea and said, 'We think your father was murdered. I'm going up to Blackheath to start the investigation.'

'Murdered?' All her conversation so far had been questions. Malone had seen it before; shock could leave some people only with questions.

'It's only a guess at the moment,' he said gently. 'It's not going to be easy to find out exactly what happened, not after so long.'

He was at the door when Dircks, foot in mouth again, said, 'You didn't tell us what's wrong with our series.'

Malone noticed that, though Venetia was annoyed, she was waiting on his reply. 'The cops solve everything too easily. It never happens that way, not in real life.'

2

A studio car had picked up Malone each week and brought him out here to Carlingford on the inner edge of the western suburbs. The studio, surrounded by landscaped grounds, backed on to a Housing Commission development; the Commission residents, battlers all, looked over their back fences at the factory where their dreams were made. They waved to the stars of the soaps who drove in every day; stars dim and tiny, but any galaxy is a relief from the kitchen sink and the ironing-board and a husband who thinks foreplay is a rugby league warm-up. One morning a woman had waved to Malone and he had waved back, hoping she had not recognized her mistake. He hated to disappoint people.

The driver got out of his car when he saw Malone come out of the front door of the administration building; but the detective waved him back. He stood on the front steps, savouring the mild sunny day. October was a good month; it brought the jacaranda blooms, one of his favourite sights. The landscape designer had planted jacarandas, interspersed with the occasional flame tree, all along the front fence of the big gardens; Malone wondered if, with the new owner, he would be told to replace them with pink blossom trees and grey gums. But Venetia Springfellow, he guessed, was an indoors person and probably never noticed the outdoors through which she passed. The seasons would mean nothing to her, except the financial ones. He wondered if he was going to finish up disliking her.

Russ Clements arrived fifteen minutes later in the unmarked police Falcon. It was a new car, so far with not a scratch or a dent in it. The State government, with an election due within months, had embarked on a new law and order policy; the police had benefited, with new cars, new computers, even a couple of new helicopters. There were fewer muggings in the streets but more in the gaols, which the government was claiming was an improvement. The voters, cynical of politics, gave no hint of how they would vote in the elections. They knew when *they* were being mugged.

Malone got into the car and Clements headed west towards the Blue Mountains. The new car had not improved his appearance; he was as unkempt as ever, a big lumbering man who looked as if he had slept in his clothes. He was the same age as Malone, still a bachelor, and Lisa Malone was forever promising to find him a wife, an offer he always received with a grin but no enthusiasm.

'So how'd the Queen Bee take it?' A gossip columnist in the financial pages of the *Herald*, a man of infinite imagination, had given her that name and now it was common usage, even amongst those who were not her drones.

'She's a cool bitch.' Why had he called her a bitch? He would have to watch out, to kill his prejudices before they grew too far. 'But I think she was shocked.'

'I was in the Springfellow offices this morning. They're my stockbrokers.' He grinned at Malone's querying eyebrow. 'It's not coincidence. I've been with them since the beginning of the year. They can't get over having me as a client. I have to keep telling 'em I'm not with the Fraud Squad.'

'She has nothing to do with the broking firm, has she?'

'Only as the biggest shareholder in the holding corporation. She has nothing to do with the day-to-day running of it.'

'So what are you doing with a broker?'

Clements's grin widened. 'I've been winning so much on the ponies, it was getting embarrassing. I was going into the bank every Monday morning putting in three or four hundred bucks every time. The tellers were starting to look suspicious. How could I tell 'em I was just an honest cop having luck at the races? So I started investing some of it on the stock market – this boom looks too good to be true.'

'The boom can't last.'

Clements nodded. 'That's why I was in their office this morning. I'm thinking of selling everything. All good stuff, Amcor, Boral, Brambles – but even they can't keep going up and up. You should've got into the market.'

'That's what Lisa's dad told me. But they won't take mortgages as a payment.'

'From what I hear, some of the yuppies have paid with nothing else. They're buying futures.'

'It's not for me.' He had never dreamed of wealth and so he would always be an honest cop.

They drove on out of the city up into the mountains where lay the bones of a man whose future had ended twenty-one years ago. Two local police were waiting for them, a detective-sergeant and a uniformed constable. They led the way in their marked car out through the small town, past the comfortable homes of retirees and the holiday guest-houses, to bushland that showed the occasional black scars of the past summer's fires. The two cars turned down a narrow side-road that led down to thick bush. Beyond and below was the Grose Valley, its perpendicular rock walls glinting in the sun like stacked metal, its grey-green forest floor thick and daunting as quicksand. Hikers were being lost in it every weekend, the police always being called in to help find them.

They started down the track that had been hacked out of the bush when they had carried out the bones yesterday. The young constable went ahead, occasionally slowing up to look back sympathetically at the three older men. He was all lean muscle and Malone wondered if he spent his spare time rock-climbing. This was the ideal beat for it.

The detective, Sam Pilbrow, pulled up to get his breath. 'There used to be a track right down here years ago. You could drive a vehicle down it for another half a mile.' He was in his middle forties, years and circumference, and walking obviously was not a hobby with him. He would never volunteer to find a lost hiker. 'Well, I guess we gotta keep going.'

At last they came to a tiny clearing where the bushes had been chopped off and thrown aside. White taping fenced the clearing, but no attempt had been made to outline where the skeleton had been.

'We didn't reckon it was worth it.' Pilbrow was a cop who would always weigh up the worth of doing anything. He had started in this town and would finish here. 'We've combed the area –' He swung a big thick arm. 'All we come up with were the ring and the briefcase and one shell. My guess is it was probably from a Colt .45. That would account for the way the jaw was smashed, with the gun held close. It could have been an execution.'

'Judges aren't executed, except by terrorists,' said Clements. 'And we didn't have any of them back in the Sixties.'

'Well, he was ASIO, wasn't he? You never know what happens in that game.' Pilbrow read spy stories.

'Who found him?'

'Some hikers. By accident – they got off the track that leads down into the valley. He could have laid here for another twenty years or whatever it was.' He really wasn't interested in such an old case.

'Any sign of clothes?'

'Nothing. If everything he wore was natural fibre, if it was all cotton and wool, the weather would have destroyed it. Or birds might've taken it for their nests. Even his shoes were gone. The briefcase is pretty worn.'

'Any bushfires through this part?'

'Not down here on the lip. If there had been, we'd probably have found the bones years ago.'

Malone looked out at the valley, wondering what peculiar fate had brought Sir Walter Springfellow to this lonely spot. Down below him two currawongs planed along, their ululating cries somehow matching in sound their oddly swooping flight. Out above the valley a hawk hung in the blue air like a brown cross looking for an altar; far down amongst the trees the sun caught a pool of water and for a moment a bright silver shard lay amidst the grey-green quicksand. He could see no sign for miles of any human activity.

'You questioned any of the locals?'

'Who'd remember back that far?' said Pilbrow. 'Yeah, we questioned them. This used to be a lovers' lane in those days, but there were no lovers down here the night he was killed. Or if there was, they're married to someone else now and got kids and moved elsewhere. I don't think you're gunna get far with this one, Inspector. There's bugger-all to start with.'

Malone nodded; then said, 'Maybe this isn't the place to start.'

He thanked Pilbrow and the constable for their help, said he'd be in touch if he wanted any more information; nodded to Clements and led the way back up the track, not bothering to wait for the toiling Pilbrow. He knew the local detective would think him rude and arrogant, a typical bastard from the city, but he felt he owed the lazy, overweight man nothing. Pilbrow would just as soon see the file on Sir Walter Springfellow remain closed.

Malone and Clements drove back to Sydney. It started to rain as they got to the outskirts and Malone looked back at the mountains, gone now in the grey drizzle. It somehow seemed an omen, a mist that would perhaps hide for ever the mystery of Sir Walter Springfellow.

'What's happening to the, er, remains?'

'They're at the City Morgue,' said Clements. 'I guess the family will reclaim them. They'll bury 'em, I suppose. You can't cremate bones, can you?'

'They do. Whatever they do, it all seems a bit late now. If there's a funeral, we'll go to it. See who turns up to pay their respects.'

'Where to now? I've never worked on a homicide that's twenty-one years old. I feel like a bloody archaeologist.'

'That's where we start, then. Twenty-one years ago. When we get back to town, go to Missing Persons and dig out the file on Walter Springfellow.'

They reached the city, threaded their way through the traffic and turned into the Remington Rand building where Homicide, incongruously, rented its headquarters space amongst other government branches. Sydney had started as a convict settlement two hundred years ago and it seemed to Malone that it was only back then that the police had been together as a cohesive unit.

Clements went across to Missing Persons in Police Headquarters in Liverpool Street. The NSW Police Department was spread around the city as if its various divisions and bureaux could not abide each other, a decentralization of jealousies.

He was back within half an hour. 'The file on Springfellow is missing. It just ain't there.'

'When did it go missing?'

'That's what I've been looking up. A file is usually kept for twenty to twenty-five years, there's no set time. Every five years they go through them, cull them. There's an index. Springfellow's name disappeared from the index a year after he went missing, which means someone lifted his file before then.'

'Do we go back to the family, then?' Malone asked the question of himself as much as Clements. 'No, we'll let them bury him first. They've been waiting a long time to do that.'

Clements looked at him, but he had meant no more than he had said.

3

'Oh Daddy! You've *resigned* from TV? And I've told everyone at school you were the director!' Maureen, the eight-year-old TV addict, was devastated.

'Well, it was crap anyway,' said Claire, the thirteen-year-old who was reading modern playwrights at school this year.

'Everything's crap,' said Tom, the six-year-old who read nothing but majored in listening.

Lisa cuffed both of them across the ear, a smack that hurt. She was totally unlike the mothers one saw on television, especially American moms who had never been seen to raise a hand against even child monsters. She had left Holland as an infant and there was none of the new Dutch permissiveness about her. Had she lived in Amsterdam she would have cleaned up the city in a week. Instead, she lived in this eighty-year-old house in Randwick, one of Sydney's less affluent eastern suburbs, and she kept it as unpolluted as she could. Malone sometimes referred to her as his Old Dutch Cleanser.

'Watch your language,' he said, 'or I'll run the lot of you in.'

'Isn't there any bad language in *Sydney Beat*?' asked Maureen. 'Oh God, Daddy, I'm so angry with you! I was going to bring all the girls home for your autograph. I wanted Mum to have Justin Muldoon home for dinner one night –' Justin

Muldoon was the star of the show, an actor who, Malone had told Clements, changed expressions by numbers.

'That's enough of that,' said Lisa. 'Dad's on a case. That's a detective's job, not sitting around a TV studio.'

'Talking to actresses, you mean?' said Claire, a junior cadet getting ready for the battle of the sexes.

'Is that what you do?' said Lisa.

'Sometimes they sit in my lap, but it's all official duty.' They smiled at each other, knowing how much they trusted one another.

'Are you on another homicide?' said Tom, who had just learned what the word meant.

'No,' said Malone, who tried to keep any mention of murder out of the house. This was his haven, something that Lisa did her best to maintain.

Later, while the two girls were doing the washing-up and Tom was having his shower, Lisa came into the living-room and sat beside Malone in front of the television set. 'Anything on the news?'

'Nothing that interests us. Which is the way I like it.'

He held her hand, lifting it and kissing it. In public he was held back by the stiffness with affection he had inherited from his mother and father, but in private he was full of affectionate gestures towards Lisa and the children. In his heart he knew he was making up for the lack of affection shown by his parents towards him, their one and only. They loved him, he knew that, but they were both too awkward to express it. He never wanted Lisa or the children to say that about him.

Lisa stroked his cheek, not needing to say anything. She was close to forty, but had kept her looks: regular features, faintly tanned skin, blonde hair worn long this year and pulled back in a chignon, blue eyes that could be both shrewd and sexy, and a full figure that still excited him. She could hold the world at bay; but, he hoped, never him.

'The stock market's still going up,' he said, but, having no money invested, it meant nothing to either of them. 'Your father must . . . Ah, I wondered if they were going to mention it.'

Richard Morecroft, the ABC news announcer, was saying, 'The skeleton of a man was found today in the bush near Blackheath. Police say it could be that of Sir Walter Springfellow, Director-General of ASIO, who disappeared in March 1966 . . .'

'Nothing about his being murdered,' said Lisa.

'We're holding back on that as far as the press goes – we're not sure of anything. We – *hold it!*' He held up a hand.

Morecroft picked up a sheet of paper that had been thrust into his hand from off-camera. 'A late piece of news has just come to hand. Charles (Chilla) Dural was today released from Parramatta Gaol, where he had been serving a life sentence for murder. A one-time notorious criminal, Dural was the last man sentenced by Sir Walter Springfellow before he left the Bench to become head of ASIO. Police would make no comment on the ironic coincidence of the two events occurring on the same day . . .'

'Bugger!' said Malone and switched off the set.

'What's the matter? It's just as they said, a coincidence –'

'It'll give the media another handle to hang on to. They've got enough as it is – Springfellow turning up as a skeleton, his missus now a tycoon and up to her neck in a family takeover –'

'It's supposed to be the daughter who's trying to take over the family firm.' Lisa read everything in the daily newspaper but the sports pages; she knew when BHP or News Ltd went up or down, what knives were being sharpened in politics, but she knew nothing of Pat Cash's form or what horse was fancied for the Melbourne Cup. Though not mercenary, she had a Dutch respect for money and the making of it. 'Justine Springfellow is only trying to emulate her mother. Two tycoons in the family are better than one.'

He looked at her. 'Who said that?'

'Someone in Perth.' Where tycoons bred like credit-rated rabbits.

'Don't believe what you read about the daughter. I met her today. She'd do everything her mother told her.'

Lisa had picked up the financial pages of the *Herald*, knew exactly where to turn to. 'Springfellow Corporation was at its highest price ever yesterday. What's this prisoner Dural like?' Lately she had developed a talent for *non-sequiturs*, and Malone, being a man, had wondered if she was at the beginning of her menopause. Which thought was a male *non-sequitur*.

'I haven't a clue. He was before my time. I've heard of him – I think he killed a cove in prison about ten years ago. But he's a stranger to me.' *And I hope he stays that way.*

Maureen came into the living-room. 'In this house a kid's work is never done. None of my friends have to do the washing-up.'

'Lucky them,' said Lisa. 'Sunday you can do the washing and ironing. That will give me Monday free.'

Malone grinned, loving the dry banter that went on in his family. He wondered what sort of banter went on among the silvertail Springfellows. Though perhaps tonight there would be nothing like that, not with the bones of a long-dead husband and father lying between them.

TWO

1

'Explain to me what's happening,' said Malone. 'You're the stock market expert.'

Next morning they were driving across the Harbour Bridge towards Kirribilli. Malone had called ASIO and they, reluctantly, it seemed to him, had invited him over. Intelligence organizations are always suspicious of police forces, who never seem to give mind to the bigger issues. Malone had read *Gorky Park* and knew how Inspector Arkady Renko had felt. But ASIO was no KGB: it could not afford to be on its shoe-string budget. Pinchpenny defence against any enemy, criminal or foreign, was a tenet of faith with all Australian governments.

'Well,' said Clements, who up till recently had been an expert only on horses, jockeys, trainers and crims, 'our Lady Springfellow owns her own company, Cobar Corporation – it's a small family company, hers and her daughter's. But now she's trying to buy out the Springfellow family interests in the holding corporation which owns the main holdings in the merchant bank and the stockbroking firm. The stock-brokers, they're the oldest brokers in Australia, own 49 per cent of the bank – the rest is owned by the public. She herself, or anyway Cobar, owns 18 per cent of the stockbrokers – she bought that when they went public a coupla years ago. The rest is owned 15 per cent by the Springfellow family, Sir Walter's brother and sister, and the rest by institutions and the public.'

Malone shook his head in wonder. 'Does Corporate Affairs know about you? They might offer you a job.'

'When you've tried to keep track of the form of horses and jockeys, the stock exchange is kids' stuff. You wanna know more about Lady Springfellow? Well, she applied to inherit her husband's estate three years after he disappeared. Her sister-in-law Emma tried to fight it but got nowhere. The irony of it was that she got her husband's old law firm to prepare the affidavits.'

'You've done your homework,' Malone said appreciatively. He was no longer surprised at the acumen and thoroughness of his partner, whom so many, at first acquaintance, took for an amiable oaf.

'This one interests me. I like to see what happens when money's involved. It's the punter in me . . . When she inherited the estate, she just took off. She used that as a springboard – no pun –' he gave his slow grin '– to start buying everything else she now owns. The radio stations, the country and suburban newspapers, part of a diamond mine, all of a gold mine. And now she owns the Channel 15 network.'

'What about the bank?'

'Springfellow and Co. started that six years ago – they were one of the few who didn't go overseas for a partner. It's done okay, but not as well as it might. A London bank and a New York one have been eyeing it. The daughter claims she's moving in to make sure it remains an Australian bank. A 21-year-old banker and a girl at that.' A true punter, he was a misogynist: he rarely backed mares.

'What do you reckon?'

'I reckon it's just greed, but I'm old-fashioned. Greed is now an acceptable thing. I'm falling for it myself.'

'So Venetia gained a whole lot when her old man disappeared?'

'I guess so. All I'm telling you is gossip and what I've read in the *Financial Review*.'

'The what? Have you given up on *Best Bets*? Have you sold all your shares?'

'I've put 'em on the market today. I'm ashamed of how much I'm gunna make. When I put the cheque in the bank, the tellers are gunna start ringing Evan Whitton at the *Herald*.' Whitton was a journalist who could turn over a spadeful of corruption with a VDU key.

They turned off the Bridge approach and circled round on to the end of the tiny Kirribilli peninsula. This was an area of tall apartment buildings bum-to-cheek with squat old houses, some middle-class grand, some just workmen's stone cottages. The population was a mix of incomes and ages, with no sleaze and mostly respectability. It also harboured the Sydney residences of the Prime Minister and the Governor-General, side by side, though the G-G's was the larger and more imposing, as if to remind the politician next door that *its* occupant was not dependent on the whim of the voters.

ASIO lived in a converted mansion on the waterfront: one had to look through barred windows, but the KGB would have given away half its secrets for such a vista. Malone and Clements were shown into the office of the chief executive, a room with a view that must have driven the Director-General, now headquartered in Canberra, subversive with envy.

Guy Fortague, the Sydney Regional-Director, was big, rugged and all smiles as if making an all-out effort to prove that spy chiefs were not really spooky. There's nothing to be frightened of, his smile assured them; a thought that had not occurred to either Malone or Clements. But he was certainly making their reception easier than they had expected.

'We were surprised when you mentioned murder to us.' But Malone suspected he was not the sort of man to be surprised by anything; if he were, he would not be in this job. 'We did think of it originally, of course.'

'Why did you change your minds?' said Malone.

'Well, we didn't exactly change our minds.' Fortague retreated a little; he was no longer smiling. 'But we had no evidence, just suspicions.'

Malone thought that one of the bases for counter-espionage would have been suspicion; but he didn't say so. 'How was security in those days? I mean national security.'

Fortague shrugged. 'We were busy – I'd just joined the organization. The anti-Vietnam business was just beginning to warm up. But we never expected murder or terrorism or anything like that, not from those here in Australia. Their violence never seemed to extend beyond demonstrations on campus and in the streets.'

'What about outsiders? Foreign agents?'

Fortague smiled. 'Foreign agents don't kill the opposition's boss – it's one of the unwritten rules in our game. Just like in yours. How many police commissioners have been murdered by a criminal, a professional one?'

Malone nodded, agreeing with the etiquette. 'Our file on him is missing. Has been for twenty-odd years.'

'Really?' Fortague's tone implied that he wasn't surprised; anything might go missing in the NSW Police Force.

Malone nodded at the thin file on the desk in front of Fortague. 'Is that your file on him? It's pretty slim, isn't it?'

All that Fortague said was, 'I'm afraid I can't show it to you.'

Behind that smile, Malone thought, there's only just so much co-operation. They don't want any coppers on their turf. 'Well, maybe you can tell me one or two things that might be in it?'

'I don't think so,' said Fortague and smiled again.

Malone hesitated, wondering where to go next. He decided to lay his cards on the table, a hand that was almost blank. 'Righto, I'll tell you what we've found. A skeleton. No weapon. No shoes, which might have been the one item of clothing that would have survived the weather. All that was left, the only things to identify the body, were the signet ring and the briefcase. But it was empty.'

Fortague tapped his file without opening it. 'I'll add those details later.'

'Righto, now the 64,000-dollar question – what was in the briefcase?'

40

Fortague took his time, the smile now gone from his big rugged face. He looked faintly familiar and Malone suddenly remembered who he was, the odd name striking a bell. He had been one of the young university recruits who had sat in on this case at its beginning. He was now an old hand at intelligence, infected by the profession's endemic suspicion of outsiders, especially other investigators.

At last he said, 'I can't tell you the specifics of what was in the briefcase – that's classified. We know what he took home with him the previous Friday. It was all labelled Top Secret.'

'He took stuff like that home with him?'

'He was an independent-minded man.' Meaning: I would never do such a thing myself. 'But I don't mean to imply he was careless – nothing like that at all. He had his own way of working.'

'What sort of man was he?'

'Brilliant. A bit hard to get to know, but brilliant. He spoke French and German fluently and when he came to us started learning Chinese and Indonesian.'

'What were his relations with the people he worked with in Melbourne?'

Fortague hesitated a moment. 'I'll tell you something off the record. He was often impatient with the ex-military types who were then running our organization.'

Malone smiled, trying to make himself an ally. 'Oh, I remember them. You probably don't remember, but you and I met here in this office twenty-one years ago. We were both rookies.'

Fortague suddenly smiled again. 'Of course! Christ – and we've both survived!' He looked at Clements. 'Are you one of the old hands, too, Sergeant?'

Clements nodded. 'I thought the scars showed.'

All at once the atmosphere had changed. Fortague looked at his watch, then out of the window at a submarine, sinister as a black shark, gliding by from the base round the point. 'The sun's well over the yard-arm on that sub. What's your choice?'

41

'I think you'd better make it a beer,' said Malone. 'We don't want to be picked up by the booze bus.'

'I've had that happen to me twice,' said Clements. 'It's been bloody embarrassing for us both, them and me.'

Fortague went to a cupboard and opened it, exposing a small fridge and two shelves of bottles and glasses. He poured a Scotch and two beers and came back with the drinks on a tray. They toasted each other's health, then he sat down behind his desk again. He was all at once relaxed, but he had once more stopped smiling. 'If Springfellow was murdered and the murderer took the papers that were in the briefcase . . . Why did he leave the briefcase?'

'I've seen it,' said Clements. 'It's his own, not government issue. His initials are on it. It's an expensive one.'

'That may have been the reason,' said Malone. 'My initials are S.M. If I'd stolen a briefcase with the initials W.S. on it, I wouldn't carry it around with me.'

Fortague nodded. 'Feasible. But what about his wallet?'

'We're assuming the murderer took that. But what if the body was found by someone who didn't want to get in touch with us? There are a lot of elements out there who have no time for the police.' Including the cast and crew of *Sydney Beat*. 'I gather Springfellow was a pretty dandy dresser. His suits would have been pretty damn expensive – or they would have been by my standards.' He dressed off the rack at Fletcher Jones; he was lucky that his clothes fitted him, because it was the price that had to fit him first. He would never make a tailor rich. 'Someone could have stolen the clothes and the shoes.'

'I can't imagine anyone stripping a dead man and then leaving him to rot in the bush.'

Malone sipped his beer. 'There are more animals out there than there are in the zoo. We come across at least one a week. Let's forget about murder for a moment. Let's say he committed suicide. So whoever took the papers and the wallet and maybe his clothes, he also took the gun.'

'So that brings us back to taws,' said Clements. 'Why would he commit suicide?'

He and Malone looked at Fortague, but the ASIO man shook his head. 'We asked ourselves that years ago. The answer was, he wouldn't have done it. He wasn't the type.'

Malone said, 'What was the domestic situation?'

Fortague hesitated, took a sip of his own drink. He hated scandal, though sometimes his profession had to use it as a weapon. 'We had no evidence that anything was wrong between him and his wife. But . . .'

Malone and Clements waited with that patience learned from experience.

'But Lady Springfellow didn't keep the home fires burning while he was away on business. I don't know whether you know, but she has the reputation of being something of a man-eater. That's not a late development. She was always like that.'

The two policemen were neither shocked nor impressed. They knew, with male certainty, that women were no more moral than men, just smarter in that fewer of them were caught. 'Why did a sober, pillar-of-the-Establishment man like him marry someone like her?' said Clements.

Malone knew the answer. Adam hadn't followed Eve out of the Garden of Eden because God had told him to go. Forget the apple: there's no temptation like a sinful woman.

'Search me,' said Fortague and looked like a man who had gathered no intelligence at all about love or lust or whatever one called it.

'I think we'll go and see Lady Springfellow,' said Malone.

'I suppose you have to follow it through?'

'You don't want to know what happened to your Director-General?'

'Of course. But you know what it's like in our game – the less publicity . . .'

'That's why you won't show us what's in that file?'

'It's not my decision. That came from Canberra.'

'From Cabinet or ASIO headquarters?'

'Ah,' said Fortague and this time the smile was forced. 'That's classified, I'm afraid.'

2

Chilla Dural sat alone in his room in the rooming-house in the side-street off William Street. He had come back to King's Cross because that had been his departure point when he had begun the journey to the twenty-three years in Parramatta Gaol. It had not been a matter of coming home but of coming back to something recognizable, a landmark from which he could plan the direction of the rest of his life. In the old days he had been able to afford a two-bedroomed flat up in Macleay Street; now, at what he could afford to pay, the estate agent had told him, he was lucky to get this room in this seedy side-street. Inflation, amongst other things, was going to blur what had once been so familiar.

He sat on the single bed, his opened suitcase beside him. It was not a large case and in it was everything he owned in the world except his bank balance and he had no idea what that was. He took out the framed photograph of his wife and two children, the woman and the two small girls as faded in his memory as they were in the frame. It had been taken his first year in prison, when Patti had still been writing to him; the girls, Arlene and Ava, had been – what? Five and six? Patti, Arlene and Ava: it had been like going home (when he had gone home at all) to a movie (though he had called them fillums in those days), a cheap movie in which he had never been the hero.

He put the photo on the varnished whitewood chest of drawers and stared at it. He had been a real bastard in those days, an absolute shit. Patti had told him so, though she had never used four-letter words. No wonder she had finally left him to rot in prison and had gone to Western Australia. *'I'm going to WA, Charlie, to try and start a new life for myself and the girls. I hope that in time the girls will forget you and I hope I do, too . . .'*

He had gone berserk when he had got the letter and had bashed up a screw. He had tried telling the prison superintendent that he had gone out of his mind at the thought of losing his children; but the plea hadn't washed. The superintendent had known him as well as he knew himself. He cared for no one but himself and his anger had come from nothing more than the fact that, at long last, Patti had put something over on him.

Five years later she had written to him, giving no address, that she had met another man (*'a good man, Charlie, he loves the girls like they were his own'*) and she was filing for divorce (*'for the girls' sake, Charlie, don't fight the divorce. For once in your life, think of them'*). He hadn't fought it; by then, Patti was no more than a sexual memory. The girls were even dimmer in his mind, small fearful shades who had never rushed into his arms as kids did in fillums. The girls would be grown up now, probably married with kids of their own, kids who would never be told that their missing grandpa had once been the notorious Chilla Dural, stand-over man, bash artist and general thug for the biggest crim in Sydney.

He had gone to prison because of Heinie Odets. A small-time operator had been trying to muscle in on Odets's drug territory; he had been warned but had ignored the warning. Dural had been given the job of eliminating the stupid bastard and had done it with his usual finesse: a blow to the head with an iron bar and then the body dumped in the harbour. Unfortunately, the murder had been witnessed by an honest off-duty cop, a species Chilla Dural hadn't believed then existed in Sydney.

Odets had hired the best criminal barrister in the State, but it had all been to no avail. Nothing had gone right; they had even copped the most bloody-minded judge on the Bench. Mr Justice Springfellow had poured shit all over him, though in educated words, and then sentenced him to life. Odets had promised to look after him when he finally got out, but

Heinie had never been a sentimental man. It had not taken Chilla Dural long to wake up to the fact that, once inside, he was forgotten.

He had been inside seven years when he had killed another prisoner. Dural, by then, had been king of his section of the yard; the newcomer had had ambitions to be the same. He had made the mistake of challenging Dural and war had been declared. It had been a fair fight: each had had a knife and each waited till he thought the other's back was turned. Dural had got another seven years, having the charge reduced to manslaughter, and his parole had been put back indefinitely. Heinie Odets had sent him a card that Christmas, hoping he was well, and that was all.

Odets was dead now. He had been buried last year in holy ground and several politicians and retired police officers from the old days had turned up at the funeral. Half of Sydney's criminal elements had been there, showing only the backs of their heads to the media cameramen. An elderly priest, who knew how to play to his congregation, had found qualities that nobody, least of all Heinie, had ever suspected in Heinie Odets. The congregation had sat stunned at the revelation that someone, especially a priest, could do a better con job than themselves. All this had been told to Chilla Dural by someone there that day who, a month after the funeral, had arrived at Parramatta to do a seven-year stretch for being, in his honest opinion, no more dishonest than the priest. Sin, he told Chilla, was a fucking class thing.

Dural put away the rest of his belongings, looked around the room again and decided he had to spend as little time as possible in it. It was clean, but you couldn't say much more for it; he had changed one cell for another. Even the single window had bars on it, something he had never had on the windows of the Macleay Street flat. The view from this room was terrific: four feet away was the blank wall of the house next door. Even at Parramatta he had always been able to catch a glimpse of the sky beyond the bars.

46

He put on his jacket and went out of the room, locking the door behind him. He was halfway down the narrow hall to the front door, aware now of the smell of the house, when the little old man came out of another room and looked at him like a suspicious terrier.

'G'day. You the new bloke? Waddia think of the place?'

Dural could be affable when he wanted to be. 'Bit early to tell. Plenty of smell, though, ain't there?'

'That's the bloody Viet Cong upstairs. They're always bloody frying rice. Me name's Killeen, Jerry Killeen.'

Dural hesitated. But he couldn't let go of the past; all he had left was his name. 'Dural. Chilla Dural.'

The old man raised an eyebrow. He was thin and bony, all lined skin and a shock of white hair; but he would take on the world, he was afraid of no one. He looked at this hawk-faced, balding man with the muscles bulging under the cheap suit and nodded his appreciation. 'Oh, I read about you. I read the papers, every page from go to whoa. There was a little piece about you this morning, about you getting out. Something to do with that feller's skeleton they found up in the mountains.'

'What feller was that?'

He hadn't looked at a newspaper since he had left Parramatta yesterday morning. He had never been a reader and he hadn't wanted to find his way back into the world through a newspaper's cockeyed view of it. He would do that through a TV set, where the view was just as cockeyed as the commercials, but you got the comic liars like politicians and union bosses.

'Springfeller, Sir Walter Springfeller.' Jerry Killeen had a photographic memory for names; he could even remember the names of strangers in the births and deaths columns. His circle of friends was those he met in his newspapers. 'You going out now? I'll leave the *Herald* and the *Tele* under your door. I'll shove 'em under so the bloody Viet Cong don't pinch 'em.' He jerked his thumb towards the stair at the back of the hall. 'They'd steal the bridle off of a bloody nightmare. You wanna come in for a cuppa?'

Dural thanked him, but said maybe some other time. He left the little old man and went out of the house, glad to leave behind the smell of frying rice and other odours he hadn't identified. There had been smells in prison that he had never become accustomed to: the b.o. of dirty bastards who didn't wash, the overnight bucket in the corner of the cell . . . He stepped out into the narrow street and filled his lungs with what passed for fresh air in the traffic-clogged city.

He walked up the street, passed a narrow-fronted shop that looked faintly familiar. Suddenly he remembered: this had been El Rocco, another cell but where you had been free to come and go, where he had come to listen to the best jazz in Sydney. Jazz had been his sole musical interest and he still had a good ear for it. He would have to find another club where it was still played. He had no time for what passed as music these days.

He went to his old bank. As soon as he stepped inside its glass walls that looked straight out on to the street, he saw there had been changes. Everything inside here was exposed to the street; any stick-up artist would be playing to the passers-by. Not that sticking up banks had been his caper; Heinie Odets had always told him that was for desperate mugs. Rob banks, yes; but at night or on weekends, taking everything that was in the vaults. Heinie had masterminded one job like that, with Dural acting as driver and look-out, and they had got away with £200,000, big money in those days. His share had been £20,000 and he had blown the lot in a year on horses, cards and women.

He took his place in the queue and worked his way along the guide ropes; he felt like a ram in a sheep-fold. At last he reached the counter and presented his passbook. The girl teller looked at the greasy, ragged-edged book as if it were a cowpat.

'Sir, when did you last use this book?'

'The date's inside.' He opened the book. 'May 23, 1964.'

The girl, plump, pretty, not really a career banker, the engagement diamond already glinting on her hand, blinked

48

at him. 'That was before I was born. Don't lean on the counter, please.'

'Eh?'

'The security shield.' She pointed to the strip of steel that was sunk into the woodwork of the counter. 'If there's a hold-up that shoots up and you get your arms chopped off.'

'Jesus,' he said. 'Banks used to be safe.'

'Not any more. Will you excuse me a moment, sir?'

She went away and Dural stood at the counter looking at the steel strip. He'd heard about bank protection methods; there was one guy in Parramatta who was said to have had his head almost taken off by something like this. It was nice to know his money was safe.

The girl came back, signalled for him to go to the end of the counter. 'The manager would like to see you, sir. We'll have to issue a new book.'

He was taken in to see the manager, a square-faced, square-minded man who was out of place in a King's Cross bank. He longed for a transfer to head office, where the chances of being held up or getting AIDS or having a passbook presented that looked like something off the sole of a shoe were practically nil.

'You *are* Charles Dural?'

Dural produced his old driving-licence, just as greasy and tattered as the passbook.

The manager looked at the licence. 'That's years out of date, Mr Dural. I guess you were driving an FJ Holden then?'

Dural wondered if he had already sent for the cops; but he humoured the smug bastard. 'It was a 3.8 Jaguar, actually. Look, Mr –' He glanced at the name-plate on the manager's desk. 'Mr Rosman, just between you and me I've been in prison for the last twenty-three years and a bit. I had a cheque account here at this branch – I suppose you'd of still been in high school then – and when I knew they were gunna send me up for a long time, I changed over to an interest-bearing account. I dunno what interest I been getting – if you

49

ever sent me any statements, I didn't get 'em. This book says I left £3,202 in it when I went in. You oughta owe me quite a bit of interest, right?'

'I suppose we do –' The bank manager looked uncomfortable. 'The truth is, Mr Dural, in this area we have to be, well, extra careful. You have no idea some of the types come in here. I've got three bag-ladies as depositors –' He stopped, as if afraid that one of the bag-ladies might be Dural's mother. 'Well, you know what I mean. We just have to be *careful*.'

'I'm glad to hear it.' Dural was surprised at his own patience; in prison he'd have blown up if he'd been interviewed by a screw like this uppity bastard. 'Now could you let me know how much you're holding for me?'

It took ten minutes to reveal that he was now worth 23,332 dollars and 22 cents. It seemed to him that he was suddenly wealthy, but the bank manager didn't appear impressed with his rich client. 'It doesn't go far these days, Mr Dural. Perhaps you'd like us to invest it for you? Interest rates are still high. Unit trusts are the thing.'

'I'll think about it.' He had heard the talk in gaol amongst the white-collar crims that this was a boom time. He had wondered why, if everything was booming, so many of them were doing time. 'I don't wanna rush into nothing.'

He drew a hundred dollars, got his new passbook and went out into the street again. He hadn't walked more than a hundred yards (he still thought in yards, feet and inches; he'd never get used to the metric system) before he was aware that this wasn't *his* Cross, not as he remembered it. It had always been an area where there were more sinners than saints; now it looked sleazy, a corner into which had been swept the dregs and grime of the city. Sex had always been sold in the Cross, but, as he remembered it, there had been a time and a place for it; now, even in early afternoon, there were girls in doorways and on street corners. He was shocked at how they were dressed; in the old days the cops would have run them in for indecent exposure. A police car drifted by, the young cops in it looking out at the girls with plain boredom.

One of the girls accosted him. She was about sixteen, her ravaged face ten years older than her body; she wore a gold body stocking and black fishnet panty-hose and smelled as if she had fallen into a vat of Woolworth's perfume of the week. 'You want a bit, luv?'

'How much?' He wasn't really interested, except in the price of nooky these days.

'Fifty bucks.' She saw the look of surprise on his face. 'You from the bush or something? What you expect, something as cheap as doing it with a sheep?'

'It's twice what I used to pay. And the sheep didn't answer back.'

'You want a cheapie, try the Orient Express down there on the corner, the Filipino. She'll give you a quicky, a knee-trembler for ten bucks.'

He shook his head and walked on, more and more disillusioned with every pace. The traffic was thicker and quicker. He stepped off on to a pedestrian crossing and was almost run down by two young men in a Toyota with two surfboards strapped to its roof. One of the young men, earring flashing, his snarl just as bright, leaned out of the passenger window.

'Why don't you look where you're fucking going, dickhead!'

Dural took two paces to his right, grabbed the young man by his long bleached hair, pulled his head halfway out of the window and punched him on the jaw. Then he shoved the unconscious youth back into the car, leaned in and said to the startled driver, 'Okay, smart-arse, move on!'

He stepped back and heard the clapping behind him. He turned round and there was a bag-lady, standing beside her loaded pram, clapping him. 'Good on ya, mate! We need more men like you! Good on ya!'

Dural grinned, then went on across the street, feeling a little better: he had done something for the old Cross where decent crims like himself, not today's shit, used to hang out. He passed a group of kids who looked as if they had spent last night in the gutter; they glanced at him and sneered, but said nothing. The sharper-eyed amongst them had suddenly rec-

51

ognized the brutal toughness in his face, the muscles under the too-tight suit. All at once he hated everyone he passed, the sleazy strangers on what had once been his turf.

A taxi cruised by and he hailed it. He got in beside the driver, a kanaka, for Chrissakes. 'The Cobb and Co.'

'What's that, mate?'

'A pub. Where you from?'

'Tonga.'

They had told him in Parramatta that the place was now overrun with wogs, slopeheads and coons. He was beginning to feel like that mug in the story, Ripper van Winkie. 'One time you used to have to pass a test before you got a taxi licence, be able to know every street in the city. Especially the pubs.'

'Mate,' said the Tongan, 'you wanna sit here and discuss Australia's history, it's gunna cost you money. The meter's running.'

'You're pretty bloody uppity, ain't you? Who let you in here?'

'Your government. I'm studying economics and you taxpayers are paying for it. We're the white man's burden. Now where's this pub?'

'The corner of Castlereagh and Goulburn.'

The driver thought a moment, then shook his head. 'Not any more, mate. That's where the Masonic Temple is now. You don't look like a Mason to me.'

'Jesus!' Dural slumped back in the seat. 'Okay, take me into town and drop me anywhere.'

'Put your seat-belt on.'

'Jesus!' He clipped the seat-belt across himself, felt he was locking himself into some sort of straitjacket; there'd been no seat-belts when he'd last driven a car. He began to get the funny feeling that he had been freer in prison.

An hour of the inner city was enough for him. He was amazed at how much Sydney had changed; the much taller buildings than the ones he remembered seemed to arch over his head, blocking out the sun. The face of the crowd had changed, too; where had all the Aussie faces, with their long jaws and narrow eyes, gone? As Heinie Odets's bodyguard (they called them minders now, so he'd been told) he had been a student of faces; it was one way of staying ahead of trouble, Heinie had advised him. He couldn't get over the number of Chinks of some sort he saw; it was like being in some part of bloody Asia. And the black-haired wogs; there had been a fair number of them in Parramatta, but here on the outside (how long would he go on calling it that?) they seemed to make up half of those in the city streets. He was the stranger come home to a strange land.

He caught a taxi back to the rooming-house. As he stepped in the front door, two young Vietnamese came down the hallway and passed him with shy smiles. When they had gone out into the street he saw Jerry Killeen peering at him from a half-opened door.

'You see 'em? The bloody Viet Cong. You wanna come in for a cuppa?' His desire for company was pathetic, it hung on his wrinkled face like a beggar's sign.

'I gotta take a lay-down,' said Dural. 'Maybe later.'

The old man looked disappointed, but nodded and went back into his room, closing the door without another word. He reminded Dural of some of the pitiful old lags in prison, the ones who would always be lonely even in the close company of a thousand men.

Dural opened the door of his own room, picked up the newspapers lying just inside it and sat down on his bed. Then he glanced at the still-open door, frowned, got up and closed it. For so many years he had been accustomed to someone else closing the door on him: the sound of good-night was the clanging of iron on iron.

He leafed through the newspapers, but none of the news meant anything to him. He knew the names of the major politicians, but they were irrelevant to him; he was like an African heathen arriving in Rome, wondering at the import-ance of bishops and cardinals. The sports pages had a few names he recognized (sport had never been censored on the gaol's TV and radio; football brawls and thuggery were enjoyed as much by the prison officers as by the prisoners), but the cricket season was starting and he had never been interested in cricket. The financial pages were a foreign language to him; once, in the prison library, a white-collar criminal had tried to explain to him how the financial world worked, but Dural had just shaken his head and said he would rather remain dumb. The newspapers, he decided, would lead him nowhere, at least nowhere that he wanted to go.

He was about to drop the papers on the floor when he remembered why the little old bloke next door had shoved them under his door. He leafed through the pages again, came to the six-inch item at the bottom of one of the inner pages of the *Telegraph*. There it was: his name and that of Sir Walter Springfellow, the released prisoner and the skeleton in the Blue Mountains bush. A strange coincidence, they called it: fucking reporters, they were always looking for an angle. He re-read the story, but there was no guts to it; even he could see that. He threw the paper on the floor and lay back on the bed, staring up at the ceiling and the single electric globe with its yellow paper shade. He had cursed Springfellow in court on the day the judge had sentenced him. The cold, stuck-up bastard had chopped him down, slice by slice, with words that had rung in his ears for months afterwards. He had raved for a couple of years against Springfellow, but in the end he had realized he was just shouting into a wind that blew back his abuse like piss in a gale. The rage and the wind had died down a long time ago and now, here, in this bare, lonely room there was only stillness. Only the skeleton in the bush could have been lonelier.

It suddenly came to him that he was lost.

3

Mosman was a suburb that, to an outsider, never seemed to change. It was a good address from end to end; unlike other parts of Sydney, it had no *poor* end. The houses, even the smaller ones, were solid and had their own gardens; the few semi-detached cottages had a shy look about them, as if their owners knew they were being tolerated only so long as they behaved themselves and kept themselves neat and tidy. Blocks of flats, known in the estate agents' argot as home units, as if they were just cards in a game of Monopoly, were lumped about the district, but high-rise development was forbidden. Mosman prided itself on its conservatism; it was a suburb not given to spontaneity, at least not in the streets. Swingers from the eastern suburbs might have called it dull, but under the dull façade there was old, real money; and real money is never dull, least of all to the swingers from the eastern suburbs. Mosman was sure of its place in the sun; it was the suburb, its residents knew, where God would have resided if ever he had emigrated to Sydney from England. A thought that God had probably never had.

Clements parked the car in Springfellow Avenue and looked around at the houses at this end of the dead-end street. 'Respectable, aren't they? You can smell it from here – respectability. You think they make love with their clothes on?'

'You look as if you do. Why don't you come over some night and let Lisa run the iron over you?'

'I'm always reading about the heights of fashion. Why doesn't someone write about the depths? I see you're wearing your best suit today. Is that for Lady Springfellow?'

'Wait till you meet her. You'll wish you'd been to the dry cleaner's.'

Clements grinned, uninsulted, and got out of the car. He was not dirty in his habits; he was a regular at the dry cleaner's. He just had the knack of being able to turn a suit into a mess of wrinkles within ten minutes of donning it. He had put polish on his shoes only once since buying them ten months ago, though he occasionally rubbed the toes of them on the bottoms of his trouser-legs. He straightened his tie and patted down the ends of his collar. 'How about that? Bewdy Brummell.'

'Bewdy,' said Malone, and couldn't have wished for a better sidekick.

Malone had only a faint memory of his first visit to the Springfellow house, but he couldn't remember any security guards in those days. But there was one now: he came down the driveway to the big iron gates when Malone tried to open them and found them locked electronically. Malone introduced himself and Clements and the security guard switched on his walkie-talkie and spoke to someone in the house. Then he unlocked the gates.

'Is this usual in Mosman?' said Clements.

'I dunno,' said the guard, an overweight, middle-aged man who looked as if he had borrowed a smaller man's uniform. 'I come, I do me job and I go. That's all I'm paid for.'

'Just like us,' said Clements. He had a cop's dislike of security guards; they were growing into another police force.

'I thought you'd be in pink and grey,' said Malone, and the security guard just refrained from jerking his thumb at the mug copper.

The two detectives walked up the driveway, past the rhododendrons, the banks of azaleas, the camellias, the liquidambars and the lawns that looked like green carpets that had been vacuumed rather than mowed. The house was a monument to Federation; one would not have been surprised to see a group of turn-of-the-century politicians, all beards and walrus moustaches, standing on the front steps. It had been built by Sir Archibald Springfellow, the grandfather of Walter, Edwin and Emma, and, true to then current ideas, had wide verandahs and narrow windows. The fierce Australian sun was to be avoided: sun worship, a later religion, was only for Aborigines and the odd health crank, neither of whom dared show his face in Mosman. At the back there was a magnificent view of the harbour, but one had to step outside the house to look at it in those days. Lady Myrtle Springfellow had never been known to take a long view; very little beyond the end of her patrician nose, usually held at a socially acute angle, had interested her. The house, like the family, suggested secrets to the occasional picnickers who came to the neighbouring bush reserve that ran down to the harbour cliffs.

The housekeeper who opened the front door to Malone and Clements was of a social mind with Lady Myrtle, whom she had never met. She looked down her blunt, unpatrician nose at the two detectives as if they were door-to-door salesmen.

'We'd like to see Lady Springfellow. We understand she is at home.'

'How did you know that?'

'Police intuition.' He had rung the Springfellow head office and he guessed that Venetia knew they were coming.

The housekeeper continued to look at them with suspicion, but before she could say anything further she was gently pushed aside by a good-looking grey-haired woman who might have problems with her weight but wouldn't let them worry her.

'Police? I'm Alice Magee, Venetia's mother.' She was the sort of friendly woman who would always use Christian names, even if dealing with the Pope or non-Christians such as Khomeini. 'Come in, come in.'

Malone could only dimly recall the dimness of the Springfellow house on his last visit. All the shadows had now gone. Venetia had widened the windows, letting in the light. All the dark panelling had been removed and replaced by grey French wallpaper that had cost as much as the original brick walls. The heavy Victorian furniture had been sold or given away; in its place were elegant Regency pieces, some genuine, some reproductions. Only the paintings on the walls, the Boyds and the Tuckers with their fear-stricken creatures and their threatening shadows, seemed out of place. But then, as Emma Springfellow often said, Venetia had never believed in making anyone completely comfortable. Emma herself was uncomfortable for a different reason. She secretly thought the house had been improved by Venetia's changes, but she would never say so. It made her uncomfortable to keep an opinion to herself. But she was not here in the house right now and Malone and Clements still had to come to know her.

'My daughter's on the phone,' said Alice Magee, leading them into a big bright sun-room that looked out on to the gardens and the harbour. There was only one picture on the wall here, a Streeton that was a painting of the scene immediately below them. 'She's always on the phone. Overseas. London or New York or Los Angeles, somewhere. I can't get used to calling the rest of the world, just like that –' She snapped her fingers; several diamond rings were a miniature flash of lightning. 'I still time myself when I'm calling Cobar – that's where we come from originally . . . Would you like a drink? Beer, whisky, tea, coffee?'

She would have made a great air hostess, Malone thought; he liked her at once. 'No thanks, Mrs Magee. How is your daughter taking the – news?'

'The –? Oh, Walter's remains. Dreadful, isn't it? Lying up there in the Blue Mountains all those years . . . I'd like to be buried as soon as I'm gone, wouldn't you?'

'I hadn't thought about it,' said Malone and didn't dare look at Clements who, trying to stifle a smile, looked as agonized as one of the men in a Tucker painting.

'When are they going to let us bury him?'

'It'll probably be a couple of weeks before the coroner releases the – remains.' A skeleton wasn't a body or a corpse; or was it? 'Did you know Sir Walter well?'

'Not really. I don't think anyone knew him well. He was a bit stand-offish, you know what I mean? Not with my daughter, of course.' Her answers would always be prompt; there was no guile about Alice Magee. 'He was a nice man, but.'

Malone had sized her up now. Despite the diamond rings, the expensive dress and the immaculate hair-do, she was still one of life's battlers. She still had the dried skin from the heat

58

of the western plains, still had the Cobar dust in her voice; her daughter might be the richest woman in Australia, but Alice Magee would never forget the need to scratch for a penny. Under her painted fingernails was invisible dirt that could never be cleaned out. Her spirit was stouter than her figure, though the latter was catching up.

Then Venetia, looking disarmingly soft in pink and grey, came out to the sun-room in good humour; she had just made another million or two. 'Inspector Malone! Has my mother told you all you want to know?'

'Give me another ten minutes,' said her mother. 'I was just about to start with the year you were born.'

The relationship between them was good, evident at once to the two outsiders. Rough-and-ready mother, smooth-as-cream (though it might turn sour occasionally) daughter: they were an odd team, Malone thought, and he wondered what the conservative, but nice, Walter Springfellow had thought of the combination.

Malone decided to waste no time; Venetia looked as if she had already put a stop-watch on him. 'We have to go right back to the beginning, Lady Springfellow. For the time being we are assuming your husband was murdered. But there are other possibilities –'

'Suicide, you mean?'

He nodded.

She shook her head. 'You didn't know my husband. He would never do that.'

'Righto, we'll scratch that off the list.' But he wouldn't: nothing was ever dismissed till something else was proved. 'Blackmail – would someone have tried that on him?'

'I don't see what you're getting at.'

'Someone might have been trying to blackmail him, he refused and they killed him.'

'You're making this sound as if it was all a personal matter. Aren't you overlooking his ASIO job? Spies disappear all the time.'

'Not spy chiefs. So ASIO tells us.'

'Not unless they defect,' said Clements.

Venetia gave him a look that should have increased his creases. 'You just have no idea what my husband was like, do you? He was a patriot, the sort that's out of fashion nowadays.'

'Have ASIO ever been to question you?'

Venetia shook her head again; Malone found himself liking the way her thick golden hair moved. 'Never. Not since he first disappeared. They've just – *ignored* me.' She sounded as if the fact didn't disturb her too much. But, Malone thought, that could partly explain why the file on Walter Springfellow was so thin.

'What about his relationship with you, Lady Spring-fellow?' He had looked directly at Venetia, but when he glanced at Alice Magee he saw the reaction he had hoped for. The plump face was frowning, the unsubtle mind remembering. 'Do you recall something that might help us, Mrs Magee?'

But Alice Magee knew where her loyalties lay; the frown cleared, her face was as bland as the swimming-pool out in the garden. 'No, I don't remember anything. They were real love-birds.'

On a table behind Venetia was a photo of her and Walter: she young and smiling, he cool and aloof: he was a love-eagle, if at all avian. 'I'm sorry I have to continue this line, Lady Springfellow. But he had no romantic interest before you?'

'You mean a jilted lover?' She laughed. 'That's mid-Victorian, Inspector.'

'It isn't,' said Clements. 'It happens at least once a month, sometimes once a week.'

'But those are the people we let in from overseas,' said Alice Magee. 'Aussies don't go in for that sort of thing.'

She had her xenophobia, though she wouldn't have recognized it by that name. She was a cousin by prejudice to Malone's own mother and father; the country was now made up of *us* and *them*, and there were too many of *them*.

'Yes,' said Venetia. 'My husband did go out with other women. After all, he was a very masculine man and his first wife had died ten years before he met me.'

'What did she die of?'

'She was killed in a shooting accident. She and my husband were on a safari in Kenya.'

'An inquest was held, I suppose?'

She gave him a sudden hard look. 'I presume so. What are you getting at?'

Malone held back a sigh. 'Lady Springfellow, if we're going to find out what happened to your husband, we're going to have to get at a lot of things. Some of them may offend or even hurt you, but it's nothing personal on our part. Sergeant Clements and I are just trying to do our job. Part of that is finding out as much as we can about the victim – that's the way we police work. Just give us a little credit for knowing the best way to go about it.'

'It's not the best way for the victim's widow, is it?' That was from the widow's mother.

'Go on,' said Venetia coldly.

Tread carefully here, Malone. 'Did your husband know much about firearms?'

'Yes. He had a collection of guns, they're still in his study. He used to go up to the Northern Territory every year, shooting crocodiles and buffalo. Until he married me, that is.'

'Is the collection still intact? There was nothing missing after he disappeared?'

Venetia hesitated only a split-second, but Malone picked it up. 'There are one or two blank spaces. I don't know when they went missing. I – I'm frightened of guns. I've often thought of selling the collection, but they were my husband's . . .'

'May we look?'

Venetia looked at her watch. 'This has gone on longer than I expected, Inspector. I'm due in the city in half an hour.'

'This'll only take a few minutes. If needs be, we'll give you an escort into town. Sergeant Clements likes to use the siren.'

'Any time.' Clements grinned at Alice Magee, who smiled back; but the smile seemed forced, she no longer looked cheerful and unafraid.

Venetia led the way out of the sun-room, back across a wide hallway and into the study; Alice, worried-looking, brought up the rear. Clements was watching her now, no expression on his big beefy face except for an occasional chew at his lower lip, an old habit.

The study had been stripped of its panelling; it was now a woman's room, except for the incongruous collection of guns in the large glass-fronted cabinet standing against one wall. Incongruous only if the woman was not Annie Oakley or one of the more ruthless prime ministers of other lands.

Malone looked at Clements, the gun expert. 'A good lot?'

Clements was examining the collection. 'As good as I've seen. A Mannlicher, a Springfield, a Sako. Even a Purdy. And these hand-guns . . . Yeah, quite a collection.'

There were two blank spaces in the array of guns, both of them amongst the hand-pieces. 'Two missing,' said Malone. 'How long have they been gone, Lady Springfellow?'

'I couldn't tell you. One of them – one of them has been missing for years.'

'I can see that.' The felt lining behind the guns showed the faint outlines. 'What d'you reckon they were, Russ?'

'The smaller one could have been a Walther or something like it.'

'Was that the one that's been missing for years?' Malone looked at Venetia.

'No. It was the other one.'

'I'd guess,' said Clements, looking directly at Malone, 'it was a Colt .45 or something as big.'

'What does that mean?' said Venetia.

'We think a Colt .45 or something like it was used to kill your husband.'

62

4

'It would be an odd sort of justice if an ex-judge was killed with his own gun. Some crim would laugh his head off at that.'

'That collection –' Clements shook his head. 'Somehow you don't expect a judge to keep an armoury. The only thing he didn't have in that case was a machine-gun and a howitzer.'

'I'm beginning to wonder if we'll ever know who the real Sir Walter was.'

They watched as Venetia went down the gravel driveway in the grey Bentley. She had declined Malone's offer of an escort, though she had not been sure that he wasn't joking. Her chauffeur would get her to the city on time; a whole forest had been chopped down to provide the paper for the tickets for speeding and illegal parking that he had accumulated. Venetia had her own traffic laws.

'Hey!' Malone and Clements, about to go down the driveway, turned. Alice Magee stood at the top of the steps. 'The other Springfellows are at home across the road, if you want to see them.'

'Why do you suggest that, Mrs Magee?'

She waved an airy hand: diamond lightning flashed again. 'Just trying to help my daughter. And you too, of course.'

'Thanks, Mrs Magee,' said Malone, trying to sound truly grateful. 'Tell me – did you know those guns were missing?'

She hesitated, suddenly not so keen to be helpful. 'Well . . . Yes. I dunno I ever thought much about the one that's been missing for years. But yes, I knew about the other one.'

'When did you notice it was gone?'

'A week ago.'

'Did you report it to the local police?'

'Why would I do that?'

'Stolen property?'

She laughed, but nervously. 'I didn't think it was stolen. I just thought someone had borrowed it or it'd been sent away to be cleaned or something.'

'Did you ask the housekeeper about it?'

'Ye-es. She didn't know anything about it. Then I told Venetia – she didn't know anything about it, either.'

'And none of you were worried about a gun being stolen from your house?'

'Of course we were!' She sounded suddenly snappish; Malone imagined he heard her false teeth click. 'But then we got the news about Walter . . .'

'You said it went missing a week ago.'

'Well, a week, three or four days ago – I dunno.' All at once she was flustered, the guileless mind caught up in an attempt at deceit. 'We're all knocked off our feet by the news . . .'

Malone decided not to press it for the moment; let Alice Magee get her story straight and then knock it down in one blow, preferably in front of another witness, such as Venetia Springfellow. He had his own guile, born of experience.

'Can we always find you here if we want you?'

'Most of the time. I'm a bush girl at heart. I like to go down to my daughter's property at Exeter. Keeps me outa mischief.' She had regained her bounce, or some of it. Malone waited for her to wink, but she didn't. 'Good luck. I suppose you coppers need it.'

'All the time,' said Clements.

They went down the driveway, nodded to the surly security guard, waited for him to let them out of the big gates, then crossed the street to a slightly smaller house, also approached by a driveway. Sir Archibald's son, the father of Walter, Edwin and Emma, had built this one in 1915, the year he had returned from Gallipoli minus half his right arm, and married the daughter of another prominent Mosman family. This house, too, had wide verandahs and narrow windows; its windows were still narrow, like the viewpoint of

64

its present chatelaine, Ruth Springfellow, Edwin's wife. Its garden was not as elaborate as the one the two detectives had just left, but it was just as ordered. Nothing grew wild in Mosman, not even weeds.

The door was opened by Emma Springfellow. Malone introduced himself and Clements and she looked at him as if puzzled they should be on the doorstep. 'Yes?'

'We'd like to talk to you and Mr and Mrs Springfellow, if they're at home. It's about your brother Walter.'

He had forgotten that he had ever met her. All he saw now was a dark-haired woman, with a single broad streak of grey along one temple, who might once have been on the way to being beautiful but had decided, of her own free will, against it. He did not see the inner woman. She was secretive, without even the phlebotomy of gossip. She had chosen loneliness and now couldn't find her way out of it.

'Who is it, Emma?' Edwin Springfellow came into the hall behind his sister; behind him was his wife. The three of them stood stockstill, like statues waiting to be moved around in the museum that was their home. 'Police? Do come in, please.'

The house was indeed a museum; everything in it seemed older than its occupants. It was all quality and in its day had probably been expensive; it had not been neglected and the timber of the tables and chairs shone with years of polishing. If there was a television set, that icon of today, in the house it was not in evidence. People, like pets, sometimes are owned by their homes and take on their appearance. The Spring-fellows were all quality and polish but suggested the past.

Malone and Clements were asked to sit down; the Springfellows arranged themselves on chairs facing them. It could have been a seance, though a medium or even a spirit would not have been admitted to this house without the best of credentials.

Edwin and Ruth looked more brother and sister than husband and wife; Ruth seemed more out of the same mould than did Emma. Both were grey-haired, had thin patrician features, looked at the world with the same superior eye. They brushed each other's hair every night and, when the occasion demanded, did the same with each other's ego. Yet Emma, self-contained, feline, was not out of place with them.

'Mr Springfellow,' said Malone, plunging straight in, 'would your brother have been the sort of man likely to have committed suicide?'

There were gasps from both women, as if Malone had accused Sir Walter of bestiality. Edwin's expression did not change.

'No,' he said in a clipped voice that sounded more English than Australian. 'He certainly would not have done anything like that.'

'What was his attitude towards guns?'

'They were for sport, not suicide.' Edwin's tone was polite but cold. 'If that's what you are getting at.'

He's too well prepared, Malone thought. He could be a lawyer instead of a stockbroker. 'Everyone seems to think we're *getting at* something. Your sister-in-law had the same idea. Don't you want to know how your brother died?'

'Of course we do!' Emma leaned forward; Malone waited for her to spring out of her chair. 'But we're not going to have his name besmirched!'

Besmirched: he had heard that word only from learned judges in libel cases. But perhaps it was part of the vocabulary one would hear in a museum like this. 'We don't want it – besmirched, either. But let's face it – this case is one of Australia's biggest mysteries. I worked on it originally for a few days – it was front-page stuff in every newspaper in the country when he disappeared.'

'I remember it.' Emma looked as if she might spit. 'Reporters! Trying to turn our life into a goldfish bowl!'

'It's started again,' said Ruth Springfellow. 'We have an ex-directory number, but somehow or other they've discovered it and are ringing all the time, day and night. Whatever happened to respect for privacy?'

'We're living in the past, sweetheart,' said her husband and, without irony, looked around the museum.

Malone tried another tack, walking on hollow eggs. 'This is a delicate question –' Both women looked at him with apprehensive anticipation; but Edwin looked offended in advance. 'What were relations like between your brother and his wife?'

Edwin and Ruth were shocked; but Emma leaned forward again. 'There were arguments. I always said they were an ill-matched pair.'

'Emma!' Edwin raised an open hand as if he intended to clamp it over his sister's mouth.

'It's true. We all want to know what happened to Walter –' She faltered for a moment and her face softened; she looked a different woman, one capable of love. Then she hardened again. 'What's wrong with the truth?'

'Nothing,' said Malone, getting in first. 'It's the only way we'll solve anything.'

'By dragging up the past?' said Edwin.

Malone gave him a steady look. 'Yes, Mr Springfellow. That's the only way we're going to do it.'

'Why not just let Walter rest in peace?' said Ruth. 'It's what he would have wanted himself.'

'No,' said Emma. 'He wouldn't have wanted it that way at all. You know as well as I do, he wasn't a man to let things rest, not even as a boy. He was like me, we always were. Let's have the truth. It's what he would have said.'

'Can any of you remember anything of the day he disappeared?'

'Nothing,' said Edwin at once and Ruth, after a glance at him, shook her head.

'I can,' said Emma, looking at neither of them. 'I was living here then with Edwin and Ruth –'

'Where do you live now?' said Clements. Malone always left it to him to take notes.

'At The Vanderbilt in Macquarie Street. I've lived there for twenty years.' She said it bitterly, as if south of the harbour were another country where she was a remittance woman not wanted at home.

Malone said, 'What do you remember of that day?'

'How can one remember exactly what happened all that time ago?' said Edwin.

Emma ignored him. 'Walter was very upset. I saw him for a moment before he left for the airport that morning –'

'What did he say?'

'It wasn't what he said – I just *knew*. Walter and I were so close – we didn't need to say things to each other. He just kissed me on the cheek and told me not to worry. Then he told me not to go near his wife.' The last word had a dagger through it.

'And did you? Go near his wife?'

'Not till the news came through that he was missing. The ASIO men came to see us, and some policemen –'

'I was one of them,' said Malone.

'Really?' She looked at him with sudden sharp interest. 'And you never found anything?'

'Nothing. We're having to start all over again.'

Edwin stood up. He had a certain dignity that was natural to him; old families sometimes bequeath other things besides money and a name. 'I think that's enough for today, Inspector. We are still upset by yesterday's discovery. I should have been at my office if it weren't for this . . .'

'We haven't finished –'

'Yes, we have, Emma. The inspector will understand. Perhaps we'll be in better shape to talk to you, Inspector, after the funeral. For the moment we'd rather be left alone.'

Emma glared at him, then abruptly stood up and without a word stalked out of the room. Ruth, as dignified as her husband, said, 'Please forgive her, Inspector. She and Walter were very close. Even after all these years she has never really reconciled herself to his disappearance. She has always believed he was still alive. And now . . .'

Edwin took her hand and once again they were as still as statues. *You will get no more out of us today*, their stillness said. Malone, who knew when to wait for another day, said goodbye. Edwin, moving stiffly, showed the two detectives to the front door. When he closed the door behind them, Malone waited for the sound of bolts being shot; but there was none. The door, however, was as stout as a castle gate. Neither it nor the family behind it would be easy to break down.

Going down the driveway Clements said, 'Emma was in love with her brother.'

Malone looked sideways at him: Clements was not usually given to such wild guessing. 'You reckon? I didn't think they went in for that sort of thing in Mosman.'

'I don't mean incest. But I saw it once before, when you were overseas on that High Commissioner case. Only it was the other way around, the brother was in love with the sister. He killed her because she married someone else.'

Malone stopped at the front gates. 'Are you saying Emma could have killed Walter?'

'I don't know,' said Clements, chewing his lip. 'I'll give you half a dozen who could have killed him. Including ASIO.'

'Keep your mouth shut on that one or you're headed for Tibooburra.' That was a one-pub town in the far north-west of the State, the NSW Police Force's farthest outpost. 'Just think it, don't say it.'

Clements grinned. 'Let's get at the truth, as Emma said.'

THREE

1

The Springfellow Corporation was headquartered in a thirty-storey building overlooking Circular Quay. The first five floors were occupied by the Springfellow Bank; the next two by Springfellow and Company, stockbrokers; the next eighteen floors by outside tenants; and the top five floors by divisions, subsidiaries or affiliates of the Corporation. The very top floor was given up to the boardroom, a dividing office and reception lobby and the office of the Chief Executive Officer and Chairwoman of the Board. The Corporation's PR chief, a woman versed in anti-sexist jargon, had tried to persuade her boss to call herself President and Chairperson, but Venetia had squashed her with, 'President has come to mean someone who's a figurehead – that's not me. Chairperson is sexless – and that's not me, either.'

Venetia sat in her office gazing out of the large picture-window at the ferries creeping into the quay, seeing them but only as on a memory screen; this had been her view for five years, ever since she had built Springfellow House. She had come an hour ago from the inquest on Walter. She felt at a loss, though of what she was not sure. She had long ago got over the physical loss of Walter; her widow's weeds had soon turned floral. In those days she had worn a variety of colours. There had been the shock two weeks ago of the discovery of Walter's *skeleton* (thank God they had not asked her to identify his bones), but she had recovered from that. The inquest this morning had been short, almost cold-blooded, and it had not upset her; she had been more concerned for its effect on Justine, who had accompanied her and who several times had shivered as if she were suffering from a chill. Then the coroner had declared that the remains were those of Walter Springfellow and that the deceased had died from a gunshot wound inflicted by a person or persons unknown and that the remains should be released into the care of the next of kin, namely Lady Springfellow. Up till then she had been calm, all her resources gathered together in her usual way, life (and death) put together as if according to the strictest of management principles.

Then, after dropping Justine off at her office on the floor below, she had come up here, come into this big room, closed the door and sat down and wept, something she had not done in more years than she could remember. She had at last dried her eyes, repaired her make-up and now sat staring out at a day she was blind to, wondering what was missing from her emotions. There was no grief, that had died long ago; no lost hope, for she had given up hope of Walter's return years ago; no anger at his murder, for she could not, after all this time, whip up the urge for revenge against a person or persons unknown. Her eyes cleared, she saw the familiar scene beyond the window, and at that moment her mind cleared. She turned back to her desk, deciding that it was love that was missing. She had lost count of the men who had been her lovers; but Walter had been the one she had married and, until now, she had always told herself she had loved him. In her fashion, maybe; but it had been a deeper feeling than she had ever felt for any other man. With possibly one exception.

There was a knock on the door and Michael Broad put his head in. He was, as usual, immaculate. A fashion dummy right out of the John Pardoe windows, Zegna all the way down to his socks, where the Gucci shoes stuck out like those of an intruder behind a curtain. Not a hair out of place, thought Venetia and, suddenly feeling better, smiled at his bald head.

71

'I have Peter Polux here, Venetia. Perhaps we could have a word before this afternoon's meeting.'

He stood aside and Polux entered, his smile as usual chopping his red cheeks in half, his white shoes as bright as bandaged feet under his dark-blue suit. He must be the only white-shoe banker in the world, Venetia thought. She knew his history, as she knew the history of everyone who worked for her or with whom she did business. He had gone to Queensland twenty-five years ago from a small town in Victoria, and had made a fortune in real estate on the Gold Coast. Seven years ago he had gone into merchant banking and become one of banking's high-flyers, taking risks declined by more staid bankers and bringing them off. He had been a founder member of the 'white shoe brigade', the new rich of the Gold Coast, and he had continued, as a thumb to the nose at the amused contempt of the supposed sophisticates of Sydney and Melbourne, to wear his white shoes on every occasion. He was a prominent Catholic, a papal knight, and he was famous for his gold rosary beads, which he often wore wrapped round his wrist like a holy bracelet. Venetia sometimes had the feeling that Polux looked upon the Catholic Church as a venture capital client: he certainly had a good deal of its business.

'Venetia old girl –' His wife had once told him he had no charm and now he was working on it; it was as heavy and rough-edged as a cannibal's table manners. 'Today's the big day, eh?'

When Venetia decided to buy out the Springfellow Corporation and turn it into a private company, she had been thinking of going to London or New York for the money she needed, but the devalued Australian dollar and the volatility of foreign currency had made her demur. Michael Broad had suggested that, instead, she call in Polux and Company. It would be Polux's biggest investment loan, they had the money and they offered good terms. After some thought, investigation and Broad's persuasion, she had agreed.

'Are we going to get any opposition from Intercapital?' Intercapital Insurance was the biggest outside shareholder in Springfellow. 'They may want to hang on for us to offer more.'

Polux shook his handsomely waved head; it was somehow an insult to the gleaming bald head sitting beside it. 'Intercapital are cautious, Venetia old girl. They don't think the bull market can last – they're expecting prices to go down after yesterday. They'll grab what they can while they can.'

'What do *you* think about the market?'

'Oh, it'll bounce back – I don't think it'll peak till just before Christmas. Friday's drop on Wall Street was just a hiccup, it happens all the time there. No worries there.' He took out his rosary beads, a gesture of habit, and ran them through his fingers. *Holy Mary, Mother of God*, thought Venetia, *pray for us bankers now and at the hour of our bankruptcy* . . . He saw Venetia looking at the beads and he laughed and put them away in his pocket.

Venetia turned to Broad. 'What about you, Michael? Are you bullish, too?'

She paid him 200,000 dollars a year, plus bonuses, and so far he had not failed her. He was greedy and ambitious, just as she was; she knew herself well enough to recognize her faults in other people. He was ruthless, too: something she only half-admitted to herself. It is not in human nature to be totally honest with ourselves; evolution still has a way to go.

'Of course. I shouldn't be recommending we go into this deal if I weren't. Now is the time to buy, when the rest of them are wondering when it's going to end.'

'We could wait till prices go down further.' She was only playing devil's advocate and both of them knew it; she was as eager as he to complete the buy-out of Springfellow. Tomorrow she would be as rich as Holmes à Court and Kerry Packer and Alan Bond, at least in assets, Boadicea up there amongst the warring men. The thought made her giddy. Feminists would write hymns (hers?) to her, Maggie Thatcher might send a message of congratulations, if she could remember where Australia was . . . She smiled inwardly at her fantasies. She had a sense of humour, something the more rabid feminists and Margaret T., too, would never forgive her for. 'It's all hypothetical, anyway. We'll have everything wrapped up by five o'clock this afternoon.'

'Absolutely!'

Broad's bonily handsome face lit up. He was the Springfellow corporate finance director, in his early forties, a little old for a whiz-kid but still called one by the kid columnists on the financial pages. A clothes-horse from an expensive stable, he was determined to impress from the first impression; he had spent almost a whole year's salary on an Aston-Martin convertible when everyone else was buying a Porsche or a Ferrari; he let everyone know, with a sort of cultured vulgarity, that he was not run-of-the-mill. But he would never go too far. The sharp observer (and Venetia was one) could always see the invisible rein he kept on himself.

He had come out of Prague in 1968, when his name had been Mirek Brod and he had been a young idealist and patriot. He had told Venetia something, but far from all, of his early life in Czechoslovakia. He had told her of throwing rocks at the Russian tanks, of seeing them bounce off and realizing the futility of it all. He did not tell her of his father, a morbid sincere Communist who committed suicide when the Russians came in; nor did he tell her of his mother, an unstable woman who went mad after his father's suicide and died in a fit. He kept all that to himself, held in by the tight rein that now guided his ambition. He no longer threw rocks, was no longer a patriot of Czechoslovakia or his adopted country, was now an egoist if not an egotist. He loved no one but himself, but he harboured dreams that some day Venetia might turn to him for more than financial advice. Or if not her, then the boss's daughter: it didn't matter. But he was too shrewd to show it. What he didn't know was that Venetia knew it.

'By this evening we'll be sitting pretty. I can't wait to read it in the newspapers tomorrow.'

'You're gunna show 'em, Venetia old girl!'

74

Venetia old girl showed her teeth; both men, blind with dreams of triumph, took it for a smile. 'Let's go and have some lunch.'

As he stood aside to let her pass out of the room ahead of him, Broad said, 'Oh, how did the inquest go?'

You cold son-of-a-bitch: he might have been asking her how a visit to the dentist had gone. 'Murder by person or persons unknown.'

'Eh?' He was startled and puzzled; it wasn't the sort of answer he'd been expecting. Up till now, Venetia's life before he had come into it had never interested him.

'The funeral will be tomorrow,' she said, went past him, crossed the outer office and went into the boardroom where a light lunch had been laid out. Behind her she heard Broad say to Polux, 'An extraordinary woman!' and Polux grunt in agreement. You don't know the half of me, she told them silently. But then, she told herself, there is a percentage of myself that even I don't know.

The board meeting began an hour and a half later. The other board members filed in: Edwin and Emma, Justine, two directors from Intercapital and three outside directors representing the public shareholders. With them was a flock of legal eagles and financial advisers. Major wars, thought Venetia, have been started with smaller gatherings than this.

Edwin nodded politely at her and Justine, as he would have even if they were bringing him before a firing squad; which, in a way, this was. Emma gave Venetia a look as blank as that of the firing squad itself; she didn't look at Justine at all. The others crowding into the big room smiled or looked deadly serious, depending upon their experience of Venetia. Though none of them had had the experience of a two-billion-dollar takeover by a woman; for some of the more historically-minded she might have been the Empress Tz'u Hsi; they walked gingerly, as if their feet were tightly bound. Some of them, Venetia noticed, had their briefcases in front of their genitals, as if afraid of castration. She must look for a small scalpel, to wear from her gold bracelet.

75

The boardroom was all pale grey but for the pink upholstery on the chairs and a single Marie Laurencin painting on one wall. Some of the older men looked as if they would have preferred to be in a darker, panelled room, a men's club, which most boardrooms in Australia were. Even the more cultured of them thought the Laurencin was out of place, especially since it was a painting of pale, semi-nude women. If it had to be a nude, give 'em a Norman Lindsay.

When they were all seated, one of the men, a newcomer, looked around for an ashtray and found none. 'Do you mind if we smoke, Lady Springfellow?'

'Yes,' said Lady Springfellow and that was that. 'Right, I don't think there is any need for preliminary remarks. My daughter will sum up why we are here and then I'll listen to what you have to say.'

Justine stood up. She was dressed in pink today, a silk dress that offset her mother's grey silk suit. They hadn't gone to the inquest wearing mourning, today was a day for battle colours, though knights who had ridden into combat under pink and grey banners might have been suspect. The younger, even the older, men looked at Justine with approval: a girl as beautiful as this had to have a soft side. She had recovered from the ordeal of the inquest; she had been upset at what had seemed to her the cold-blooded formality of it all, as if declaring a man legally dead meant no more than taking away his driving licence. Still, the ghost of her father, even though a gentle one, had at last been exorcized and now she was her mother's daughter completely.

'First, let me say when we take over the various elements –'

'*When?*' said Emma, soberly dressed, even wearing a hat and gloves: old Mosman keeping up standards. 'Nothing has been decided yet.'

'Yes, *when.*' Justine looked across the table at her aunt. The older men looked slightly embarrassed; women should not fight, at least not in the company of men. The younger ones sat up, hiding their grins by lowering their heads; this was going to be even better than they had anticipated. Then Justine went on: 'The Springfellow name will be retained. We shall do that out of respect for tradition and for the value of the name. It's a name I'm proud to have myself.'

She looked across at Edwin, who visibly annoyed Emma by nodding.

'So –' Justine had learned a few tricks from her mother: the value of a pause, for instance. 'So we are offering six dollars fifty for all Springfellow and Company shares beyond those my mother and I own, subject to the usual minimum acceptance conditions. On top of that we are offering nine dollars fifty a share for all those shares in Springfellow Bank beyond those owned by Springfellow and Company, again subject to the usual conditions.'

'Those should be two separate transactions,' said one of the Intercapital directors.

'They will be,' said Justine. 'I am merely summarizing here. But we do not want any hiatus between the two deals. We want them wrapped up together. Payment will be in cash, payable within the usual thirty days. The corporation will then become a private one, though certain of you will be invited to join our board.' That was a carrot thrown in front of the horse drawing the tumbril and everyone recognized it as such.

Especially Emma. 'Very generous. Do you expect us to respond to that sort of bribery?'

'Not you, Aunt. I wouldn't expect it of you,' said Justine coolly. Oh, I'm proud of you, thought Venetia and sat silent. 'We are just hoping you will take the money and run.'

'I've never run away from anything in my life,' said Emma, peeling off her gloves, which were not kid but suggested chainmail. 'We real Springfellows never do.'

Beside her Edwin tried to look like a man who wasn't already bending to the starting-blocks. Seemingly there was less fight in him than in his sister; it was as if he knew the battle was already lost and he wanted to retire, if not run, with dignity. In his secret heart, which he never opened, even to his wife, he knew that Venetia had taken over the Springfellow empire at least five years ago; indeed, almost from the day, long before that, when she had legally inherited Walter's estate. Also in his secret heart he had hoped that Walter might some day reappear and save them all. But tomorrow that hope would be buried for ever with Walter's bones.

'I am not selling,' said Emma, gloves now off, 'no matter what you may offer. Nor is my brother.' She did not even look at Edwin; he was leaving all the fight to her. They *were* fighting, he knew that, but he had lost all heart for it. 'We have the capital to buy up a major block of shares in Springfellow and Company and we are doing that at the moment.'

Justine looked up the table at her mother; Venetia looked at Michael Broad. He spread his hands in an almost Jewish gesture. 'Unless it's happened in the last hour . . .'

'It has,' said Emma, bare-knuckled. 'You should have kept track of the stock exchange board.'

As if on cue but a trifle late, like a wounded messenger from another part of the battlefield, there was a knock on the door and one of Venetia's secretaries came in and put a sheet of paper in front of her. Venetia looked at it, then sat up straight. Justine sat down at once, recognizing she had just lost her status. Her mother was not the sort of general who stayed in the background when the tide of battle went against her.

'Seven dollars a share is being offered for Springfellow and Company. Four million shares have been bought in the last half-hour –' She looked at the sheet of paper. 'I don't know who the sellers are –'

'We are,' said one of the Intercapital directors. He was a man named Safire, in his fifties and an advertisement for creature comforts; if ever he were reduced to the breadline, he would ask for croissants. He had a voice full of rich plums, a vocal orchard of over-ripe fruit. Venetia had never liked him, nor he her. 'We arranged the sale this morning, but

78

didn't let the market know till half an hour ago. When this meeting was timed to start.'

'Thank you, Erwin. I hope Intercapital's policy holders are treated better than you've treated me. Do you cut their throats as their policies mature?'

'I think that's uncalled for,' said the other Intercapital director, a thin under-nourished man named Newstead, seemingly chosen to contrast with Safire's sleek corpulence. 'Business is business, Venetia. We are in business to do our best for our clients.'

'My sister-in-law must have an awful lot of insurance with you. Is the sale of shares finalized? I'll give you seven-fifty.'

Safire and Newstead looked at each other like men who suddenly realized they had jumped before ascertaining the depth of the pool. Emma said, 'You can't renege, Mr Safire. The sale has already been through the exchange. It wouldn't look good for Intercapital if I reported you to the Companies and Securities Commission.' She had them by the throat and she looked up the table at another throat, Venetia's. 'That raises our holding in Springfellow and Company to 19.9 per cent.'

'Still less than ours,' said Justine, shooting cross-fire.

'But still too big for you to buy out over our heads.'

'I don't suppose you'd tell us where you got the money?' said Venetia.

'You're not that naïve and neither am I,' said Emma. 'You'll find out eventually, but for the time being that's our business. You'd be surprised how many people are prepared to put up money to fight you.'

Venetia bent her head for a whispered conference with Broad and Polux, both of whom looked as if they would cut Emma's throat if there were not so many witnesses. Everyone else, except Justine, seemed at a loss for somewhere to look; one man got up and closely examined the Marie Laurencin, as if he had just been called in to appraise it. All the men in the room were, in these days of takeovers, accustomed to seeing blood spilt. But this was family blood, almost blue, and abruptly they were squeamish.

Justine leaned across the table towards Emma; for a moment she looked a younger, darker version of her mother, all sharpened steel. 'You won't win, you know that. You've done nothing but draw dividends all your life, never contributed a thought or a suggestion to the firm –'

For once Emma was cool and controlled. 'I've contributed something now, haven't I? The other shareholders, the public who have never had a spokesman, may canonize me.' She looked smug enough to do the job herself, if no one else would.

Safire and Newstead both smiled at that, throwing petrol on Justine's smouldering fury. 'Goddamnit, Emma, you're doing this out of spite!'

'Partly,' said Emma, still cool; she and Justine were alone in their own arena. 'It adds taste to it. But the main reason, as Edwin tried to explain to you when you first made your horrible offer, is to keep the firm, the name, where it started and has always belonged – in the Springfellow family, the *real* Springfellows.'

'The real Springfellows will die with you and Uncle Edwin! There's no one after you – except me! I'm a real Springfellow, I have my father's name –'

'Perhaps so,' said Emma and for the sharper ears in the room there was an enigmatic note in her voice. 'Unfortunately, there isn't a hint of him in you. You are your mother's daughter through and through.'

Justine was leaning across the table, her voice low but strained; she seemed on the verge of reaching for Emma and doing her harm. Emma just sat and stared at her, only moving to gently shake off Edwin's hand as he tried to put it restrainingly on her arm. There was dead silence in the big room; the air was full of taut invisible wires. Then a man coughed and it sounded thin and shrill, like a castrato caught halfway to a wrong note.

'That will be all,' said Venetia. 'The meeting is adjourned.'

'You mean you withdraw both your bids?' said Edwin and looked suddenly relieved.

'No,' said Venetia and looked directly at Emma. 'I mean the war is just beginning.'

2

'Venetia darling,' said the Prime Minister, 'I had to call you –'

'You took your time, Philip.'

'Don't you read the papers? I've been in New Zealand with that lesbian PM of theirs. Christ, don't ever try to work out a defence treaty with a dyke . . . Don't you follow my movements at all?' He sounded more bewildered than hurt, as if his minders had fallen down on their job of letting the voters know where he was.

'I was looking for a little sympathy. They've discovered the phone in New Zealand, haven't they?' She was leading him on, being perverse. She really hadn't wanted to hear from him at all, least of all this morning.

'Well, just let me say this –' It was the politician's catch-cry. Every night, on the TV news and the current affairs programmes, heads were bobbing emphatically, like horses' heads on a carousel, and voices were demanding, *Just let me say this* . . . Television had bred a new breed of politician, mechanized clones from all parties with interchangeable clichés and platitudes. 'Nobody has greater respect for you, Venetia, than I do. And that's not just the politician in me speaking.'

'That's sweet of you, Philip.' She wondered if he realized how pompous he sounded.

She had known him for twenty-five years. They had been occasional lovers, but there had been no love and no mention of it. He had once been the biggest TV star in the country, his chat show out-rating every other programme; if Armageddon had occurred on a Friday night, 65 per cent of the nation's viewing audience would have told it to wait. Then a kitchen cabinet of rich industrialists had pushed him into politics and, after a decent interval, into the prime minister-ship. He was politically inept, almost stupid, but he under-stood what his advisers told him, if they kept their words and their sentences short, and he could memorize any speech written for him after no more than two readings. On television, which was now an annexe of the voting booth, he looked and sounded sincere. He was also handsome, charis-matic and had more sex appeal than any two other Members of Parliament. Those who knew him intimately, including Venetia, knew that to go to bed with him was like being laid in a voting booth. He was the sort of lover who wanted a pat on the front after the exercise; you were expected to vote him the best stud since Errol Flynn or, if your fantasies were kinky, since Hyperion – the horse, not the god. The voters, those not in his bed, had heard hints of his dalliances, but, unlike Americans, Australians never expected too much morality of their leaders. It was the natives' only show of political sophistication.

'I can't come to the funeral, of course –'

'Of course not. You never knew Walter.' Going to bed with Philip didn't make him a friend of the family; at least not in Mosman. 'Thanks for your call, Philip. I'll be in touch.'

She hung up in his ear: something even the lesbian PM from across the Tasman would not have done. She was in no mood for the hypocrisy of a part-time lover, even if he was the Prime Minister.

She looked at herself in her bedroom mirror, turning her face to the frank light of the morning sun. She was long past the need of vanity to prop herself up; an honest woman knows what is best about herself. She had never been strictly beautiful, but she had had the sort of face that the early days of Australian television, with its awkward lighting, had demanded: cheekbones that could be highlighted, good strong teeth that were not shadowed by her upper lip, hair that reflected the light and didn't look thin under it. Since then the years, and an expensive beautician, had treated her well. She was forty-seven, but everything, including her confidence in herself, was still firm. She had gone through the menopause in a hurry, brushing it aside as if it had been no more than a minor bad business deal, and had come out the other side as lubricious as ever; if there had been any hot flushes, they had been due to passion from the several affairs she had also been going through. There had been no thought in her agile mind that from now on life would run downhill. Yet for the first time in her life she felt this morning a certain fear; she had never before had to bury anyone close to her.

Justine, already dressed for the funeral, came in. 'Mother – you're not dressed! It's almost time to leave. Funerals aren't like weddings – they like you to be on time.'

'What do you know about funerals?' Venetia began to dress. 'Black doesn't suit me. Nor you, either.'

Justine looked at herself in the tall cheval mirror. 'No. Who are we trying to impress – the dead or the living?'

'Your father, I suppose. He always wore the right thing for the occasion.'

'Why did you love him?' Justine was still examining the dark stranger in the mirror. 'He was handsome and all that. But he was so much older than you. You must have had lots of young guys running after you . . .'

'I don't really know.' She did know, exactly. She had been looking for a father figure, someone to replace the drunken shearer who had been killed in a pub brawl when she was five years old. But no one would believe that, except her own mother. 'He was kind – well, he was to me. He had the reputation of being very tough when he was on the Bench – he had no time for anyone who broke the law. But with me . . . He loved me,' she said simply.

Justine turned away from the mirror, irritated by what she had seen. The Italian black suit had cost her 2,000 dollars at Maria Finlay's and she couldn't imagine that she would ever wear it again. 'May I borrow some pearls?'

'Take your pick.' Venetia gestured to her jewel box. 'Leave the single strand – I'll wear that. There, how do I look?'

'Ghastly.'

'After all this time – widow's weeds. But it's what he would have wanted.' Her father had been the same, when he was sober; so her mother had told her. To be more exact, he had been conservative towards women and what he expected them to be. Walter had been very much like that, though she had realized it too late. 'The family will expect it, too.'

'After yesterday, I don't care a damn what they expect.'

She and Venetia had talked for four hours yesterday evening, but both had known that their thinking had not been too straight. They had had one shock too many.

'We're on our best behaviour this morning,' said Venetia. 'Don't forget that.'

'Is Nana going to be there?'

'No, she's staying home to organize the reception afterwards. The wake, if you like.'

'What did Nana ever think of Father? They couldn't have been far apart in age.'

'I think she was in love with him.' *More, I think, than I was.*

Justine looked at her curiously. 'Was there any jealousy between you?'

'Of course not. Nana was happy that I was happy. But she was – still is – a romantic. Walter was everything she'd dreamed of in a man. Sometimes she couldn't believe her daughter was married to him.'

'So she must have missed him as much as you when he disappeared?'

Venetia nodded. 'She's never really got over it.'

'Have you?'

Venetia had a last look at herself in the mirror, looking for the truth in her image. 'Yes.'

They went out to the grey Bentley (more chic than a Rolls-Royce, Venetia had told her daughter). She had thought of having pink upholstery as a joke; but that would

84

only have brought more sneers from the family. Occasionally the sneers rubbed her raw and she tried to avoid them. The chauffeur, dressed in grey with a pink shirt and a dark-grey tie, drove them, out of habit, at his usual brisk speed to the cemetery. His mistress, he knew, prided herself on her punctuality and he wondered why she had been a little late coming out of the house this morning.

Walter Springfellow was being buried in the family vault. The first Springfellow had been buried here ninety-nine years ago when the cemetery had first been opened. It was called the Field of Mars and Justine thought it an ideal meeting place for the warring family. She hoped that, for the sake of the father she had never known, there would be no battle today.

An old jacaranda stood just behind the vault, its blossom lying like purple snow on the white marble. Two magpies sat in branches carolling a warning to the humans below: don't hang around or you'll be dive-bombed. A bulbul, as cocky as its red crest, sat on the cross atop the vault. A blimp drifted by overhead, tourists in its gondola busily snapping the grieving ants far below. Edwin Springfellow had used his influence and the media photographers had been stopped at the gates. Some of the more enterprising, however, were perched like magpies in distant trees. Cameramen hate to see grief kept private, especially if it is moneyed. The public, while t'ch, t'ching in disgust, never turns its eyes away from the pictures.

Malone and Clements were also there, though standing well away from the mourners; looking, indeed, like visitors to another grave. Venetia had asked that the burial be kept as private as possible, but at least fifty mourners had arrived, most of them elderly. Malone recognized several retired judges; Fortague, from ASIO, was there too. There was one surprise mourner: John Leeds, Commissioner of Police.

'What's the boss doing here?' said Clements.

Malone was watching the neat-as-always Commissioner standing in the background, making no effort to approach those gathered around the vault. Malone was too far away to see the expression on Leeds's face, but the Commissioner did not seem to have his usual stiffly upright stance. It was hard to tell whether he was grieving or suffering from lumbago.

Venetia turned away as the door of the vault was closed until another day, another death. Edwin stood in front of her, looking at the closed door as if expecting it should have been left ajar for him. She touched his arm. 'Not yet, Edwin. Perhaps you'll be next, but not now.'

'What a cruel thing to say!' Emma had come up behind them.

Edwin, recovering his focus, shook his head; he wanted no scene today. 'No, Venetia has hit the nail on the head. As usual.'

'There's a time and place for hitting nails on the head.'

The three of them were slightly apart from the crowd of mourners. Their voices were low; good manners were everything in front of non-family. Emma and Edwin came of an old school where even murder, if committed, would be in a low key; Emma's behaviour yesterday in the boardroom had been an aberration, something for which Edwin had berated her, in well-mannered terms, on their way home. She had not welcomed the admonition, had secretly enjoyed being bad-mannered and outspoken.

Edwin said, still in a low voice, 'Let's behave ourselves. We still have to come back to your house, Venetia. We're still welcome, I take it?'

'Only for today.'

'I shan't be coming,' said Emma.

'Yes, you will,' said Edwin quietly but firmly. 'We keep up appearances today. Out of respect for Walter.'

Emma said nothing. She glared at them both, then turned and walked away, stumbling in her blind anger over a nearby grave. As she passed the other mourners she managed to produce a smile that sat on her face like a slice of thrown pie. Justine, hurrying by her towards the Bentley, gave her aunt a look of hatred that only the more elderly, dim-sighted bystanders missed. Accustomed to hypocrisy at funerals, some of the women were shocked. The retired judges and the ASIO chief, more accustomed to hypocrisy, wondered what the man they had just laid to rest would have thought of this enmity.

Venetia left Edwin, who had been joined by Ruth, his wife, and moved amongst the crowd as it began to straggle away with that lack of direction that affects mourners at a funeral, as if for a moment they have lost their grip on life. Everyone treated her warily and none with affection; these were Springfellow family friends. All except Roger Dircks and Michael Broad, who were wary but not cool.

'You must be glad that's over,' said Dircks, stating the obvious yet again. As axeman, he would have told Anne Boleyn the same thing.

'It's not over, is it, Venetia?' said Broad solicitously.

'Not really. Did you sleep well last night?'

'No. I don't know what we're going to do about your sister-in-law.' He looked worried, even slightly creased. 'Did you look at the messages this morning?'

She shook her head. 'I've had this –' she waved a hand back at the vault '– on my mind.'

'The New York market crashed last night, five hundred and eight points. That means the local market will go down today.' He looked at his watch. 'It's probably already started.'

'Jesus, of course!' Dircks looked at his own watch; the dead man was forgotten, he had never known him anyway. 'We'd better be going. We'll call you later, Venetia. Nice funeral.'

He moved off, not waiting for Broad. The latter looked after him. 'We'll have to get rid of him. He's bloody embarrassing. What do we do if the worst comes to the worst? I mean our share holdings?'

'Call me as soon as you get back to the office and see what's happening. Who knows? This may be our salvation. If prices do drop, we may be able to buy up enough to drop the bucket on Emma and Edwin.'

He looked at her admiringly, though there was still strain in his lean face. 'You never give up, do you?'

'Never.'

She turned away from him and pushed her way through the mulga scrub of polite hostility; these mostly elderly conservatives had never taken to her. She was surprised when she came face to face with a sincere, if restrained, smile. 'John! Oh, it's been so long –'

'Hello, Venetia. I had to come – I felt it was time . . .' John Leeds opened his hand in what, in a less self-contained man, might have been mistaken for a helpless gesture.

Once upon a passion she had been at the point of falling in love with this honest, conscience-stricken man. He seemed hardly to have changed, except for the grey in his hair and the few lines in the square-jawed face. He was as neat as she remembered him: everything about him was neat, including his pride and his conscience. It had been that in the end that had stopped her from falling completely in love. Someone else's conscience was harder to live with than one's own. Or was for her.

'You've avoided me all these years. I looked for you at some of those official functions, but you always looked the other way.'

'It was best, Venetia. I've been married for years – it's been a happy marriage –'

She nodded, understanding; but half her lovers had been married men. She looked past him and saw Justine coming towards them. 'You've never met my daughter, have you? Justine, this is John Leeds, the Commissioner of Police. He was an old friend of your father's.'

'His protégé,' said Leeds. 'He persuaded me to take a law degree, said it would help me in the Force. It did, so I have him to thank. Hello, Justine. I'm sorry we should meet on such an occasion.'

'I never met my father. At least now I've met one of his old friends.' She said it naturally, without any apparent effort to say the right thing. She was surrounded by her father's old friends, but, as with her mother, they had never been hers. She liked this quiet, sober-faced man at once, aware that her mother, too, liked him. 'We're ready to go back to the house, Mother. Will you come, Mr Leeds?'

'Unfortunately, I can't.' He watched her as she went off and Venetia watched him. 'She's a beautiful girl. Walter would have been proud of her.'

'Would you have been?'

'What does that mean?'

'She could have been your daughter.'

'Is she?'

But she didn't answer that, merely said, 'Why did you come, John? After all these years. Did you feel safe?'

'Straight and to the point, still.' He smiled, though it did not appear to come easily. 'No, it's you I'm concerned for.'

'Me? Well, yes, I have some problems –'

'The takeover? No, I didn't mean that. You probably read about this man Dural who was released from prison a couple of weeks ago . . . I could have sent someone to warn you, but I thought I should come myself.'

'Warn me?'

'I looked up the reports on the case after Walter increased his sentence – I wasn't on the case myself. He threatened he would some day kill Walter. It's too late for that . . . The man's a psycho, Venetia. He could switch his revenge to you. For some years he continued to rant against Walter while he was in gaol. I think you could do with some protection.'

'Not police protection, John, please. The media would get on to it and that might only make this – this psycho worse.' He had to admire how quickly her mind could see a problem. 'I have my own security men. I'll just double them. But thanks . . .' She looked at him steadily. 'That wasn't the real reason you came, was it?'

'No,' he said after a long moment; an old love, no matter

89

how fleeting it might have been, is hard to relinquish. He was happily married, had been for eighteen years, but one can't help wondering what might have been. We create our personal mysteries, sometimes, out of nothing. 'But there's no answer, is there? Goodbye, Venetia. Take care.' He meant there were more dangers for her than a vengeful psycho.

Venetia watched him as he departed, also wondering what might have been. He had been one of half a dozen lovers in that last year of her marriage, but he had been the only one with whom she wanted to lie after the love-making. That had always been her test of men. She sighed, then straightened herself and walked briskly across towards the Bentley.

'Time to go,' said Malone, still standing beside the distant grave.

'Do you think the Commissioner saw us?' Clements watched the Commissioner's car drive off.

'He saw us, all right. He never misses anything.'

'So why was he here? That was a personal little talk he had with her ladyship.' Clements, discreetly, had been using small binoculars to scan the crowd of mourners. 'I wish I was a lip-reader.'

'You might have read more than you wanted to know.' Malone had the greatest respect for the Commissioner. He had cleaned out the Force and at last it also had regained some respect, from the voters.

'Well, where do we go from here?'

'I'm buggered if I know. I've got a feeling this one is going to go into the Too Hard basket.'

They walked across to their unmarked car and drove away. Though he had had little hope of solving the case, Malone was disappointed. He had found himself wondering about Venetia Springfellow, what made her tick. He had seen the uses of power by powerful men; he wondered at its uses by a powerful woman. Most of all, he wondered about her as a woman. He would not mention his wonder to Lisa.

90

3

The driveway and the street outside were lined with cars: Mercedes, Jaguars, Volvos; the two or three small Japanese cars looked shamefaced, like queue jumpers. The security guard walked up and down them like a parking officer, frowning at the occasional passer-by who stopped to stare up at the Springfellow house.

Inside, Venetia glided amongst her guests. At last she came to a stop beside Edwin, whom she had once, for Walter's sake, tried to like. It had not been easy.

'It's like old times,' he said, doing his best to be friendly; he was not by nature an aggressive man. 'So many old faces.'

'*Old* is the word. I find it hard to believe – if Walter were still alive, he'd be seventy-two.'

'I'm seventy. It's unavoidable – getting old, I mean.'

'I'm doing my best to avoid it. I still *feel* young.'

'Is that why you started this fight?' He hadn't meant to bring up the subject.

She looked at him, not wishing to fight him. They were out in the garden, away from the others. She looked at him and then up at all the other old men on the wide verandahs. Once they had been young boys; where had all their energy gone? Why hadn't they stored some of it for days such as they had to live now? If Walter had lived, would all his energies have gone, would she have been far too young for him in bed and out of it? She looked back at Edwin, saw he had no energy for a fight.

'It wasn't meant to be like that, Edwin. It was meant to be a rationalization. You've just said it yourself – you're old. So is everyone on the board, except me. You should talk to Justine, she works amongst the young people in the corporation. Ask her what *they* think. In the foreign exchange section of the bank we have 22-year-olds earning a hundred thousand dollars a year.'

'They're not worth it!'

'They think they are.'

'The young people aren't the ones who have to find the money for all you want to do. You're too ambitious, Venetia.'

She nodded. 'I know. So is Justine.'

He had always found difficulty in arguing with her; she seemed to mock him by agreeing with him. But then Emma came up as a reinforcement.

'We've done our duty. We can go now, Edwin.'

'I'll be in touch,' said Venetia. 'I'm not finished yet.' Michael Broad had called her only a few minutes after she had reached home; he had sounded panic-stricken, told her the market was plunging like a broken dam. 'We'll be back to you.'

For a moment Emma looked uncertain. 'None of this would have happened if Walter had still been alive.'

'No, that's true. If Walter were still alive, I might still be the dutiful wife. Which is what you would have wanted me to be.'

'You were never that.' Emma couldn't control her venom; like cancer, it had got worse with time. 'Walter was fortunate he never learned the truth about you. I saw you today with one of your old boyfriends –'

'Emma, that's enough!' Edwin's usually mild voice was unexpectedly sharp.

For a moment it looked as if Emma might turn her venom on him. She stared at both of them; Venetia would not have been surprised if she had pointed a finger at them and called down a curse. Then abruptly she turned and stalked stiff-legged across the lawn and up into the house. At the top of the steps that led up to the wide verandah she was confronted accidentally by Justine. They stood face to face, something was said that made the guests on the verandah turn their heads, then Justine stepped round her aunt and almost ran down the steps and across the lawn to her mother.

'What's the matter?' Venetia had never seen her daughter so upset.

'What's the matter with that woman?' Justine was on the verge of tears. 'In front of everyone she asked me did I know whose bastard I was!'

There was a gasp from Edwin. He put his hand on his niece's arm, the first time he had touched her in years. 'I don't know what's come over her lately, since the discovery of Walter's . . . Take no notice of her, my dear –'

'That's not easy,' said Venetia, looking up towards the house; Emma had disappeared inside and now all those on the verandah were gazing down at the three of them. 'Taking no notice of her, I mean. You will have to do something about her, Edwin.'

'I'll try.' But he sounded as if he had little hope that he would.

Venetia took Justine's arm and walked her towards the garden's back boundary. The garden had once been a local showpiece, thrown open every year by the Springfellows for charity; Sir Archibald had been one of the nation's more famous camellia growers. There were flowers and shrubs that had been brought from all over the globe; the natural world had been brought to order in these couple of suburban acres. Venetia no longer opened the garden to the public, not even for one day; instead, the Royal Blind Society got a cheque but no invitation. She knew that, though the day was for the benefit of the blind, those who had paid to come were as keen-sighted as Aboriginal hunters, missing nothing, especially her. She had been more on display than any camellia, rose or rhododendron.

'Darling, Emma is a sick woman –'

'What did she mean – whose bastard am I?' Justine herself felt sick. She was thoroughly modern, didn't believe marriage was necessary if two people wanted to live together, saw no shame in an unmarried mother; yet she felt as if muck had been splashed all over her when her aunt had asked *that* question in front of all those stuffed shirts, male and female,

93

who were her mother's enemies. She had never thought of herself as a bastard; to be accused of being one with no known father shattered all her up-to-the-minute attitudes. She was more Mosman than she had realized: there are degrees of illegitimacy that are unacceptable. She *wanted* to be a Springfellow.

Venetia looked out past the rhododendrons towards the harbour. A lone yacht fluttered its sails, like a pariah gull; a Manly ferry hooted for it to get out of the way. *Walter*, she said to the man she hadn't spoken to in years, *what do I tell her?* But Walter, for all his kindness, had never been a forgiving man: lifelong standards had propped him up like callipers.

'I've never thought of anyone but Walter as your father,' she said at last.

Justine looked sideways at her. 'But you've had your doubts?'

'I didn't say that.'

'No, but you're thinking it. You've puzzled me sometimes, but not always. You and I think alike. That's how I know you better than you think I do. So someone else could have been my father?'

Venetia hesitated, then nodded. 'It's possible.'

'Who?'

'No, it wouldn't be fair to them. It was all so long ago and they're leading other lives now.'

'What about being fair to me?' Justine's anger was being switched from her aunt to her mother. If she was a bastard, she wanted to know whose. She felt lop-sided. 'You said *them*. God, how many were there?'

Venetia shook her head. 'No, I'm not going to tell you that. I wasn't any angel, I never have been – you know that. We're alike, Justy. We can't do without men.'

'Even when you were married to –' All at once she couldn't say *Father*; for who was he?

Venetia smiled, though it was only camouflage. 'Are you just going to call him Walter from now on? Darling, I'm sorry this had to happen. You'd never have known it if it hadn't

94

been for that bitch Emma. Yes, there were other men while I was married to Walter. But only in that last year when he spent five days a week down in Melbourne. It might have been different if I'd been a stay-at-home housewife –' She knew in her heart that it would not have been different; she'd have found a lover or two, perhaps even amongst the tradesmen calling at the house. Her sex drive in those days had exhausted Walter and she guessed he had realized the dangers of it. 'But I was working at the studio – there were plenty of attractive men who wanted to take me out . . . So long as Walter didn't know, I didn't see any harm in it. I've never thought much about sin. Neither have you.'

'Speak for yourself,' said Justine, suddenly prim.

'Well, all right, if that's the way you feel . . . I'm sorry Emma had to be such a bitch towards you. It was no way for you to learn . . .'

'Would you have told me some day?'

Venetia thought about that for a moment. 'Probably not. It might have been a pretence, but I've always thought of Walter as your father. Perhaps because that was the easiest thing to do.' She could be remarkably honest with herself at times; but it hurt her now to be honest with her daughter. 'It never really mattered to me who your father was. You were *mine*.'

'Like everything else.'

'You really are being a bastard, aren't you?' She had never before quarrelled with Justine. Her life had been full of enemies, but never one so close to her as this; for she could sense Justine turning into an enemy. So she softened her tone, put out a hand to take Justine's, but the latter drew hers away. 'Don't let's fight. I love you, I really do. Isn't that enough?'

Justine looked at her, not coldly but with no warmth. She felt abandoned, a bastard left on a doorstep. There had always been a streak of romanticism in her: inherited, she now wondered, from whom? 'I don't really know, Mother. I'd like to go home and think about it.'

'Stay here – this is home. I'll get rid of the crowd –'

'No.' She had her own apartment in a luxury block overlooking Circular Quay, a million-dollar twenty-first birthday gift from a loving mother. 'I'd like to be on my own for a while. Everything's all of a sudden, I don't know, *changed*.'

Venetia said fiercely, 'I could kill Emma!'

'We're going,' said Ruth Springfellow right behind them. She and Edwin had come silently across the thick buffalo grass, moving in that quiet way that some elderly people have, as if afraid of disturbing the air about them. 'Thank you for asking us to come.' She spoke as if they had come a great distance instead of from just across the street. 'It was nice to meet all of Walter's old friends.'

'Like old times.' Edwin had an old man's habit of repeating himself. 'Goodbye, Justine. Black suits you. It doesn't always suit a young person.'

'I'm going, too. I'll walk out with you.' She hadn't the panache of her mother; she was afraid of exits. 'Goodbye, Mother.'

'I thought you two would want to stay together on a day like this?' said Ruth, an arranger of other people's moods.

'No,' said Venetia. 'I think it's a day for each of us to be alone with our thoughts.'

'I shouldn't worry too much about Emma,' said Edwin as if listening to another conversation.

Ruth gave him a sharp glance. 'You all worry too much about her. Walter was the only one who kept her in check.'

Venetia watched the three of them go round the corner of the house, avoiding those guests still up on the verandah. She turned and looked out at the harbour. Rain was coming up from the south: it would be a good day for misery. Over in the city fortunes were crashing, greed had given way to fear. For once, however, she was not thinking of the making or losing of money.

She had felt like this only once before, the day they had come to tell her Walter had disappeared. She had always liked to think that since then her character had been based on rock; some might have thought it flint. Now she could feel fissures in herself, a crumbling to sand.

'You all right, sweetheart?' Alice Magee had come down from the house. She was dressed in black like her daughter and somehow looked more at home in it. She was of an age when funerals could be regular events, though she did not go to many; her old friends, the ones who were dying, were too far away, in Cobar and points west. 'I saw you and Justy – what was going on?'

'Did you hear what Emma said to her?'

Alice nodded. 'I won't ask if it was true. That Justy's father could be someone else. I'm just glad Walter couldn't hear her say it. He was looking forward to being a father.'

'How do you know?'

'He told me, once. He never confided in me much, but he told me that. You cheated on him, sweetheart.'

'Don't rub it in, Alice. You've never been the Mother Superior.'

'I couldn't be if I tried. I wonder what they think of you in the convent back at Cobar? Where you are now. What you are. Poor Justy. Someone should hit that Emma bitch on the head.' She was talking to herself, her thoughts jumping around like fleas. 'Walter would have hit her. He could've been a violent man, I think.'

Venetia turned to her. 'How did you know that?'

'I didn't miss much, sweetheart. He was something like your Dad, only he never got drunk like Dad did. Did he ever hit you?'

'No, I still remember what Dad did to you, even though I was so young. Walter knew I'd have left him if he'd hit me.'

'Strange, how most people didn't know him. He was nice, but. I liked him.'

'You *loved* him.' She didn't say it accusingly, but her gaze was steady, a kindly prosecutor's.

'Yes,' said Alice. 'But he didn't know. And I'd never of tried to cheat on my own daughter.'

4

'It'll mean a new sort of garage sale,' said Lisa. 'Porsches and Ferraris will be going like old washtubs.'

'Serves 'em right,' said Con Malone, bugle voice of the workers. 'Greedy buggers.'

'Wash your mouth out,' said Brigid Malone, who would have protected her grandchildren from even a nun's mild imprecations.

'I said beggars. Me teeth slipped.'

'It sounded like buggers to me,' said Tom, whose ears would have been worth a fortune in industrial espionage.

'Don't listen to him, Tom,' said Brigid and stroked the head of her youngest saint.

She never stroked my head, thought Malone, not even when I was Tom's age. But his mother had softened in her latter years, affection was beginning to peep out like a tiny flower between old bricks.

'The papers will be full of it for the next week,' said Lisa. 'At least we shan't have to keep looking at photos of Jonno and Danno and Jenny Kee.'

'Who are they?' said Con, who read only the political and sports pages and wasn't interested in ordinary celebrities.

'I haven't the faintest idea,' said Lisa airily; she could tell small lies with the smoothness of the best of them, but a big lie would tie her tongue in a painful knot. 'I suppose the Springfellows lost a packet?'

'I wouldn't know,' said Malone, tucking into the apple cake and whipped cream, the dessert Lisa made for Con every time he and Brigid came to dinner. 'Russ will fill me in tomorrow. He's the stock market expert.'

'What's your homework, Claire?' said Lisa.

'The Depression of the 1930s.' Claire wrinkled her nose. 'Sister Catherine whipped that one in on us this afternoon, after she'd heard the news. I think she's a sadist.'

'She believes in capital punishment,' said Maureen.

'So do I,' said her grandfather.

'Caning?'

'No, hanging.'

'They don't go in for that at Holy Spirit Convent,' said Malone.

'Pity,' said Con Malone and grinned mock-evilly at his three grandchildren, who reacted with mock horror. All three were older in the head than he thought: they knew that the wrinklies had to be humoured.

Con was shorter and broader than his son; he was sixty-six years old and it seemed that every year had made its mark on his long-lipped, broad face. He and Brigid came every second week for dinner; in the other week Lisa's parents, Jan and Elisabeth Pretorius, took their turn. Malone welcomed the visits, if for no more than to see the effect on his own children, who adored being adored by all four grandparents. He was often at odds with his father, a cloth-cap Labour man; not because he himself had become anti-Labour, which Jan Pretorius was, but because experience had made him apolitical. Sometimes, however, he envied his father's simple outlook on the world and its evils. If prejudice was the child of ignorance, as he had once read, then he was not his father's only child.

'The Yanks are to blame,' said Con.

'What for? Capital punishment?'

'No, the stock market crash.'

'You blame the Americans for everything,' said Lisa amiably. She tried to have a fair opinion of the world, but sometimes found it difficult.

Con nodded in complete agreement with her and Brigid said, 'He'll never forgive President Reagan for being part-Irish.'

Brigid was the one who had given Malone what looks he had. She was plump and always plainly dressed, a chaser after bargains; but there were hints in her plump face of the pretty girl who had gone to the altar with young Cornelius

99

Malone. She had a narrow view of life, believed in the efficacy of prayer and thought holy water was an elixir. She loved everyone to whom she was related, but had great difficulty in showing it.

Later Malone drove his parents home to Erskineville in his five-year-old Holden Commodore. The older Malones had never owned a car and, when not being driven by their son, still went everywhere by public transport, flashing their pensioners' concession cards like gold badges.

'I was at a funeral this morning,' Malone said out of the blue, trying to stop the flood of his father's diatribe against the greed of capitalist bludgers. 'Walter Springfellow's.'

'His missus is another of them capitalist bludgers.' Con Malone could sidestep a subject like a rugby league winger.

'She's a widow,' said Brigid from the middle of the back seat. 'I always feel sorry for widows, no matter how much money they've got. Money doesn't make you happy, does it, Scobie?'

'I wouldn't know, Mum. You and Dad never made me rich.'

'Are you trying to find out who killed Springfellow?' said Con, executing another sidestep.

'Trying.'

Con looked almost sympathetic; it had taken him a long time to accept his son as a mug copper. He was the unrecognized grandfather to the cast and crew of *Sydney Beat*. 'Why don't you give up on it? He's been dead for years.'

'We have to tie up the loose ends.'

'He was never much good, not to the unions. He always had them spooks of his spying on us in the union.' Con had worked for years on the wharves and in the construction trade, where union politics had always been Far Left. Malone sometimes wondered if his father had been a Communist, but had never dared ask him. If he had been, it would have killed Brigid; or anyway had her on her knees for a month, praying for his soul. 'Give up.'

100

'Did you ever give up on anything? You've been fifty years trying to resurrect Keir Hardie and Karl Marx.'

'I'd shoot him if ever he brought back that Karl Marx,' said Brigid from the back seat, sitting back there like the poor man's Queen Mary, hat on head, hands folded over her handbag as if it held the crown jewels.

'That's the only thing you've ever given me,' Malone told his father. 'Bloody-mindedness.'

'I've always said that,' said Brigid. 'He was bloody-minded the day I married him. He wanted to knock the priest down on the altar. I've forgotten why.'

'He wanted to lecture me,' said Con, who would knock God down if He tried to lecture him. 'So you're gunna keep on with the case? What good will it do?'

'I don't know,' said Malone. 'A cop only gives himself a headache when he asks a question like that.'

'That only proves what I've always said about coppers,' said Con, satisfied.

They drew up outside the narrow house in the narrow street in Erskineville. There were no front gardens here, no vacuumed lawns, no blazing banks of azaleas. Behind the narrow terrace houses were tiny back yards backing on to other back yards; the biggest blooms there were the washing on the lines. Malone looked out at the house where he had been born and grown up and tried to be sentimental about it. But sentiment becomes a dry fruit when squeezed.

'I wish you'd move away from here.'

The elder Malones got out of the car. Con looked up and down the terrace. 'They're all strangers. The street's full of Wogs, we even got some of the bloody yellow peril here, too. But it'd be just as bad, no matter where we went.'

'One thing,' grinned Malone, 'you've got no capitalist bludgers down here.'

'Give 'em time, give 'em time. The Wogs and the Chinks will always make money. Thanks for bringing us home.'

'Good-night, Scobie.' Brigid half-raised a hand as if she might pat his shoulder, then let it drop. 'Don't take no notice of Dad. I actually seen him talking to Mrs Van Trong the other day.'

'I was only asking her wasn't there any boats going back to Vietnam,' said Con, never giving up.

Malone laughed and drove off before he embarrassed both of them by getting out of the car and kissing them.

On the way home to Randwick he thought about Walter Springfellow. By the time he had turned into his garage he had made up his mind. He would be bloody-minded, he would not give up.

FOUR

1

He got nowhere in the next two weeks. He sent Andy Graham, one of the junior detectives in Homicide, up to the State Library to ferret his way through newspapers for the period March–April 1966.

'Find out if anyone else went missing at that time. If they did, check Missing Persons here and ask the Victorians if they'd check theirs – maybe someone from Melbourne, a crim or a radical, was gunning for him.'

While Graham lost himself in the State Library, Malone and Clements kept losing themselves in dead ends. Malone rang ASIO, but was told Mr Fortague had been called down to Canberra to headquarters; no, they didn't know when he would be back. He tried to make an appointment with Venetia, but, one of her secretaries said, Lady Springfellow was interstate. He rang Edwin Springfellow at Springfellow and Company, but met a blank wall – 'We have nothing more to say, Inspector,' said Edwin politely and, impolitely, hung up in his ear. Twice he called at the Springfellow apartment in The Vanderbilt in Macquarie Street and twice the doorman told him that Miss Emma Springfellow was away.

Trying to take his mind off the case, he went one night with Lisa to see *Les Misérables*, a booking Lisa had made months in advance. He sat there depressed by the whole show, sympathizing not with Valjean but with Inspector Javert; thirty-nine dollars a ticket to see a cop give up and jump off a bridge. He had noticed several of the more respectable crims in the audience and they all clapped at the death of Javert. He went to work the next morning wondering if he should give up, though he would not jump off any bridge.

'I feel like trying for a warrant and bringing them all in here and keeping 'em here till they tell us something.' He and Clements were sitting facing each other across their adjoining desks in the big room at Homicide, lunching on pizza. 'That's what they'd do in *Woolloomooloo Vice*.'

'What about the daughter?'

'What would be the point with her? She wasn't born when her old man disappeared. How are she and her mother going on their takeover bid?'

'I dunno. There's been nothing in the papers and nobody's talking at the brokers. I gather they're all running around like headless chooks since the Crash. The young guy who sold my shares for me says he wishes he'd followed my example. That made me feel good, coming from someone I pay commission to for advice. Do I look smug and self-satisfied?'

'Every inch of you. My old man would hate you as a capitalist bludger.'

Clements grinned, reached for his phone. 'I think I'll call my bookie. I've made up my mind for the Cup.'

It was the first Tuesday in November, Melbourne Cup Day, the country's holiest day of the year; down in Melbourne, south of the border, it was a public holiday. Elsewhere in the nation, at 2.40 this afternoon, everything would come to a standstill. Right-wing bosses and left-wing shop stewards would stand arm-in-arm in front of television sets; patients on operating tables would be left wide open while doctors and nurses turned up their transistors; bank hold-ups would go into freeze-frame while robbers and staff watched the horse race. If Judgement Day arrived on the first Tuesday in November, the Lord Almighty would have to wait. Unless He, too, was a punter. Which, when one looked at some of those He had created, He might very well be.

'What's your tip?'

'I think I'll go for Kensei. You want me to put a bet on for you?'

'The last time I backed a horse he bit his jockey and raped the mare in front of him. It was like being back on the beat in Newtown.'

Then Chief Inspector Random came down towards them. Clements put down the phone. Random was a tall bony man, with hair that had started to turn grey when he was twenty-one and eyes that had been middle-aged all his life. He had a slow way of moving, as if sleep-walking, but his mind was always a street ahead of his appearance. He was chief of the thirty-six detectives in Homicide, but soon, with the Department's reorganization into regions, he was ticketed for transfer. Malone, as the next senior man, already holding a rank that should have taken him off day-to-day investigation, was tipped to succeed him here in this office. A prospect that Malone was not looking forward to.

'Don't get up.' Malone and Clements hadn't moved. 'Pizza, eh? I thought only pimply kids ate that, and gummy Italians.'

'What's your problem, Greg?' said Malone. 'You look even more unhappy than usual.'

'The wife's gone down to Melbourne with her sister. She's spent five hundred dollars on an outfit she won't be game to wear anywhere else and she'll put two bucks on a horse and come back and say she's had a wonderful time.' He grinned, showing slightly buck teeth. 'Actually, I was glad to get rid of her. I can catch up on my reading – I've got five Elmore Leonards. You ever read him? Oh, there's a homicide.'

Malone was not surprised at Random's way of telling them they had a job; it was his habit, his way of saying that murder was nothing to get excited about. Random hated excitable cops.

'They've found the body of a woman in her apartment in The Vanderbilt in Macquarie Street. Emma Springfellow.'

Malone choked on his slice of pizza and Random looked at him out of those aged grey eyes. 'I thought that might spoil your lunch. Get down there as soon's you can. I'll alert Scientific and the rest of 'em. Can I try a piece of that?'

Malone handed him the rest of the pizza. 'Watch your pimples.' Then he looked soberly at Random. 'Emma Springfellow. They sure it's murder?'

'What makes you say that?'

'It wasn't suicide?'

'I don't know. The uniformed chap who phoned it in said it was murder. A bullet in the chest. You make up your own mind.'

'Greg, can I stay with this one? I'm still on the Walter Springfellow homicide.'

'I wasn't thinking of putting you on anything else. Why?'

'I just want to be bloody-minded.'

Random looked at him, then grinned his slow grin. 'You were always that. Why change?'

He went away back up the room to his own desk. Malone stood up, put on his jacket after wiping his fingers on a paper napkin. 'Righto, lunchtime's over.'

'Hold it a minute.' Clements dialled his phone. He waited a moment, jotting down some figures on a slip of paper, then: 'Sid? Russ Clements. I want five hundred each way on Kensei.' He hung up, saw Malone's raised eyebrows and grinned. 'Okay, it's more than I usually bet. But it's the one day of the year. And while my luck's in . . .'

Malone led the way out of the room, wondering what his own luck was going to be from here on in.

2

Clements parked their unmarked car under a No Standing sign in the lane beside The Vanderbilt. They got out of the car and the heat instantly wilted them. Coming down from Homicide, Clements had switched on the car radio and a news report had told them that the temperature was 34 degrees Celsius ('94 on the old scale,' the announcer advised for the benefit of any ancient who might be listening) and still climbing. Malone hoped that Emma Springfellow's body was in an air-conditioned room.

They walked back into Macquarie Street and up the steps into the old but well-preserved apartment building. The doorman saw them coming and opened the glass doors to them at once. He was a small, thin man and his brown uniform, shiny at the elbows and knees, hung on him as if he had lost weight since the original fitting. He had bright friendly eyes that couldn't be dimmed by the pain and puzzlement in the rest of his face. This was the most exclusive apartment block in the city: murder, most of all, should have been excluded.

'Police?' He had a thin, chirpy voice. 'Oh yes, I remember you, Inspector. I'm Joe Garfield, I found Miss Springfellow. I went up –'

'Can you get someone to relieve you down here?' said Malone. 'We'd like to see you upstairs. What floor is it on?'

'The tenth. She owns – owned the whole floor. I'll be up in a jiffy, soon's I get someone.'

Malone and Clements went up in the automatic, timber-panelled lift, one that climbed slowly, as if it had been designed not to bring on giddiness in anyone who travelled in it. There were residents in the building who had lived here for fifty years or more, elderly voters who had no wish to travel speedily, especially towards heaven. The two detectives stepped out into a small hall, also panelled, and went through the open front door into the Springfellow apartment.

'She lived here all alone?' said Clements to no one in particular.

There were eight rooms to the apartment, every one of them expensively furnished; it was difficult to place the sour, dark woman amidst all this light elegance. There was nothing modern about it; this was the past at its best. There were two shieldback chairs by Chippendale, a sideboard by Hepplewhite, other furniture in the style of those craftsmen by the

107

best of Australian makers; there was no wall-to-wall carpet, but rugs that covered almost the same area. On the silk-papered walls hung a Pissarro, a Degas, a Monet, all paintings that would not offend the sensibilities of a maiden lady; there were no robust Tom Roberts or any of the vulgar later Australians. The robust policemen, capable of vulgarity, were all that was out of place.

The uniformed sergeant had met Malone on other cases. 'She's in the main bedroom, Scobie. Two bullets, I think. They couldn't have missed her heart.'

Malone stood in front of the air-conditioning in the window, cooling off. The building had been built long before built-in central air-conditioning; every window, as far as Malone could see, had its own small unit. They were effective and he was glad for Emma Springfellow's sake. She might offend people while she was alive, but she would not want to offend when she was dead.

'G'day, Jack. How long's she been dead?'

'Hard to say. Some time last night, I'd guess. The rigor mortis is starting to loosen up.'

'Any weapon?'

'No sign of it so far.'

'Go through the flat, Russ. I'll have a look at the body. Which way, Jack?'

Jack Greenup, the sergeant, led the way down a narrow hallway to a big room that looked out over the Botanical Gardens to the harbour. Malone's first thought was: all the Springfellows, while they lived, had to have a view of the harbour. It must have been a pool from which they loved to drink. But then there were three million other voters who, if they could have afforded it, would have loved to drink at the same pool.

'There she is.' Greenup was a heavily built man with a battered face; but law-abiding footballers had done that to him, not criminals. He had been a prominent rugby league forward up till a couple of years ago and still missed the roar of the crowd and the sweet malice of an uppercut in a scrum.

But he was not without feeling and he looked down now at Emma Springfellow with compassion. 'Poor woman.'

Malone looked at the bedroom first. This was as elegant as the outer rooms, though more feminine: a room, he guessed, in which any woman, even a punk rocker, would delight to waken. The bed was queen-sized, though he wondered with whom Emma would ever have shared it; the silk coverlet had been half-dragged off it and one of the bedside tables had been knocked over. Two or three books lay scattered on the floor. Malone remarked the title of one of them: *Unquiet Souls*.

Then he walked round the bed and looked down at Emma. She lay on her back, one hand still clutching the coverlet, an ugly dark stain on the breast of her white blouse. Malone looked at the mask out of which she would never look again; there was no malice on it, no contortion, just a cold still peace. She looked strangely young, but then corpses often did.

She was one of the privileged; yet it had availed her nothing. She had finished up at the most democratic level, dead. He stepped over the body and pushed up the window; there was no balcony. Ten floors below, workmen were busy in Macquarie Street, preparing for the nation's 200th birthday celebrations that would begin in a couple of months. It was one of the most attractive boulevards in the whole country; and one whose mention suggested power, at least in Sydney. Up the street on the far side was Parliament House, the bear-pit where State politics were fought out behind an elegant colonial façade; on this side were the brass plates of the city's specialists, the medical oligarchy who believed in their own feudalism. There were few, if any, ugly buildings in its length; it was a street that, without effort, suggested dignity, even permanence in a city that was constantly changing. Murder had been done, even if only politically, in Parliament House; but that was to be expected. Otherwise, it was not a street for violent crime.

He pulled down the window, turned round as Clements came to the door. 'The Scientific fellers are here, Scobie.'

'Get them started. What about the doc?'

109

'He's on his way. Oh, the doorman's come up, too.'

Malone went out to the living-room; or would Emma have called it the drawing-room? Garfield, the doorman, was there, fidgeting anxiously. He had freshly combed his sparse dark hair sideways across his sallow scalp; it lay on his head like a black lace doily on a melon. He kept putting his hands in his pockets and taking them out again. He was not accustomed to being surrounded by police.

'How did you come to find Miss Springfellow?' asked Malone.

'I brought her paper up first thing this morning, the same's I do with all the flats. That would have been just after eight, when I come in. She usually went for a walk over in the Gardens every morning about ten. I didn't see her this morning, but I didn't think nothing of it, it could of been too hot for her. Then about, I dunno, three-quarters of an hour ago, maybe more, a lady phoned me downstairs, a lady from, I dunno, somewhere, Pymble, I think. She said she was expecting Miss Springfellow for lunch, a Melbourne Cup lunch, and she hadn't turned up and she hadn't been able to raise her on the phone, would I go up and see if anything was wrong. I come up and I saw the paper was still outside her door. I knocked, but I got no answer. So I used me pass-key and I come in and I found her. I phoned you blokes and that was it. I still can't believe it. Not her.'

All this had come out almost without his taking a breath. He was a decent man, not a gossip, a doorman who respected doors that were closed; but he would talk about this for the rest of his life, beginning tonight. He could not wait till he got home to tell the wife and family. Miss Springfellow – murdered! Her, of all people: you wondered who might be next.

'Were you working last night?'

'Nup. I do me shift from eight to eight, four days a week. Next week I do three days. There's another bloke, Paul Kosciusko, same's the mountain, works with me.'

'So there's no one on after eight p.m.?'

'Nup. There's a security lock, a good 'un – you'd have to break the glass in the doors to get in. All the tenants have their own key.'

'Did Miss Springfellow have any visitors before you went off last night?'

'Yeah.' Then he hesitated, as if he suddenly realized he might be pointing the finger at someone. After a moment he went on: 'Her niece come in about five minutes before I went off.'

'The niece. Justine?' The doorman nodded. 'How was she?'

'How'd you mean?'

'Did she look normal or was she upset or anything?'

'She seemed all right. I don't know her well – I've only seen her once or twice before. I've seen her in the papers, of course.'

'She wasn't a frequent visitor to her aunt?'

'Eh? Frequent? No, no. This was the first time I'd seen her in, geez, I dunno how long.'

'Did you call up Miss Springfellow to let her know her niece was coming?'

'We do that all the time – it's part of the security.'

'How did she sound?'

'I dunno. The same as usual, I suppose. She was always a bit cold, always a lady, but. I put Miss Springfellow, the niece, into the lift and then I knocked off.'

'So you didn't see her leave?'

Again the hesitation: 'No-o. Look, I don't wanna put anyone in, Inspector –'

Malone gave him a reassuring smile. 'You're not, Joe. We don't arrest people just because they've been visiting someone. We need more than that. That's why all these fellers are here.'

Garfield looked around the room at the Scientific men, the photographer and the two uniformed officers. He had followed the government medical officer into the apartment and now he and Malone had to stand aside as two men from

111

the funeral contractors came in with a stretcher. Murder has its own bureaucracy.

'Geez, I didn't know it took so many of you.'

'Union rules,' said Malone and saw that Garfield wasn't sure whether to take him seriously or not. 'If Miss Spring-fellow had any other visitors, after you'd gone off, how would they get in?'

'They'd speak to her on the intercom and she'd just press the button in the flat here. It's out there by the front door.' He nodded back over his shoulder. 'It's a standard system, the same as you find everywhere else.'

'Righto, Joe. Could you give Sergeant Clements a list of all the other tenants?' He looked over at Sergeant Greenup. He always respected protocol; he never gave orders to another officer's men. 'Jack, could you have your chap go down and start asking them if any of them heard any shot or saw anything suspicious?'

Greenup looked at his constable, a good-looking boy who had all the alertness of a young pointer: he looked as if he might go bounding down the fire-stairs looking for a scent. 'Okay, Gary, you've always wanted to be a detective. Now's your chance.'

'If someone comes up with something,' said Malone, 'bring 'em up here. Be polite.'

'Yes, sir.' The young policeman went off, nose held up to the wind, followed by the doorman, who went with some reluctance. It would have been something to tell the family tonight, to explain how the police worked.

'He's a good boy, that Gary,' said Greenup, who was content to remain in uniform; detective work meant broken shifts and too many hours. 'You might keep an eye on him. He's got more intelligence than he knows what to do with.'

'We don't want him with us, then,' said Clements and put on his dumb look.

Malone turned as the police surgeon came through the door from the bedroom. He was a red-faced, balding man with a large belly and he preferred corpses to be found on

112

beds rather than on the floor; like an overweight penitent, he always had difficulty in getting up from his knees. He was dusting down his trousers now as he stopped in front of Malone.

'Two shots to the chest, Scobie, one right through the heart, as far as I can see. Death would have been instantaneous. Both bullets are still in the body. The empty cases are missing. What sort of killer housekeeps after a murder?'

'Any idea when she died?'

'I'd be guessing at this stage – I'll let you know after the autopsy. But I'd say between ten and eleven o'clock last night, give or take an hour or so. Can they take the body now?'

Malone glanced at Clements. 'Okay?'

'The Scientific guys have done their bit. Yeah, it's okay.'

The police surgeon went back into the bedroom and Malone nodded at the framed photograph and the leather-bound book Clements was holding. 'What have you got there?'

'I'll tell you later,' said Clements and looked at Malone warningly.

The GMO came back, followed by the two funeral men, the green-shrouded body of Emma Springfellow on the stretcher between them. As they passed the door of a room off the living-room, the man at the front of the stretcher pulled up sharply. The man at the rear kept walking for a pace, driving the stretcher into the front man's back. Emma Springfellow made her last involuntary movement, sliding forward on the stretcher to kick the bearer in the behind, something she would never have done while she was alive.

'For Chrissakes, Des –'

'There's a TV in there.' Des, a beefy man who looked as if he might have started carting carcasses in an abattoir, twisted his arm to look at his watch; Emma rolled to one side and for a moment looked as if she might slide off the stretcher. 'The Cup's just about to go.'

Everyone in the room, the Scientific men, the photo-

113

grapher, even Jack Greenup, looked at Malone. He looked at Clements, sighed and grinned. 'I don't think Emma would have minded. She was going to a Cup lunch anyway.'

The funeral men took the stretcher into the room, which seemed to be a den, put down Emma and stood aside while all the other men crowded in beside them. Malone stood in the doorway, Emma Springfellow's shrouded corpse at his feet. Someone switched on the television set and the picture came on the screen.

'They're off! Just in time!'

Excitement throbbed in the room as, six hundred miles away, twenty-one horses thundered round Flemington racetrack, today's altar for the nation. Only Emma and Malone remained unexcited: she because she was beyond all odds, he because he had no interest in horse-racing, not even in the Melbourne Cup. He was lucky he had his rank, otherwise he might have been arrested for being un-Australian.

'You beaut!' Clements stepped back as his bet, Kensei, went past the post a head in front. His heel caught under the stretcher and he would have sat on Emma if Malone hadn't caught him. He looked down between his legs at the green plastic shroud. 'Sorry, old girl.'

Nobody else had backed Kensei. They all looked morosely at the grinning Clements. Des, the stretcher-bearer, said, 'How much did you have on him?'

'Just ten bucks,' said Clements. 'I'm not a betting man.'

Everybody began to file past him and Malone. Des and his mate picked up Emma Springfellow and she left her apartment for the last time, going out head first, no way for a lady to depart.

When they were alone Malone said to Clements, 'For a non-betting man, you know how to pick the ponies.'

Clements grinned. Then abruptly he sobered and held up the silver-framed photograph. Two men in bush trousers and shirts, rifles held in the crook of their arms, stood with a foot each resting on a huge crocodile. In the bottom corner of the photo a neat hand had written: *Roper River, June 1963. With much love.*

'The Roper River – that's in the Northern Territory.'

'That's it. You recognize the two guys?'

'The one on the right, that's Walter Springfellow. The other one – no, I don't think so.' He knew who it was, but, unaccountably, was reluctant to say so.

'It's him! It's the Commissioner. Twenty-four or five years younger, but it's him, all right.'

Malone made a pretence of studying the photo. 'Yeah, it's him. Who wrote the inscription – him or Walter?'

'Walter, I think. Here, have a look at this.'

Malone took the leather-covered diary, opening it where Clements had placed his finger. It was an expensive Italian edition, the paper too good for mundane social jottings; Emma seemed to have used it as much as a journal of her thoughts as a record of her daily events. Her handwriting was almost copperplate, small but with character and written with a thin-nibbed pen; no biro for her.

Malone read the entry for Tuesday, October 20:

They buried the last of Walter today; with it they buried the last of my love. Even after all these years I cannot believe I shall never see him again. But, of course, I shan't . . . Venetia's old lover made a reappearance. One supposes he felt an obligation to – as Walter's supposed friend. I had a scene with Justine, who could be his bastard. I am ashamed of myself for letting it happen in public, but sometimes true feeling has to break out. I had to speak for Walter –

The entry broke off with a scratch, as if she had not been able to control her pen.

Malone looked at Clements. 'Put these in your murder box, put the lid on it and lock it in your desk.'

Clements's concern was a mirror of Malone's own. He went to a desk against one wall, fumbled in several of the

115

drawers and came up with a large manila envelope. He put the photo and the diary in it. 'What do we do next?'

'You're the expert on form. Tell me how we're going to pick a winner on this one.'

3

They left the Scientific men still working in the apartment and went out to the lift. Going down, it stopped at the seventh floor and the young constable got in. 'Nothing so far, sir. Most of the tenants are out. Those I've seen say they heard nothing – they said they'd have been watching TV about then. They're a pretty elderly lot here, sir – they'd have the volume turned up pretty high, I reckon.'

Malone grinned, holding the lift door open as they came to the sixth floor. 'You should hear my kids when they watch TV. What's your name?'

'Gary Sobers.'

'You're kidding.'

The young constable returned Malone's grin. 'No, sir. My old man thought Gary Sobers was the greatest cricketer he ever saw. Our name's Sobers, so he called me after him.'

'You play cricket?'

'With a name like mine? Would a guy named Joe DiMaggio play baseball in the States? No, sir, I stick to golf.'

Crumbs, I'm old. I played against Sobers and now here's a kid who was named after him. 'I'll be back at Homicide in an hour. Call me there and let me know what you've dug up.'

Sobers got out of the lift and the two detectives went on down to the ground floor. Clements said, 'You trust the kid? I think we should get some of our own guys down here.'

'I'll send 'em down. I want a search for the gun, in case the killer got rid of it. They can try the Gardens over the road. *Gary Sobers.*' He shook his head. 'He makes me feel I'm ready for my pension.'

The doorman rushed to open the front door for them.

'Good luck – Inspector. I mean – I mean I hope you find out who done it. If I think of anything, I'll let you know.'

'If you do, we'll be truly grateful.'

Outside in the heat Clements said, 'Truly grateful?'

'I think it was him opening the door for me. Nobody ever does that for me at Homicide.'

Clements opened the passenger's door of their car and stood back. 'Let's hear that truly grateful bit again.'

He went round the car, took the parking ticket from under the windscreen wiper, tore it up and dropped it in the gutter and got in behind the wheel. Malone said, 'How much did you win on the Cup?'

'I dunno. Kensei would've been about tens, maybe twelves, something like that. I guess I'll come out with about six thousand for the win and another fifteen hundred for a place. Say seven and a half grand all up.'

'What are your bank tellers going to think? You must be richer than the Springfellows.'

'Where to now?'

'Springfellow House. We've got to go and tell Edwin Springfellow his sister is dead.'

'And then?'

'And then we'll have a chat with Justine.'

Clements took the car down to Circular Quay and swung into the garage of Springfellow House. There was no attendant in sight, so he parked the car in the vacant space beside the grey Bentley. Police parking privileges are priceless.

Edwin Springfellow's office was on the seventh floor, a darkly panelled room that suggested quill pens and abacuses and a leisurely approach to the making of money. There were no computers here, no hint of the feverish activity that usually shook the walls of the floor below. Though nothing was shaking on the sixth floor this week, except the staff: the effect of the Crash two weeks before was still being felt. The headless chooks, as Clements had described them, had their heads back on but held there only by the Scotch tape of

117

desperate hope. Edwin, however, was calm; he had the sort of money that never sinks, that rides out recessions and depressions with the flotation of royal wealth.

He was calm, that is, until Malone and Clements brought him the news of his sister's murder. He seemed to shrink in his high-backed leather chair, to age visibly like a man who had suddenly had all substance drain out of him.

'You're sure? Murder? But of course you're sure, it's your job, isn't it? First Walter, now Emma –' He looked around him, as if looking for the third gun, the one that was meant for him. 'Who, for God's sake? Who would want to kill her?'

'When did you last see your sister?'

Edwin was shocked; but not numbed. 'Are you suspecting *me*?'

'Why would you say that?'

Edwin looked flustered; he waved a helpless hand. 'I don't know . . .'

'Mr Springfellow, we're just trying to trace her movements last night.'

'I saw her at the weekend. Sunday – she came for lunch.' Edwin was collecting his thoughts; he sat up in his chair. 'I spoke to her on the telephone last night about – I suppose it was about six. Just before I left the office.'

'How did she sound?'

Edwin hesitated. 'Tense, a little tense. She's been like that for several weeks. This family takeover battle . . . I advised her to put it out of her mind for today. She was going to a Cup luncheon at a friend's. She liked that sort of thing, women getting together.'

'Did she say anything about expecting a visitor last night?'

'Well, no-o . . .'

'You mean yes.'

Edwin fiddled with a silver fountain pen; he, too, would never soil his fingers with a biro. 'She just said she was expecting someone to drop in during the evening. She said she might have a surprise for me next time she talked to me.'

'She gave you no hint of what the surprise might be?'

'No. She didn't say who was coming by.'

'You're sure of that?'

'Of course I'm sure! Dammit, Inspector . . . I'm sorry.' Edwin could not shed his good manners; as the trapdoor opened, he would raise his hat in farewell to the hangman. 'No, she didn't say who. My sister could be – could sometimes be, well, a little secretive. Maiden ladies can sometimes be like that. Perhaps it's because they have no one to confide in.'

'Bachelors can be the same,' said Malone and looked sideways at Clements, who didn't smile, just gave him a secretive look. He was holding the big manila envelope on his knees, but Malone didn't ask him to open it and show the contents to Edwin.

He looked back at Edwin. 'I'd got the impression that you and your sister were close.'

'On the strength of one interview with us? Do you have any siblings, Inspector?'

Malone had to remember what a sibling was. 'No, I'm an only child.'

'Do you have children of your own?'

'Three.'

'Ask them how much they confide in each other.' Not bloody likely, thought Malone. His kids' secrets were their own. 'My sister kept her confidences to herself.'

'Did she ever confide in your brother?'

Edwin fiddled with his pen again. 'Ye-es. Yes, they were close. They were – *friends*, real friends. Brother and sister often aren't. Emma and I weren't.' There was no hint of regret or bitterness in his soft voice. 'Do you think there's any connection between her murder and my brother's?'

The thought hadn't occurred to Malone; he hid his surprise that Edwin's mind should have gone in that direction. 'Who knows? We'll let you know if that's the way it turns out.'

Malone and Clements left Edwin and went up to the

twenty-ninth floor. They were admitted, after their credentials had been checked as if they were newly arrived immigrants, into Justine's office. It was not a large office, there was no title on the door; but it was on a corner and it had a splendid view of the harbour. Location gave it its cachet.

They had no sooner told Justine of her aunt's death than Venetia came down from above in a pink-and-grey storm. 'Why didn't you come to see me first? How dare you upset my daughter like this –'

'Calm down, Lady Springfellow,' said Malone.

'Don't you tell me to calm down!'

'Please yourself,' said Malone and stood patient and calm; Clements looked equally at ease. The temperature in the room began to drop.

'All right, Inspector, I apologize. But this dreadful news –' She went round behind the desk and put her hands on Justine's shoulders as if she were going to give her some relaxing massage. 'My brother-in-law called me –'

'Another – *murder*?' For the second time shock was prompting only questions from Justine. 'How? Why?'

'We're hoping you might be able to help us,' said Malone, going off the deep end.

Justine, ashen-faced, looked at him in puzzlement. She put a hand up to her shoulder and squeezed her mother's fingers. Venetia asked the question for her: 'How can she help? How do you mean?'

'She might have been the last person to see her aunt alive. Except for the murderer, of course,' he added, though his voice was flat and had no hint of sympathy in it.

Venetia turned her daughter's face up towards her, as one might a child's. 'Did you see Emma last night?'

Justine pulled her chin out of her mother's hand, nodded her head almost defiantly. 'I know you told me not to go near her. But I called her yesterday afternoon –'

'When was that?' Clements was making notes.

'Oh, I don't know. Before I left here, about five, I guess. I went home – I live just across there –' She nodded out at the block of apartments by the Cahill Expressway. The Wharf was not as exclusive as The Vanderbilt, but it was more expensive; the money in it was so new one could smell the ink as one drove past. 'Then I went up to see Aunt Emma about eight o'clock.'

'Why?' Venetia was ready to hold her own interrogation.

'I – I thought she might listen to a new offer. I knew she was never going to listen to you –'

She's lying, Malone thought; either for her mother's benefit or for ours. 'What time did you leave her?'

'I'm not sure. I'm not very good about time – I never look at my watch.' She looked at it now, a gold-strapped one, as if to make sure she was still wearing it. 'I suppose I was there an hour or so –'

'Just talking?'

She looked at her mother first, then back at Malone. 'Arguing, most of the time. But I never got – *violent*. I mean, I didn't threaten her or anything.'

'Nobody has said you did, darling,' said Venetia and looked threateningly at Malone.

Malone didn't take up the challenge. 'Did your aunt mention she was expecting someone else?'

'Yes,' said Justine. 'She said someone was coming to see her.'

'She didn't say who?'

'No.'

'When you left, did you part on a friendly note?'

'No-o. It was impossible to be friends with Emma. It was for me.'

'How was she with you, Lady Springfellow?'

'We were never close. And lately – you've read the papers, I'm sure. We were business enemies, one of the columnists called us.'

'I didn't read that,' said Malone, who had sent for back issues of the newspapers after attending Walter Spring-fellow's funeral and read every word about the family war. 'So there was bad feeling between you and the deceased?'

'Yes.' Venetia's hand tightened just slightly on Justine's

121

shoulder; Malone saw the material of the daughter's dress drawn up in a crease. 'Why lie about it? It was common knowledge.'

'We miss out on a lot of common knowledge,' said Malone. 'We live a pretty sheltered existence in Homicide.'

'Balls,' said Lady Springfellow. For a moment the cultivated voice coarsened, she was the young girl down from the bush and determined to take on all-comers in the tough, dirty city. She had been younger than Justine was now, but tougher, much tougher. 'Don't beat about the bush with me, Inspector. If you have something to accuse us of, do it!'

'Calm down,' Malone said again. 'We've only just started on this. We don't rush in without all the evidence we can round up.'

'How much have you got? Is that evidence?' She nodded at the manila envelope in Clements's big hand. 'Have you been taking things from Emma's flat? Can you do that?'

'We could strip the flat,' said Clements. 'Carpets, everything. We'd give the next of kin a list, of course.'

'Is what you have in there on the list? What is it?'

'You're not the next of kin. Her brother Edwin is that.'

'Let Lady Springfellow see the photo,' said Malone.

Clements raised an eyebrow; then without a word he took the photo out of the envelope. 'Do you recognize these two men?'

'The one on the right is my husband.'

'Who is the other one?'

'I haven't the faintest idea,' said Venetia.

Clements turned the photo towards Justine. 'Miss Springfellow?'

She leaned forward to look at the photo; her mother's hand slipped off her shoulder. 'Yes, the man on the right is my – my father. I don't recognize the other man. What does the inscription say?'

'"Roper River, June 1963,"' said Malone. '"With much love." Do you recognize the handwriting, Lady Springfellow?'

'No,' said Venetia.

Women, generally, don't show the gall that men do as liars. They are subtler and sometimes their subtlety shows, especially when there is no time to weave it properly. These two are lying, Malone thought, telling different lies but lying all the same.

'What else do you have in the envelope?' said Venetia.

'There's a diary,' said Clements, but didn't take it out of the envelope. 'We can't let you read that. That's the deceased's property.'

'And yours, of course.'

'And ours,' said Malone, 'of course.'

Clements stood up, looked at Malone, who nodded. Justine stood up beside her mother; they were shoulder to shoulder but they did not look indomitable, not even Venetia. But she faced them full on, because that was her best side; and anyway, to turn in profile is to half-retreat. This one won't retreat, thought Malone. But Justine, ah: she was already in retreat, front on.

'We'll be back,' he said.

4

On their way back to Homicide Clements said, 'I was surprised when you showed her the photo.'

'I don't know whether I did the right thing. It's out in the open now, a little bit anyway. She's lying, though. She knew who the second man was.'

'Do I still lock it away in my desk or do I tell Greg Random?'

'He'll know about it eventually. I guess we might as well show it to him now.'

But when they got back to Homicide Chief Inspector Random had left the office and wouldn't be back till the next day. Clements got out his 'murder box', the repository of a thousand items from a hundred crimes, an old shoebox held together by what looked like metres of Scotch tape; he was superstitious about it, to lose it would be like saying goodbye to all his experience. It was empty now, ready for a new crime. He tried to put the framed photo in the box, but it wouldn't fit. He put the photo and the diary back in the manila envelope.

'Maybe I'd better start a new box for the Springfellows.'

'Maybe you'd better. We still have Walter's murder on our hands.'

'What about the Commissioner?'

'That's Greg Random's problem,' said Malone; but little did he know.

FIVE

1

'I had to come and see you,' said John Leeds. 'I thought it better that I see you here at home.'

Venetia had been surprised when he had called her; even more surprised when he said he had to see her at once, preferably where they would not be disturbed. She had left her office immediately and had been at home in Mosman only ten minutes when he had arrived. She had noticed that when he had driven up the driveway he had been in what she assumed was his own car. He was not in uniform and she wondered if he had changed before leaving the office. She never missed a detail, especially about men.

'Did you tell the security guard who you were?' She held his hand as she led him through to the back of the house, but she did not attempt to kiss him.

'That I was the Police Commissioner? No, I just said my name was Leeds and you were expecting me. He may have recognized me, but that's a risk . . .'

'Why all the secrecy, John?'

'Because I *am* the Commissioner and as such I shouldn't be here.'

Her memories of him weren't as sharp as she had imagined. Had he always been as ill at ease as he appeared now?

'I got the news about Emma's death a couple of hours ago. It was pure accident – I usually don't get reports, summaries, till the next day. I was trying to make up my mind whether to call you –'

'Why? To offer sympathy? Tea?' She poured two cups. A tray with a fine china tea-set was waiting for them in the sun-room. 'I'm sorry Emma is dead, but you'd be wasting sympathy on me, John. She'd have felt the same way about me if I'd died.'

'Venetia – it was *murder*!' He was still an innocent man in some ways; he couldn't bring himself to believe the depths of enmity some women have towards each other.

'I know. Biscuit? I'm sorry she died that way – it's horrible. I'm not callous, John, just honest. Now why did you come? Why all the secrecy?'

He stirred his tea without looking at it; he might have been stirring his reasons into some sort of coherence. He was here for reasons that went against the whole grain of his training and character. Like her, he had claims to honesty; perhaps more, he thought, than she did.

'I went to see Emma last night.'

She frowned, her cup stopped halfway to her mouth. 'To see Emma? But you haven't seen her in God knows how long . . . Have you?' She hadn't meant to, but she abruptly sounded suspicious.

'I haven't seen her since a week or two after Walter disappeared. We saw each other at his funeral, but we just nodded, that was all. She called me yesterday morning and asked me to go and see her. She said she had something important to discuss with me. I got there about nine, a few minutes afterwards. Venetia –' He paused, put down his cup and saucer. 'I was just coming down Macquarie Street when I saw Justine come out of The Vanderbilt. She was running and she had her hand over her face, as if she were upset. She ran down Macquarie Street, going home, I guess. She lives in The Wharf, doesn't she?'

Venetia nodded. She put down her own cup and saucer. 'Yes, I know she'd been to see Emma. The police know, too – your Inspector Malone and Sergeant Clements. They've already been to see us.'

Leeds nodded morosely. 'I might have known it. Malone doesn't miss much.'

'Did you go up to see Emma?'

'Yes.'

'Was she still alive?'

'Of course! Good Christ, Venetia, I'm not saying –'

'That Justine might have killed her? I know you're not. She's not as tough as I am and I'm not a murderer. Neither are you, John.'

'Of course I'm not!' He picked up his cup, took a long swallow of tea, as if his throat had suddenly become dry. Then he sat back, re-arranging himself in his usual mode, neat and calm. It was a mask, but it was a familiar one and he felt more comfortable in it.

'What did Emma want to see you about?'

'She accused you of having Walter murdered.'

'She *what*?' Venetia lost her own control. She almost sprang out of her chair, began walking up and down, stiff-legged but with her body trembling. 'Good God – what a bitch! I knew she hated me – she was ready to start spreading dirt about you and me after all these years – but to say something like *that*! What did you say?'

'I said it was ridiculous.'

'That's all? That it was ridiculous?'

'No, if you must know, I lost my temper. We had quite a row.'

'She seems to have spent last night having rows – she had one with Justine.'

'Did she make the same accusation to Justine?'

'No, not as far as I know. If she did, Justine hasn't told me. What did Emma actually say?'

'That she was going to tell Inspector Malone to start looking into your past, that you had reason to have Walter killed because he had found out about your – your lovers.'

'Did she include you amongst them?'

He hesitated. 'Yes.'

Venetia paused, leaned on the back of her chair. 'She'd

127

gone crazy, I think. Even Edwin said she was far worse over the past few months than she'd ever been before.'

'It could have been a late menopause.'

She gave him a dry laugh. 'Oh, come on, John! God, you men blame everything on that. Emma went through the menopause ten or fifteen years ago. She was a natural-born bitch even before she got into puberty. No, she just went round the bend naturally. *If* you go crazy naturally,' she added; she had a pedantic grasp of her own sanity, she would know exactly the reasons if ever she went mad.

Then she said, 'Do you think I hired someone to kill Walter?'

'No.'

She sensed he was holding something back. 'What do you know that I don't? About Walter?'

He hesitated again, looked uncomfortable. 'I don't know everything, but I can't tell you the little I do know.'

'John, he was my husband! Your friend! God Almighty, how can you keep secrets from me on something like that? I didn't have Walter killed. I have a right to know who did, if you know!'

'I don't know. All I know is there was a cover-up.'

'Why? Who by? ASIO?'

He nodded, reluctantly. 'I was never on the case – I deliberately dodged it. You know why,' he said, the old conscience-stricken lover. 'Everything was just suddenly pulled out of the files. It wasn't just ASIO – I understand the word came from higher up than that. From the Prime Minister's office.'

There would be a blank wall there, she knew. The Prime Minister of the time was himself dead; he, too, had disappeared, while surfing. There had been suggestions of mystery about that, bizarre theories that, in retrospect, were laughable. She wondered why Harold Holt, an uncomplicated man if what history told her was true, would have ordered all enquiries on Walter's disappearance to be stopped.

'He'd have done it on ASIO's advice,' she said.

'Of course. But you don't think you're going to get anything out of them, do you?'

'Do you think Emma's death has anything to do with Walter's disappearance? Could she have sent for someone else to see her after you?'

'Who else would it have been? Another – lover?' It was difficult for him to be cruel, but he was a policeman as well as an ex-lover.

She shook her head, saddened that he had to put such a question. There was still some of the old feeling left for him; old love that is not chopped off by bitterness lingers in the heart, if not in the mind. She had not really looked into her heart in a long time. Our deepest feelings are a hundred fathoms deep: most of us are not capable of diving so far.

'You didn't have to ask that, John. I was never an angel, you knew that. But I never went to bed with devils.'

'That sounds like something out of a Channel 15 soap opera.' But he smiled, suddenly relieved.

She smiled, too. 'I know. I get that way sometimes. I don't read any more, not like I used to. Except company reports and business magazines. I look at TV now for relaxation. Sometimes I think I'm a character in *Dynasty*.'

'So do a lot of other people,' he said not unkindly.

'We're beating about the bush, John. We still don't know if there's any connection between Emma's death and Walter's. If there is – if it comes out . . . Too much may come out about you and me. Inspector Malone has an old photo of you and Walter. I said I didn't know who you were.'

'That was foolish. Malone is no fool.'

'I'm beginning to appreciate that. I was just hoping to protect you.'

He nodded, put his hand up to fix his already perfectly knotted tie. He said carefully, 'Venetia – is Justine my daughter?'

'Did Emma mention that last night?'

'Yes.'

She sat down again, pulled her chair close to his and put

her hand on his. She could see him last night with Emma as the latter raked up old coals and hauled him across them. 'John, I honestly don't know. There would have to be a blood test and I'm never going to put that to Justine – or to you. She wants to be Walter's child, that's the way it's always been with her and that's the way it's going to stay. You're happily married – you told me that at the cemetery that day. Why complicate things for yourself?'

'If she were, I'd feel responsible for her –'

'Don't you think I can look after her? What about your wife and children? You have – what? three, haven't you? Oh, I looked you up in *Who's Who*, when I came back that day from the funeral. What about your responsibility towards them? Don't be chivalrous, John – it's too late for anything like that. And I never expected it – not of any of my men.'

'Ah, if only things had been different –' Then he smiled. '*That* sounds like something out of a soap opera.'

'I'm surprised you look at them. John – stay for dinner.' She wanted his company, not sex.

He leaned forward and kissed her on the lips. 'It's too late, Venetia. Even for us to be just friends.'

She wiped the pink lipstick from his mouth: she could not leave her trademark on an old lover. 'You're right. I shouldn't have suggested it.'

When he had gone she went and sat in the window-seat of the sun-room, looking out across the lawns and shrubs to the harbour. The sky to the west was bright red: it was wonderful, she thought idly, how Nature could sometimes get away with such bad taste. Bright colours were not her taste, though there were few more colourful figures in Australian business. ·

Her colours had been dimmed in the past couple of weeks. Engrossed in the takeover bid, she had kept only half an eye on the stock market: that had been Michael Broad's domain. When the dust had settled after Black Tuesday, she had been shocked at the extent of their losses, the corporation's and her own. She was candid enough to admit, to herself if to no one else, that greed had blinkered her; if she had brought off the takeover, she would have had only one or two peers in the whole country in power and wealth. She was philosophical about the loss of her wealth; to be worth 500 million instead of 700 million takes only a minor adjustment, a shrug of the shoulders and no less respect from one's bank. The loss of the prospective power, however, was a body blow. She had been on the road to being an empress, but had finished up still a commoner. Which, being philosophical again, she supposed was better than being common.

Emma, and perhaps a lot of other women, had thought of her as common. That was because of her men; history has always had less respect for whores than for rakes. She had never stolen another woman's man, at least not for more than a night and she had never considered that theft; sex was not love and so long as the man took love home to his wife, no harm was done. She had cheated on Walter, but love there had died six months after they had married; she had become pregnant, on his insistence, trying to save the marriage, but she had known, even before his disappearance, that it would not work. She had been on the verge of falling in love with John Leeds, but she had known in her heart that marriage to him would be a failure, too.

There had been a dozen proposals over the past twenty years, but she had always said no. She was capable of love, but not of sacrifice; and marriage demanded both. She loathed partnerships; in marriage she would always be making takeover bids. Only lately had she begun to recognize that amongst her dividends was loneliness.

2

Russ Clements had gone home and Malone was putting on his jacket, ready to follow him, when the phone rang. 'Inspector Malone? Scobie, this is the Commissioner. Can you come over and see me?'

'Now, sir?'

'Yes, now. And Scobie – for the moment, don't mention this to anyone. You understand? *Anyone.*'

Malone hung up, smelling politics again; but this might be the worst of all, personal politics. *Do I take the photo and the diary?* But they were locked away in Clements's desk, safe from even hands like his own.

He walked across to Police Headquarters in College Street. The evening was still warm; the sky was turning from red to pink. He was checked in at the desk and was about to get into the lift when Assistant Commissioner Zanuch stepped out.

'Malone, how are you? Coming up to see me?'

Why would I be coming to see you? 'No, sir. I'm on my way up to the Commissioner.'

Zanuch was the best-dressed man in the Department, every bit as spruce as Leeds but more relaxed, less of a band-box dummy. He was as well known at society functions as any of the charity queens or free-loading celebrities; he was a social mountaineer, though the heights he scaled didn't take one's breath away. He was also a good policeman, honest and incorruptible. Blatant ambition was his only sin, but in Sydney that was considered only venial.

He drew Malone aside. 'What case are you on? The Springfellow one?'

'Both of them, sir. The sister, Emma, was murdered last night.'

'Yes, I heard that. What's the Commissioner's interest in it?'

'I don't know if he has any, sir. I just got the call that he wanted to see me.'

Zanuch was itching with curiosity, but he didn't scratch himself. Instead he just smiled, nodded and went on his way out of the lobby with, 'Good luck with the cases, Inspector. I'll look forward to hearing of an arrest or two.'

Malone got into the lift, wondering at what rivalries went on here where the brass polished itself every day. He rode up to the twentieth floor and was shown into the Commissioner's office by a secretary who had already refreshed her make-up, ready to leave. She said good-night and Malone and the Commissioner were left alone.

'You're wondering why I sent for you?'

Malone took it carefully. 'I hope it's not politics again, sir.'

Leeds smiled wryly. 'If only it were as simple as that . . . You're on the Springfellow cases, both of them, right? Any progress?'

'Not much. I –'

'Yes?'

'I'm here because you're somehow connected with them, sir. Am I right?'

Leeds said nothing for a moment, tapping with a brass ruler on his tidy desktop. He was renowned for his insistence on neatness and the slobs in the Department were always running for cover. Everything had to be in its place; but now, suddenly, things were starting to unravel. He hated the thought that he was now having to confide in a junior officer, even though one for whom he had the greatest respect.

'I understand you have a photo you took from Miss Springfellow's flat – one of me and Sir Walter. Where is it?'

'Locked away in Sergeant Clements's desk. I haven't shown it to Chief Inspector Random yet.'

'You'll have to, of course.' He waited for Malone to agree and after a moment the latter nodded. 'There's something else. You may find out eventually or you may not, but I think I'd better tell you. I visited Emma Springfellow last night. Someone else had been there before me, as I gather you already know.'

'Yes, Justine Springfellow.'

'Emma was still alive when she left. I saw her leaving, when I was coming down the street.' Malone remained silent and Leeds said testily, 'I'm telling you she didn't murder Emma.'

'She could have gone back after you left, sir.'

'For God's sake, Scobie!' Malone had never seen him so agitated. They had had awkward moments between them on three or four other cases, but they had involved politics; this

133

was different and the awkwardness now had spikes on it. 'The girl didn't do it! Don't start building a case against her on nothing –' Then he stopped abruptly, put down the brass ruler and steadied himself. 'I'm sorry. I shouldn't have flown off the handle like that. You do what you have to.'

'What sort of state was Emma in when you got up to see her?'

'Quite a state. Angry, a little hysterical –'

'Did she quieten down?'

'Yes.'

'Why did you go to see her, sir?'

Leeds hesitated, then shook his head. 'I'm not prepared to say at this stage. It was a – a family matter.'

Malone drew a deep breath, slumped back in his chair. 'I think I'd better ask Greg Random to take me off this one. I have too much respect for you. I don't want to have to start nailing you to the wall with questions.'

Leeds gazed steadily at the younger man. There was reciprocated respect; there was no more decent, hard-working man working under him. Malone was an example of what he had tried to make the Department. He was handicapped by his own decency, by his own ambitions for the Department: 'Thanks, Scobie, but no. You have to stay on it.'

Malone said nothing for almost half a minute. Beyond the Commissioner's head he could see the lights now bright in the valley of Woolloomooloo; the towers of St Mary's Cathedral stood on the slopes like medieval watch-towers. The windows were closed and the sounds of the city were shut out. The silence between the two men seemed to expand to fill the room. At last he said, 'Righto, I'll stay with it. But I may have to come back and ask awkward questions.'

'I know that.' Leeds sighed, seemed to shrink down in his chair. 'The past has a habit of catching up, hasn't it?'

'If it didn't, we wouldn't solve half our crimes. Did you leave any prints in the flat, sir?'

Leeds sat up again, frowned. 'What? I suppose so. Yes, I did. I was holding a glass – I had a whisky and water.'

134

'Scientific will have found it. Emma hadn't washed any of the glasses – I noticed them on a tray on a sideboard in the living-room. Justine's prints are probably on a glass, too. We'll have to check hers.'

'What about mine?'

'If nobody saw you going up to the flat – did they?'

'No, I don't think so. There was nobody in the lobby – Emma herself let me in through the security intercom. I'm not asking for favours, Scobie –' But he was, and they both knew it. 'There should be a third set of prints. The person who did the killing.'

'Yes,' said Malone non-committally; he could see the riptide and he was doing his best to avoid it. 'Anyhow, yours may never be traced. What time did you leave the flat?'

'Just after nine-thirty. Nobody saw me leave.'

'You saw nobody waiting to go in?'

'No.'

'Sir, do you carry a gun?'

Leeds stared at him. 'You're really grilling me, aren't you? No, I don't. I have an issue Smith & Wesson at home, but I don't carry it around with me.'

'We don't know what she was shot with, not yet. The bullets are still in the body.' A spark glowed in his memory. 'You were a friend of Sir Walter's. You used to go shooting with him –'

'Just the once. On that trip in the photo, up to the Roper River.'

'Did you ever see his collection of guns?'

'Yes. He lent me a couple of guns for that trip – I can't remember what they were.'

'Can you remember the hand-guns?'

'No. Why?'

'The collection is still there in Lady Springfellow's home. Two hand-pieces are missing. One's been missing for years – we think it might've been a Colt .45. The other's been gone only a couple of weeks. It's a smaller piece, maybe a Walther.'

135

Leeds didn't flinch. 'It was a valuable collection – Walter would have had it insured. Lady Springfellow may not have kept up the insurance, but there'd be an inventory in the files somewhere. I hope you're not suggesting *she* killed Emma?'

'I'm not suggesting anyone at the moment, sir. Were you a friend of hers as well as Sir Walter's?' *How did I get into this situation? Did Corporal Kafoops ask Napoleon why he'd lost the battle of Waterloo?*

Again Leeds's voice and gaze were steady. 'Yes.'

'A close friend?'

'Yes.'

'That's what you meant, wasn't it? The past catching up with us.'

Leeds picked up the brass ruler again; for a moment he looked as if he was trying to snap it in half. 'It was something I'd rather not talk about. I'm not proud of it.'

'Will it come out if I continue with the investigation on him?'

'It may. I hope not.'

Malone was silent once more; then he stood up. It was dark outside and dark in here, too: the Commissioner had turned on no lights. 'May I go, sir? I think I'm getting a headache.'

Leeds put down the ruler, managed to rake up a smile. 'I'm sorry I've got you into this bind, Scobie. Yet I'm glad. I'd rather you investigated me than some of the others in the Department.'

'I don't mean to be rude, sir – but thanks for nothing. You wouldn't care to transfer me to Tibooburra?'

'I may be there before you.'

3

Chilla Dural was getting ready to hold up a bank.

Life on the outside, he had decided, was too complicated. He had once been as self-reliant as any man in Sydney: 'I can always trust you to look after yourself,' Heinie Odets had told

136

him. But it hadn't turned out that way, not these past few weeks.

In gaol he had been able to look after himself. There had been problems when he had first gone in; the screws had been at pains to let him know who were the bosses. Those were the days when a pick-handle had been an accepted form of persuasion. He had made the mistake of trying to fight them; it had taken him quite a while to realize that that wouldn't work. The system would always beat you unless you joined it. After a year he had joined it, had acknowledged who were the bosses and taken his own place in the pecking order. He had never acknowledged any other con as a boss in the yards and that had resulted in a couple of running wars; in the end he had been recognized as his own boss, except for the screws, and he had been left alone. There had been a certain code in those days, but it wasn't like that any longer. Drugs ran the gaols these days: he who had the supply ran the system and a code was only something that gave you a runny nose in winter. He had never taken any drugs and he had knocked down several dealers who had tried to sell them to him.

Two or three queers had tried to mate up with him, seeing him as a protector, but he had had, and still had, an almost religious priggishness towards homosexuality. When he had gone into Parramatta there had been some, but not much, of it; now, it seemed, it was as common as masturbation had once been. Once, as an act of revenge, a yard boss had organized four homos to gang-bang him; they had made the mistake of trying to take him while he was dressed and not stripped in the shower-block. He had had a knife and he had used it effectively; nothing deflates an erection so quickly as its being chopped off at the base by a sharp knife. From then on he had been left alone.

In time he had become friendly with some of the screws, though he had never let them turn him into an informer. He got to know of their families, though he never met any of them; in the carpentry shop, where he had become head of

137

the shop, he made toys for their kids. One of the screws had, like himself, a fondness for jazz; he brought in records for Dural, old classics by Beiderbecke and Bechet and Art Tatum. Life had settled into a pattern and, though he had dreamed of freedom and what he would do when his time was served, he had never fretted about it. He had nowhere to go, but he had felt he was getting somewhere, even if standing still.

Now he was getting nowhere and still had nowhere to go. He had bought himself some new clothes and gone looking for a job; but no one wanted a 58-year-old ex-con, not even the new nightclub owners, his last resort. He had hoped at first for a decent, honest job; he had worked for one day as a carpenter on a building site. Then the union rep had come round, asked for his ticket, refused to let him join the union when he said he had no ticket and had told him to get lost. He had king-hit the union rep and walked off the job. So much for rehabilitation. He had, unenthusiastically, gone to a half-way house run by ex-cons, but half an hour there had been enough: he had listened to more politics in twenty minutes than in twenty years in Parramatta.

He had talked it over with his parole officer, Les Glizzard. Because he had been serving a life sentence, he had not been released on parole but on licence. Once a fortnight he had to report to Glizzard and he was not allowed out of the State. He was not to apply for a passport, to consort with known criminals or to break the law in even the slightest way.

'I could throw a brick through a window,' he had said. 'You'd have to pull me in for that.'

Glizzard had shaken his young curly head. He had a broken nose but he still looked like a cherub, one who had been vandalized but not knocked off his feet. 'You're wasting your time, Chilla, thinking like that. The coppers bring you in here for that, I'd just tell 'em to forget it. We don't want you back, Chilla. The gaols are chock-a-block, we want your space. You've done your time, we can't go on providing you with a home.'

138

'Mr Glizzard –'

'Call me Les.' That was his trouble: he was everybody's friend, a mate of all and sundry, especially the sundry. He should have been a nun, he saw too much good in too many of the world's worst.

'Les, I don't like it out here. There's real shit in gaol, I know that – they had a better class of con when I first went in.' He was not given to many jokes, but he grinned now. 'But I can handle that shit. Out here –' He shook his head.

'You've got to be patient, Chilla. You're still in an institutional mode. Once we've got you into a work mode –'

'A what?'

'What?' There was a language barrier, even though they were both speaking in their native tongue. 'Oh. Well, once we've got you *working*. Once we've got you in that mode, out there at the cutting edge of getting you on your feet, you'll be okay, it'll be a different scene.'

'I don't think so. I think I'll be back here in a coupla months at the outside, with the cops telling you I've knocked down some young punk or I been consorting with some of the old crims I used to know –'

Glizzard was not to be denied his role as guardian angel. 'Not a chance, Chilla. I'm going to give you every opportunity. This is the cutting edge of our new policy, the rehabilitation mode. We've got to take risks and I'm betting you're a good risk.'

'I'm gunna disappoint you, Les.'

He had been out of gaol, had left home, only a month; but already he knew where he belonged. Or anyway didn't belong. He had given up looking for a job, trying to get into a work mode, and gone looking for means of getting back to prison. It would have to be something so serious that Glizzard, for all his bleeding heart and good intentions, could not brush it aside.

He spent a week doing a reconnaissance, looking for an old bank where there was no new-fangled technology. The world was being taken over by bloody technology; he had become so reactionary, he longed for the horse-and-buggy days that only his grandfather had known. He found what he wanted out in Leichhardt, a bank built before the First World War and soon to be replaced by a new building close by. There was no sky-rocketing steel shield mounted in the counter; there were remote-controlled cameras in the corners of the ceiling, but they would be a help, not a hindrance. They would help him to be identified, if he should walk away with the hold-up money.

He bought a gun, knowing where to go from the old days: a Walther PPK .380, a formidable-looking gun that would frighten the pants off any sensible bank teller. He did not, however, buy any ammunition; he was not looking to get into a shooting match. The object of the exercise was to fail, not to succeed; bullets were not necessary for failure, unless you were going to commit suicide. So far, he was not *that* depressed.

He put the gun in the cheap briefcase he had bought, put on his new straw hat, debated whether to wear a jacket and decided against it, and went out into the hallway, locking his door behind him. Jerry Killeen, as always, was waiting in his own doorway.

'G'day, you going out? It's bloody hot, I can tell you. I just been up the road and I was bloody glad to get back for a cuppa, I can tell you. You want one before you go out?'

A few nights ago he had spent the evening with Killeen. On the spur of the moment, feeling sorry for the little bugger, he had asked him to go with him to the jazz club up the street. Killeen had been bored by the music and Dural had been embarrassed at his boredom and remarks. He had decided that from now on he would keep the little man at arm's length.

'I can't, mate. I got an appointment with my parole bloke.' He had found it best to be frank with Killeen, up to a point; otherwise the old coot would just keep asking questions. 'We're gunna rob a bank together.'

'Well, good luck. On the way back, knock on the door. I'm

always here.' He sniffed the air. 'You notice anything? The Viet Cong have stopped frying rice. They must be trying to become more like us Aussies. They're gunna take over the bloody country, I can tell you. Definitely.'

Dural left him, the little Aussie battler besieged by slant-eyed invaders, and went out into the heat of the morning. He hailed a cab and got into the back seat, not wanting to have to belt himself into the front seat; he wondered if breaking the seat-belt law could result in his being sent back to prison. The driver was an Aussie, a change from the bloody foreigners who had been picking him up for the past month. This one was a *real* Aussie.

'You don't like riding in the front?' Meaning: *you too good to sit up here beside me?*

'I'm nervous.'

'You afraid I'm not a good driver? Listen, sport, I been driving a cab for twenty-five years, never had an accident, not so much as a scratch. This is me own cab, I own it, paid a hundred and fifty grand for the plate and don't owe a penny on it. I'm as good as the next man, I always say.'

'As good as your passengers, that what you mean?'

'Every time, no matter who they are. No offence.'

'Not bloody much.' Dural took the Walther out of the briefcase; it was a spur of the moment decision. 'I'm not gunna shoot you, *sport*, nothing like that. But I don't like uppity cab drivers, you know what I mean? Now shut up and just drive.'

'Jesus, I told you – no offence, mate.'

Dural put away the gun and the driver drove in silence for the rest of the journey, keeping a watchful, fearful eye on his passenger in the rear-view mirror. Dural caught the glance and grinned at him.

'Relax, sport, I'm not gunna hurt you. I just like cab drivers who know when to shut up.'

The driver kept his silence, but Dural knew that once he had got out of the cab, the man would be on his radio to report a gun-toting crazy he had just had as a fare. Within minutes the police would have a patrol car cruising the area looking for him.

'Here will do,' said Dural abruptly and the cab driver swung into the kerb so sharply he almost mounted it.

'Forget the fare, sport –'

'No,' said Dural. 'I never take charity. Keep the change and learn to keep your mouth shut.'

He walked away, knowing that before he had turned the corner the driver was already on his radio. It was a ten-minute walk to the bank; halfway there he wondered why he had not just remained beside the cab while the driver called the police. But that would have been too obvious: Les Glizzard, the angel's advocate, would have pleaded for him and, who knows, some bleeding-hearted magistrate or judge might have listened to him. No, it had to be the bank: the police could pick him up there.

The bank was in a side-street off Parramatta Road: twelve miles up the road was home. Or nineteen kilometres, if you wanted to be modern: that was another thing he could not get used to, metric measure. The bank was an old building, built of stone, the sort of institution where you expected pounds, shillings and pence still to be the currency across the counter. Dural went into the bank and took his place in the roped-off queue. Queueing for a hold-up; even he, without much sense of humour, had to grin at the thought. Though it was a nervous grin, more a tic of reaction. He was suddenly uptight, afraid that things would go wrong, that he might be carried out of here feet first.

He had decided on the quiet approach to the teller, just presenting a note and a sight of the pistol. He had listened to discussions in gaol about bank hold-ups. The mode (one con had actually used that word) these days was to threaten violence, to go in shouting with all the violent language you could think of, waving your gun and looking ready for murder. The psychology of fear, the cons had said: the mode was to frighten the shit out of everyone in the bank. But that wasn't for Dural. Walk softly, speak softly, Heinie Odets

142

had advised in the only hold-up he had master-minded, and you'll be gone before they get over the shock.

'Move along,' said the woman who stood behind him. 'We no can stand around all day.'

The district, a working-class one, had been named after the German explorer Ludwig Leichhardt; but there had been few German settlers in Sydney and it had never resounded to Wagner or even to the music of a glockenspiel. It had, with post-Second World War immigration, become almost a Little Italy. When he had been scouting here a couple of days ago he had gone looking for somewhere to lunch on steak and chips and grilled tomatoes, but every café and restaurant he had passed seemed to offer only pizza and pasta. The names above the doorways of the shops were straight out of the Rome or Naples phone directories: there was even a P. Mussolini, Fruit and Veg. Dural now became aware of the fact that he was standing in a queue of Italian women. When he drew the gun there was going to be a panic that they would hear at the top end of Italy.

'I no seen you here before,' said the woman who had spoken to him. She was young but already middle-aged plump, an Italian momma years ahead of schedule. She had a friendly, pretty face and a voice that suggested she might be able to carry a song. 'You new around here? Is a nice place to live, you know? Lots of life, things always going on.'

She had no sooner said that than things started going on. The front door of the bank burst open and three men came in with stocking masks over their heads. They were waving sawn-off shotguns and they were shouting at the tops of their voices, their language as violent as their behaviour.

'Okay, okay, on the fucking floor – everybody! On the fucking floor or we'll blast the shit outa you! On the floor! Fuck you – move!'

One man kept yelling, waving his gun back and forth as the other two rushed at the counter and leapt at it. There was a shriek from the woman behind Dural; she fell into him, carrying him to the floor with her. Christ, he thought, this ain't happening! These bloody cowboys, drug-drunk, are spoiling everything for me! His straw hat had been knocked off as he went down, he had dropped his briefcase as he grabbed at the woman. He lay flat on his back under the shaking jelly of her; it was like being underneath a vibrating bed. He turned his head and saw the briefcase had burst open and the butt of the Walther was sticking out. Oh Jesus! He turned his head and looked up past the woman's tangled hair and distorted face and saw the gunman standing over him.

'Quit that fucking row!' The gunman kicked the woman in her well-padded behind; she lurched forward on Dural as if trying to rape him; he was smothered by her big bosom, could see nothing but black satin. 'Shut up, you bitch, or I'll kill you!'

The woman suddenly went limp, as if the language itself had shot her. Dural lay beneath her, waiting for the gunman to see the butt of the Walther, pull it out of the briefcase and then start in on him. The crazy junkie might even kill him.

Then out of the corner of his eye, through a curtain of the woman's black hair, he saw the gunman's feet turn away. He lay still, the unconscious woman still covering him, heard more violent swearing; the gunmen were shouting at each other now. All around him people were stretched out on the floor, faces against the cold tiles; some had fainted, like the woman on top of him, others were weeping in sobbing gasps. An old man just lay and stared across the floor at Dural with a sort of resignation, as if he felt no surprise that his time had come at last and like this.

Then: 'Okay, don't fucking move for five minutes – no one, understand! Move and you're fucking dead!'

The two men who had been behind the counter jumped over it again, encumbered by the two airline bags each of them carried. A canvas bank bag spilled out of an airline bag and fell with a clunk right beside Dural's head; but the gunman who had dropped it didn't stop to retrieve it.

Dural, with one eye, saw the robbers go. They went on the run out of the front door, straight into the patrol car as it pulled up outside the bank looking for the gun-toting taxi passenger. The two policemen in the car reacted at once; the driver swung the car up on to the footpath and drove it straight at the three gunmen. The leader let fly a round, but the shot went high, bouncing off the roof of the patrol car. The car hit him, kept going and collected the other two robbers. It was like something out of *Dirty Harry* and if Chilla Dural had seen it he would have remarked how different things were from the old days.

But he saw nothing of what went on out in the street. He slid out from under the woman as she moaned and regained consciousness. He reached for his hat and the briefcase, pushing the Walther back into it and closing the flap. He also reached for the canvas bag; it was heavy, full of coins. Then he stood up and looked around as the other customers slowly came to life and began to struggle up from the floor. The bank staff appeared above their counter like soldiers rising out of their trench to see if the war was really over. Out in the street there was shouting and the sound of an approaching siren. In a moment or two the police were going to burst into the bank. It was time to go.

Dural picked his way through the customers, stepping over those who still hadn't the strength to stand up. The old man who had been ready to die sat up and looked at him as he passed.

'Not yet?' he said in a shaky voice.

'Not yet, Pop,' said Dural.

He found a back door, unlocked it and stepped out into a small yard. He opened the canvas bag; it was full of dollar coins. He crossed to a gate, unlocked it and walked out into a narrow lane. He straightened his hat, put the canvas bag in his briefcase, tucked the case up under his arm and walked unhurriedly up the lane.

There were probably five hundred bucks in the bag, so the morning hadn't been entirely wasted. Les Glizzard would be happy at what had happened, though he would never tell him. He just wished that he had had ammunition in the

Walther; he could have shot all three of the gunmen; he hated the bastards and nothing would have given him greater pleasure. But then Glizzard would have had him declared a hero and he would be more lost than ever.

SIX

1

'I've been through the newspapers, Inspector,' said Andy Graham. 'For the whole of March and April 1966. There's plenty on the Springfellow disappearance, but nothing on anyone else missing, no one that hasn't been accounted for since. Same with Missing Persons, those files that are still there. I've drawn a blank.'

Graham was an oversized young man who had only recently transferred from the uniformed division; he was all enthusiasm, but he had to be taught that detective work was 95 per cent plodding routine. He had just had his first lesson and looked suitably chastened.

'That's just the start, Andy. I want you now to go looking in places where missing persons wouldn't be reported.'

'Right, Inspector,' said Graham, looking blank.

'You know where I mean?'

Graham coloured, ran a hand like a crab up and down his thick thigh. 'No, sir.'

'Radical hang-outs, embassies, consulates. Walter Spring-fellow was a spy chief, don't forget that.'

'Will I need a warrant to get into any of those places?'

Malone grinned. 'The embassies and consulates would just tell you to get stuffed and they'd be within their rights. As for the radicals, if you can find 'em, just barge in and then apologize afterwards. It saves a lot of bother. They'll ring up that Civil Liberties bloke and he'll go to the news-papers, but nobody'll read the story. The voters don't care about civil liberties in this country, not unless it's their own.'

Graham nodded, his enthusiasm regained; this was like his old days in uniform. 'About the embassies, Inspector – they're all down in Canberra, right? Do I go down there?'

'Only at your own expense and in your own time. Get the Federals to do all that for you.'

'Right,' said Graham, disappointed.

He stood up and galloped off and Clements, who had sat silent during the instructions, said, 'You're a bit tough on him, aren't you?'

'Right,' said Malone. 'You want me to be the same with you?'

'No, thanks. When you've got shit on the liver, it's time for me to find something else to do.' Then he said with concern, 'What's the matter with you, Scobie? You've been like a guy who prayed for rain and got acid instead.'

Malone leaned back in his chair. 'I think I've got too much on my plate. Maybe I should ask Greg to give the Walter Springfellow case to someone else.'

'You asked him to let you keep it. Why not let someone else take the Emma case? I'll take that one over, if you like. You and Andy can keep on with Walter and his bones.'

I can't do that. The Commissioner has told me I have to stay on Emma's case. But he could never tell that to Clements, no matter how much he trusted the latter to keep his mouth shut.

'I'll give it another week or two, see how we go. What have you come up with so far?'

Clements opened up his desk, took out the manila envelope and extracted Emma's diary. 'I've been through this line by line. She was a sour old bitch – she doesn't seem to have had a good word for anyone except Walter, not even for her other brother, Edwin, and his wife. As for Lady Venetia and the daughter –'

'What about the daughter?' Malone tried to keep his voice casual.

148

'Emma accuses her of being someone's bastard, though she doesn't say whose. Three months ago – here, August 15 – she says something about the "old friend" – that's in quotes – does he know about his bastard child? That's what she writes, *bastard child*. That's almost biblical. Then there's another entry –' He flipped through the pages. 'Last Sunday. "J. –" it's just the initial – "J. phoned me and threatened me."'

'J. could be anyone.' J. for John Leeds, for instance: he shot down that thought as soon as it rose in his mind. 'What about Venetia?'

'Oh, the diary's full of her for the past month – she gets a guernsey practically every day. But it's Emma threatening her, not the other way around. She's going to wipe the streets of Sydney with Venetia – those are her words in one of the entries.'

'What about Edwin and his wife? And Venetia's mother?'

'Nothing really bitchy about Edwin and his missus, just sort of cool. Alice Magee – yeah, she cops it a coupla times.' He dropped the diary back into the envelope, put it back in his desk and locked the drawer. 'Emma made her own enemies. I think she was around the twist, myself.'

'Are there any other diaries?'

'If there are, we haven't found them yet. We've been right through the flat. There's a storage basement in the building, but we didn't find anything there of hers.'

'I'd like to go through that diary myself some time, just in case you missed something.' Clements looked offended and Malone grinned. 'Come on, you know four eyes are better than two. Now what about Ballistics – you heard anything from them?'

'Came in this morning. They took two bullets from her, both .380s, round nose profile. Ballistics say they could have come from a Walther. I checked with the insurance company – it was Intercapital – and Walter's gun collection was insured with them and Venetia had kept up the insurance.

149

There was a Colt .45 and a Walther PPK .380, both automatics, in the collection. They are the two that are missing.'

'Scientific?'

'So far all they've come up with are some prints on three drinking glasses – one set of prints are Emma's. The others are a small set, could be a woman's, and a man's. There's a fourth set on the doorhandle of the bedroom.'

'The doorman's? He went into the bedroom to find her.'

'I dunno. We have to check that. There's a fifth and sixth set, but they could be old ones, a day or so old. The maid who cleans up didn't come in on Monday, she had the 'flu or something.'

'Seems there are bloody prints all over!'

Clements nodded glumly. 'I know. They found a couple of threads on the key in the front door, as if someone had brushed against it, maybe in a hurry, and torn their dress. Blue threads.'

'Dress?'

'So Scientific think. They don't think it's from a feller's shirt, unless Emma was entertaining a ballet dancer.'

Malone grinned. 'Have you ever been to the ballet? Some of them have bigger balls than the front row from South Sydney.'

Clements had been saving something; he looked uncharacteristically smug as he produced it: 'Justine went back to The Vanderbilt a second time Monday night.'

Malone felt a sudden weight, as if John Leeds had slumped against him. 'Someone saw her?'

'Two of the tenants, a couple named Pandon. They flew down to Melbourne yesterday morning to see the Cup and came back late last night. Our guys hadn't had a chance to talk to 'em till this morning.'

'What did they have to say?'

'About eleven on Monday night they came back from a concert at the Opera House. Justine was pressing Emma's intercom buzzer. They knew her slightly, they're pretty

150

social types, I gather, always in Dorian Wilde's column, you know the sort –'

Malone didn't; but he said patiently, 'Go on.'

'Well, they let her in with their key and she went up in the lift with them. They live on the sixth floor.'

'They'll give evidence?'

'I gather Mrs Pandon will do anything that'll get her name in the papers. They're old money, but vulgar. Or anyway she is.'

'You're becoming a snob in your old age.' Malone was silent a moment, feeling a burden he hadn't anticipated already settling on him. Then he sighed and stood up. 'Righto, I think we'd better start all over again with Justine. She looks like our best bet.'

The best bet would be to forget the whole thing and get a transfer to Traffic Branch: Malone could already see the traps beginning to show through the roadside undergrowth. He could not, however, flash the red light on Clements, not too obviously and not yet. He stood up, felt like a man standing in the middle of a road on which accidents were going to happen at any moment, a traffic cop whom everyone was, wittingly or unwittingly, ready to run down.

He said, trying to keep the reluctance out of his voice, 'Let's go down and see Miss Springfellow.'

They drove down to Springfellow House, persuaded the parking attendant of police parking privileges and rode up in the lift to the twenty-ninth floor. Miss Springfellow's secretary came out to the reception area. She was in her late twenties, just the right side of plainness, a girl who had tried to make the most of herself by being as up-to-the-minute stylish as possible. Her clothes were expensive, possibly more than she could afford, and her hair was a mass of ringlets; Malone thought it looked like a bird's nest hit by a strong wind, but he was a man of simple tastes when it came to coiffure. He guessed that the secretary was not afraid of men, not even *police*men.

'Miss Springfellow is not in this morning.' Her tone

151

implied that *they*, too, should not be here this morning. 'She was *shattered* by her aunt's murder. We all were.'

'Could we go somewhere a little more private?' said Malone. Through a big glass partition they were being watched by half a dozen girls, crouching behind their computers and typewriters as if behind machine-guns. There wasn't a man in sight, no one to infiltrate behind the lines. 'I think we're keeping your staff from their work. You're Miss –?'

'Quantock – Ms.' It came out as *Mizzzz*, squeezed out like a hiss. 'We'll go into Ms Springfellow's office.'

She led the way into the office where the two detectives had been two days before. She sat behind the desk and waved Malone and Clements into the chairs opposite her. Crumbs, thought Malone, trying hard not to be a male chauvinist and barely succeeding, this building is riddled with masterful (mistressful?) women. Ms Quantock was sure of her destiny.

'I'm not entitled to speak for Ms Springfellow –'

'Oh, I thought you were,' said Clements, never one to dodge being a chauvinist; he tried occasionally for chivalry, especially towards Lisa Malone, but, being an Aussie, it gave him a hernia. 'Sitting there . . .'

She gave him a look that buried a knife in his groin; then she looked at Malone, who appeared reasonably civilized. 'What was it you wanted to ask me, Inspector?'

'Have you seen Miss Springfellow since the murder of her aunt?'

'Yes. She came in yesterday morning, but went home after an hour. I went across to see her this morning at her apartment. She is *shattered*.'

'Yes, so you said. Did Emma Springfellow ever come up to this floor to see Justine? A business visit? A family one, you know, aunt visiting niece?'

'I don't think Miss Emma –' *Miss*, not *Ms*: Emma, Malone guessed, would have cut anyone dead who called her Ms '– I don't think she would have been seen –' She stopped abruptly, for the first time lost her composure.

152

'Been seen dead? Well, she wasn't, was she? Seen dead up here.'

Elizabeth Quantock sat silent, suddenly looked plain, all her sense of style gone; the wrecked bird's nest of hair only added to the impression that she had crumbled. Malone all at once saw that he and Clements so far had been shown only the façade. This organization to which she belonged, this building where she worked, had helped create her image. She was one with all the money-making that went on on this floor and the floors below; she had done her best to be part of the Scene. Beneath her feet were the $100,000-plus-a-year whiz-kids with their green-lined computer terminals, their phones growing out of their ears like a malignant growth, their high-pitched yells and the feverishly excited faces of the money-mad. Or that was how it would have been down there up until three weeks ago. Now the Crash, the postponement of the takeover bid and the murder of Emma had reduced the Scene to a shambles. Perhaps she was engaged to one of the whiz-kids; a diamond ring glinted on her finger; the future no longer was as bright as the diamond. She had nothing but her own original character to support her and suddenly she was having difficulty in locating it.

There was a knock on the door and a bald head appeared as the door was pushed open. 'Oh, I'm sorry –' said Michael Broad. 'I thought Justine was in –'

'Mr Broad, this is Inspector Malone and Sergeant Clements.' She was a good secretary; she remembered names. 'Mr Broad, our finance director.'

Broad nodded to the two detectives. Years ago he would have shaken hands with them in the European fashion; but he had learned in Australia one did not shake hands with policemen. The rumour was that too many policemen had taken bribes that way, though Broad would never descend to that level. He was a venal snob.

'Are you interrogating our staff, Inspector?'

'Not the staff, Mr Broad. Just Miss Quantock, just

checking on a few things about Miss Springfellow. Justine, that is.'

'In what connection?'

'Are you Justine's employer, Mr Broad?'

A warmer-blooded man might have flushed at that; but Broad just smiled coolly. 'You know better than that, Inspector. But I think in all fairness you should be interviewing Miss Springfellow herself, not subjecting Miss Quantock to some awkward questions.'

Ms Quantock had stood up as soon as Broad entered the office; she stood awkwardly behind the desk, like a lady-in-waiting caught on the throne.

'Our questions are always awkward, Mr Broad,' said Malone. 'We may have to come and ask you some, at the proper time.'

'You'll be welcome,' said Broad, realizing he had been dismissed and knowing when to go, without further argument.

When Broad had gone, Malone wondered why Broad had not asked what the questioning would be about.

But Clements was already back on the attack with Elizabeth Quantock: 'Justine is a rich young girl. Has anyone ever threatened her?'

'Justine?' She had sat down behind the desk again, but all her composure had gone. 'What do you mean?'

'Rich people are always under threat,' said Clements. 'Kidnap, that sort of thing. Did she ever carry a gun for protection?'

That's it! thought Malone. Clements had put the questioning back on track. He realized that, subconsciously or otherwise, he had been trying to protect Justine; or, rather, he was protecting John Leeds. He, and not Clements, should have asked a question about the gun; he was troubled, uncertain that he would have raised the matter of the gun at all. He felt a weight settling on him like an iron saddle.

Elizabeth Quantock shook her head. 'No, she never

154

mentioned anything like that – I'm sure she would have. I did see –' Again she stopped.

'You saw what?' Clements at times could be remarkably gentle with his questioning. 'A gun or something?'

She nodded, reluctantly. 'Yes, a gun. It was in the desk here.' She pulled open a drawer, looked relieved to find there was no gun there now. 'I didn't mention it to Justine. It was gone the next day – I never saw it again.'

'When was that?'

'Is any of this relevant, Sergeant?' She was loyal to her boss; she tried for some of her old assurance.

'Everything's relevant when we're talking about murder,' said Clements, voice still gentle.

Nicely said, thought Malone; and wished he were miles out of town, say on the traffic beat in Tibooburra, where three trucks and a pick-up would be the peak-hour crush. In his mind's eye, that nervous tic that afflicts the imaginative, he saw John Leeds coming out to join him in the accident lane.

'Justine said nothing about it?' he said, hoping he might take the line of questioning away from Clements before it got too dangerous; but he had no idea how he was going to do that.

'No.'

'When did you see the gun?' said Clements, not letting go.

'About, I don't know, about three weeks ago, maybe a bit more. I just saw it and then shut the drawer – I'm scared stiff of guns. Nobody should be allowed to have them.'

'That's what we think, too,' said Malone and stood up.

'One thing more,' said Clements, rising. 'Was Miss Springfellow wearing a blue dress on Monday?'

Ms Quantock thought for a moment, with that concentration that some women have for remembering what other women have worn. 'No, she was in yellow. She has several blue dresses, but she wasn't wearing one on Monday.'

'Thanks,' said Malone. 'That will be all, Miss Quantock.'

155

'It's Ms,' she said almost automatically, as if she spent half her time battling chauvinists like him.

'I never try to pronounce anything with no vowels in it,' he said with a grin. 'I once ruptured my tongue trying to book a Polish feminist. Don't bother to call Miss Springfellow and tell her we've been to see you. We'll tell her ourselves how loyal you've been.'

He and Clements left Ms Quantock and went out to the lift. He said, 'What did you think of Mr Broad? I could feel you in there, wanting to get up off your chair and thump him.'

'I'm beginning to get pretty shirty about this Springfellow outfit, from the boss lady downwards. They're an uppity mob, aren't they?'

'Wait till you've banked your first million. You'll be the same.'

They caught the lift and went down past the floors where euphoria, not so many days ago, had threatened to burst the windows. Two young men in broadly-striped shirts with white collars and their $125 Hermès ties got on at the foreign-exchange floor, their faces slack and pale. They looked at each other and shook their heads.

'You, too?' said one.

The other nodded. 'Leave Friday.'

'Just been fired?' said Clements.

They looked at him, decided he looked solicitous and concerned, proving they couldn't read faces. 'Yeah, just this minute.'

'Tough titty,' said Clements and grinned as if he had just seen a 100-to-1 shot come home in the Derby. 'You going to swap the Porsche for a skateboard?'

'Up yours,' said one of them as they got off at the fifth floor.

'Who's got shit on the liver now?' said Malone as the lift doors closed. 'You made a fortune on the market and you put the knife into those blokes.'

'It's being middle-aged,' said Clements, unrepentant.

'Kids like that making the money they did! It's criminal. Nobody should be successful till they're middle-aged like me.'

'Alexander the Great was successful at twenty-one.'

"You mean Greg Alexander, plays for Penrith? Don't try to make me feel a mean old son-of-a-bitch – you're not gunna be successful at that. I'm gunna be just as shitty towards Justine when we see her. I think deep down I'm a Commo. I usedn't to be, but it's all these rich yuppies.'

'I always thought you saw nothing wrong with being rich.' Over the past few weeks Malone had heard at least two snide jokes a day about the young high-flyers who had crashed. Nothing binds the lower orders together more than malicious envy, not even patriotism.

'I don't. So long as you're middle-aged.'

They got to the ground floor, crossed the pink-and-grey marbled lobby and went out into the hot morning. They walked across to The Wharf and climbed the granite steps to the brass-and-glass entrance. A doorman seated at a desk behind the glass wall spoke to them through an intercom, asking whom they wanted to see. Clements just flashed his badge, saying nothing. The doorman peered through the glass, then he pressed a button and the doors slid open.

'We're very careful here.' He was a tall thin man with hunched shoulders, as if he had spent his working life bending over to explain matters to rich old ladies. 'We have the tightest security in Sydney, with the people we have living here. You wanted to see –?'

'Miss Springfellow,' said Malone. 'You'd have seen her if she'd gone out?'

'Oh, sure. Unless she went straight down to the basement, to the garage. I'll buzz her.'

'Not just yet.' Clements put his hand on the doorman's arm as he reached for his house phone. 'Were you on duty here Monday night?'

'Monday night? Yeah, sure. I only started day shift this morning. Yeah, I was here Monday night. There was a big

157

party upstairs, at the Poluxes'. A Melbourne Cup Eve party, it was.'

'Peter Polux, the banker – he has a flat here?'

'We don't call 'em flats, they're apartments. Other people live in flats. Like me.' He grinned. 'Mr Polux has the penthouse, right above Miss Springfellow's apartment.'

'Was she at the party, do you know?'

'Not as far as I know. No, I don't think so.'

'Lady Springfellow?'

'No. I didn't know everyone who came in. I think Mr Broad was the only one from across at Springfellow's. He's the finance director or something.'

'We've met him. What's your name, incidentally?'

'Stan Kinley.' The doorman frowned, his long thin face suddenly lost in a maze of lines; he worriedly watched as Clements made a note of his name. 'What's this all about? I dunno I'm supposed to talk to you about the residents here.'

'It's about people's movements, that's all,' said Clements. 'Did Miss Springfellow go out at all on Monday night?'

We already know that, Malone thought; but he held back. Clements, probably without his realizing it, had taken over the investigation. Sooner or later Malone would have to wrench it back from him; but for the moment he found it safer to remain silent. He didn't want Russ Clements asking *him* questions he'd rather not answer.

Kinley hesitated a moment. 'Well, yes, she did. Early in the evening, I dunno exactly when, just after I come on duty, she went out. She didn't take her car or ask me to call a cab or anything. Then she come back, I dunno, I guess about nine o'clock, maybe a little later. She went out again about eleven – I was seeing some people from Mr Polux's party out and she went out at the same time. Again no car or taxi. She come back about half an hour later, maybe a bit more.'

'How was she?'

'How'd you mean? She was all right, a bit quiet, now I come to think of it. But she's often like that, a bit up and down in her moods, you know what I mean? Don't quote me, though.'

'Never,' said Clements. 'Now would you like to tell Miss Springfellow that Inspector Malone and Sergeant Clements would like to see her?'

Kinley looked at Malone with sudden new interest. 'You're not *Scobie* Malone? Geez, I saw you play at least a dozen times. I never knew why you weren't picked for Australia.'

'My sentiments, too,' said Malone modestly.

As they waited for the lift he was grinning. Clements said, 'That makes you feel good? Maybe I'd better start patting you on the back.'

I'd feel better if you were less enthusiastic about kicking the rich in the bum.

They rode up in a lift that was all brass and glass; the carpet on the floor felt thick enough to be straight off a merino's back. Everything in The Wharf was designed to show the residents where their money had been spent. Discretion was something only the poor should afford.

Justine was waiting for them at the door of her apartment, tension in every line of her, in her voice, too: 'My secretary rang to say you'd been over there questioning her –'

'We thought she might,' said Malone. 'It's just routine. Did Mr Broad ring you, too?'

Justine looked puzzled. 'No. Should he have?'

'I don't know,' said Malone blandly. 'I don't know how things work in the Springfellow Corporation.'

They followed her into the apartment. There was plenty of glass here, black glass; though no brass. The big living-room opened out on to a wide balcony, though these days anything larger than a pigeon roost was called a terrace; the harbour lay immediately below, the ferries seemingly coming in to berth in The Wharf's basement. An interior decorator had been let loose in here, allowed his or her head. Black and white were predominant: black glass walls, white carpet, black and white leather couches and chairs, black glass tables on white metal legs: it was like being trapped in a modernistic nightmare. The abstract paintings on the walls, with their

159

vivid reds and greens and yellows, were somehow a relief to the eyes, as if reassuring any visitor that he hadn't lost all sense of colour. Malone knew nothing about interior design, but he had the feeling that this was all old hat; when he described it this evening to Lisa, as she would insist that he did, she would tell him that it was definitely old hat, something that had gone out with Fred Astaire movies. If this was a rebellion on Justine's part against her mother's pinks and greys, she had gone all the way. How will my kids rebel against me? Malone wondered. But let that question remain in the future, the best place for problems.

Someone materialized out of all the black glass, as if stepping out of a magician's mirror. It was Alice Magee, who would never be at home in anything like this, not even with Fred Astaire.

'I thought my granddaughter would like some support. You're going to make a nuisance of yourself, aren't you, Inspector?'

'Only if we have to, Mrs Magee. Have you been waiting for us?'

'I'm just surprised you haven't come sooner.'

'We work to union rules, Mrs Magee. Slow and easy.' The banter was done with a smile, but he wondered why she should have been waiting for them. Had Emma Springfellow had everyone as expectant as this when she had been alive?

'Do sit down,' said Justine in a tone that suggested Malone and Clements had been galloping about the room. They sat down, the black leather sighing embarrassingly beneath them; the designer evidently had never been troubled by flatulence. Justine and Alice perched themselves on the edges of steel-framed chairs, like birds on a roost. Now they were together the resemblance could be seen, though Alice had the weathered, coarsened look that would never mar Justine. It had nothing to do with the fact that the granddaughter could afford the best of cosmetics and beauticians: she just could not imagine the life her grandmother

160

had lived forty or fifty years ago. Circular Quay was more than a mere 700 kilometres from Cobar.

Malone decided he had better do the questioning; Clements had to be held back. 'Miss Springfellow, you've already told us you went up to see your aunt on the night of her murder. You got there about eight and you thought you left there about nine or so. Did you come straight home? Here, I mean.'

'Yes.'

'Were you here Monday night, Mrs Magee?'

'No, I was down at Exeter. My daughter has a property down there. I told you.'

'With Lady Springfellow?'

'No. I'm still down there. I just came up today to do some shopping. And to see if Justine wanted me to stay with her?'

She looked at her granddaughter, who shook her head. 'No, I'm all right, Gran . . . Inspector, why are you here? Just to repeat your questions?'

'No, to ask a few more. Did you go out again on Monday night?'

She hesitated a moment. The two detectives and the two women were sitting on opposite sides of the big black-glass coffee table. There were six white-glass drink coasters on the table, like blank eyes in a black face. Justine picked up one and began to handle it nervously.

'Ye-es. Yes, I did. I went out about eleven.'

'Where did you go?'

'Nowhere in particular. I just went for a walk – I went up Macquarie Street as far as Martin Place, then I came back – I don't know, I can't remember whether I came back down Pitt Street or Castlereagh. No, it was Pitt.'

'That end of town is pretty deserted that time of night. Do you usually go for late-night walks?'

'No. I was – I was upset. I've already told you I had the most fearful row with Aunt Emma. It was about the family takeover. There's a tremendous amount of money involved –' She was her mother's daughter, keeping the priorities prominent. She rolled the coaster through her fingers, as a gambler would a gambling chip.

'When you walked up Macquarie Street, did you stop and think of going into The Vanderbilt?'

'What was the point? Talking to Emma was like talking to a brick wall. I wasted my time going there in the first place.'

'You should've listened to your mother,' said Alice.

'We should all do that,' said Malone, but couldn't remember a single piece of advice Brigid had ever given him, except not to forget his prayers and to keep his shoelaces tied. 'Was that the only reason you went out, that you were upset?'

'Well, no-o. Peter Polux upstairs rang down several times, trying to get me to go up to his party. I, er, don't like Mr Polux.'

'Mr Broad was there. Does he like him?'

'I don't know. They're just business acquaintances, I think.'

Then Malone said abruptly, deciding the plunge had to be taken before Clements dived in ahead of him, 'When you went for your walk, did you take the gun with you?'

It was almost as if he had produced it and pointed it at her. '*What gun?*'

'The .380 calibre Walther you took from the collection in your mother's house. Your father's gun.'

'Who said I took the gun?' She held the coaster as if she might throw it at him. Then she put it back on the table, as if putting temptation out of reach.

Malone didn't answer her question, but looked at Alice. 'Did you know she had taken it, Mrs Magee?'

The two women stared at each other; this was something they had not expected. Then Alice Magee said, 'Yes, I knew. I suggested it – I thought she needed something for protection, living alone here in this flat.' It was a flat to her, not an apartment.

'You didn't tell us that when we talked to you before. Why?'

162

'I – I knew she didn't have a licence for it. I didn't want to get her into trouble.'

'She's in trouble now,' said Clements, saying something at last. 'Her aunt was killed by two .380 calibre bullets that could have been fired from a Walther.'

Both women's hands tightened on the arms of their chairs; Justine's hands looked particularly white, almost skeletal. She said huskily, 'Are you accusing me of murdering my aunt?'

'We're just asking questions at the moment,' said Malone before Clements took them too far down that road. 'Do you still have the gun?'

'No.'

'Where is it?'

'I was frightened of it. I took it back to my mother's house. I don't know when –' She was flustered; all intelligence seemed to have dropped out of her face. 'Yes, I do. It was the day of my father's funeral. I took it with me and put it back in the collection, in the gun cabinet.'

'Did anyone see you put it back? You didn't tell your grandmother?'

'No, I don't think so. My mind's a bit hazy about that day – I'd never been to a funeral before –'

You're lucky, thought Malone. Twenty-two years old and she'd never been even remotely touched by death. Now, in the space of a few weeks, she had been hit, violently, by violent death. 'Is the gun still there?'

'No,' said Alice Magee. 'I'll save you the trouble of going over to Mosman. It's gone again.'

'Did you see it after Justine returned it?'

'No. If she put it – when she put it back, it couldn't have been there long. I'd have noticed it.'

'Are you in the habit of checking the gun collection?' said Clements. He was not taking notes. His notebook lay on the table beside the white coasters.

'No. I just *notice* things, especially about the house. I've got a housekeeper's eye, so my daughter says.'

163

'What about *the* housekeeper? Would she have noticed it?'

'I don't know. You'll have to ask her.'

'Miss Springfellow, was your argument with your aunt about money?'

'Of course.' She sounded as if she believed all arguments were about money. Then abruptly she softened, something else coming out from behind the hard shell she had tried on in her mother's image: 'Well, no, it was not all about money. There were other things – undercurrents. Mother and I and my grandmother, we were always treated as outsiders by Emma. She hated the thought that Mother and I had the Springfellow name.'

'She thought Magee was common,' said Alice, who had her own hard shell; snobbery would bounce off her like rocks off a tank. 'She hated anything that smacked of the Irish or Catholics.'

Malone grinned at Clements. 'I wondered why she didn't like us that day we met her. I thought it was just because we were cops.'

'Had you ever threatened her?' said Clements, taking up the questioning again. Malone noticed that in Clements's approach to Justine there was a trace of the antagonism he had shown towards the two yuppies in the Springfellow lift. Clements had never before given even a hint that he would take up any proletarian cause; indeed, in his uniformed days he had relished the opportunity to rough up demonstrators, particularly any leftist trade unionists or students. Now, all at once, he was beginning to wave a banner, if only in his manner. He had developed a sudden resentment of the rich, especially the young rich.

'Threatened her?' Justine was puzzled, the hard shell cracking even more. She plucked nervously at the blue dress she wore.

'There was a note in her diary said you had done that.'

That's not entirely true, Malone said silently; the entry said that *J.* had threatened her. But he wasn't going to contradict Clements in front of the two women. At the same time he

164

realized that, sooner or later, he would have to ask the question himself of the other J., John Leeds.

Justine looked dumbly at her grandmother; Alice Magee stepped into the breach. 'We all threatened her at one time or another – we had some real donnybrooks. I threatened to throw her out of my daughter's house one day. She was a real nasty woman, but somehow I felt sorry for her. She was around the bend, I think. It's tougher for women, being alone like her.' She had a natural sympathy for the underdog, even a rich one. 'She thought the whole world was against her.'

'I know the feeling,' said Malone; then looked directly at Justine. 'Miss Springfellow, we don't think you're telling us all of the truth.'

Justine seemed to go totally rigid, as if even her young flesh had calcified. Her voice rasped: 'What do you mean?'

'You did go back to see your aunt a second time. A Mr and Mrs Pandon let you into The Vanderbilt and you went up in the lift with them. That was around eleven o'clock, when you went out for your walk.'

'Don't say anything, sweetheart.' Alice Magee stepped into the breach like a professional bodyguard.

Justine said nothing for a moment; then the stone crumbled, just a little. 'Yes. Yes, I did try to see Emma again.'

'Why didn't you tell us that the first time?'

'I – I was frightened. I still am.'

'Sweetheart –'

'No, it's all right, Nana. I haven't *done* anything, I mean not to Emma. Yes, Inspector, I went back there. I went up to Emma's apartment and rang the doorbell, but it wasn't working. Then I knocked, but I got no answer. I didn't know whether she guessed it was me or whether she had someone else in there. I just gave up and went back down in the lift. Then I went for the walk I told you about. I didn't see Emma the second time. That's the truth, Inspector.'

Malone looked at her, wanting to believe her. 'You saw no one else going into or coming out of The Vanderbilt?'

'Only Mr and Mrs Pandon.'

'I don't think they're suspects,' he said drily. He knew she should be questioned further; but abruptly he stood up. 'I think that'll be all for the moment, Miss Springfellow.'

'Not quite,' said Clements. 'I think we need some fingerprints. Would you come up to Homicide with us?'

'No,' said Alice. 'Not unless you're going to charge her with something. That's the law.'

'You know something about the law?' said Clements.

Whatever happened to my authority? Malone wondered. But he let it go: he hadn't yet got his bearings, for attack or defence.

'A little,' said Alice. 'I had a husband who was always in trouble. I don't think my granddaughter ought to say any more without her lawyer.'

Clements stood up, bending over the coffee table to pick up his notebook. At the same time Malone glanced at Justine. She was standing now, her back straight. She's scared stiff, he thought, but there's a lot of her mother in her. And of her grandmother, who went on, still talking to Clements, 'Justine didn't murder Emma. You'll never make a case against her.'

'I've heard that before, Mrs Magee.' Clements straightened up, slipping his notebook into his jacket pocket. He hadn't raised his voice, but Malone could sense the hard antagonism in him. 'You'd be surprised how many times they've been wrong.'

2

Going down in the lift Clements said, 'What did you make of that?'

Malone looked at himself in the brass-framed glass; he was surprised to find he hadn't changed, that he still looked calm and unworried. 'Why did you try that dumb trick? You were never going to get away with it. As soon as you got her into Homicide, she'd have been on the phone to her mum. Then we'd have had Lady S. down on us with a battalion of lawyers raising bloody hell. I can do without that.' He could do without a lot of things, including a sergeant who was, unexpectedly, turning nasty. 'Russ, what's the matter with you?'

Clements looked into the mirrored walls, as if looking for an answer there. Then he shrugged. 'I don't bloody know. I think I've all of a sudden got shit on the liver against the rich. I've never been a red ragger – the Commos wouldn't touch me with a forty-foot pole. I've never resented other people having money, but all of a sudden, with these bloody Springfellows –' He stepped out of the lift with a last look at himself in the mirrors. 'They tell me there are always reasons for prejudices, but I dunno – I think it's just like catching a cold. One day you're okay and the next . . .'

'You're richer than I am. Are you going to give your money back to the bookies?'

'I'm prejudiced, but I'm not bloody stupid.'

But you're going to be a weight round my neck on this case: Malone looked at his friend, the albatross. 'Just tread carefully, Russ. We don't know how much clout the Springfellows have.'

'Clout has never worried you before.'

'Maybe I'm like you. I'm feeling middle-aged.'

Then Clements took out his notebook. Something slipped out of it and he held it gingerly by its narrow edges: it was a white drink coaster. 'I lifted this.'

'The one she was handling? For Chrissakes, Russ –'

'I'm not going to use it officially. I'll just get Don Cheshire out at Fingerprints to put it on file, no names, no pack-drill. Just so's we'll have something to refer back to, if and when.'

'If and when what?' But he knew.

'If and when we nail her. She did it, all right.'

They retrieved their car from the garage in Springfellow House and drove back to Homicide. The air-conditioning had stopped working, a frequent malfunction in police vehicles, as if the taxpayers, even the honest law-abiding ones, occasionally put a hex on it to remind policemen who paid their wages. Malone and Clements wound down their windows, but the hot air that blew into the car did nothing for their comfort. As they passed Hyde Park Malone looked up through the trees and saw the Archibald fountain sparkling like falling ice-drops in the sunlight. They pulled up at some traffic lights and a girl crossed in front of them, looking as cool as a mermaid in a pale-green sleeveless dress.

'Sometimes I wish I was a drag queen,' said Clements, 'so's I could dress like that.'

Malone looked at the hulk beside him. 'You'd set sex back five thousand years.'

They grinned at each other, their faces glistening with sweat and, yes, affection, though both of them would have shied away from the word. I couldn't wish for a better sidekick, thought Malone. It was a pity, though, that Clements wasn't on vacation right now, somewhere out of the State or even out of the country.

When they got back to Homicide Malone's phone was ringing. He picked it up; the Commissioner was on the other end. 'I've had a call from Lady Springfellow, Inspector. I believe you've been harassing her daughter.'

'Harassing, sir?' Malone felt himself get suddenly hot and not with the summer heat.

'Her word, Scobie. I hope you haven't been – harassing her?'

'No, sir. Just questioning her.'

'I thought I told you I saw her leaving The Vanderbilt?'

What's happening to the man? He had never known the Commissioner to interfere like this. 'Yes, sir, you did. But I just can't *stop.*'

'You could direct your enquiries elsewhere, for a start.'

'I'll do that too. Unfortunately, sir, I'm not on this case on my own.' He looked down the long room at Clements, who had stopped to talk to Andy Graham. 'Sergeant Clements is working with me – and he's pretty dogged.'

168

There was silence at the other end of the line; then Leeds sighed, sounded weary. 'I'm sorry, Scobie. Do it your way. The right way.'

<h1 style="text-align:center">3</h1>

Malone had a moment of inspired hope. After hanging up the phone he had sat utterly dejected; Clements, coming up to sit opposite him, had spoken to him but he hadn't answered. The silence between the two men was threatening to become bitter; Malone was aware of it and was desperate to break it. Then he had his inspiration.

'Maybe we're barking up the wrong tree.'

Clements gave him a hard look. 'What tree's that?'

'The Springfellow tree. What about that cove Dural who was released the same time we found Walter's bones? He was a raver against Walter for refusing his appeal. Maybe he's revenging himself by killing off someone else in the family.'

'You're stretching it,' said Clements, unexcited.

'Maybe. But it's worth a try. Corrective Services will give us an address on him. I think I read he's out on licence.'

They went to see Chilla Dural, Clements showing no enthusiasm at all for the venture. Dural was just coming out of the front door of his rooming house when Malone and Clements drew up at the kerb. As soon as he saw the two tall men get out of the car parked in a No Parking zone, he recognized them for coppers. He felt something flutter inside him: was he going to be pinched after all? He gave them a genuine smile of welcome.

'Could we go inside, Mr Dural?' said Malone after he had introduced himself and Clements. 'It's a little hot out here.'

Dural led them back down the hallway. At once Killeen's door opened, the wrinkled face appeared, the watchdog eyes wary. 'Trouble, mate?'

'I don't think so, Jerry. I'll call you if I need you.'

He ushered the two detectives into his room, closed the door. The room was still bare of any identification except for the photo on the dressing-table; he wasn't prepared to declare this as home. He gestured to Malone and Clements to sit down on the room's two chairs and he stood leaning against the dressing-table.

Malone came straight to the point. 'You've probably read about the murder of Emma Springfellow, Mr Dural. She was the sister of the judge who sent you up twenty-odd years ago.'

Dural went cold: for Chrissakes, they weren't going to pin a murder rap on him, were they? He wanted to go home to Parramatta, but not with another murder marked against him.

'I read about it.'

'Where were you last Monday night?'

Dural relaxed, though only inwardly; he showed the bulls nothing. 'That's easy. I was up at a jazz club up the street. I went up about, I dunno, nine o'clock, something like that, and I come home just after midnight.'

'You have someone who'll vouch for that?'

'The little bloke next door, Jerry Killeen. He come with me. He'll remember it, 'cause he hated it. He's no jazz fan, he kept asking the band to play some Nelson Eddy songs. Nelson Eddy, for Chrissakes! I remember it, all right, the night, I mean. I never been so bloody embarrassed in me life.'

Clements grinned and Malone, who knew a little about jazz, nodded sympathetically.

'Okay,' said Clements, 'we'll take your word for it. But while we're here – do you know anyone around the Cross who'll do a knock job if the price is right?'

'Mr Clements, I been outa the game for years. I dunno none of the rough 'uns that are around today. Was she done by a hit man? I dunno I'd wanna know anyone who'd hurt a woman, I mean a *decent* woman. I done a few knock jobs in my time – I wouldn't of been in Parramatta if I hadn't – but

I'd never do domestics. You know, hurting a woman 'cause some bugger paid for it. How was she done? Shot, wasn't she?'

'Yes,' said Malone. 'Two .380s, probably from a Walther.'

Dural was suddenly aware of his own Walther in the drawer against which his right buttock was resting. Possession of a weapon, if the bulls wanted to search his room, could have his licence revoked. For a moment he was tempted to produce it: Parramatta beckoned. But in the same drawer were what remained of the five hundred dollar coins from the bank robbery at Leichhardt. He didn't want to be connected to that. Those goons had shot at the police and that was a no-no in his book. He wanted to be on good terms with the screws when he went back home.

'I don't think it'd be a hit man with a piece like that. Maybe, but I don't think so. He'd use a sawn-off .22, something like that, something he'd screw a silencer on to. I mean, if he was a professional. Fitting a silencer to a Walther ain't easy.'

'We don't know that a silencer was used.'

'You mean you ain't found the gun yet? Then how d'you know it was a Walther?'

Malone stood up. It had been a stupid forlorn hope that Dural might be the killer; anything that would lead them away from Justine and get John Leeds off his back. 'Right, Mr Dural, we just had to check. You're staying out of trouble, I suppose?'

'Doing me best, Mr Malone.'

He opened the door for them and they stepped out into the hallway. Killeen was there, broom in hand, making a mountain out of a molehill of dust. 'Just cleaning up. Everything all right, Chilla?'

Dural nodded, grinning inwardly at the old stickybeak. 'Just a coupla old friends, Jerry. Inspector Malone and Sergeant Clements. Just checking where I was Monday night.'

'What happened then?'

171

'Nothing,' said Malone, but didn't believe Killeen's innocent look. The old man would know all the news that was printed or broadcast, and a great deal that wasn't. 'You and Mr Dural were together that night, he says. Where'd you go?'

'You think I could forget it? No offence, Chilla, but that was the night we went up to the jazz club. Jeez, what a night! You wouldn't believe it, Inspector, they never heard of Nelson Eddy!'

'Hard to believe.' Malone shook his head in sympathy.

'Who's Nelson Eddy?' Clements was straight-faced.

'Come on,' said Malone and led the way out to the police car. Inside it, he said, 'Why pick on the little feller? You know who Nelson Eddy was.'

'I should be picking on you, bringing us out in this heat. That was a waste of time, Scobie. I tell you, we don't have to look outside the Springfellow family for Emma's murderer. Least of all, look at Chilla Dural. If ever I've seen an old lag who doesn't want any more trouble, it's him.'

'Do a further check on him. Have Andy Graham check the jazz club.'

All at once he wished that Chilla Dural was the murderer, but he knew in his policeman's heart, a suspect organ amongst crims, that life was never that simple.

4

'That film only proves that happy innocence isn't possible, even for fools,' said Gil Holman.

'Yves Montand's character was typically French,' said his wife Jean. 'If the story had been set today, he'd have been letting off bombs in Gérard Dépardieu's back yard.'

Her accent on the names was perfect: she taught French in one of the better private schools. She and Gil were both teachers, he at a State high school. Jean and Lisa had gone to university together, had lost contact and then, a year ago,

172

had met again. Malone suspected that the friendship, on either woman's part, was not a deep one; he also suspected that Lisa had taken up with the Holmans because they offered her some intellectual stimulus, even in their limited outlook, that he couldn't give her. Though he would never have told her so.

'I'm always half a street behind what's going on when I see a foreign film,' he said. 'By the time I've read the sub-titles, the actors have changed their expressions.' It wasn't much of a contribution to the discussion, but he didn't want to embarrass Lisa by sitting there like a log.

They had been to see *Jean de Florette* at the Village cinema here in Double Bay and then come across to the International Café for supper. The Holmans had no children and so didn't have to worry about baby-sitters; the Malone children were staying the night with Lisa's parents at Rose Bay, probably still up way past their bed-time and making the most of their grandparents' indulgence. Some day, when Jan and Elisabeth Pretorius died, the children would be indulged even further: a trust had been set up for them that would give each of them a very comfortable start in his or her adult life. Malone was unsure how he felt about the intended inheritance; he would have liked to have been responsible for the assurance of his children's future himself. That, too, was something he would never mention to Lisa.

The International was Double Bay's principal meeting place. The tiny inner suburb, five minutes by car from the city centre, was also known as Double Pay; *bargain* was a rude word, except between wholesalers and retailers; customers who came looking for bargains were as optimistic as the hunters who came to the International looking for virgins. Here amongst the expensive boutiques, the European delicatessens and the coffee lounges, the post-war European immigrants, those with money or memories of it, had begun to meet in the 1950s at the International Café. They would sit, as they had in cafés in Vienna and Berlin and Budapest, sipping their coffees and watching the passing

173

parade and each other. At one time it was said that anyone with an Australian accent would not be served, but those reverse xenophobic days had gone. Now there were far fewer older immigrants, one heard much less foreign language, and the younger set had moved in, those with money of their own or with parents who had it. They still did what was expected of them: they sipped their coffee and watched the passing parade and each other. To Malone's jaundiced eye, that of the boy with the mark of Erskineville still on him, they looked to be all from the same family, their smugness a distinguishable feature like a hereditary birthmark.

Three young men came in, peacocks in white John Lane outfits, gold gleaming round their necks and their wrists. They sat down, turned their chairs to face in the same direction, and, as it happened, looked directly at Malone in his Fletcher Jones checked shirt and his 49-dollar Hagger fawn trousers. He might have been wearing a bikie's leathers; they looked at each other as if to ask how he had got in here. They were black-haired, darkly tanned and handsome: they could have been Italian, Greek or Lebanese. Above a certain level of affluence, Malone thought, all Wogs look the same. And at once heard his father's voice in his ears and felt ashamed. What was the matter with him? Where, all of a sudden, had his prejudices come from? Had he, like Clements, suddenly caught the virus of them?

'What's the matter?' said Lisa. 'You look as if you've swallowed a cup of cold coffee.'

He wondered what she would say if he told her what he had been thinking. He couldn't, however, tell her in front of the Holmans. They were the sort who claimed they had no prejudices, except against the French, the Reagan Administration, the Nationalist Party, the Returned Servicemen's League and all loggers and saw-millers and any anti-conservationist. He looked over Lisa's shoulder and was saved.

'There's Justine Springfellow.'

The other three turned; as had most of the big café's customers. 'My God, she's beautiful!' said Jean Holman.

174

'She's just made the most of herself, that's all,' said Gil, the expert on women.

'We all do that,' said Jean and smiled at Lisa. 'Or we try to.'

'Have you met her?' Lisa said to Malone.

'A couple of times. I had a session with her today.'

'Who's the guy with her?' said Gil.

'His name's Michael Broad. He's her old lady's financial director.'

'Her old lady,' said Lisa. 'That's how you describe Venetia Springfellow? How would you describe me to your mates in Homicide?'

'You're my old lady,' said Malone and grinned. If they had been alone he would have taken her hand; but not in front of the Holmans, not in front of the International crowd. 'Or my kids' old lady, if you like.'

Lisa smiled at him. 'I don't know why people say Aussie men have no charm.'

'Ah, break it down,' said Gil, who, Lisa had once confided to Malone, had as much charm as an empty beer bottle. 'We're just different, that's all.'

'Different,' said Jean, and for the first time Malone wondered if things were quite as congenial between the Holmans as they made out. 'Yes, I think that's the word. *La différence*. That Michael Broad is different.'

'He's as smooth as the top of his head,' said Malone.

Lisa ran her hand over his thick unruly thatch. 'So are you.'

Without thinking, Malone had turned his chair round, like the three peacocks at the nearby table; he was an animal observing its prey. Or Clements's prey: the big sergeant should be here, not himself.

The café a moment ago had seemed full; but somehow Justine and Broad had found an empty table; money, real money, has its own magic. Justine, well aware of the circle of stares ringing her, sat down, arranging herself with the unnatural grace that is natural to a model; Lisa, who knew

175

that *the* Miss Springfellow had never had to earn a living as a model, wondered where she had acquired the gift. Malone, for whom sitting down was no more than putting a bum on a seat, just continued to observe.

Then Justine looked across the café and saw him. The International was well-lit; it was a place designed not for rendezvous but for recognition; the Viennese owner knew his customers better than they knew themselves. She stared at Malone, her eyes opening as if she were suddenly frightened; then she leaned forward and said something to Broad. He turned and looked across at Malone, his gaze coolly aggressive.

'Her boyfriend doesn't like you,' said Gil Holman.

Lisa had turned back, was picking at her cheesecake: she knew she made better herself. 'I don't think he's her boyfriend. He is just her minder, a hanger-on.'

Malone looked sideways at her. 'What makes you say that?'

Lisa smiled at Jean. 'Do you agree with me?'

Jean nodded. 'She's far too casual with him. When she walked in, she might as well have been on her own, for all the attention she gave him.'

'Listen to 'em!' said Gil. 'You two oughta be in the police force. Cagney and Lacey. What do you think, Inspector?'

'I never argue with a woman in public. Certainly not with two of them.' He looked back across the café. Justine and Broad were no longer staring at him; but neither were they looking at each other. They had the detached appearance that a brother and sister might have in public; or Justine did. 'But it's given me something to think about.'

On the way out the Malones and the Holmans had to pass Justine's table. As they did so, Malone paused. 'I'm glad to see you relaxing, Miss Springfellow. You didn't look very relaxed this morning. I'm sorry about that.'

She was wearing a blue linen dress, but he guessed it was not one she would wear to the office: it was a shade too revealing. He wondered if it was the dress she had worn on Monday night.

'I don't think Miss Springfellow needs your sympathy or your attention,' said Broad, smiling broadly; people were looking at them and he attempted to look as if he and Malone were exchanging pleasantries. He was dressed in a white silk jacket and blue shirt and trousers. Malone, standing above him, might have been his gardener caught in an off-duty moment and being told how to mow the lawn tomorrow. Except that no gardener could afford the International's prices. 'You don't have to stop and talk to her in public. Not here, anyway.'

Malone grinned, though he was not amused. 'I didn't think I looked *that* much like a cop. Sorry, Miss Springfellow. Next time I'll wear my Gucci gear.'

As he caught up with Lisa she said, 'I heard that. You trying to sound like those cops in *Miami Vice*?'

'It's reading those scripts for *Woolloomooloo Vice*.' *That*, thank Christ, was behind him; some other poor mug had been drafted as technical adviser. 'I don't even know why I stopped to speak to her.'

'You couldn't help yourself. She's a very pretty girl and you have the seven-year itch.'

'Is that all?' He grinned at her, took her hand; they were out of the International now. 'I thought it was something serious, like a cop's sadistic streak I'm always reading about.'

They said good-night to the Holmans, who drove off in their Volvo with the Anti-This, and Anti-That stickers on the rear window. As they got into the Commodore, with not a sticker in sight but the registration label, Lisa said, 'What did you mean when you said I'd given you something to think about?'

'You never forget a line, do you?'

'That comes of being a married woman. Freud or Havelock Ellis or Dorothy Dix said that.'

'It sounds more like Dolly Parton.' He waited till she had started up the car and pulled away from the kerb; when they went out at night he preferred her to drive. 'I think we've been concentrating too much on Justine.'

177

'I could have told you that, if you'd asked me.' They had discussed his day's work on the drive over from Randwick to Double Bay. 'What about Venetia? Isn't she a suspect? Or Venetia's mother, Justine's grandmother? From what you said, she's tough enough.'

'Maybe. So's Michael Broad. From what I've heard of him, he's as ruthless as the lady he works for.'

'Well, yes, I suppose you could put him on your list. But I'd stick to the women. What about the other sister-in-law, Edwin's wife?'

'You really have got it in for the women, haven't you?'

'I just don't want you spending all your time with one of the prettiest, the richest young girl in town. No, seriously –' She kept her eyes on the road as they drove up through Woollahra, under the tunnel of big trees along Ocean Street, with the fruit bats scratching their ragged lines across the early summer moon. 'You haven't got your heart in this, have you? Not even with Justine?'

'How do you know?'

'Darling, you're like an open book sometimes. It's almost as if you want me to read you, instead of you telling me something. Now are you going to tell me or not?'

They crossed Oxford Street and went on down past Centennial Park, dark as an unmapped continent on their right. He looked out at the darkness beyond the high iron railings: it was a good place for telling secrets. So he told her about the intrusion of Commissioner John Leeds into the case.

'Was he a boyfriend of Venetia's?'

'I'd say so. He might be more than that. He might be Justine's father.' It was only in the last few years that he had begun to discuss his cases in detail with her; but he knew she could be trusted, though he worried sometimes that he burdened her with his own need for support. She was a sounding-board and sounding-boards were supposed to absorb a certain percentage of what was bounced off them. He wondered at the cumulative effect.

178

'Was Venetia ever a suspect in the disappearance of her husband?'

'I don't know. From what I gather, the lid was put on that case quick smart.'

'What about Venetia's mother? Was she ever questioned about Walter Springfellow? Mothers-in-law have been known to be very nasty.'

'Yours isn't. Neither is mine.'

They agreed that Brigid Malone and Elisabeth Pretorius would never murder anyone and they drove on in silence for a while. Then Lisa said, 'Let's forget the Springfellows. I'm not going to waste tonight talking about them.'

'What did you have in mind? It's bed-time.'

'That's what I had in mind. This is the first opportunity I've had in weeks to make love without holding my breath.'

'Is that why you dumped the kids on your mother?'

'Of course. I'm going to moan my head off if you do your part properly.'

'What if the neighbours hear you?'

'They'll think you're murdering me. What a lovely way to go!'

She put the car in the garage and, hand in hand, they walked into the house to the queen-sized bed, the capital city of the country of marriage, where the small death might occur every time they made love, but never murder.

5

Venetia could not believe what she was being told.

'It's true,' said Peter Polux. 'I'm stone motherless broke. All bets are off, Venetia old girl.'

'But –' Then she paused, suddenly afraid she was going to stammer; she had cured herself of that impediment years ago. There had been too many shocks in the past month; the nervous system could take just so much. 'Two months ago,

179

when we signed our agreement, you gave us proof you had the money. Five hundred and fifty million, less your 10 per cent success fee.'

'Well, at least you won't have to pay that.' But his smile was nervous. 'Venetia, I *had* the cash, honest to God. But that was before Black Tuesday.'

She noticed for the first time that he was no longer wearing his white shoes; his feet, which were tiny for a man of his bulk, were in mourning, in black brogues. He was still, however, fumbling with his gold rosary beads.

'I had a silent partner, Steinburgers in Zurich – it was Brunei money we were going to use. I was borrowing from them and on-lending to you at a spread.' He grinned again, like a boy confessing to stealing apples from her orchard. With every moment she was now seeing him for what he was, a high-flyer who had soared far too high for his ability to stay airborne; she wondered at her own lack of judgement. Then she looked at Michael Broad, who had recommended Polux so strongly. 'But as soon as the crash came, they reneged. I've been tearing around like a blue-arsed fly since then, trying to raise the cash.'

'For us or for yourself? You said you were broke.'

'I am, God's truth.' She waited for him to hold up the rosary beads, but he didn't. 'Everything I own has gone down the gurgler. I was over-extended to buggery, Venetia. You were going to be my saviour.' He was trying candour now: it hung on his face like a lop-sided mask.

Venetia looked at Broad again. 'You recommended him. You said you'd had him checked out 100 per cent.'

'I did. I had our best people on the job. He was just too clever for us.'

Polux looked unoffended that they were discussing him in front of him. His brashness was an armour-plating. Venetia began to wonder if he would use his rosary beads as a sling-shot.

'How long have you known he was going to be of no use to us?'

'A few days.' Broad had hesitated for a moment. 'I was hoping I could salvage something, find another banker.'

'And did you?'

'No.'

'All right, Mr Polux –'

'Peter.' With an ingratiating grin.

'No – *Mr Polux*. You were never going to be a friend of mine, not even if our deal had gone through. We owe you nothing, right?'

For the first time he looked as if he might turn nasty; he had been dismissed before, but never by a woman, one as ruthless as this bitch. 'You might need me in the future, *Lady* Springfellow. I'm not going to be broke for ever.'

'You'll always be bankrupt as far as I'm concerned, Mr Polux. See yourself out, will you?'

'I'll see you out, Peter –'

'Stay where you are, Michael. You and I have something to talk about.'

Broad shrugged, gestured with a helpless hand to Polux. The latter put away his rosary beads and stood up; if he was bruised or scarred, it did not show. But as he walked out of the room he was limping, as if the black shoes were pinching. He was a white shoe man, a fair weather banker.

When the door had closed Venetia said, 'All I can say is, I'm glad we found out now instead of further down the track.'

'I'm sorry. I should have been more careful with him.'

'Why weren't you?'

'I trusted those I had working on him.'

'Michael, you always double-check everyone who works for you. That's why I pay you what I do. Why didn't you do it this time? When you found out he couldn't raise the money, why didn't you come to me immediately?'

He looked away from her for a moment, but she knew that he was not looking at the view from her window. He ran his hand over his bald head, a nervous gesture she had never seen before. He was not a nervous man; she had heard it said

181

that he had more balls than any two men in Sydney's financial world. That touched off a thought that eunuchs, so it was said, never went bald. She smiled at the irrelevancy, but when he looked back he mistook the smile for malice.

'Are you planning to fire me, too?'

That put her on her guard. 'I haven't made up my mind what I'm going to do. You still haven't answered my question. Why did you neglect checking your feasibility team?'

'I – I had something else on my mind.' Again the nervousness, this time in the normally steady, deep voice.

She said very evenly, 'Michael, was Polux going to give you a cut of his success fee?'

'No.' He faced her openly, but she knew he was lying.

'Then what was on your mind?'

'Venetia – I'm in trouble. Not as badly as Peter, but bad enough. I've been buying futures. When things crashed . . .' The hand crept over the shining skull again.

'How bad?'

'I'll have to sell my car.'

God, she thought, how grown men value their toys! He made the Aston-Martin sound like a family estate.

'And I'll have to take out a second mortgage on my apartment. I may even have to sell it and move into something smaller.' He had an apartment in Double Bay that, she knew, was worth probably $500,000, though he had paid nothing like that for it four years ago.

'Have you sold your Springfellow shares?'

'No. I – I'm over-committed there.'

'Why? You've owned them for some time, you got them at a good price – you could sell them without capital gains tax. You have – what? – fifty thousand?'

'A hundred and fifty thousand. I – I bought up when we first started to put the takeover deal together.'

'You could be in a lot of trouble. That's insider trading. You'd better sell them.'

'I can't, not at the current price. I'm in enough of a hole, I don't want to dig it any deeper.'

She stared at him. She had never entirely trusted him, but it was her philosophy that trust was a luxury in today's business; all one could do was rely on one's judgement. And her judgement of him had been way off line.

'Why did you go out on a limb like this, Michael? Don't I pay you enough?'

He stared back at her, less nervous now. 'Greed, I suppose.'

Our virtues are often connected to our vices. She had often told herself that her own greed for power and money financed her generosity to charity. But she doubted that Michael Broad had any charity in him. He would look upon even ten cents in a blind man's tin cup as a tax deductible item.

'I thought you'd understand that.' He was suddenly blatantly, if coolly, aggressive. He had argued with her, had never allowed her to walk over him as she walked over others; she had respected him for that, no matter how much he might have annoyed or angered her. But this was downright rudeness.

'Watch yourself, Michael. You're digging a bigger hole than you think.'

'Don't lecture me, Venetia. What I was after was the same thing as you were after – it was just a difference of degree, that was all. Everybody in town was bitten by the same bug.' *Everybody* was those tied by their computers to the stock exchanges of the world; it was another world from that of the man in the street, one where money was the visa needed and the dream desired. She understood what he meant. 'I learned from you, Venetia. I should not have taken so much notice of you.'

He had lost tens, perhaps hundreds of thousands; she had lost millions. She felt no self-pity: she had gambled and lost. She could, however, see him filling the hole he had dug for himself with self-pity and diving into it. All at once she was not only angry at him, but despised him.

'I think you and I are coming close to saying goodbye. You're not indispensable, Michael.'

She saw the sudden frightened look in his face; he began to retreat. 'I'm sorry – perhaps I've expressed myself too strongly. One says things when one is worried . . .' His accent seemed to have thickened, he was speaking with the precise English he had had when he first joined Springfellow. For a moment he was the newly arrived immigrant, one foot on the ship, one on the land where he had to begin a new life. 'We can still perhaps salvage a deal for the takeover. In the last couple of days I've been in touch with Steinburgers in Zurich, asking them if they would come to the party on their own. With the dollar down, we'll have to pay more in interest –'

'What did they say?' She might forgive him if he did manage to salvage something from the wreckage. There are uses for charity: it isn't all done with the best of intentions.

'Well –' He knew that what he had held out was an empty promise. 'At the moment they're not interested. But . . .'

'But nothing, Michael. I'll think about what I'm going to do with you. That'll be all.'

He tried a last bluster: 'You'll have to buy me out –'

She laughed. 'I'll buy you out by promising not to let the NCSC know about your insider trading.'

His bony handsome face was abruptly as expressionless as his bald scalp. He said nothing, just got up and walked quickly out of the office. He didn't slam the big heavy door: he had more sense of style. She had made another enemy, but the fact didn't disturb her. The battlefield was too crowded for her to worry about another sniper.

She got up and went to the largest of the windows, the one that looked out on to the harbour. Diagonally across from her she could see The Wharf; Justine's daily maid was sweeping the apartment's terrace. Beneath her feet was the prize she had been trying to win. Not visible from her office but only half a kilometre up behind the Springfellow building was The Vanderbilt, where Emma had schemed against her and been murdered. Within spitting distance, as it were, were all her problems. It was small comfort, but it meant she could keep in touch, even if she couldn't solve them.

She felt suddenly weak, but she resisted the temptation to sit down; that would be surrender. She prided herself on her strength, though she had never been one to boast. Boasting was a staff of those with a weakness; she had weaknesses, but she liked to think she had them under control. Her liking for men, the physical side of them, was a weakness; but she had been discreet about her choices, or thought she had been, and so far there had been no problems there. Except, of course, twenty-one years ago . . . The finding of Walter's remains had revived her guilt about him, but nothing could be done about that. Guilt is a weakness, but only to the honourable and she had never claimed to be one of those.

She had been bitterly disappointed at the collapse of the takeover bid. She had set her heart on taking over the Springfellow empire: from then on, the Springfellow name would be hers and Justine's and all other members of the family would soon be forgotten. She had wanted the name and the power; the riches would be incidental. That she had been denied them had wounded her more deeply than she showed. But the opportunity was still there; the death of Emma had removed the major obstacle. A pox on Polux: she would look around for other finance. She was indomitable; or anyway optimistic. It was optimism that had brought her all the way from Cobar.

Her intercom buzzed. 'Mr Edwin is here to see you, Lady Springfellow.'

He had made no appointment; Edwin was always so meticulous about not dropping in. It was not *Mosman*. 'Ask him to come in, Shirl.'

Shirl, middle-aged and sensible, with a sensible name, a secretary who would keep any boss's feet on the ground, opened the door and showed in Edwin. She gave him a wide smile; she had always liked Mr Edwin, a gentleman of the old school. 'Would you like some coffee?'

'No, thank you, Mrs Miller. Perhaps a double Scotch, though? No, I'm only joking.'

185

Shirl gave him another smile and went out and Venetia said, 'A double Scotch at this time of day? Are you taking up the grog, Edwin?'

'I've been tempted once or twice in the past months. I don't think I have the strength of character to surrender to it.' He had never been one for irony, either; he was changing day by day. She hadn't seen much of him since the day of Walter's funeral, but even the occasional glimpses had shown her that he was no longer the predictable Edwin she had known for more than twenty years. 'Forgive me for bursting in on you like this.'

She smiled. 'You'd never *burst* in on anyone, Edwin.'

He smiled in return, made himself comfortable, in his stiff way, in his chair. He was immaculately dressed as always, but one had to look twice to see the effect; everything about him was understated. She knew that he, like Walter, had always had his suits made by Cutlers; he bought his shirts in Jermyn Street on his annual trip to London; he always wore custom-made Lobb shoes. His ties, too, were always sober: plain dark colours with sometimes a discreet stripe. But not today: the white shirt was – disfigured? Was that the word? – by a green-and-blue-and-white creation tie – could it be a Hermès?

'I like your tie. Very dashing.'

'Thank you. It was a present from Ruth.' *Was she stepping out, too?* 'I had a birthday a week ago. Before Emma . . . But Ruth says no one wears black any more, not for weeks, as we used to.'

'Only Greek and Italian widows.' She was wearing a grey linen suit and a pink shirt. She would wear the unflattering black again to Emma's funeral, when her body was released by the coroner.

Edwin composed himself for an announcement. 'I'm announcing my retirement. I thought you should know first.'

'No! Edwin, you'll never retire –'

'Yes. You said something to me a few weeks ago – you said I was *old*. I've never thought of myself as such, but you are

186

right. I don't understand half of what goes on around me, not any more. It's a different world. Not one that I particularly like.'

'What will you do? Springfellow's has been your life.'

'I'll find something. I'll do more charity work –' He was on the boards of half a dozen charities, duties inherited from his father. It only occurred to her now (had she remarked it at the time?) that Walter had never interested himself in charity work. 'Ruth and I will do more travelling. See more of Australia, take more time to see Europe.'

'Well, I'll miss you, Edwin.' She meant it. She was surprised she felt no elation at his going; he had never been one who had tried to exclude her as a Springfellow. 'We haven't always seen eye to eye, but now I think about it, you've always been a steadying influence on me.'

He smiled at that. He had always liked her more than he had ever shown; or perhaps admired was the word. She was a handsome woman, more complimentary in his lexicon than calling her beautiful: beauty, these days, was something that could be manufactured. She also had sex appeal, but he would never have mentioned that to anyone. His sex life with Ruth had been adequate, but there had been the occasional dream . . .

'I don't think I ever influenced you one iota. But thank you for the thought. Now, there's something else . . .'

'Two surprises in one day?'

'Yes, I suppose this will surprise you. Emma's will has been read to me. I've inherited all her estate, except for a few bequests to her favourite charities and all her paintings going to the Art Gallery. Everything else is mine. Ruth and I don't need it and we have no children to pass it on to. As I said, I'm retiring and that means leaving Springfellow altogether, a clean break. I want to sell you all of Emma's shares at whatever is the going price. It would mean, of course, that you would have to make a full bid.'

She felt her breath rise in her throat. At today's prices she would be gaining full control of the family company and the bank at far less cost than she had ever dreamed. 'I'll have to think about it, Edwin.'

It was his turn to be surprised. 'Good heavens, why? I thought you'd leap across your desk at me, grab them before I changed my mind.'

'The situation is a little different now from what it was a few weeks ago.'

He might be old, but he was still sharp: 'You mean you no longer have the finance?'

'Something like that.' A month ago she would have lied to him.

'That man Polux has let you down? I could have warned you about him, but it wasn't my place.'

'Will you sell to someone else? Intercapital or one of the other institutions?'

He deliberated a moment. 'No, I'd rather keep it in the family.'

'Thank you, Edwin. For still thinking of me as family.' Then she said, 'Where did you and Emma get the finance to buy out the other shares?'

'That was Emma's doing, not mine. She borrowed against everything we already owned.'

'You let her do *that*?'

'Venetia, I was sick of all the fighting. Truth to tell, I was sick of *her*. I gave in to her. It was against the grain of my whole life.' He sounded genuinely ashamed.

'If things get worse –' Already there was talk of a depression, one to match that of the 1930s. With the exception of Hong Kong, the Australian market had plunged further than any of the world's markets; the euphoria of the past year had suddenly given way to the deepest pessimism; the jeremiahs were having a field day. 'Your backers, whoever they are, could end up being the major partners in Springfellow. How will you feel about that?'

'Worse than you will,' he said sadly. 'The family will turn in its grave. Particularly Emma.'

'Who was your bank?'

'Asian-Malaysian, from Kuala Lumpur.'

There had been a time when, as an old-fashioned Australian, he had looked upon Asian money as slippery coin. Xenophobia, like so many other things, had been bought out.

She smiled wryly. 'Perhaps I should have gone to them instead of Polux.'

'Did you know about Polux's failure before Emma was – murdered?'

'No.'

'Who did?'

'You mean in Springfellow? Only Michael Broad. He's just told me. It was as big a shock to me as it was to you. I'm tempted to fire him.'

'Is this the time to do that? Who else could you call on as a financial adviser?'

'You.' She smiled as she said it, but she was half-serious.

He shook his head. 'No, Venetia. I'm too ethical. I'm not boasting when I say that – it's just that they have a different way of doing business these days. Sydney, Melbourne, Perth – they've all become modern Babylons. Greedy, hedonistic – all that's missing are the Hanging Gardens.' She knew nothing of the ancient world, but she didn't interrupt him. 'It's not for me, Venetia, not any longer. They'd shear me like a lamb. One of my old friends, the managing director of an overseas bank, it had better be nameless, he told me of one of his whiz-kids –' the slang term was as stiff as a foreign phrase on his tongue '– this young man made two and a half million dollars last financial year. He was tacking his own orders on to institutional orders, buying at their discount. My friend sacked him.'

'I'd probably do the same.'

'I don't mean any offence, Venetia, but I don't think you would. You would do what the overseas bank's headquarters did. They told my friend to reinstate the whiz-kid. They said that if he was that bright, they couldn't afford to lose him to the competition.'

'What did your friend do?'

'He reinstated the young man and then resigned as M.D. The bank told him he was a fool, but didn't try to persuade him to stay. He was expendable, he's in his late fifties, but the young man wasn't. I'm afraid when you've given yourself time to think about it, you'll feel the same way about Michael.'

She knew he was right. She had arrived in Sydney from Cobar almost thirty years ago, plain Mary Magee then, bringing with her a country air, a stammer, an itching ambition and no sense of ethics at all. Nineteen fifty-eight was a time when the sharks that abounded today were just toothless minnows; honesty might not have been the best policy, but the financial men were still trying to find a better one. She had not, of course, known any financial men then; she had headed straight for a television station and got a job as a typist. It had meant dating the personnel manager; that had been her first lesson in ethics, or the lack of them. She was not a virgin – she had lost that status to a jackeroo from a sheep station outside Cobar; he, with all the grace of a bush lover, had referred to her as his favourite ewe – but she had managed to convince the personnel manager that she was. By the time he gave up chasing her she was settled in the typing pool and had attracted the attention of the senior executive producer, who was further up the station totem pole than the personnel manager. She still hadn't learned anything about ethics, but she had learned what opportunism was. Now, after all these years, she fully understood what ethics were, but had decided that Mother Theresa was the only woman who could afford them. In a sea of sharks, mermaids get nowhere just by singing.

She changed the subject. 'The first thing we have to do is find out who killed Emma.'

He nodded, put his hand over the modest brightness of his tie; he really should have worn black. 'I hope you're not thinking of doing that? Doing your own detective work?'

'No. I think Inspector Malone will do all that for us.'

'I just wish he'd leave it alone. I'm afraid if he persists, we'll learn more than we want to know.' He was silent a moment; then: 'Emma had left some things in our attic – Ruth let her use

190

it as a storeroom. Paintings, things like that. Some childhood things. And a suitcase, one of Father's old leather ones. It had all her diaries in it, going back to her schooldays.'

'Is there anything in them?'

His shock was genuine. 'You don't expect us to have read them?'

'I would read them.' She couldn't see that the dead were entitled to their secrets. Once she herself was gone, the world would be free to know everything it wanted to know about her. Once in the grave, she would be safe; as Emma now was. 'They can't hurt her, not now.'

'They could hurt some of us who are still alive.'

'You and Ruth? Me?'

'Possibly. No, Venetia, I opened the suitcase and shut it at once as soon as I saw what was in it. When things have quietened down, I'll have it burnt, with the diaries in it.'

'There may be something in them that would give us a hint why Walter was murdered.'

Edwin sighed. 'As I said, I'm old. I don't have the mental energy any more to try solving old mysteries. I'm ashamed to say it, but I shan't be disappointed if the police don't solve Emma's murder. I think it's time we Springfellows were left in peace.'

Venetia said nothing to that. She knew that peace was a condition she had never contemplated.

SEVEN

1

'I'd like to pay another visit to Mrs Magee,' said Clements.

Am I imagining it, thought Malone, or has he always been as eager as this? He was starting to make Andy Graham look like a lead-swinger. 'Why her?'

'I think she's the one with the loosest tongue in the family. And she knows more than she lets on.'

Just like me; I must watch I don't let my tongue rattle loose. Then his phone rang and he picked it up. With John Leeds on his mind, he feared it might be the Commissioner. Instead, it was Sergeant Greenup.

'Scobie, we've found the murder weapon, I think. My boy Sobers did some fossicking over in the Gardens. He found a PPK .380 Walther under some bushes. What do you want done with it?'

'I don't want too much handling of it. Send it direct to Fingerprints, then tell 'em to pass it on to Ballistics. Tell 'em the reports are to come direct to me. Give my thanks to your constable.'

'Are you getting anywhere with the case?'

'Just plugging on, Jack.' He hung up; but the phone immediately rang again. 'Inspector Malone.'

'Ah, Inspector –' It was Assistant Commissioner Bill Zanuch, suave as a con man on one of the more expensive cruise ships. 'Just checking on the Springfellow case. Both of them. Any progress?'

There were seven Assistant Commissioners. The Assist-

ant Commissioner, Administration, did not check on homi-
cides. 'We're making marginal progress, sir.'

'I have an interest in these cases. I was on the original one,
when Sir Walter disappeared.'

'Yes, sir, I remember. I was with you for a week or two.'

'Of course, so you were!' The bugger hadn't forgotten at
all. What was his game? Then, oh so casually, 'The Commissioner probably has an interest, too. He was a protégé
of Sir Walter's.'

'I didn't know that, sir.'

Zanuch waited, as if he was expecting further comment
from Malone. But Malone, too, could play the waiting game
and after a moment the Assistant Commissioner said, 'Well,
keep me informed if anything interesting turns up. I'm
always here.'

'Yes, sir. Thanks for your help.' Malone waited; you
didn't hang up in a senior officer's ear. There was silence for
a moment, then Zanuch hung up.

'Who was that?' said Clements.

'Zanuch.'

Clements frowned. 'What the hell's worrying him?'

'I wouldn't know,' said Malone blandly, but wondered if
politics was going to invade the Police Department. Should
he warn John Leeds? Then decided against it. He could read
between the lines and he did not want to be caught between
them.

'Let's go and see Mrs Magee,' he said and in his own ears
sounded reckless. 'Is she down at The Wharf or over at
Mosman?'

'When we left her yesterday she said we could always find
her at Mosman.'

But they didn't find Alice Magee there. Instead they found
only Mrs Leyden, the housekeeper. 'Mrs Magee has gone
shopping. She likes to do it herself.' It was difficult to tell
whether she was resentful or relieved; neither Malone nor
Clements had had much experience of housekeepers. 'I'll
tell her you called.'

193

'Perhaps we could come in and talk to you for a few minutes?' said Clements, carrying the ball again.

'I have nothing to say, I'm sure.' She was a good-looking woman who put on a plain face when holding unwelcome visitors at bay.

'Just a few questions, Mrs Leyden.' Clements didn't have one foot in the door, but looked as if he did.

She led them through the house and out to the kitchen; that was her ground, where she would feel safest. It was a big room: in the old days, one could imagine, the Springfellow children would have had their meals here (though Malone could not imagine Emma and her brothers as children). Today, one could not imagine even the most modern child in it. It was clinical, stainless steel and plain grey tiles; the triple oven looked as if it might house scientific experiments. But Mrs Leyden looked at home in it, as house-proud as a Nobel laureate.

She offered them coffee, freshly brewed: none of your instant muck here. Playing hostess seemed to soften her: 'I don't really think I can help you much.'

'Let's try it,' said Clements, up and running as he sat down. 'Were you at home here on Monday night?'

'Monday?'

'The night Miss Emma was murdered.'

'You don't think –? Of course you don't. No, I wasn't home, at least not till about one o'clock. Monday is my night off. And my husband's – he's Lady Springfellow's chauffeur.'

They still say *chauffeur* here in Springfellow Avenue, thought Malone. Everyone else, even the Prime Minister and the Governor-General, had a *driver*.

'Where did you go?'

'To the early show up at Mosman – we always go to the movies on Monday night. Then we went down to the Manly Leagues Club for dinner.' She was sounding more human, less starched, by the minute.

'What about Lady Springfellow? Was she home here on her own?'

194

'You'd have to ask the security man, the night one. He's not on duty now. He comes on at six.'

'Was Lady Springfellow home when you left?'

'No, she was working back, she does that a lot on Monday nights. She has her dinner sent over from the restaurant in the apartments where Miss Justine lives.'

'How does she get home if your husband isn't there to drive her?'

'A hire car picks her up.'

'Was she home by the time you got home?' Clements was doing all the questioning.

'Oh, yes.'

Clements suddenly changed tack. 'That gun collection in the other room. Did you notice the Walther missing? The smaller hand-gun?'

'Oh, that one. Yes, I noticed it was gone, the first time.'

'The first time?'

'Yes, just before they discovered Sir Walter's – remains. Then it was back in the cabinet for a day or two, then it was gone again.'

'Did you mention it to Lady Springfellow?'

'No-o. She had enough on her mind – I mean with Sir Walter – turning up after all that time.'

'What about the other missing gun?'

'Oh, I don't know a thing about that. You'd have to ask my aunt. She was the one who really knew all about the family. She was with them for forty years.'

'Your aunt?'

'Mrs Dyson. She was the housekeeper and cook here for years. When she retired, she got me and my husband our positions.'

'Is she still alive?'

'Oh yes. She lives in a retirement village out at Carlingford.'

'Near Channel 15?'

'Just down the road.'

'Does Lady Springfellow visit her?'

195

Mrs Leyden looked at her cup, as if searching for scum on the coffee. 'Well, no, not exactly. She and my aunt didn't see eye to eye, if you know what I mean. Well, maybe you don't.'

'No, I'm afraid we don't.'

She looked up again. 'Well, I'm not going to tell you. That's in the family. Lady Springfellow doesn't visit her, but she looks after my aunt. She pays for everything and my aunt gets a nice pension. I don't think Aunt Grace complains.'

'Forgive me asking,' said Malone, feeling he'd better ask something, 'if Lady Springfellow and Mrs – Dyson? – didn't see eye to eye, how did your aunt last so long? And why did she accept your aunt's recommendation of you?'

He hadn't meant it to sound so much like a barrister's cross-examination; Mrs Leyden took a moment to straighten it out. 'I – I think Lady Springfellow sometimes has – I shouldn't say this – well, she has fits of conscience. It seems like that. Sometimes she's come home with an expensive present for my aunt, a nightgown or something like that, but she always asks me to take it to her. She's really a kind woman at heart. My aunt just never understood that.'

'Does your aunt refuse the presents?'

Mrs Leyden smiled. 'No. She's an old lady. Old ladies like to receive presents. So do old men, I should think.'

'I'll let you know when I get there,' said Malone.

'We'd like to talk to your aunt,' said Clements. 'She's not too old to answer questions, is she?'

Again Mrs Leyden smiled, the plain look gone from her blunt-nosed, good-looking face. Policemen were not such ogres after all. 'My aunt likes to talk. There's not much else to do in a retirement village, except talk and watch TV.'

And wait to die, thought Malone.

He and Clements drove out through the heat of the day, away from the coast breezes. He wondered why Mrs Dyson, having lived for forty years cooled by harbour breezes, should have chosen to retire away from them. But perhaps she had had no 'choice: when someone else was paying the bills, you went where you were sent.

'What do you reckon about the guns?' said Clements.

'I don't know.' Malone was cautious. 'Anyone could have taken them.'

'Any one of the family, you mean? Yeah, I guess so.' But Clements's mind was already starting to set.

Despite the stationary air that felt as if it had escaped from a furnace and been filtered through a wet screen, Pleasant Oaks was not a hell-hole. The cottages and apartments were attractive, built of dark brick and with green-tiled roofs, fitting neatly into the landscaped grounds. Malone had a sudden dim memory of visiting his grandfather, his mother's father, in an old men's home somewhere in the southern suburbs, where the roof leaked, the rooms smelled damp and the season, it seemed, was always winter.

Mrs Dyson had a one-bedroom apartment in the main wing. 'When we get on a bit, they move us in here so's they can keep an eye on us. Everybody's indoors today – it's so hot. So you two are policemen, eh? You're an inspector, eh? They must make 'em younger these days.'

She was in her late seventies, her back beginning to bend but not her mind. Her eyes, behind their glasses, showed how alert she might be; Malone only wondered about her memory. His own memory, at least of her, was dim; he couldn't remember the woman who had opened the door to him and Zanuch twenty-one years ago, yet he was sure it would have been her. She was not tall, but she sat up as straight as she could in her straight-backed chair and he could believe she would have been a formidable guardian of the Springfellow privacy.

'Lady Springfellow? Well, yes, I worked for her –' there was a pause '– when she married into the family.'

'It's going back a long way, Mrs Dyson –' Malone decided it was time he did the questioning; he had given Clements enough rein. 'Can you remember when Sir Walter disappeared?'

'Of course. How could I forget?' Then her eyes clouded, as if the memory was too much for her and she *wanted* to forget.

'Did anything unusual happen about that time?'

'How do you mean?' She had made them some tea as soon as she realized they were going to spend some time with her; once a housekeeper, always a housekeeper. 'Have a biscuit. I believe they call 'em cookies now. Everything's American. How do you mean?'

'Well, did Sir Walter or Lady Springfellow do anything that wasn't usual with them?'

'They had a terrible row.' Then she looked at them cautiously. 'I shouldn't tell you that. I'm not a gossip.'

'Giving information to the police isn't gossiping, Mrs Dyson.'

But gossip is a great help; it oils the wheels and sometimes gives them a shove. Tell it not in Gath, whisper it not in the streets of Askelon: no Philistine policeman ever gave that advice.

'Well –' She was dubious; but she was afraid that if she said nothing, they would leave her. Company was company: she looked out the window at the empty grounds. 'We-ee-ll, some time that weekend, I can't remember which night, they had this terrible row. I don't know what it was about – my bedroom was at the other end of the house. It was unusual, all right – Sir Walter never raised his voice. *She* did – in those days she was . . .' She didn't finish, but Malone made a guess: Venetia was *common*.

'Were they still, well, *cool* towards each other when he left on the Monday morning?'

'I think so. I'm sorry. When you ask me things like that, I mean the little things, I can't remember as well as I used to. Your memory goes, you know, when you get on. That's why I keep so many of my things out, to remind me.' She looked around the small living-room; framed photos formed a broken frieze on side-tables, a bookcase, the television set. A hearty-looking man with a laugh that could be heard even in the photo looked out at her from a silver frame. 'That was

198

my husband, we never had a cross word in our whole married life.'

'You were lucky, Mrs Dyson. Had anything happened during the previous week, while Sir Walter was down in Melbourne, that might have caused him and Lady Spring-fellow to – to disagree?'

She was silent for a while, staring at her dead husband. She closed her eyes and for a moment Malone thought she had dozed off; then she opened them and said firmly, 'Yes, I remember something. A young man came to see her. Inspector Leeds had come to see her – I don't know what night, the Tuesday or Wednesday.'

Malone avoided Clements's glance. 'That was Inspector John Leeds?'

'Yes, he was a friend of Sir Walter's. He's the Police Commissioner now. But I suppose you know that.' She smiled, showing what looked to be still her own teeth.

'Vaguely,' said Malone, smiling back at her; he had a gentle way with old women, though he didn't know where he had learned it. 'Was Mr Leeds a frequent visitor?' *Christ, why did I ask that?*

'Did he come with his wife?' said Clements.

'He wasn't married then, not that I know of. He'd come when Sir Walter was home and sometimes he'd come and take her out to dinner. That was after Sir Walter had joined that spy lot and gone to work in Melbourne. They were very friendly.'

'Who were?' said Clements.

'Mr Leeds and her.' Her mouth tightened, like a drawer snapped shut; she had said too much, some things should be locked away in the past. 'No, I'm not going to say any more about them. That would be gossiping.'

Malone nodded, taking the ball away from Clements again. 'You mentioned a young man coming to see Lady Spring-fellow. Who was he?'

'I don't know. We didn't have a security man in those days. The family was well off, but nothing like she is today. It was different then – people were *safe*.' Again she stopped and

199

closed her eyes. The two detectives waited patiently. Then she opened her eyes and went on, 'He just came to the front door that morning – I think it was the Thursday, I'm not sure, but – and he said she was expecting him. She must have been, because she came into the hall before I could go and tell her and said to let him in.'

'You'd never seen him before?'

'No. He was a foreigner, I think, he had an accent. But that's no help, is it? The place is full of foreigners these days. We even have them in here.'

Con Malone would make a good neighbour for her, battling the invaders. All at once Malone wondered what would happen to his parents when they became too old to fend for themselves.

'Can you remember what sort of accent?'

She shook her head. 'How can I remember something like that? You young people don't know what it's like to be losing your memory. I'm only remembering this because I had to remember it once before, when that spy lot – ASIO, is that it? – came to ask me questions.'

Malone and Clements exchanged glances, then Clements said, 'So you don't know why he came to see her?'

She shook her head again. 'All I remember is, I went in to see if she –' It was *she* all the time now, never Lady Springfellow '– if she wanted me to serve tea or coffee. She was giving him money, quite a lot of it, in bundles. Like, you know, the way they have it in banks. She got angry with me for coming into the room. In front of him, too – ladies didn't do that in my day, tick off their help in front of guests. I remember *that* distinctly – it's why I remember seeing all the money she was giving him. He was putting it in a briefcase.'

'Did she say anything to you after the young man had gone?'

'She apologized to me for getting angry. But the damage had been done.' And persisted to this day.

'She didn't mention the money?'

'No.' All at once she looked tired: her memory might be dim, but parts of what she had left weighed heavily.

'We shan't keep you any longer, Mrs Dyson. One last thing. Do you remember Sir Walter's gun collection?'

'Of course. I was always wanting to dust it, but he would never let me. He used to oil the guns himself.'

'The guns never frightened you?'

'I grew up in the bush, Inspector. My father always had a gun or two in the house. No, I was never frightened of them. But she was.'

'Can you remember one of the guns went missing about the time Sir Walter disappeared?'

'Yes. It was a pistol, the big one.'

'It was a Colt .45, an automatic,' said Clements.

'Do you know what happened to the gun, Mrs Dyson? Did you mention it to Sir Walter?'

'No, not that I remember. I think I only noticed it had gone *after* he disappeared.'

'Did you mention it to Lady Springfellow?'

'No, I don't think so.'

'To the Commonwealth police or the ASIO men?'

'I may have. I don't remember.' All at once she looked tired again; her memory had run more than its usual distance today. 'I'm sorry, Inspector. It makes me sad to remember those days . . . I had a lot of time for Sir Walter.' But not for *her*: she would be a hostile witness there.

The two men stood up. 'You've been a great help, Mrs Dyson.'

'If you see Mr Leeds, give him my regards. I think he might remember me. But it was all so long ago . . .'

They let themselves out of the tiny flat, leaving her sitting stiff-backed in her chair, unafraid while death lapped at her like a rising tide.

Outside, the elderly residents were now visible, moving through the heat in slow motion, like mirages, as they

201

headed for the communal dining-room in the main building. Some of them smiled at Malone and Clements, glad to see new faces, especially younger ones. One or two couples had a buoyancy about them, but either the heat or the environment had got to most of them. They knew that, for all its pleasant surroundings, Pleasant Oaks was the end of the road.

'It makes you sad, doesn't it?' said Clements, chewing his bottom lip.

'No,' said Malone, remembering where his grandfather had lived his last years. 'They'd be a bloody sight sadder living in one room in Redfern or the old blokes dossing down in the Matthew Talbot.'

'Why do you always look on the bright side?'

'It's the Irish in me.'

'Bullshit. The Irish can be the most mournful buggers on earth, especially when they're drunk.' They got into the car and Clements switched on the air-conditioning; it was working again. Then he said, 'You've got something on your mind, haven't you?'

'What about? The Irish?'

'Come on, Scobie, don't muck about. Yesterday when we were questioning Justine, you were holding back. The same today. Is it something to do with the Commissioner?'

'What gave you that idea?'

'Just the way you reacted when his name came up back there with the old lady.'

'She was gossiping.' He was treading carefully, not wanting to put himself too far offside with Clements. His loyalty should lie with Clements, his sidekick; but he could not break the confidence of John Leeds. 'Yes, I've got something on my mind. I'm beginning to wonder if Lady Springfellow is a double murderer.'

It was fanciful, but he had to say something to throw Clements off the subject of John Leeds. But Clements said, 'I'm thinking the same thing. Who was the guy she paid the money to? A hit man?'

2

'We're in a bad way,' said Venetia.

'We'll get out of it,' said Justine.

'Of course we shall. But it's not going to be easy. I had them do a quick check on where we stand. We've lost 170 million since the Crash. Most of it on paper, but not all of it. There's about 80 million we'll never get back. Then there's the servicing of our debt – that runs to 60 per cent of our cash flow. We're going to have to sell off some assets.'

'We've been cutting back on staff. I laid off another two girls from my department today.'

'Darling, people aren't assets, not at that level. They're disposable. No matter how much we pay a man or woman to join us, when they leave us we don't get any transfer fee. Business isn't like football.'

Justine said nothing to that. Sometimes she was shocked at her mother's ruthlessness. She was further shocked that it might be in her own genes: she dreaded the day when she would control Springfellow's.

They were in Justine's apartment. Venetia, wanting a break, had come across from her office when all her personal staff had left for the day. She did not like the apartment's décor and never felt at ease in it; but she recognized it for what it was, a rebellious expression, and she never made any comment on it. She just made sure that Justine's decorator never got any work on any Springfellow project.

'I was going to say fire Michael –'

'He's told me his head is on the block,' said Justine.

'When did he start confiding in you?'

Oh God, she's not jealous of me, is she? 'He's not *confiding* in me. I went out with him the other night to a movie and some coffee afterwards.'

'I don't want anything starting up between you and him.'

'There's nothing like that. But don't tell me who I can go out with. I'm not sixteen any more.'

'What did he tell you?'

'It was this morning. He said you and he had had a run-in and he might get the chop. He didn't seem too worried. He's just so cocky, in his own quiet way. I don't really like him, yet I find him *interesting*.'

'He's conceited, all right. But we need him – he's one asset we have to keep, for the time being, anyway. There isn't time to go shopping for someone else. Though Sydney at the moment looks like a game of musical chairs – I can't keep up with the hirings and firings. We'll keep him. We have to raise money again and he's the one who knows where it is. When he took you out the other night, did you go in his Aston-Martin?'

'Yes. Why?'

'He said he was going to have to sell it.'

'Oh God, that'll kill him!'

Venetia smiled. 'Life has its small satisfactions.'

But Justine was too young for ironies. She had other worries besides those of the Springfellow business interests. 'Changing the subject . . . Mother, I think Inspector Malone suspects me of having something to do with Emma's murder. I didn't want to worry you, but . . .'

'How do these policemen get so out of hand? I'll get on to John Leeds.' So much could be done with a phone call, if one knew the right number. History is full of networks; all that differs is the scale and the instrument. Business leaders and bureaucrats have replaced kings and ambassadors, the phone has replaced the post-chaise and the king's messenger. 'He'll call off Malone and that other one, the big slob, Sergeant What's-his-name.'

'Won't that make Malone more suspicious? I saw him the other night at the International at Double Bay. He was with someone, probably his wife. They were discussing me. Do you think cops tell their wives about their cases?'

'Probably. She's probably some dowdy little mum, it'd be the only excitement in her dull little life.'

204

'She's not dowdy. She's beautiful and very smart-looking.'

'How did he manage it? I'll have to have another look at him. He looked and sounded so *suburban*.' She was deliberately sounding casual, frivolously snobbish. Justine had to be protected; she recognized there was less steel in her daughter than in herself. 'Don't worry. John will take care of it.'

'Mother, this is *murder*! It's not a traffic ticket – I haven't been pulled up by the booze bus – Malone thinks I *killed* Emma!'

'Has he said so?'

'No-o. But I *know* what he's thinking. And so does Nana. You ask her. It all has something to do with me borrowing that gun, the Walther or whatever it was. I'm frightened, Mother.'

'Nothing will happen to you, I promise.'

'How can you be so sure?'

But Venetia couldn't answer that. She was standing on shifting sands, financially and emotionally. Life, all at once, was turning into a bad dream, though she had never been a dreamer but a doer.

She stood up, kissed Justine, then paused and looked out through the glass walls. Across the water, shining like the black glass here in the apartment, she could see the lights of Kirribilli nesting like electric gulls in the apartment-cliffs. 'The harbour always looks so peaceful at night.'

'I sometimes sit here and look out at it and read Kenneth Slessor's *Five Bells*. It's not just about the harbour, it's about the death of a friend, but he gives me the picture.'

Venetia looked carefully at her. 'I've never read it.'

'It goes:

'And tried to hear your voice, but all I heard
Was a boat's whistle, and the scraping squeal
Of seabirds' voices far away, and bells,
Five bells. Five bells coldly ringing out.'

She stopped, embarrassed; she had not recited poetry aloud since she had left school.

Venetia looked at this sudden stranger. 'You read *poetry*? You never told me.'

'There's a lot I haven't told you. You never had time to listen.'

There was nothing to say to that, no defence except the retreat of, 'Good-night, I'll see you tomorrow.'

She went down in the lift, looking in the mirrors for some recognition of herself. But there was a stranger there, too: she could not believe she knew the puzzled uncertain woman who looked back at her with her own eyes.

She got out of the lift and literally bumped into Peter Polux. Instinctively she looked down at his feet. He was wearing black shoes: he was still in mourning for his lost fortune.

'Venetia, old girl –' He sounded like a desperate sales-man. 'I've been ringing you at your office all this week –'

'I know, Mr Polux. There's nothing we have to talk about. Save your money – you need it.'

She stepped past him before he could reply, and went out of the lobby. She had made a huge error of judgement with him and she did not like reminders of her mistakes.

As she came out of The Wharf and paused on the footpath before crossing the road to the Springfellow building, where Leyden and the Bentley would be waiting for her, a man all at once appeared beside her. He was a burly man, older than herself, with a battered face split by a mocking grin.

''Night, missus. You wouldn't have a dollar for a cuppa coffee?'

'Don't bother me or I'll shout for a policeman.'

'Ain't none around here or I wouldn't of asked you.' The man looked round him, the mocking grin still on his face. 'I'm not gunna rape you or anything, missus. All I asked for is a dollar. You look as if you could afford it.'

She hesitated, then she opened her wallet and gave him a two-dollar note. 'Are you broke?'

'No,' said the man. 'But this beats working. You'd be surprised how many kind-hearted people there are like you.'

'Balls,' she said and stepped off the kerb and began to cross the road.

'Thanks,' he called after her. 'You're a real lady!'

'I know,' said Lady Springfellow.

3

Chilla Dural watched her go. He was planning a kidnapping and hadn't yet decided who the victim should be: Lady Springfellow or her daughter. The idea had come to him yesterday when he had paid his fortnightly call on Les Glizzard.

'Chilla, you've got to get a grip on yourself. You've been kidnapped by apathy.'

'Kidnapped?'

'Yes, by apathy. And apathy leads to despair. Or vice versa.' Les Glizzard knew that the emotions went in a circle, but he was not sure if they went clockwise or anti-clockwise. Night school sociology was often dim-sighted in the bright light of day.

'What's the ransom?' said Dural, a practical-minded man.

'Ransom? Who's talking about ransom?'

'You are. You were talking about kidnapping.'

'Chilla, it was a figure of speech,' said Glizzard, close to despair and battling apathy; sometimes towards the end of the week he wondered if his work and devotion were all worthwhile. 'I'm trying to save you from yourself. You never did a kidnap job, did you?'

Dural shook his head. 'It's never really been worth it in Australia. Not up till now, not like in the States. But I suppose with the money that's around now . . .'

'Don't even think about it!'

'Don't think about what? What are you up to now, Chilla?'

Tom Binder had come into Glizzard's tiny office. He was the senior probation officer, a small dried-out man with a cowlick and black-rimmed glasses that camouflaged the shrewdest eyes in the business. Chilla Dural thought he would have made a top boss if he'd been a crim: he could think of no higher compliment.

'We were talking about kidnapping,' said Glizzard, looking at Dural with disappointment.

Binder sat on the edge of Glizzard's desk, lit a cigarette and coughed two or three times. He had been in the Department of Corrective Services for almost thirty years, long before it had been given such a new-fangled, sociologically-oriented title: he was one of the old school who called a spade a spade or a darky, a crim a crim and bugger the soft approach. He suspected he would die of lung cancer, but he still smoked two packets of cigarettes a day and to hell with the new government directive that there was to be no smoking in work areas. He and Chilla Dural understood each other and the way the real world worked.

'Chilla, you're not working along those lines, are you? It's different from when you went in – they're tougher now. You kidnap someone and before you can name the ransom, they'd have the SWAT boys and the Tactical Response fellers surrounding you with shotguns and tear gas and Christ knows what. They'd fill you so full of holes you'd look like my wife's knitting.'

Dural grinned. 'You just talked me outa it, Mr Binder. No, it was just a – figure of speech, right?'

He looked at Glizzard, who nodded. 'Right. We were talking about apathy, Tom.'

'What's that? Is that what I feel every Monday morning when I come in here?'

'Well, not exactly,' said Glizzard, who came in every Monday with enthusiasm that had been stoked up over the weekend. He would never give up striving to rehabilitate the criminal classes; he would have been in seventh heaven in convict days with all that material on his doorstep. He had read Robert Hughes's *The Fatal Shore* and it had thrilled him as much as if it had been a book of erotica.

'Stay out of trouble, Chilla,' said Binder through a cloud of

208

smoke. 'Don't make us start another file on you. You buggers have no idea how much paperwork you cause. How are you holding out for cash?'

'I've got enough, Mr Binder. I can always hold up a bank if I run short.'

'Well, don't get caught. Or you might get hurt. Look at those buggers out at Leichhardt the other day. One dead and two in hospital. That could happen to you. It'll only mean more paperwork for us.'

He stood up, winked and went out of the office, dry as the smoke he left behind him. If ever he turned crooked, Dural thought, I'd go to work for him.

'A good bloke,' he told Glizzard.

'I suppose so,' said Glizzard. 'He's just so old-fashioned in his ideas, that's all. He's not what you'd call state-of-the-art.'

'What?'

That had been yesterday. He had gone home with the word *kidnap* tickling his brain like mental lice. As he had let himself in the front door Jerry Killeen, the gatekeeper of the hallway, had opened *his* door.

'G'day, Chilla. I was just gunna make a cuppa. How about one?' He was holding a copy of the *Mirror*; Dural saw the headline: KIDNAP! It hit him like an omen. 'Come in. I just got some fresh cakes, good old-fashioned ones, none of the Frog patsy-whatever-it-is stuff.'

Dural followed him into the room. Up till now he had managed to dodge the invitations; he knew the little old man had sometimes been hurt, but he had never been openly resentful. He was the lonely sort who was ever hopeful that someone would recognize him; Dural had seen dozens like him over the years in Parramatta.

'Siddown. Here, have a look at the paper while I put the kettle on.'

He tossed the paper at Dural, who caught it and opened it. The kidnapping story was not a local one; this was the early edition, when most of the stories were cable items. A minor TV star, someone Dural had never heard of, had been kidnapped in Los Angeles; the victim played a cop in a series and the kidnapping was a real-life replay of a series episode. Since Dural could never tell one TV star from another, he wondered if the series producers would bother to pay the ransom demanded; they would probably cast another look-alike actor and the kidnappers would be left with an actor who no longer rated. He put the paper aside; then picked it up again. The name Springfellow had caught his eye.

'Take it with you,' said Killeen, spooning tea into a chipped china pot. 'I've read it. Dunno why I buy it, there's nothing in it.'

Dural folded the paper for later reading, then looked around the room. This was Killeen's home: one room with, it seemed, his life papering the walls. Dural had never seen so many photographs: family groups, army groups, football teams, single photos of Killeen at various ages. The room was meticulously neat and clean; just like Killeen himself. Dural's cell at Parramatta had been as neat and clean, but there had been no walls of photographs. Only the one of Patti and the girls.

'You looking at the footy pictures, eh?' Dural hadn't been, but now he did so out of politeness. 'I used to play scrum-half for Western Suburbs back in the Forties. You probably remember me?'

'Killeen? Oh sure, I never connected . . .' He couldn't remember a single footballer from that long ago.

The old man beamed as if he had just figured in the Honours List. He put down a plate of cakes on the small table between him and Dural; they were fresh, but they reminded Dural of the cakes he had eaten back in the Forties or even before. There was even a chester cake, that heavy cube of pastry and pudden filling that, if one bought enough of them, could be used to build a house. The two men sat down and, like schoolboys, bogged into the museum fare.

'Waddia gunna do for Christmas dinner?' said Killeen, wiping mock-cream from his chin. 'I always go to the Salvos. They turn on a good spread.'

210

'I dunno,' said Dural cautiously. He didn't want to spend Christmas Day with a lot of other lost souls at a Salvation Army hostel. He had begun to think of himself as a lost soul only since Les Glizzard had told him not to. He tried a quick lie: 'My probation officer wants me to have it with him. I might do it, just to keep him happy.'

They drank tea, ate cakes and chatted for another twenty minutes. Then Dural decided he had given the old man enough of his company. He stood up, picking up the paper, and opened the door. He had never been one who didn't know how to make a quick exit. A good many times, a quick exit had been obligatory if he hadn't wanted his head kicked in.

'Thanks, Jerry. See you another time.'

'You gotta go? I'll put the kettle on again, make a fresh cuppa –'

'No, thanks. See you.'

He closed the door on the wrinkled, disappointed face, feeling a right bastard but knowing the right time to escape. As he opened his own door he sniffed, turning his face towards the back stairs that led to the upper floors. The Vietnamese were frying rice again; they must have retreated from trying to be dinkum Aussies. He wondered what they would think of Jerry Killeen's good old-fashioned cakes, especially the chester cake. One of them lay in his stomach, having smashed a couple of ribs on the way down.

In his room he opened up the *Mirror*. The feature article on the financial page dealt with the Springfellow holdings; it was evidently one of a series on tall poppies that had been lopped in the Crash. There were pictures of Lady Springfellow and her daughter Justine: two good sorts, if ever he'd seen 'em. He didn't take in all that the article tried to tell him; bloody economics writers wrote for each other. But he got the gist of it: Venetia Springfellow (Venetia and Justine? Patti would have loved those names) had done a packet in the stock market crash. She was still worth at least five hundred million, give or take ten or twenty million. It only proved, said the writer, the difference between the rich and the wealthy. The wealthy could go bankrupt, but the rich never.

Dural looked at the two women: which one would be easier to snatch? And how would he go about it? The actual snatch might be the easiest part of the exercise; kidnappers were usually caught when they tried to collect the ransom. He would have to work that out, get the old brain working again. It was a pity Heinie Odets was dead: Heinie had been a great one for solving problems. Of course the object would be to *get caught*, but so far down the track that the do-gooder Les Glizzard couldn't interfere.

The first thing, though, was to get to know the routine of the Springfellows, mother and daughter.

And so, tonight, he was standing outside the apartment building where the daughter lived when who should come out but Lady Springfellow herself. He had looked her up and down, seen the slight breeze coming down the narrow gorge of Phillip Street and moulding her dress against her body and thighs and got a surge of feeling in his crotch. She'd be the one to take, someone more his own age. She was the one with the money, too.

He began to make plans.

EIGHT

1

'Inspector –'

'G'day, Andy, where've you been? I thought you'd resigned from the Department or something.'

'I've been following those suggestions you gave me.' Andy Graham grinned; he had learned that you could relax with Malone, just so long as you did your job. 'The Feds have been really helpful on this one.'

Malone looked across at Clements. 'Do they owe us something?'

'I don't think so.' All the police forces, State and Federal, were fiercely independent, sometimes even mistrustful, of each other. They were bureaucracies and being in uniform made them no different from other bureaucracies. Clements, a State chauvinist, had no time for Canberra. 'The PM must be calling an election and is looking for votes.'

'Who'd vote for Phil Norval except little old ladies?'

Andy Graham waited while his two seniors discussed Canberra. Then he said, 'At the same time as Walter Springfellow disappeared, a Third Secretary from the Russian embassy went into smoke. The same weekend, March 27 and 28, 1966.'

'You get his name?'

Graham looked at his notes. 'Alexis Uritzsky. According to the Federal, the Russians never issued a comment. They did inform External Affairs, as it was then, that he'd been recalled to Moscow for personal reasons.'

213

'Did anyone make a connection between his and Spring-fellow's disappearance?'

'I don't know. I guess only ASIO would know that. I tried contacting them, but they just brushed me off. I don't think they talk to detective-constables.'

Malone grinned at Clements. 'We'll try a higher rank, see how we go. Right, Andy. Good work. See if you can dig up anything more on – what's his name? – Uritzsky.'

'Right.'

After Graham had galloped away, Malone picked up his phone and dialled the *Herald* and asked for the editor-in-chief. 'Jack Montgomery? Jack, this is Scobie Malone. Could I drop in to see you for a few minutes?'

'So long as it's in the next hour. After that I've got to look as if I'm working.'

Fifteen minutes later Malone and Clements walked into the *Herald* building uptown and went up to Editorial on the sixth floor. Jack Montgomery, tall and stooped, grey-haired and slow-talking, looking and sounding more like a battling farmer than one of the most highly regarded newspapermen in the country, took his feet down off his desk as the two detectives came into his office. He took his pipe out of his mouth, a major concession.

'They never had editors-in-chief when I first started as a copy boy. I still don't know what it means, but it's a nice-sounding title and they don't expect you to work too hard. What can I do for you?' He put his pipe back in his mouth, where it would remain for the rest of the conversation.

Malone introduced Clements and then came straight to the point, explaining that he was working on both the Springfellow murders. 'Jack, you were in Canberra in the 1960s, weren't you?'

'I was working for the *Age* in those days. I was chief political hack.' Montgomery had a gentle sardonic way of putting himself down; he was the general commanding on this floor, but he would never write self-extolling memoirs.

'What year are we talking about? The year Walter Spring-fellow disappeared? That was 1966.'

Malone was impressed that the newspaperman hadn't paused in remembering the date. 'March 28, 1966. That same weekend a Third Secretary from the Russian embassy dropped out of sight. A cove named Alexis Uritzsky.'

Montgomery frowned, chewed on his pipe. The flat drawl and the pipe constantly in his mouth made him difficult to understand; Malone wondered how foreigners ever carried on a conversation with him. 'Yeah, I remember that. Not very clearly – I had no facts to go on. A feller in External Affairs tipped me off that a Russian just wasn't around any more – I think it was about a week or so after Springfellow disappea-red. I tried to get something out of the Russians, but they were worse then than they are now – they hadn't coined the word *glasnost* back then. There was a rumour that Uritzsky – that his name? – was a KGB man, but I was never able to check that – you never can. He was a bit of a party-goer, even in those days – he liked the cocktail circuit. I can't remember him too well – he was young and he liked women. I did a piece on his disappearance, but the story was spiked. I learned later that ASIO had offered some reasons why it shouldn't run – I didn't learn what the reasons were. Just after that I came up to Sydney to join the *Herald* and I never followed it up. There was a lot of funny stuff went on about then. The Springfellow thing was allowed to die as if Springfellow himself was no more than some wino who'd disappeared from Belmore Park.'

'You said Uritzsky liked women. Did he have any particular girlfriend?'

'I couldn't say, Scobie. I never cultivated him – he only became interesting after he disappeared. And then only for a week or two.'

'Did you connect him with Springfellow?'

'I suppose I thought about it – that was probably the reason I wrote the story. But I got no encouragement, so I didn't pursue it. The *Age* in those days wasn't interested in investigative journalism. Muck-raking, if you like.'

The two detectives stood up. 'I'm all for muck-raking, Jack, so long as you don't run the rake through us cops.'

Montgomery took the pipe out of his mouth. 'Scobie, you're safe. Just do me a favour. If you crack this case, or cases, let me know. I'd love to show these hot-shot kids who work for me that some old coves still know a good story when they see it. Some of them think editor-in-chief is a euphemism for pensioner-in-chief.'

When they got outside the *Herald* building, Clements said, 'Where next? ASIO?'

'How'd you guess?'

They drove over to Kirribilli through a brilliant day, one that invited an escape to the beach. Fortague, the ASIO chief, was not pleased that the two policemen had dropped in on him without warning.

'I'd have liked a little notice, Inspector.'

'Forewarned is forearmed, isn't that what they say? I'm sure you security fellers work on that principle.'

'So you're trying to catch me on the hop, is that it?' It was hard to tell whether Fortague was genuinely annoyed or putting on an act to discourage Malone and Clements from further unannounced visits. He certainly wasn't offering them a drink, though the sun was well over the yard-arm; he didn't offer them even a cup of coffee. 'I take it we're still talking about the Springfellow case? Sir Walter's, not his sister's. That was tragic,' he said, softening for a moment. 'I never met the poor woman, but women don't seem safe any more, do they? Not even in their own homes.'

'That's where most of them are killed.' But Malone wasn't here to discuss the demography of murder. 'Let's go back to March 1966. When Sir Walter disappeared, at the same time a Third Secretary from the Russian embassy, a cove named Alexis Uritzsky, vanished. Do you remember that?'

Fortague was stone-faced. 'Jog my memory a bit.'

'The story never got into the papers. It was all hushed up and as far as we can tell Foreign Affairs – or External Affairs

216

as they were called then – went along with the act. So must have ASIO. Why?'

'And you expect me to know the answer?'

'Not off the top of your head, no. But I thought you might help us find the answer. Look, Guy –' Malone tried the old mates' act. It is no different from the old boy network, just more proletarian. It binds Australia together more than blood ties or school ties ever could. 'I've got to get to the bottom of this – the Commissioner is breathing down my neck.' Which was only partly true: John Leeds was certainly breathing down his neck but for a different reason. 'Russ and I are a stubborn pair of bastards – we've got to keep at it, otherwise we'll finish up out at Tibooburra. Where do they send spy chiefs when they foul up?'

Fortague suddenly smiled. 'Haven't you read all the spy books? They usually promote us. Okay, Scobie, I'll see what I can do. But it's not my decision. I'll have to contact the Director-General in Canberra. What exactly do you want to know?'

'Why a black-out was put on Uritzsky's disappearance, why did External Affairs co-operate, was there any connection between Uritzsky and Springfellow, does anyone know where Uritzsky is now.'

Fortague smiled again. 'And that's all? Canberra may not co-operate.'

'Tell them that if they don't, a certain newspaper may start asking whether ASIO wants to know who murdered its former chief or doesn't it care any more.'

'You've been to the newspapers with this?'

'No,' lied Malone. 'But I know there's a certain journalist who'd like to talk to me about it. I've been dodging him up till now.'

Fortague thought a moment, then promised to do what he could. Then he offered them a drink. When Malone and Clements left twenty minutes later, they felt they had the ASIO Sydney chief on their side. But Malone knew that a lone player in the espionage business was like a lone player in a police force: more often than not, they took the ball away from him.

When they got back to Homicide, two visitors were waiting for them.

'How's that for service?' said Sergeant Don Cheshire from Fingerprints. 'Right to your door.'

Malone looked at the other visitor, Constable Jason James from Ballistics, who said, 'I'm here for the same reason as Sergeant Cheshire, sir. Anything to get out of the office.'

'That's it, Scobie. You get service and we get a break from the office.'

Malone grinned. He had pulled the same trick himself when they had tried to chain him to a desk in his junior days. It was the old army and police academy trick of going walkabout; so long as you carried a piece of paper, nobody queried what you were doing. 'Righto, where are your pieces of paper?'

Cheshire, the senior man, produced his first. He was a thirty-year veteran of the force, the last twenty years in Fingerprints. He was a big man, at least twenty kilos overweight, with a double chin and bloated cheeks hiding what once might have been a handsome face. He had a rough, gruff voice and, having been passed over for promotion in favour of younger, better educated officers, he had no respect for anyone. There was, however, still no one better than he at his job.

'Well, I've come up with some matching prints. I took the prints off of that drink coaster you gave me – they were clear. You didn't give me any name on them, so I've marked them down as Print X. Then I had a look at the gun, the Walther.'

Malone wondered why he felt such trepidation at what Cheshire might say next.

'The butt of the gun's been wiped clean, but I got a fraction of a print off of the end of the barrel. It was a faint one, but it come up under the Xeon lights. I can't say it's a man's print – it's too faint and there's not enough of it to be sure. It could be a woman's. It's not someone who's ever done any hard yakka, that's for sure. You get some little bloke with soft hands, some poofter ballet dancer or something like that, and you'd have trouble telling his prints from some woman's, especially a female with big hands like some of those Wog peasants.'

Malone, Clements and James kept their faces blank. Cheshire knew all there was to know about fingerprints, but he knew nothing about community relations.

'Okay, that second one is Print Y. Then I started looking for what else I could find. Like I said, the butt and trigger had been wiped clean. So I took out the magazine from the butt and lo and behold –' He was a dreadful actor, a navvy playing Shakespeare. 'Lo and behold, there was another print. I give it the beery breath treatment.' He gave a demonstration, breathing heavily on the imaginary magazine. 'A fingerprint is 99 per cent moisture, oils et cetera. You give it a little humidity and it shows up, even after it's faded.'

'How old would this print on the magazine have been?' said Malone.

'It don't matter, Scobie, so long as it's been protected from drying out completely. Like as if it had been lying out in the sun. A coupla years ago they brought me a pile of silver coins that had been under a house for eight years, where it was pretty damp. They were the proceeds from a bank robbery that the guy didn't want. I found a print on one of the coins and it matched the suspect's. It wasn't easy, but we did it. He's doing six at Parramatta.'

Malone shut his mind to the thought of Justine doing time in some women's prison. 'So what about this print on the magazine?'

'Well, whoever fired the gun hadn't taken the magazine out to wipe it clean. Stuck up inside the butt, it was protected and so was the print. Lo and behold –' He raised his hands again. 'It matches Print X on the drink coaster. They're the same, I'll swear in court, if you like. No argument.'

'Good,' said Malone, trying to sound convincing. 'Thanks, Don. That gets us halfway there. Now what about you, Constable?'

'I'm afraid my job was much easier, sir.' James was a young man who looked too small to be a policeman; one could not imagine his being called in to help with crowd control. He was baby-faced, with small delicate hands; he was lucky Sergeant Cheshire had not already branded him a poofter. 'The weapon's serial number checks with that on the Springfellow inventory. The bullets hadn't been damaged going into the body and they remained there. I checked the lands and grooves, the rifling, and there's no doubt those bullets came from that particular Walther PPK .380.'

'You'd go into court on that?'

'Yes, sir.' He hesitated a moment: 'There's just one thing. I think a silencer might have been used. The outside of the barrel has been threaded to screw on a silencer.'

'There was no mention of a silencer in the insurance inventory. But then they're illegal in New South Wales, so it wouldn't be in it, anyway.'

'The threading looks pretty new,' said James. 'Silencers on automatics work okay, but not as you see in the movies.'

'Silencers mean premeditation.' Clements looked directly at Malone from the other side of the desk. 'It's beginning to look bad for you-know-who.'

Malone nodded reluctantly, knowing there was nothing more he could do to hold back any further investigation of Justine Springfellow. 'Righto, have you got copies of your reports for me? Good, leave them with Russ, plus the evidence. I'll let you know when we make an arrest and you can hold yourselves ready for the magistrate's hearing.'

'You don't want us for the coroner's inquest?'

'No, not that soon.' Putting off the evil day.

'Who's the suspect, Scobie?' said Cheshire.

Malone sat back in his chair. He would have preferred to have brushed the question aside till he had seen John Leeds; but he couldn't do that, not with Clements sitting across from

220

him. 'Keep it under your hat – we still have a few things to tie up. It's Emma Springfellow's niece, Justine.'

Cheshire pursed his lips, but didn't whistle; he was long past surprise in the matter of murder. 'Christ, the media is gunna make a meal of this.'

'Just don't give them an early serving, Don. Keep it under your hat, like I say. Don't even tell your mates in your section. The same goes for you, Jason.'

Both policemen promised to remain silent and went away looking as if they were egg-bound. 'They'll rupture themselves if they can't tell *someone*,' said Clements.

'I know. It's a risk we've got to take.'

'So do we go and bring in Justine and charge her?'

'Let's hold off a day or two, till we hear from ASIO.'

'What are you trying to do?' Clements looked puzzled; or suspicious.

'I'm trying to see if there's any connection between the two murders.' He hoped he sounded convincing; at least there was some truth in what he said. He hoped he could see the Commissioner before he had to take another step. 'Let's wait till we hear from Fortague. Take a breather, spend the rest of the day counting your money. You must be the richest cop in Australia by now. The richest *honest* one.'

'I went into the bank this morning to put in my Melbourne Cup cheque. The girl behind the counter asked me if I was married or anything. She did everything but rip the buttons off her blouse for me.'

'They do that with all the male customers now. It's part of the new competition amongst banks.'

Feeble jokes were part of the cement that bound their friendship; it was the lighter side of the old mates' act. Yet Malone felt a troubling sense of disloyalty towards Clements.

'Do we tell Greg now what we're going to do?' said Clements.

'I guess we'd better.'

221

Malone, however, felt relieved when one of the other detectives told him that Chief Inspector Random had gone home with an early summer virus.

2

Clements went out to the toilets and Malone picked up his phone and asked for the Commissioner. 'I'd like to see you, sir. Something's come up.'

There was a pause at the other end of the line. 'I think it would be better if we didn't meet here. Did you bring your own car in today?'

'Yes, sir.'

'Okay, pick me up. I'm not in uniform today. I'll see you in ten minutes up in Oxford Street, opposite the Koala Hotel. You can take me for a ride.'

More likely you're taking me for a ride. 'I'll be there, sir. I have a grey Commodore.'

He left a note on Clements's desk saying he had gone to do some shopping for Lisa, and escaped before Clements came back. He would be glad when he could start telling Clements the truth, the whole truth and nothing but the truth. So help me, Commissioner.

Leeds, neatly dressed as always, looking like a successful lawyer or doctor, was waiting as Malone brought the Commodore into the kerb. 'Don't look at the mess in the back, sir. I have three kids –'

'So have I, all at high school. Old enough to –' Then he said no more, his lean, strong-jawed face clouding over.

Malone drove up Oxford Street. It was the homosexual community's Main Street, but in today's hot sunlight it looked only shabby and dully suburban. A couple of punk girls crossed at the Taylor Square traffic lights, hair bright green and red, their black stockings polka-dotted with holes, but they were the only exotic wildlife to be seen. Malone turned south and drove on out to Centennial Park, the huge green oasis only four miles from the heart of the city.

He parked by a line of palm trees that bordered one end of the park's longer lakes. Brown ducks, mallards and a couple of black swans glided in on the lake's still waters towards two elderly women who had just got out of a car with two large plastic bags full of bread scraps. The bread flew through the air and the wildfowl started a riotous assembly.

'I hope there're no undercover photographers out here,' said Leeds.

Malone grinned, remembering photos taken of a prominent lawyer meeting an even more prominent underworld figure under some of the park's trees. 'I think we're safe, sir.'

'I don't think so, Scobie,' said Leeds, and Malone caught his other meaning.

'Well, no, maybe not. We've built a case against Justine.' He outlined it as it would be presented to a magistrate. 'It doesn't look good.'

'She didn't do it, you know.'

'How do you know?'

Leeds looked away for a moment, out at the two elderly women still throwing manna to the ducks and the swans. Some gulls had arrived from somewhere and, more aggressive than the ducks, were throwing their weight around. Leeds noticed that they stayed away from the two majestic swans. There were always king-pins who had to be left alone: it had been the story of his official life once he had got to a certain rank. But now things were different. He was fighting to protect the girl who might be his daughter, but, let's face it, he was fighting to protect himself, too. He was a king-pin who might be exposed.

Up till a few weeks ago his personal life had been as smooth as the lake on which the waterfowl floated. There had been the family life, as solid as the house in which they lived in Waverton, on the lower North Shore: his wife Rosemary, his daughter, his two sons. The sins of the past -- he was a churchgoing High Anglican who thought in terms of

223

sin, which, as a policeman, he knew was different from crime – the sins of the past were in the past, almost forgotten, certainly never thought about. He had been startled when, coming home from Walter's funeral, he had been asked by Rosemary if there had ever been anything between him and Venetia Springfellow. He had laughed at the suggestion, but he had wondered how good a liar he was. He was not by nature a liar: he remembered the pain of his deceit all those years ago.

'I don't know,' he confessed. 'I don't even know the girl. I've met her only once, just for a few moments.'

'I have to ask this, sir. What's your interest in this? If you and Lady Springfellow were – *friends* all those years ago, what do you owe her?'

A third swan was crossing the road, its black neck curved in a question mark. Leeds watched it as if its destination was important to him. It came up behind one of the elderly women and nipped at her behind. She jumped and swung round, showering the swan with bread; some of it lay on its black back like a tiny snowfall. Malone, also watching the scene, smiled, but Leeds's face remained stiff.

Then he said, 'I was hoping I wouldn't have to explain this. Scobie, Justine could be my daughter.'

Malone was silent, moving his lips up and down over his teeth, as if words were stuck between them. At last he said, 'Do you know that for sure?'

'No, and I'll never know. But there's a fifty-fifty chance that she is. If you put her to trial and you get a conviction, how do you think I'm going to feel for the rest of my life?'

Malone slumped in his seat, bounced his hands up and down on the steering wheel. 'Jesus, I think I'd rather be in Tibooburra . . . I can't ditch the evidence we have. Russ Clements would start asking questions . . . There's something else I'd better tell you. We're picking up evidence against Lady Springfellow – I mean about her husband's murder.'

224

Leeds, who had been half-watching the swan harassing the two women, suddenly jerked his head round. 'You're crazy! God Almighty, Scobie, what started you on that track?' He was even more agitated than he had been in his office three days ago. He put a hand on the dashboard; it was shaking, like that of an old man with ague. 'You're getting carried away with this – you're letting suspicion get the better of you! You're –'

Malone interrupted: there was no rank between them now. 'You're letting your *feelings* get the better of you. Why the hell do you think I'd have any axe to grind on this, on either of these cases? I'm not some bloody left-wing crank out to chop down the silvertails. Christ, I thought you had more respect for me than that!'

It was no way to speak to one's Commissioner; but Leeds was in mufti, plainclothes as it was called, they both were, and Malone's anger was anger plain, man to man. Leeds, an honest, sincere man, recognized Malone's right to say what he sincerely thought. He backed down.

'I'm sorry – I apologize . . . But how? How can you come up with that sort of charge against her?'

'I'm a long way from charging her.' Malone cooled down. He valued Leeds's friendship, though it would always be constrained by the difference in their rank. Perhaps, when they were both retired, they could become real friends; but by then, Malone knew, it would be too late. This confidence Leeds had given him would always stand in the way of other, more relaxed confidences. 'All I have against her at the moment is that she gave money, quite a bundle of it, to some feller, a bloke with a foreign accent who'd never been to the house before. About then the Colt .45 went missing from Sir Walter's gun collection. The following Monday he disappeared. Twenty-one years later we find his bones, with the lower half of the skull blown away by what could have been a large-calibre gun, a Colt .45.'

Leeds shook his head. 'Are you trying to say she hired a hit man?'

225

'I don't know at this stage what she did. There's another angle.' He told of Uritzsky's disappearance. 'He could have been the cove who came to see her, the one she gave the money to.'

'Why would she give money to a Russian? I told you, you're – no, I'm sorry. You're not prejudiced against her. Are you?' he asked doubtfully.

'No, I'm not. She rubs me up the wrong way occasionally, but that's been happening to me ever since I became a cop.'

'She's – *harder* than when I first knew her. She was never exactly, well, *vulnerable*, but she was much softer than she is now. Maybe that's what happens to you when you make your first hundred million.' He sounded suddenly cynical, an endemic condition with policemen; but this was personal. 'I wonder what Walter would think of her now? He wanted her to give up her career when they married. In those days she wasn't a tycoon.'

The elderly ladies had distributed all their bread upon the waters; the ducks and swans and gulls had picked the waters clean. The women smiled at each other, folded their plastic bags neatly and walked back to their car, an old square-nosed Rover as sedate as themselves. The ducks and swans glided away without a backward glance, unbothered by having to look grateful for the charity. The gulls squabbled amongst themselves for the crumbs left on the grass and two currawongs flew down to watch the proceedings, like lawyers looking for clients.

'Well,' said Leeds after a long silence, 'what are you going to do? Arrest Justine and charge her? And then her mother?'

'Forget the mother for the time being. I'll bring Justine in and question her again. But I can't see any way out of it – I'll have to charge her on the evidence. The motive was there. Emma left a diary and there are some pretty incriminating entries in it about Justine. Incidentally, she refers to Justine as "Venetia's bastard child".'

'Bastard child? That's an old-fashioned phrase.'

'Biblical, Russ Clements called it. Russ is our problem. He

226

knows as much about this case as I do. He's flat out to bring in Justine.'

'Am I mentioned in the diary?'

'No. She mentions "Venetia's old friend", but that could be anyone. Unless they question Lady Springfellow and she dobs you in. There's an entry that says, *J. threatened me.* J. could be John, but I don't think any Crown Prosecutor is going to read it that way. He'll read it as Justine.'

'I had a row with Emma the night she was murdered, but I didn't threaten her.'

'No, this was an earlier entry. She was killed before she wrote down anything for the last day and night.'

'Are there any other diaries? For other years?'

'We haven't found any so far, but I'm sure there were. They could be in a safe deposit box somewhere. There is a safe deposit we've turned up, but it only had her jewellery in it and some papers.'

Leeds was silent again; then he sighed. 'Okay, Scobie, do what you have to do. All I can do is pray my name is kept out of it. I'm happily married and I have three kids I love very much. I don't want something I did years ago, before I was married, to ruin their lives. It was reprehensible, betraying a friend the way I did Walter. But . . .' His voice trailed off; decent men sometimes cannot understand their sins. It's the bastards of the world, thought Malone, who can afford peace of mind. 'Let's go back.'

Malone started up the car, but had to wait while a black swan crossed the road in front of them with pompous flat-footed dignity, its neck arched in another question mark.

3

'It's strong enough.' Chief Inspector Random blew his nose for the third time since Malone had sat down opposite him. He should not have come to the office this morning; Malone wished he had not. 'You could put a case against her and any magistrate would listen to it. It's going to have the media howling like a pack of wolves. If you put it up, you'll have to make it stick. They'll be looking for a conviction, especially since she's Venetia Springfellow's daughter. You know what they're like – if they can't chop down a tall poppy, get the tall poppy's son or daughter. You see it all the time, but especially since the stock market crash. There is an air of sort of malicious revenge.'

'There's another thing,' said Malone, getting everything off his chest; why did he feel he was confessing some sort of sin? It was like being back at the Marist Brothers school, going to Confession every first Friday in the hope of the salvation that the brothers thought you so desperately needed. 'I'm building up half a case against Lady S. herself on the disappearance of her husband.'

Random blew his nose again; it sounded like a snort of derision. 'Are you developing some sort of vendetta against the Springfellow women? Are you anti-feminist?'

'You've met Lisa, Greg. She'd cut my balls off if I showed anything like that.'

'You're not anti-the-rich?'

Malone's grin was lopsided, like his feelings. 'I accused someone else of that. No, I'm not. I don't love 'em, but I'm not going to go out of my way to shoot 'em down.'

'Okay, what have you got against the mother?'

Malone told him. 'I'm waiting to see how much further I can get with ASIO.'

'As you said, you've only got half a case. Not even that. Watch your step, Scobie. This lady has friends in Canberra, like all those tycoons.'

She has a friend right here in the Department. 'I'm not going to shove my neck out, Greg. I'll only bring something against her when I'm absolutely certain.'

'Are you absolutely certain about the daughter?'

Malone hesitated before replying: 'Ninety-nine per cent. Do I bring her in now?'

Random blew his nose again, sighed loudly with irritation.

'Bloody virus – I feel lousy. I think I'll go home again. You take over. Do whatever you want.'

'I think I'll wait till we get the coroner's report.'

'Okay. Just keep an eye on her, in case she tries to piss off out of the country. We don't want another bloody extradition foul-up.' The Department had not had much luck with its last few extraditions of wanted criminals. 'I think we should take some lessons from the Israelis. Just go in and grab who you want.'

'Go home, Greg. You're starting to sound like Rambo.'

Random, still blowing his nose, went home and Malone was left in charge of the bureau. He did not want, however, to sit at his desk making decisions on other detectives' cases. When Fortague rang and invited him to come over to Kirribilli, he went, taking Clements with him. He was not afraid of assuming responsibility; like Random's virus, it was something he did not want, at least for the moment. When in doubt, go out.

He and Clements went out to Kirribilli, to the air-conditioned view from Fortague's office. It seemed, from the ASIO chief's demeanour, that he had turned up the cold air in his room.

'I'm afraid the black-out remains on Uritzsky. The file was closed a month after he disappeared.'

'Why are you defending a Russian? Did he come over to our side and have you given him a new identity?'

'I can give you no explanation. The matter has been marked Top Secret.'

Malone and Clements looked at each other. Every bureaucracy has its secrets. The Chinese, who invented bureaucracy, understood the reasons for secrecy: it is the sauce that makes dull work palatable. Sometimes, of course, it makes corruption palatable. The two detectives had dealt in secrets of their own, but that didn't make them sympathetic towards ASIO and its clandestine frame of mind. Murder was a public affair, or so the policemen thought.

Clements said, 'Then did Springfellow defect? If he did, why was he shot?'

229

'I told you, I can tell you nothing.' The air-conditioner hummed in the background, getting chillier.

'Let me tell you something,' said Malone, coolness creeping into his own voice, 'we're working on the possibility that there was a contract out on Springfellow, that he was killed by a hit man.'

'Who put out the contract? Uritzsky?'

Malone grinned. 'For the moment, that's Top Secret.'

Fortague was silent for a moment, head cocked as if listening to the air-conditioner; its humming seemed softer, as if someone somewhere else in the building had decided the chill was too much. Fortague must have decided the same. He smiled. 'We're playing games, aren't we?'

'I guess we are,' said Malone, relaxing; he could tell when a man was going to talk. Twenty years of interrogation teaches you a lot about the looseness of the human tongue; its natural function is to say something. Fortague, whose trade was secrecy, was only a little different from all the other men with whom Malone had sat in rooms, waiting for questions to be answered. 'But we're on the same side, aren't we?'

Fortague nodded. 'I should hope so. Look, I can't tell you everything I know – you appreciate that. Furthermore, I don't know *everything*. I'm 2 i/c of ASIO, but I doubt if I'll ever know, not unless I get to be Director-General.'

'Tell us what you do know. We've got to put the lid on this case one way or the other. The newspapers aren't going to let us alone.' It was an empty threat.

'Stuff the newspapers,' said Fortague. 'If we took any notice of them, we might as well go out of business . . . All I can tell you, because there was talk of it at the time, it was no secret, at least not then, was that Uritzsky had a girlfriend. Her name was – Jennifer –' He turned over a small pad on his desk. 'Jennifer Acton.'

Malone remarked that Fortague had had the name at hand: he must have been half-prepared to make a concession or two. The room had warmed up a little. 'What happened to her?'

'She hung around Canberra for several months after he disappeared, then she moved to Sydney. She was a very pretty girl, but apparently didn't have much up top. She was a hostess, he met her in some restaurant. I don't think his interest in her was serious, he just liked to go to bed with pretty girls and she was the most available. Evidently she was in love with him.'

'Have you kept tabs on her?'

'We did up till about ten years ago. By then she'd married and had kids and forgotten all about Uritzsky.'

'What was her married name?'

Fortague looked at the pad again. 'Mrs Clive Ventnor. He was a truck driver.'

'A flash name for a truckie,' said Clements. 'I thought he'd be at least a banker with a monicker like that.'

'No, this guy was a tough one. A wife-beater.'

'So are some bankers.'

Fortague looked surprised, as if he thought bankers were like spies, gentlemen through and through. 'Well, I suppose it takes all sorts to make a world.'

Malone wondered if the world of spies was much smaller than he had imagined. 'Where was Mrs Ventnor when you last heard of her?'

Fortague once more looked at his pad. 'She lived out at Paradise Valley. It's a Housing Commission estate out past Mount Druitt.'

'She still there?'

'I couldn't say. We gave up surveillance ten years ago.'

Malone stood up. 'Thanks, Guy. Tell me something – why did you decide to be on our side and tell us about Mrs Ventnor?'

Fortague was tearing up the sheet from his pad, dropping the tiny pieces into his waste basket; from there, Malone guessed, they would go into a shredder. 'I decided to show you and Russ that we're human. Not all of us think that you and the rest of them out there –' he waved at the window '– are a mob of subversives. I don't think you're going to find

231

Uritzsky by interviewing Mrs Ventnor, but at least you can't say I was a totally obstructive bastard.'

'Oh, I never thought of you as that,' grinned Malone.

Fortague's rugged face broadened in an answering grin. 'Thanks. Incidentally, Alexis Uritzsky was a grand-nephew of the Petrograd chief of the Cheka, the forerunner of the KGB. He was shot in 1918.'

'Is that what the KGB did to our Uritzsky?'

The ASIO man's grin was now enigmatic. 'I wouldn't know, Scobie. Good luck.'

Fifty yards up from where Clements had parked the police car was a phone-box. Malone walked up to it, found the phone-books inside it were intact; Kirribilli must be an area that vandals hadn't yet discovered. He looked up the Ventnors: there was a C. Ventnor at a street in Paradise Valley. Then he called Jack Montgomery at the *Herald*.

'Jack, did you know Alexis Uritzsky had a girlfriend called Jennifer Acton?'

Montgomery drawled an obscenity; Malone sometimes wondered if his farmer's image was an act. 'I'd forgotten all about her. Yeah. I tracked her down once, but I didn't get much out of her.'

'She was a restaurant hostess, pretty but on the dumb side.'

'I wouldn't know about the dumb bit – I can never fathom women.'

'You should read your women's pages. Jack, keep turning your memory over. If you come up with something, *anything*, let me know.'

'If *you* come up with something, let *me* know.'

'Don't write anything for the moment, Jack.'

'Scobie, have I ever stabbed you in the back? Okay, I'll keep mum. But if anything breaks, you owe me.'

'You'll be the first to know, Jack.'

He went from the phone-box back to where Clements waited in the car. 'The bloody air-conditioner's gone on the blink again,' said Clements. 'We going back to the office?'

'We're going out to Paradise Valley.'

'The bloody Outback? Burke and Wills died out there.'

They drove out to the far western suburbs, into heat that seemed to increase a degree for every kilometre they covered. They went beyond Parramatta, out along the Western Highway and at last turned off and drove several kilometres across gently rolling terrain where drab houses seemed to crouch exhausted beneath the burning heat. Then they came to Paradise Valley, several hundred acres of planned living that had never come to life. Houses that had all the charm of large packing cases stood in tiny plots where grass struggled to punctuate the hard yellow-brown earth; a few householders had tried to cultivate gardens, but the flowers and shrubs had the withered look of those in untended cemeteries. The police car drove through a small shopping centre, but the shops looked deserted; two of them had For Lease signs plastered across their windows. Malone caught a glimpse of a poster in the window of a video shop – ESCAPE . . . He couldn't read the rest of it and he didn't know whether it was the title of a movie or a shout of desperate advice. There was no McDonald's, no Pizza Hut, no sign of a cinema or a community centre. The planners, secure in their inner-city environment, had lost either their enthusiasm or their imagination before the pioneers had moved into Paradise Valley for the new life that died at birth.

The Ventnors lived in one of the drabbest of the packing cases, on a plot where no attempt had been made to grow a lawn or start a garden. A battered, dirty Toyota, wheelless, squatted on blocks in the narrow space beside the house. A mongrel dog under the car growled at the two detectives as they came in the wire front gate, but was too listless to come out and challenge them. Maybe nothing and nobody inside the house was worth defending.

Jennifer Ventnor opened the door to their knock. She looked at the two tall men and Malone at once saw the apprehension in her hazel eyes.

'Police? Is it Clicker? Is he hurt? In trouble?'

233

'Clicker?'

'My hubby. Clive.' She spoke in gasps, as if the heat was too much for her. 'You *are* coppers, aren't you?'

Malone produced his badge and introduced himself and Clements. 'No, it's nothing to do with your husband, Mrs Ventnor. Could we come inside?'

Despite the heat women had come out on to the front steps of the houses on either side. One of them, tall and thin, with a thin, high voice, called out, 'You all right, Jenny? Everything all right?'

Jenny Ventnor just nodded, turned and led Malone and Clements into the house. 'Shut the door, I'm trying to keep the heat out. I'm having a cuppa coffee. You want one?'

The small house was a mess: Jenny Ventnor was no housekeeper. Children's clothes and toys cluttered the front room; Clements trod on a doll and it protested with a thin squeal. The kitchen was a far cry from the kitchens one saw on TV commercials: there was no Persil sparkle, no Sunbeam blender whipping up a soufflé, no mum who oughta be congratulated. Malone, remembering Mrs Leyden's kitchen in the Springfellow house, thought it looked like a garbage tip.

A radio was playing, some housewives' friend making a comment on the day's news; Malone wondered why all these battling women made heroes of these richly-paid, right-wing gurus. Spread out on the table, from which the breakfast dishes hadn't yet been cleared, was the *Good Living* supplement from the *Herald*. Malone wondered what escapism Jenny Ventnor found in a supplement written by well-paid journalists for supposedly well-heeled readers. A food critic recommended a $60-a-head restaurant for a reasonable night out.

Jenny Ventnor made three cups of instant coffee and they all sat down at the cluttered table.

'Well, what's it all about?'

She had been pretty once, but it had all faded behind the dusty windows of the years. Once she might have had a good figure, but now she was fat and unhealthy-looking. She had

234

the voice of a crow: from shouting above the crying of her kids, from yelling at her husband who came home from work and turned deaf as soon as he entered the house. It takes a sensitive ear to recognize that a whine is sometimes a cry for help. At the moment Malone was not attuned to Jenny Ventnor.

'Some time ago, twenty-one years ago, you knew a Russian man named Alexis Uritzsky.'

She suddenly frowned and shook her head, looking at him with a hurt stare as if he had struck her. 'Aw, Jesus, why –? Is he back here in Australia?'

'We don't know,' said Malone. 'Nobody's had any trace of his movements since March 1966.'

She nodded, the hurt look slowly disappearing from her plump sad face. 'Yeah, that was the last time I saw him. I dunno the exact date, it wasn't the sorta weekend I wanted to remember. He was all sorts of a bastard in a way. But I – we were in love.' She looked at them as if pleading with them to believe her. She then looked down at herself, at her fat body sloping down like a steep hill under the faded blue sun-dress she wore. Her work-worn hands rested on an illustration of a $700 dress: the slim beautiful model smiled out at her with smug superiority. On the opposite page an article began: *As you talk with your husband or live-in lover over your Sunday morning coffee and croissants* . . . 'I was good-looking then, believe it or not. I was a size twelve. Now . . .' She closed her eyes, put her hand over her quivering mouth.

Malone and Clements looked away; neither of them, despite the years of experience, had ever learned to feel comfortable with a woman's tears. Malone looked out of the kitchen window: a breeze had sprung up from somewhere and a Hills clothes hoist turned slowly, creaking like a windmill, the children's dresses and the man's shirts fluttering like defeated banners. This is battlers' territory, he thought, a sunburnt Siberia.

Out of the corner of his eye he saw Jenny Ventnor wipe her eyes with her hand; then she croaked, 'Sorry. I haven't thought about him or any of that in years. My hubby would kill me if he knew.' Without thinking she caressed a dark bruise on her fat upper arm. 'I'm just glad he's not home now, while you're here.'

'He need never know we've been here. If your friends next door –' He knew the dangers of next-door neighbours; they could kill with curiosity as well as kindness. 'If they ask who we were, just say we were from Social Welfare, but everything was okay, there'd been a computer mistake. You can always blame anything on computers.'

'They wouldn't believe me.' She suddenly smiled, the ghost of the girl from the past came out of the plump plainness. Her teeth were still good, white and even, and her eyes for the moment were no longer full of pain. 'If you stay longer than ten minutes, they'll think I've been having a bit on the side with both of you.'

'Well, at least they won't tell your husband *that*.' Malone returned her smile. 'Tell us about Mr Uritzsky.'

She looked out of the window as if looking for 1966 on the hot blue screen of the sky. 'He didn't wanna go back to Russia. He was gunna defect, he told me, take me with him and we'd start a new life somewhere here in Australia, Queensland maybe. He liked the heat. I only half-believed him. I wasn't as dumb as he thought I was, like a lot of people thought I was. I only got to be dumb later on, when I . . .' She looked back at them, then at the messy kitchen. Malone began to wonder what Clive, Clicker, Ventnor was like. 'I think Alex was gunna disappear on his own.'

'Did he have any money?'

She laughed, a harsh giggle. 'You kidding? The Russians don't pay their people anything, leastways they didn't in those days. That was why he picked me up in the first place, I used to tell him. I used to fiddle the bill at the restaurant where I worked. He got a cheap meal and a free lay. I *sound* cheap, don't I?'

'No,' said Malone gently. 'If you fell for him . . . I believe he was very attractive to women.'

236

'Oh, he was that, all right. He was a real ladies' man. I was flattered he paid me more attention than he did the others. You don't believe I was a good-looker then, do you?'

'Why not? Sergeant Clements once was handsome and slim.'

She looked at Clements, then laughed softly: the Jenny Acton of twenty-one years ago peeped through the fat screen. 'I'll believe you if you believe me.'

Clements smiled. 'I've never doubted a lady's word.'

Reassured, Jenny Ventnor looked back at Malone. 'You were talking about money. No, Alex never had any. But he told me that week before he disappeared that he knew where to get some. He said he had two – sources? Is that the word? – who were gunna come good. I remember him saying it was gunna be easier than winning the lottery.'

'Did he say how much?'

She shook her head. A lock of hair fell down and for the first time Malone noticed how much grey there was in the light-brown hair. 'No, he could shut up, just like that, sometimes when we were talking. As if he was scared he was gunna tell me some secret or something.'

'He was rumoured to be one of their KGB men at the embassy.'

'Alex? A spy?' Again she shook her head; more hair fell down. 'Well, I dunno, I suppose he could of been. Nobody ever told me what happened to him. I went to the embassy to find out, after I hadn't seen him for a coupla weeks, but they just told me to get lost.'

'Did ASIO interview you?'

'ASIO? Oh you mean our crowd? Yeah, they come to see me. You'd of thought *I* was a spy, the way they treated me. They aren't like James Bond, are they? You guys are much politer.'

'We have more experience with women. ASIO doesn't meet many women spies – they think it's a man's club, like Rotary. So you never heard from Alex again after he disappeared?'

'Nothing, not a word. I suppose he's in Siberia or wherever they send 'em. Poor devil.' She'd forgive him, no matter what he had done to her. Then she looked out of the window again, saw her own Siberia and a note of self-pity crept back into her voice: 'I often used to wonder where I'd be if he'd taken me with him.'

'One last question, Jenny. Did he ever mention the name Springfellow to you?'

'Springfellow? That's them that's been on the news lately, right? I remember now, the ASIO guys asked me that. No, I don't think he ever mentioned them. On the last night I saw him, the Wednesday I think it was, I'm not sure but I think it was the Wednesday or it might of been the Thursday, he said he was going up to Sydney to see if one of his – sources? – was gunna help him. But he didn't mention no names. He just said it was a woman who had more money than sense. No, not sense. What's another word?'

Malone thought a moment. 'Discretion?'

'Yeah, that's it.' She smiled again. 'You could say that about me, I guess. No money, but no discretion, either. A lot of women are like it. We're a dumb lot when it comes to you men.'

Malone couldn't argue with that; he had seen too many willing victims. He and Clements stood up. 'Thanks, Jenny, you've been a great help.'

'Are you trying to find him after all this time? If you do, don't tell him you saw me, okay? I wouldn't want him to see me . . . Jesus, how does life get away from you?'

Malone put his hand on her fat, bare arm; even there he could feel the sobs quivering to get out of her gross body. 'I'm sorry we had to come, Jenny. It would've been better if we hadn't had to drag up the past. But it has a habit of coming back . . .' *As my Commissioner would tell you if you asked him for sympathy*. 'Don't forget – if your neighbours get nosey, we were from Social Welfare and it was all a mistake, a computer mistake.'

She managed a smile, the sobs subsiding before they could

surface. 'I might keep 'em guessing. Two good-looking guys . . . Will you have to come back?'

'No,' said Malone, having caused her enough pain. 'Good luck, Jenny. Don't say anything to Clicker about our visit.'

'Are you kidding?' Her hand went again to the bruise on her arm.

They left her on that. At least she was smiling and the whine had gone from her voice. For a few minutes, though unhappy, she had been Jenny Acton of long ago and far away from Paradise Valley.

NINE

1

'It was unavoidable,' said Justine. 'It was all arranged months ago.'

'It just seems – *inappropriate*,' said Ruth Springfellow. 'Going to a coroner's inquest, then going home to get dressed for *this*.'

'You didn't have to go to the inquest, Aunt Ruth.'

'I thought I should.' Ruth had a sense of what was proper about death and sickness: one had to *attend*. Emma, of course, had not died from sickness (unless one thought of murder as a sickness): murder had made her death a public affair and Ruth had had to attend to ensure there was proper respect and decorum. As if an inquest stood the chance of turning into a circus. 'Fortunately, the media stayed away. But they're here tonight. Or anyway the gossip columnists are. They are hounding Venetia.'

'I doubt very much if the Vandals and the Goths could hound her,' said Edwin, and smiled at Justine. 'Your mother has a certain impregnability about her.' Edwin at times could sound like a third-rate academic. He hated occasions such as these, but he was an Art Gallery trustee and had had to attend. He had no cocktail talk and so settled for draught beer.

Venetia came towards them, brushing off a gossip columnist as if he were a union picket. She had once walked through a line of pickets when Springfellow House was being built and the rough, tough building labourers had folded like a jelly of gigolos. She was dressed as usual in pink this evening, the only grey being her pale grey wallet and shoes and stockings; she always wore stockings because, as she had told one of her lovers, pantyhose locked in her juices. She wore no jewellery other than two small diamond earrings – 'I am not here to distract attention from the paintings,' she had told the columnist.

But, of course, she was incapable of not attracting attention. The cream, a lot of the skim milk and a few curds of Sydney were here in force tonight. Captains of industry and commerce (no one seems to rise above the rank of captain in the financial ranks) and their Other Ranks ladies mingled with free-loading artists and writers. Politicians trusted voters enough to shake hands with them; ambassadors, up in town from Canberra, and consuls-general, down in rank for the evening, exchanged smiles and hypocrisies. The artists looked at the paintings and told each other they could do better: the Americans, they said, always, like their foreign policies, just missed out. The American ambassador, a patient, tolerant man, though from Texas, listened and smiled. Envy is a form of flattery, he knew; he was a Roman scholar, though from Dallas, and took a broad view. Envy was what turned most of the women to look after Venetia; the men looked out of lust, though two artists held hands and looked at each other. Venetia swept on through the rooms, past the canvas of America.

People turned from a portrait of George Washington or a Winslow Homer seascape to stare after her; what was a Sargent painting of Mrs Jack Gardner against a living, breathing Lady Springfellow? This evening was the gala night of the year for the Art Gallery of New South Wales. Venetia had, through the Springfellow Corporation, sponsored this huge collection of American art. It was a motley collection, from Copley through Remington to Stella, but the gallery had solved the problem by dividing it and hanging the paintings of different periods in separate rooms. John Singer Sargent would have chased Venetia; but so would de

Kooning. Between them they might have captured her on canvas.

The Springfellows, the rest of them, were in the Early 19th Century Room, where Edwin, at least, felt at home. Venetia approached them gladly; she was in no mood for strangers tonight. 'God, why did I choose tonight for the opening?'

'Exactly what I said.' Ruth also had a proper sense of occasion, though she could never bring herself to miss one.

'How was the inquest?'

'So – so cold-blooded.'

'That's what inquests are about. Blood that has run cold.' Venetia saw the slight crease of pain on Edwin's face and she put a hand on his arm. 'I'm sorry, Edwin. I'm uptight tonight. What did the coroner say, Ruth?'

'Murder by person or persons unknown. The same as he said for Walter. It was the same coroner.'

'The police offered no evidence? I mean, they didn't name anyone as a suspect?'

'Should they have?'

Venetia looked at Justine, then back at her in-laws. 'They suspect Justine murdered Emma.'

Ruth felt for her niece's hand, but didn't take her eyes off Venetia. Edwin said, 'Where on earth did you hear that?'

'John Leeds told me. That Inspector Malone is building up a case against her.'

2

Outside the Gallery, Malone and Clements sat in their car on the opposite side of the road. A marked police car had already been along and told them to move on; but police never move along for other police, unless they are out-ranked. The two constables in the marked car apologized and themselves moved on. Malone and Clements continued to munch on their Mars bars, while thirty metres away

242

diners in the Pavilion on the Park toyed with their Tasmanian salmon and drank their 1982 Chardonnay.

The dark park of the Domain, by day a green playground in the heart of the city, by night a green-black lake, stretched away on their left. At its far edge was the rear of Parliament House and the parliamentary offices; the politicians had gone home or were at the Art Gallery reception, while the cleaners were at work, vacuuming the visible, if not the political, dirt. Farther over, the city office blocks, gold-riveted by their lighted windows, appeared to have no more substance than a stage back-cloth. To the detectives' right, the pillared front of the Gallery was floodlit, the gleaming cars of the guests drawn up in front of it like chariots before a temple. There were no gods in the temple, however, just a few impersonators.

One of them had just arrived, not in a chariot but in a Commonwealth car. 'There's the PM,' said Clements. 'He's opening the show.'

Malone watched the famous blond head run up the steps to the entrance. He paused at the top and looked back. 'He thinks he's going into Parliament House. He's waiting for the media to interview him.'

'When we arrest Justine, you think we should ask him to say a few words?'

'He's never said a few words in his life. We haven't got all night.'

'There's a rumour he's one of Venetia's boyfriends.'

'Could be. She's had more boyfriends than Catherine the Great.' He wondered how John Leeds felt about being part of a stable, even if he had long left it.

'You're a great one for all these Greats. Alexander the Great, Catherine the Great. Where'd you learn about 'em?'

'On SBS.'

SBS was the multicultural television channel, founded and funded by a benevolent government that thought all the immigrant ethnics would be clamouring to see all the Greek, Italian, Turkish, Egyptian and Brazilian classic films that

243

they had missed at the local cinema in Larissa, Salerno, Eskisehir, El Faiyum and Santa Maria. Instead, it was said, the culturally deprived immigrants were devoted fans of Australian soaps, while SBS's minuscule audience was made up of academics and would-be intellectuals who were fortunate enough to live in areas where their aerials could pick up SBS's weak signal. Malone watched it because Lisa, neither an academic nor a would-be intellectual, watched it. He had always been weak on history; living with Lisa, he had gleaned some knowledge of world history but still remained not uncommonly ignorant about Australian history. The nation's bicentenary was only a couple of months away and he sometimes felt he should educate himself in Australia's history. Try as he might to avoid it, he was intellectually hamstrung by his job. History is full of homicide; the trouble with Australian history was that it was all at a mundane level. No kings here to order murder, no presidents to be assassinated: the truth was, he guessed, he liked history to be spectacular.

The Prime Minister disappeared into the Gallery and Malone said, 'I don't think now's the time to pinch Justine. What if she and Venetia come out with the PM?'

Clements chewed his lip. 'Well, if that happens, we call it off. Otherwise, tonight's the night to grab her. It'll make a good spread tomorrow.'

Malone looked at him sourly. 'You were never one for publicity. What the hell's got into you?'

'I told you,' said Clements, unrepentant, 'I'm dead set against the rich yuppies.'

'She's no yuppie.'

'She's rich and she goes around with yuppies. She did her aunt in, no two ways about it, so why not grab her and get as much publicity as we can? The Department's had some bad publicity lately, with those bent cops they got rid of. This'll look good, show we play no favourites, that the Police Department doesn't go in for rich mates.'

Clements had always been the most easy-going, almost

244

phlegmatic of policemen; he did his job methodically and conscientiously, but he had rarely, if ever, become exercised about it. True, there had been some particularly brutal murders that had aroused him, but the anger had been directed at the particular murderer or murderers and not at a group or class. Now he was acting like Wat Tyler, who had been on SBS only last week.

When Clements had first proposed coming here this evening to arrest Justine, Malone had demurred. His first reaction had been: what would John Leeds think of such a stunt? But his demurral had been half-hearted; he had to agree with Clements that all the evidence pointed to Justine's having murdered Emma. They had gone to The Wharf apartment as soon as the coroner's inquest was finished, but Justine had not been there. Nor had she been with her mother and grandmother at Mosman, nor at her office. It was Andy Graham, who evidently read the social columns, who had told them that Justine would be with her mother at tonight's opening of the Art Gallery.

'Then we'll grab her there,' said Clements, and Graham had nodded in vigorous agreement. 'Maybe even the art critics will do a piece on us.'

It was no laughing matter, but Malone had somehow managed a laugh to match those of the other two. In the end he had reluctantly agreed to the timing of the arrest.

Only Clements had attended the coroner's inquest. It had been agreed that no more than factual and physical evidence of Emma's murder should be tendered, that nothing linking Justine to the murder should be mentioned. Malone, hoping against pessimism that something else would turn up in the meantime, had insisted on the delay; to his surprise, Clements had agreed. Only later had he realized that Clements did not want the coroner to steal his thunder. Clements, the least thunderous of men, suddenly wanted to shake the rich to their foundations.

Now, in the unmarked police car, Malone ate the last of his Mars bar, screwed up the wrapper and threw it out of the window. A park ranger, on duty for the evening, walked across the road and picked up the wrapper.

'We have to clean up this park after you people mess it up with your litter.' He tossed the wrapper in the open window. 'Now move on before I give you a ticket.'

Malone looked at Clements. 'Isn't that some sort of sign? An omen?'

Clements leaned across Malone and looked at the park ranger, a small bespectacled man who could toss a candy wrapper but never a 100-kilo cop. 'Jack, we are police. If you toss any more of your litter in our car, I'll arrest you for littering, loitering with intent, soliciting, obscene language and pissing your pants in a public place.'

'He means it, I think,' Malone told the ranger.

The little man grinned. 'Would you like to gimme back my wrapper? Sorry, sport. I think I'm cranky because of all them silvertails going in there. Especially that bastard Phil Norval. They shouldn't put Labour voters on a duty like this. You're not a fan of them silvertails, are you?'

'He's a Commo,' said Malone.

'Good on you, comrade,' said the ranger. 'Chuck out as much litter as you like.'

He went away and Clements said, 'You see? That bloke and all his mates, 99 per cent of the population, will cheer like buggery when they read about us pinching Justine at tonight's do. The *Mirror*'s circulation will go up 50 per cent.'

3

Chilla Dural was also watching the Art Gallery. He had rented a small Datsun and for the past week had been following Venetia's grey Bentley. At times it had not been easy; the Springfellow chauffeur had Grand Prix dreams. But whenever Dural had lost the Bentley, he had gone back to Mosman, parked the Datsun in a nearby street and gone down to continue his surveillance of the big house at the end of Springfellow Avenue. He had established that, except for the chauffeur, Lady Springfellow had no other security riding with her. The chauffeur, for all his mania for speed, looked as if he would be no trouble; he was a weed who barely filled the grey uniform he always wore. Snatching Venetia Springfellow, once he had finally decided on where and when, would not be difficult.

He had decided that tonight was the night, though here at the Art Gallery was not the place. She had arrived here with the old duck who was her mother; they would presumably be going home together. He would follow them home to Mosman and pull in behind the Bentley, get out and present the Walther to the head of the chauffeur as he waited for the security guard to open the front gates. The danger was that the guard might open fire, but that was unlikely if the Walther was held against the chauffeur's head. He would order Venetia to get out of the Bentley and into his own car; he would utter threats about not calling the police and then drive off with his kidnap victim. With a bit of luck the police should pick him up within ten minutes at the outside and from there on it would be Parramatta, here I come.

He was busting for a leak and he stepped behind a tree to relieve himself. 'You can't do that,' said the park ranger, coming round from the other side of the tree. 'It kills the grass.'

'If that's all it kills,' said Dural, wondering for a moment if he should forget the kidnapping and just king-hit the ranger; but that bloody do-gooder, Les Glizzard, would find excuses for him, 'it won't be too bad. I'm not wanking, sport, just having a leak.'

'Are you one of the drivers?'

'Yeah. I'm driving one of the Rolls-Royces.' Dural shook himself and did up his fly.

'You should of pissed on the Rolls-Royce,' said the park ranger.

He wandered off, looking for more class warfare, and

Dural went back to watching the front steps of the Art Gallery. Then he saw his target come out into the flood-lights.

4

Venetia was wishing that Philip Norval had not been invited to this evening's reception. She knew, since the Art Gallery board had confided in her, it had been an invitation difficult to withhold; when the Canberra minders let it be known that the PM would be pleased to launch the American collection, the two or three other nominees had been swept off the table. A television personality for ten years and a politician for the same length of time, Philip Norval had forgotten, if he had ever known, what modesty was; given a choice of sunlight or limelight as health insurance, he would have taken the limelight. That he knew nothing about art was no handicap; he knew nothing about most things. The Lucky Country survived despite him.

He was only one of a dozen of Venetia's lovers here tonight. At the moment Norval entered, she was talking to one of her ex-lovers, John Leeds. With him was his wife Rosemary, whom she had never previously met.

'There's the Prime Minister.'

Rosemary Leeds was a pretty woman, as neat as her husband in appearance and speech. Venetia, never having passed through suburbia on her way from Cobar to stardom, had developed a snobbery towards things suburban; in her mind's eye she saw the Leeds home, the cushions fluffed up and arranged like fancy cakes in a shop window, the magazines laid out with geometrical precision on the coffee table, the bed-clothes turned back each night with set-square sharpness for mathematical love-making. She wondered if John Leeds had married Rosemary out of a need for safety. He had confessed once that he had never felt safe with herself.

'I hear you know him well.' Rosemary turned her neat, innocent face towards Venetia.

Venetia looked at her, saw all of a sudden that the big brown eyes were not innocent at all. I must be losing my grip, she thought; she had always been able to size up other women as quickly as she did men. 'Only at a political level.'

'There isn't much to know at that level, is there? I believe the real Dead Centre of Australia is between his ears.'

'Steady there,' said John Leeds, as if he were calling a parade of cadets to order.

'He can't fire you, sweetheart,' said Rosemary, patting his arm proprietorially. 'You're State, not Federal. I can't see what women see in him, can you, Venetia?'

'He's handsome and he has that marvellous voice.' What had *she* seen in him? 'That's all some women look for. And, of course, he has power.'

'I suppose power turns some women on.' She seemed to be losing her neatness by the moment; the preciseness had gone out of her voice. She sipped her champagne. 'I suppose powerful *women* turn some *men* on. Do you find that happens?'

Venetia had the distinct feeling that she and Rosemary were alone in the Art Gallery, the empty halls echoing around them. Suddenly she felt sorry for John and wanted to protect him. 'No, not at all. Men are frightened of powerful women. I suppose I'm looked upon as having power of a sort, so I should know. You'd be surprised how men shy away from me.'

'You mean there are lonely beds at the top?'

Venetia wondered if Rosemary was always as sharp-tongued as this or whether she was having too much champagne. Australian and Californian champagne were being served in honour of the occasion; the French Ambassador was drinking Perrier water out of patriotism and a misplaced regard for his palate. A group of yuppies who, for at least a year, had drunk nothing but Bollinger, the only French name they could pronounce correctly, were practising for penury and sipping local champagne while dropping witticisms about 'Aboriginal piss'. Rosemary, no connoisseur, would-be or real, drained her glass with a flourish, no longer pretending to be neat or even polite.

'You'd better run along, Venetia. We can't monopolize our hostess, not when the PM is making eyes at you. Nice meeting you.'

Venetia glanced at John Leeds, who had turned to stone. Which was better than jelly, the natural condition for men caught in feminine crossfire, especially unexpected crossfire, as this had been. As she left them, he said something to Rosemary, who tossed her head, displacing a curl and further cracking the neat image.

Philip Norval, *sans* wife, was waiting for her. 'Venetia, my dear, you look stunning, as usual. Like a goddess.'

The goddess's mother appeared. No deity herself, least of all Minerva, the Goddess of Tact, she said, 'You already have her vote, Phil. Why don't you campaign for mine?'

Norval gave her the famous smile: he was all men to all women, so long as they were old enough to vote. 'Alice, you know how much I love older women. But what would the under-twenty-ones say? We'll have to meet in secret.'

'I'll get in touch with your minders,' said Alice, winking at him and floating off. She walked well and had bequeathed her walk to her daughter and granddaughter.

Norval looked after her. 'What a pleasure it is to meet an honest woman.'

'Your wife is honest,' said Venetia honestly.

Norval wrinkled the famous classical nose. 'Anita wanted to come up with me, but I persuaded her to stay at home at The Lodge. I was hoping you and I might –?'

'Not tonight, Phil. I've got too much on my mind. It's been a bad couple of months.' She had been with him the night Emma had been murdered. She decided, out of malice, to frighten him. 'I may need you as a witness if and when they find Emma's murderer.'

The famous tan turned yellow. 'For God's sake! You mean

last time we –? You can't do that to me, love. It'd be – be –'

'Treason?'

'Yes. No. You know what I mean.' He was flustered, caught without his teleprompter. He saw Hans Vanderberg, the State Premier, his arch enemy, bearing down on them, and he greeted him with relief, almost embracing him. 'Hans, you old bastard, how are you? Great to see you!'

Hans Vanderberg, The Dutchman to political columnists, looked exaggeratedly over his shoulder. 'Who's behind me? Ronald Reagan? Mrs Thatcher? Oh, you're talking to me? What have I done now, Phil?'

'No politics tonight, Hans, please. We're on neutral territory.'

'No, we're not,' said the Premier, never one to concede a point. 'This is the *State* Art Gallery. I dunno why Venetia here didn't ask me to open this collection.'

'I didn't know you were an art lover,' said Venetia.

The old man grinned his evil grin. He was the most powerful politician in the whole country, though he could have been mistaken for a pensioner down on his luck; he always looked as if he dressed in the dark and no tailor in town ever claimed credit for dressing him. He had, however, stripped better-dressed men naked in Parliament, including the Zegna-suited man beside him, and on the hustings nobody any longer mistook The Dutchman for anything but what he was, a political cannibal.

'Venetia love, the only American artist I know is Norman Rockwell – I used to get the *Saturday Evening Post* when I was young. But that still puts me one up on Phil here. The only one he knows is Walt Disney.'

The two men smiled at each other; they looked like two sharks about to go at each other's throat. Norval said, 'I'll miss you when you retire, Hans. Or get booted out by the voters.'

'I've decided to see out the century,' said the Premier. 'Even Venetia has asked me to stay on.'

He grinned at them again and walked on, a shark cruising

251

in waters where even the conservative voters clung to him like pilot fish. He turned no women on, nor would he have wanted to, but he exuded power. He came up to Justine and Alice Magee.

'Evening, ladies. You still voting for me, Alice? You gunna vote for me next time, Justine?' He grinned once more: it was a joke. He knew as well as anyone that one didn't win votes at functions like this. Votes came out of pockets, not out of champagne glasses. Then he sobered, said sincerely, 'You Springfellow ladies have had a bad trot lately. You got another funeral tomorrow, right?'

'My aunt's.' Justine felt a fascination for this ugly old man, a love-hate feeling that younger men never aroused in her. She was just old enough to appreciate what power meant.

'How are the coppers treating you?' Besides being Premier he was also the Police Minister.

'You could call 'em off, Hans,' said Alice Magee. 'They keep bothering us.'

'They've got to do their job, Alice. But if they worry you too much, gimme the word. I'll speak to John Leeds. Who's worrying you in particular?'

'Inspector Malone. Do you know him?'

Vanderberg nodded. 'I know him, all right. He's a bugger for getting in other people's hair. Even mine, sometimes.' He ran his hand over his mottled bald head.

Another bald head, unmottled, appeared; light gleamed on the polished pates as from the women's jewels. Michael Broad said, 'Mr Premier, you look great! How do you manage to stay so healthy in that bear-pit you call Parliament?'

'Practice.' The Dutchman, who had arrived in Australia forty years ago, could not stand this other immigrant, who had been here only half that time. The newcomer had gone for the money, and Vanderberg, who knew more than any two other men in the State, knew that Broad had lost a packet in October. The Premier, for all his political vices, had one virtue: he was not a venal man. He sold favours, but

252

never for money; when he retired there would be no apartment blocks around Sydney in his wife's name, no lush property in the country, no Swiss bank account. He was not against greed for power, he was guilty of that himself, but he had only contempt for those who were greedy for money alone. Like all devils, he was capable of moralizing. 'You don't look so good, Mr Broad. You're not one of them who lost on the stock exchange?'

'Not a penny,' said Broad, avoiding the gaze of the two women.

'Good for you,' said Vanderberg and the two liars smiled at each other. 'Well, ladies, if that feller Malone keeps worrying you, let me know.'

He moved on and Broad said, 'Malone? Who's he?'

'Inspector Malone,' said Alice. 'He's been harassing Justine about Emma's murder. There should be a law against the police.'

'You know him, Michael,' said Justine sharply. 'Why are you pretending you don't?'

'Of course I know him. I meant, who does he think he is? He's got a cheek, harassing you. Venetia should have him pulled into line.'

The two women nodded and Alice said, 'I saw her talking to the Police Commissioner a while ago. Maybe she was doing it then.'

'Let's hope so,' said Broad. 'The police do tend to over-step themselves.'

Then Roger Dircks joined them. Alice Magee looked him up and down. 'Why don't you relax, Roger? You always look so – so *starched*.'

Dircks gave her a starched smile. Unlike her, he was still ill at ease in top circles. He had the rigid neck common to learner-drivers; the effect was heightened by the stiff collars and three-piece suits he wore. He was encased in his clothes, rather than wearing them; his wardrobe, it seemed, also strait-jacketed his mind. He had a wife somewhere, but no one ever saw her: she was either more frightened than he of

253

the upper social circles or she had the sense not to care about making the effort.

'I thought you might like to know it's going to be announced first thing tomorrow that Peter Polux has applied for bankruptcy. Our early-morning business programme has got a beat on it.' He could not keep the note of smug satisfaction out of his voice. He had the natural jealousy of any decent, ordinary Australian; there was no more satisfying feeling in the national psyche than to see a tall poppy, especially one taller than oneself, chopped down.

'My God, it'll kill him!' said Justine, who thought all deprivation was a mortal wound. 'He'll commit suicide!'

'No,' said Alice. 'He's shot himself in his white shoe. That is as far as he'll go. You're not going to shoot yourself, are you, Michael?'

'Why should I?' said Broad warily.

Alice tried to look innocent, but she missed by about seventy years. 'I thought you were on the verge of bankruptcy.'

'Where on earth did you hear that?'

'Oh, I heard it.'

She didn't look at Justine, but the latter gave herself away: she still suffered from innocence. Broad looked at her with a sudden hatred that shocked her.

Then Alice said, 'We'd better move into the main gallery. It looks as if Phil Norval is ready to make one of his long, long speeches.'

As they moved as a group towards the congealing crowd in the main gallery, Dircks leaned down close to Alice's ear. 'Everybody seems to be falling apart. What else can happen?'

'A lot,' said Alice. 'Quite a lot, I'm afraid.'

5

'I wish it didn't have to be so *public*,' said Malone.

'It won't be that bad. It would've been worse if we'd

pinched her at the coroner's inquest or at tomorrow's funeral. At least tonight all the TV cameras have gone home. It'll be in all the papers tomorrow, but nothing on TV.'

'That'll disappoint you, won't it?'

'You're still shitty. What's the matter with you, Scobie? If I'm doing something wrong, get it off your – There she is!'

The crowd had been leaking out of the Art Gallery for the past twenty minutes, flowing down the broad steps to their cars. Chauffeur-driven Rolls-Royces and Mercedes lined up for their owners; rented Mercedes and Fords edged forward, the drivers not sure that they would recognize those who had hired them for the evening. Several couples crossed to their BMWs and Jaguars: the men got in behind the wheels of those cars, proclaiming their skill; they were *drivers*, men who didn't need to be driven anywhere, except, perhaps, by their wives, whose driving sometimes was metaphorical. The grey Bentley drew up at the end of the waiting line.

Malone and Clements got out of the police car and crossed the road, Malone almost breaking into a trot to catch up with Clements. They reached the three Spring-fellow women as they were about to enter the big car.

'Could we see you for a moment, Miss Springfellow?' Clements kept his voice low, bending his head close to Justine's like a lover arranging something for later in the night.

Venetia, about to enter first, turned back. She shot a quick glance at Justine, then looked at Clements. 'Can't it wait till tomorrow?' Then she saw Malone. 'Oh, it's you, Inspector. What the hell's going on?'

'Sergeant Clements will tell you,' said Malone evenly.

Clements frowned at him, then turned back to the women. 'We'd like you to come with us, Miss Springfellow, for questioning.'

'You've asked her enough questions!' Venetia was

255

beginning to stiffen with rage. 'Mum, go and find John
Leeds –'

'He's gone home,' said Alice. 'I saw him leave before the
PM made his speech. Can't this wait till tomorrow, Sergeant?'
She was the calmest of the three women.

'No,' said Clements flatly. 'I think it's better we do it
tonight. We have our car over there. Don't make a fuss – it'll
be better if you don't –'

'Where does she have to go?' said Venetia in a more
controlled voice.

'To Homicide, up in Liverpool Street.'

'We'll follow you in our car. My daughter will ride with us.
I'm not having her taken in in a police car.'

'Fair enough,' said Malone, deciding it was time he took
charge again. Thank Christ, John Leeds had gone home,
though he hadn't seen him come out of the Art Gallery. 'I'll
ride with the ladies, Russ. You bring our car in.'

Clements's look, even in the semi-dark, was full of
suspicion. But all he said as he walked away was, 'I'll be right
behind you, Inspector.'

The three women got into the back of the Bentley and
Malone got into the front seat beside Leyden, the chauffeur.
The latter looked even more shocked than the women; or at
least more shocked than two of them. Malone turned in the
seat and looked back at Justine. She sat in the corner, hunched
in on herself like a little girl, her full lips bitten into a straight
line as if she were trying not to sob, her beautiful eyes staring at
him as if they were sightless. He felt a sudden compassion for
John Leeds: if this were my daughter, I'd be doing everything I
could to protect her. Even if she was a murderess.

'You'd better get your lawyer,' he said to Venetia. 'We're
going to charge Justine with the murder of her aunt.'

The chauffeur's hands jerked on the wheel; the Bentley
snaked along the road for a few yards. Venetia took her
daughter's hand, held it tightly. She knew the dangers of
maintaining a rage; anger and clear thinking did not mesh.
'You're making a terrible mistake, Inspector.'

256

'It won't be the first time. But all we can do is go on the evidence. Justine will have her chance to defend herself.'

'What evidence have you got?' said Alice. Malone noticed that she was the most at ease with the police; her husband, whoever he was, must have exposed her to plenty of experience.

'We'll tell her lawyer that.' He turned back, said to the chauffeur, 'Do you know where Homicide is?'

'No, sir,' said Leyden. 'Why would I know that?'

6

Chilla Dural had seen the Springfellow women come out of the Art Gallery and down the steps to their waiting Bentley. He was about to turn to hurry back to his own rented car when he saw the two vaguely familiar figures cross the road towards the Springfellow women. He stopped, then moved back towards the far end of the steps, watching the small group now gathered by the open door of the Bentley.

With a shock of disgust he recognized the two men with the women: the two bulls, Malone and the other guy – Clements? For a moment it looked as if an argument was going to develop between the women and the bulls. Then the women got into the Bentley and Malone got in beside the driver. The big guy almost ran back to his car on the opposite side of the road. A moment later the Bentley drove off, the unmarked police car doing a tyre-screeching U-turn and following it.

Dural let out a curse that turned the heads of two couples passing him on their way to their cars. He had been thwarted once again; his aim was to fail, but how could you fail if you couldn't bloody well get started? He should have invested in the stock market; with his luck, the Crash would probably have made him a fortune. He cursed again and the two couples hurriedly fled to their cars, complaining to each other that crazies like the big thug back there should be locked up for life. The police, they said, were never around when you needed them.

TEN

1

The Springfellow lawyer was a sensible man who knew from experience that battles with the law were more often won if concessions were made at the beginning. He conceded that the evidence Clements presented was strong, though, of course, he didn't believe it would be enough to *convict* Miss Springfellow.

'Convict me?'

Justine had recovered to some degree. She seemed to have drawn on some hidden steel within herself once her mother and grandmother had been excluded from the scene. Venetia and Alice had demanded that they be present while Justine was questioned, but Malone had firmly but adamantly told them to wait at the far end of the Bureau's big room. Brownlow, the Springfellow lawyer, had quietly supported Malone.

'I'm speaking purely hypothetically, Justine.'

'Don't you dare speak like that, even hypothetically! Jesus, Mr Brownlow, don't you realize what these men are trying to do to me?' Her control was suddenly on the point of collapse, the steel had proved flawed.

'Of course I do.' Brownlow was a small man with a thick moustache that grew down round the ends of his small mouth, and a thick mop of dark hair; he wore unfashionably thick-rimmed glasses and one had the temptation to wrench him out from behind all the camouflage. He was not a criminal lawyer and in these murder waters he was treading

259

carefully, looking for rocks to stand on. 'But they are only doing their job.'

'I'm innocent, can't you understand that? I'm not a bloody murderer!' Suddenly she burst into tears, hunched her shoulders as if trying to curl herself into a ball.

Brownlow looked at Malone, then he leaned across and tentatively touched Justine's arm. 'Tomorrow we'll call in a barrister who's experienced in matters like this. It may be that you'll have no case to answer. In the meantime, you won't object to bail, Inspector?'

'No,' said Malone. 'We'll take her over to Police Centre, charge her and fingerprint her. We'll hold her overnight –'

Justine, face tear-streaked, all her beauty wrecked, look-ed up as if Malone had kicked her. 'No! No, you're not going to lock me up – I won't go –'

Venetia came running down the room. She fell on her knees beside her daughter and gathered her to her. Alice Magee arrived a moment later, stood in front of Malone and glared at him.

'What are you doing to the girl?' Her voice was rough, like a smothered scream.

'We're charging her with the murder of her aunt,' said Clements before Malone could reply. 'We don't want the onus of letting her go on bail, so we'll hold her overnight –'

When it got through to the distraught Venetia what the police were planning to do with her daughter, she almost blew the top off the Remington Rand building. The use of money can be an explosive charge; the use of a lot of money has ambitions to be nuclear. She made phone calls in all directions, lighting fuses, but they all spluttered out. Malone noted that one call she did not make, though he had expected it to be her first, was to John Leeds. It was comforting, somehow, to find that someone else was intent on keeping the Commissioner's name out of this. He was doing it out of respect; he wondered what prompted Venetia. Love? Everyone was capable of love: with some it just needed a major mining operation.

'Can't we come to some arrangement?' said Brownlow, blinking behind his glasses, twitching his moustache as if it had suddenly begun to itch. 'Lady Springfellow will go surety for her daughter – you know the family's standing in the community –'

'No,' said Clements.

Jesus, thought Malone, come down off the barricades, Russ. There would never be a revolution in Australia; everyone would be at the beach or at the footy or on strike. Get used to the idea, Russ: the rich, like the poor, are always going to be with us.

'All right,' he said, not looking at Clements. 'She can go home with Lady Springfellow tonight. But we'll want her at Number One Magistrate's Court tomorrow morning at nine sharp, on the dot. We'll be asking for top bail, the surrender of her passport and that she report to the local police twice a week till the committal proceedings.'

'Emma is being buried tomorrow,' said Alice, who had been silent up till now.

'I'm sorry, she will have to miss the funeral.' He could not afford to appear too lenient in front of Clements. These people would be out of his life within six months at the outside; he would have to go on working with Russ Clements for God knew how many years yet. If he lasted so long . . .

Venetia was not insensitive; she grasped that there was some conflict between the two policemen. She tried for grace, but found it difficult: 'Thank you, Inspector. My daughter and I will be at the Magistrate's Court. I'd just ask one more favour – do the media have to be there waiting for us?'

'Sergeant Clements and I are not publicity hounds. If they're there, it won't be us who'll have brought them.'

'You're human after all,' said Alice Magee.

Malone sighed, smiled at her. 'It's an effort sometimes.'

When the Springfellow women and Brownlow had gone, Clements sat back in his chair, bit his lip and said, 'That's the first time I've been kicked in the arse by a mate.'

'I'm sorry, Russ.'

'Yeah, you could be. You look it. But it doesn't explain why.'

'Trust me.'

Clements chewed his lip again, looked away down the long room. It was empty now, all the detectives gone home for the night or out on cases. Only the duty officer sat at his desk near the door. The room had the emptiness that comes much more late at night, as if the darkness beyond the windows had drained it of life. It would not remain like this all night: soon the night duty men would be returning with yet another homicide suspect.

It seemed that Clements felt the emptiness of the big room because when he looked back his big broad face seemed empty, too.

'I guess I'll have to trust you. But it's something I never expected you to ask me.'

2

Venetia lay in her big bed staring sightlessly at the sunlit window. The bed this morning felt empty, yet she had had no man in it with her since Walter had disappeared; all her affairs had been conducted elsewhere. Justine, when she had lived here in the house, would come in in the mornings and get into bed with her; but that no longer happened, not since Justine had moved to her own place in The Wharf. Alice never got into bed beside her: she would sometimes come in and sit on the end of the bed, but there was always something that held them back, each of them, from the warm intimacy of mother and child. That had not happened since the Cobar days and Cobar, now, had been left behind for ever.

She closed her eyes, felt the tears inside her lids, fought against the temptation to let herself go. She sat up abruptly, reached for the phone and opened the grey suede-covered book beside it. Then she began calling for, demanding, pleading for help. She called the State Attorney-General, who owed her favours: not sexual ones but financial ones. She called Premier Hans Vanderberg, who owed her no favours but had more power here in this State than she could ever even aspire to. She made other phone calls, getting some men out of bed, interrupting others at their breakfast, getting some in their cars on the way to their offices; but all to no avail. Suddenly all her wealth, all her connections, all her *power*, meant nothing. All the men she had called would, in other circumstances, have come to her aid; but not in the circumstance of murder. Even over the phone she had seen them drawing away from her. Their scruples in politics and business, she knew, were paper-thin; but murder, it seemed, especially a murder in the family, was a different thing. She put down the phone on the last call, utterly defeated. The one man she had not called was John Leeds.

3

Justine was granted bail of $100,000, her passport was surrendered, she was ordered to reside at her mother's home and she had to report to the Mosman police twice a week. She and Venetia did not attend Emma's funeral; the media cameramen attended, but decided there was no one worth wasting film or tape on. Edwin and Ruth were there, and Alice Magee and Michael Broad; but they weren't considered newsworthy, not at a funeral, and so Emma was buried without fuss, as she would have wanted. Edwin and Ruth wept, but Alice and Broad remained dry-eyed. Malone did not attend, but sent Andy Graham instead.

The newspapers, who went to their morgues for pictures of Justine and Venetia, spread the story of Justine's arrest across their pages as if she were Mary Magdalene resurrected and back in her original business. Reporters and cameramen camped in Springfellow Avenue; retired Mosman couples on their daily constitutionals extended their walks to come to the end of the street and watch the circus. It was a decorous circus, of course: Mosman was not like the eastern suburbs, where the rich were often raffish and the media were encouraged rather than discouraged. Neither Venetia nor Justine appeared in the three days that the circus was in the street, but Alice came to the front gates and, in a tone very restrained for her, made a statement that said Lady Springfellow and her daughter asked only that their privacy be respected and that, because the matter was *sub judice*, a phrase Alice had a little trouble with, nothing could be said at the moment. The media men and women grumbled, but eventually gave up and went away. The local spectators, left exposed once the circus had gone, also went away. One had to show good manners, no matter how much one was bursting to be otherwise.

Malone and Clements, their relationship still a little stiff, kept their investigation simmering. A week after Justine was granted bail Andy Graham came to Malone's desk.

'I've got nowhere trying to trace any other diaries by Emma. But the doorkeeper at The Vanderbilt says he now remembers that about six or eight months ago, Emma had some stuff moved out of the basement. All he can remember was that there were some pictures, but there was some other stuff. It wasn't much, it went into a small van.'

'Where did it go?'

'He doesn't know. But I thought it might be worth asking her brother Edwin.'

'Try him.'

Graham was back in the afternoon, lugging a heavy leather suitcase. 'He was pretty upset, at first he didn't want to answer any questions about whether Emma had sent him any stuff. His trouble is, he's decent and honest.'

'You're learning,' said Malone.

Graham blushed, as if he had been accused of being too just towards an ordinary citizen. 'He really is. This job would be no strife at all if everyone was like him. Anyhow, finally he said yes, he had a suitcase full of Emma's diaries. This is it.'

It was the sort of suitcase that, in these days of air travel, one never saw. It was solid leather, battered and scuffed but still strong. The labels on it were symbols of another age, of travelling not cruising: P & O stickers, Cunard, Matson; Emma, or her parents, had travelled sedately and in style. Andy Graham opened the suitcase and there were the diaries, leather-covered, some of them freckled with mildew, all with her initials stamped in gold on the covers. They were not loose, but bound in bundles of five by rubber bands, the years marked in a neat hand on strips of faded pink cardboard inserted in the rubber bands. Emma had arranged everything meticulously in her life, except her death.

Malone looked up at Clements, who had joined them. 'You and Andy take the last five years, up to 1986. You may come up with something you can cross-refer to in the one you have for this year, the unfinished one.'

'What about all the others?' Clements said.

Malone fished through the bundles. 'They go back to 1938. She'd have been – what? She was sixty-five when she died. So she started these when she was sixteen. I'll skip through the early ones, then I'll start at 1966 to '70, when Walter disappeared, see if she has anything interesting to say.'

The three of them settled down to read Emma Springfellow's life. Malone felt a certain guilt, as if he had crept in on the woman in her bedroom. She had had one or two affairs, but the entries on them were discreet; only initials were mentioned and there were no comments on the men as lovers. She had lost her virginity at nineteen to someone named L.; it had been a disastrous event in her life and L. was never mentioned again. W. appeared on almost every second page, though not as a lover; but a stranger, reading the diaries, might never have suspected that W. was her brother. Incestuous love must, of course, be kept in the family, but never in the family history.

The diary for 1966 was full of woe for the lost W. *Has she had him killed? Where has my beloved W. gone?* It was like glancing through a Victorian melodrama and Malone missed a lot, as if he were reading it with averted eyes.

He finished the 1966 diary, having skimmed through it looking for names. Then he went back to read it more carefully. Phrases had caught his eye, but hadn't registered; now they started to come up like invisible writing that had been treated. There was an entry for March 24, the Thursday before Walter disappeared.

I spoke to a young man standing outside W.'s gate this afternoon. He looked suspicious to me; he had been standing there for some time. He said he was looking for Lady S. He had an accent. He went into the house after I spoke to him. When he came out he was carrying a briefcase. Who was he?

The entry for the Friday said:

I mentioned the young man to W. this evening – how I miss him during the week while he is in Melbourne! – He appeared disturbed, but then told me not to worry. But of course I do worry! How can he be happy with that whore?

Malone began to take notes. He found the diary depressing and irritating; Emma's bitterness got beneath his skin. Why had she stayed so close, just across the street, to the situation that was so obviously ruining her life? But Malone, unlike most men, knew a woman's capacity for masochism. One doesn't need whips for self-flagellation.

He opened the diary for 1967. September of that year brought a spate of entries on the one subject:

She can't wait to get at W.'s money . . . Already she is borrowing against his estate . . . She has bought a country radio station! What next? . . . How will she bring up the child, whose ever it is?

266

He closed the diary, feeling soiled: one shouldn't have to face such private venom. 'You fellers come up with anything?'

Clements had been making his own notes. 'She had it in for Venetia just before Venetia started the takeover bid. Evidently she was thinking last year of letting the NCSC know that Venetia had done something fishy in putting a deal together. She must have forgotten the idea because there's no more about it.'

'Anything about Justine?'

'She calls her a whore, like her mother.'

Malone looked at Andy Graham. 'Anything in yours?'

'Nothing that will help us much. In November of this year –' he held up the diary: it was for 1985 '– she evidently had a real donnybrook with Alice Magee. They actually hit each other.'

'I didn't think that was allowed in Mosman. Any more references to Mrs Magee?'

'Occasional ones. She doesn't seem to have a good word for anyone who lived on the other side of the street. She doesn't have much time for Ruth Springfellow, either. They fell out occasionally. She calls Ruth a hypocrite, but doesn't say why.'

'What about Edwin?' There had been references to Edwin in the 1966 diary, but they had been non-committal. He could have been a brother in name only. Had he been a widower or a bachelor, she might have shown more concern for him: he would have profited by being Ruth-less.

'He just seems to annoy her. She thinks he's too cautious about everything.'

'Any fights with him?'

'None in here. She says at one point –' Graham riffled through the pages. 'Here. April 21. *Why does Edwin always walk away from a fight? Nothing is ever won by turning the other cheek.*'

'She sounds like a rugby league coach,' said Clements. He re-opened the 1986 diary. 'There's something here about J.

267

That would be Justine – she only used initials all the time, I guess.'

'It's only initials in mine,' said Malone, and Graham nodded.

'She writes: *J. threatened me today, told me that some day I'd go too far. Too far to ruin them or to get rid of them? How could I go too far?* Emma was asking for trouble.'

Malone nodded. 'But not to be murdered. She was a real bitch, but we've got to forget that. Let's have another look at the 1987 one.'

Clements opened his desk drawer, ferreted beneath his murder box, then handed the unfinished diary to Malone. The latter flipped through it, stopping at random pages. Then he saw the initials NCSC. 'Here she is again, thinking about the Companies and Securities Commission. You said she did that in 1986?' Clements nodded. 'Righto, listen to this for October 15 this year. *Someone* – no initial – *should be reported to the NCSC. How do these people get away with such swindles?*'

'That was probably Venetia, trying to tie up things before the takeover went through. Justine probably knew what Emma had in mind when she went to see her. That was why she killed her, or one of the reasons. She didn't want her mother to go to gaol.'

Malone threw the diary back to him and stood up. 'I've had enough of this war between women. I'm going home. First thing tomorrow, before I come into the office, I'm going over to see Venetia about her husband. You two start getting everything together on Justine's case. I want it watertight.' He didn't, really: he would have preferred it to look like a sieve, one that he could have presented to John Leeds as a gift. He had no sympathy for Justine as the murderer, but he had less sympathy for Emma as the victim. And that troubled him.

He went home to Lisa, who had no venom, who would never succumb to masochism, not even if she were chained and whipped. He kissed her passionately, and the children, who had come silently (for a change) in the door, stood and looked at them.

'Terrific!' said Maureen. 'Just like Kathleen Turner and William Hurt in *Body Heat*. It was on TV the other night.'

Malone and Lisa drew apart. Malone said, 'How did you see that movie? You were supposed to be in bed.'

'We sat out in the hall,' said Claire, nudging her sister for giving the game away. 'We kept very quiet and you didn't know.'

'I was asleep,' said Tom, hoping for some reward.

'Anyhow,' said Maureen, 'what are you kissing Mum like that for?'

'Is there a law against it?'

'No-o. But it's not – *decent*, parents kissing like that.'

'Is that what the nuns teach you at Holy Spirit?' He looked at Lisa. 'Take 'em away from that school the end of the week. I don't want my married life ruined by celibate nuns.'

'What's celibate mean?' said Tom, who would be sure to ask one of the nuns tomorrow.

Claire, the sophisticate, said, 'It means they don't –'

'Never mind what it means,' said Lisa. 'Wash your hands for dinner. And no educational talks while you're in the bathroom, understand?'

'You're not a modern parent,' said Claire.

'And ain't you lucky I'm not. Now get!'

Oh, and ain't I lucky, thought Malone. He put his arm round Lisa's waist and followed her into the kitchen. 'I think I'll retire. Just stay at home with you and be inde-cent.'

'Another bad day?' She recognized the signs.

'I had a peek into someone's private life today. I didn't enjoy it.'

'Want to tell me about it?'

'No, I want to forget it – at least till tomorrow. What's for supper?'

'Fish casserole. And trifle – it's Tom's favourite. I think he gets drunk on the spoonful of sherry in it.'

269

He kissed the back of her neck, not passionately but still lovingly. 'How's your body heat tonight?'

'I've got a headache.' She smiled, kissed him in return. 'You're out of luck. I've got my period.'

'I'll see you at the weekend then. We'll send the kids to Tibooburra.'

4

He rang Venetia at 7.45 the following morning, apologizing for the early call.

'Don't let it worry you, Inspector – and I'm sure it won't. You're lucky I'm an early riser. Why do you want to see me? Is it about my daughter?'

'No, it's about your husband.'

The line was silent for a long moment, then she said, 'I think you'd better come here, instead of to my office.'

He drove over to Mosman, edging his way over the Cahill Expressway and across the Harbour Bridge in the peak-hour traffic, and by the time he pulled into Springfellow Avenue he was not in a good mood. He was not a man who was prone to bad moods, he was too even-tempered for those. But everyone has a liver and his, like everyone else's, sometimes took in the wrong juices.

The security guard let him in the gates and Mrs Leyden let him in the front door. She had reverted to her original stony-faced self; he was the enemy again. She led him out to the sun-room beyond the drawing-room, where Venetia was waiting for him. He was glad to see that Justine was not present.

'My daughter has gone to report to the local police station. We'll be alone, Inspector. I take it that's what you wanted?'

She was not antagonistic this morning; she was wary but pleasant. She was dressed in her usual pink and grey, ready for the office. He wondered if, here at home, she ever changed into other colours.

270

He sat down facing her. They were both in deep lounge chairs in pastel floral covers, a glass coffee-table between them; facing south, the room did not get the morning sun, but out beyond the big picture window a bank of red azaleas glowed like a coke fire in the bright day. Mrs Leyden brought them coffee. It was all very homey in a rich way that he could never afford.

Venetia crossed her Fogal-clad legs, the shimmering silk highlighting their graceful shape. 'What do you want to know about my husband?'

He came straight to the point. Beating about the bush with women is profitless for men; women are mistresses of the art. 'It's about you, Lady Springfellow, that I want to know.'

Her expression didn't change. 'Go on.'

'A man came here, a young man with an accent, he came here on the Thursday before Sir Walter disappeared. Who was he?'

'You expect me to remember that?'

'Yes.' Bluntly.

Her expression still didn't change. 'Do you mind telling me who told you the young man came here?'

For the moment he wanted to protect Mrs Dyson; he didn't want her pension and her living in the retirement home suddenly taken away from her. 'We've read Emma's diaries. She spoke to him out in the street before he came in here.'

Her expression did change now; she said sourly, 'Emma never missed much.'

'No, it would seem so. She didn't miss the fact that when he came out of this house he was carrying a briefcase that he hadn't had when he came in. I presume you gave him the briefcase.' She nodded. 'What was in it?'

'Emma didn't know that?' she said sarcastically.

'No. But I think I know. There was cash, quite a lot of it.'

She frowned, waited a moment before she said, 'I think I can guess where you got that information. Why did you have to go worrying that old woman?'

271

'Because we were getting nowhere with you or the rest of the Springfellows. I hope you're not going to take it out on Mrs Dyson?'

'I like to think I'm not vindictive, Inspector. No, Mrs Dyson will still be all right. I have a debt to her, for my husband's sake, and I'll continue to pay it.'

He warmed to her a little for that thought. 'I'm glad to hear it.'

'I'll be better off than Mrs Dyson, but I'm not looking forward to being old. Are you?'

'No.'

She had softened and he was looking at her now with a different eye. She was a remarkably good-looking woman and there was a sensuality about her that he hadn't noticed before. She was wearing some sort of knit dress that clung to every curve of her body; she still had the sort of body that could wear such a dress. He began to understand why she might have had so many lovers; it was not the scent of her money that drew so many men into her bed. He knew her age from her entry in *Who's Who*: she was forty-seven. Twenty years ago he would have thought of her as practically an old crone, dried out and way past sex. Now he remembered the title of an old book: *In Praise of Older Women* . . . He might delicately discuss the subject some time with Lisa. Then, on a quick second thought, he decided he had better not.

She was aware of his look and the hint of a smile turned up one corner of her mouth. 'You look to me like the sort of man who will age gracefully, Mr Malone. A lot of men don't.'

He grinned, unembarrassed. 'If I do, it'll be because of my wife's influence.'

'That's a charming thought.' Now it was her turn to look with a different eye. This policeman had more to him than his badge and the authority of the law.

Malone saw the conversation going down a side-track; he wrenched it back. 'I think we had better get back to the young man. Who was he? Was he a Russian named Alexis Uritzsky?'

272

She was surprised at that. 'How did you know?'

'I have a very patient young detective-constable working for me. Did you pay him any money?'

It was a moment before she said, 'Yes.'

'How much?'

'Five thousand pounds.'

'That was a lot of money in those days. How did you give it to him?'

'As I remember, I'm not sure, it was in fifty-pound notes. I had them waiting for him in the briefcase.'

'Yours or your husband's?'

'Mine.'

He was disappointed. 'I thought it might have been the one we found, with your husband's initials on it. Did you give Uritzsky anything else?'

She was puzzled. 'Anything else? Such as?'

'The Colt .45 that went missing from the gun cabinet at that time.'

Every muscle in her face and body seemed to stiffen. 'Just what does that mean?'

Malone hesitated, aware that he was out on a limb. 'I think I'd better warn you at this stage, Lady Springfellow. If you don't want to say any more without your lawyer being present, you're quite within your rights.'

'I know that.' Her voice harshened; it was her fighting voice. 'I think it better that you and I settle this between us, Inspector.'

He paused, then shrugged. 'Righto, we'll play it that way if you prefer. But I have warned you – I hope you'll remember that when the time comes.'

'When what time comes?'

'When I may have to charge you.' He knew he was on dangerous ground here; he could ruin everything by being impatient. Yet he felt he would get more out of her being alone with her than with a lawyer present. He began to suspect she had a certain honesty or frankness, call it what you like, that she couldn't deny.

273

She was looking at him now as an opponent. He became aware of a certain sexual tension between them; he knew it could happen. Danger could heighten the sex in some people; not everyone's blood ran cold with fear. 'What will you charge me with?'

'Conspiracy to murder.'

She tilted her head at that, almost comically. 'To murder my husband? You're out of your head!'

'Maybe. You still haven't told me why you paid Uritzsky five thousand pounds.'

She relaxed a little; or at least the stiffness seemed to go out of her body. 'He was blackmailing me.'

'What about?'

She said cautiously, 'How much of this will go into your official report?'

'I'm promising nothing.' They had stopped calling each other by name: they had reached a degree of intimacy, almost that of lovers.

She looked out of the window, then she shrugged, as if she knew some things were unavoidable. 'Things catch up with you, don't they?'

'You mean the past? Yes, it does.' Had she talked with John Leeds about this?

'Mr Uritzsky had some photos of me. Not in bed with someone, but they were incriminating enough. I didn't want the other person hurt.'

'Mr Leeds?'

She looked sharply at him; pain flashed across her face. 'How did you know about him?'

'He's talked to me. I'm trying to protect him, too.' Then he wondered if he should have told her that.

She had folded her hands in her lap, a demure pose if one could think of her as demure. She looked down at them, then back up at him. 'He was my husband's closest friend. Walter didn't have many friends, lots of acquaintances but few friends. John Leeds was the closest of them. Do you look at other women?'

The question was so sudden it caught him off-balance; but he recovered: 'Yes. I guess every man does.'

'But you don't go any further?'

'No.'

She smiled, but not maliciously. 'Most men would have said yes, even if they didn't – it's that stupid macho thing. Unfortunately – what's your first name?'

'Scobie.'

'Scobie. That's unusual. Unfortunately, Scobie, I'm not, never was, as decent as you. I was very attracted to John Leeds – I might have been in love with him, I'm not sure. My husband was away in Melbourne five days a week . . . No, I'm only making excuses.' She made a gesture with her hands, as if she were throwing something away. She looked directly at him, then said, 'I like men, Scobie, that's the simple truth. I'm not a nympho, at least I don't think so. I liked John Leeds better than any of them.'

He had had women make confessions to him before; he had just not expected her to be so confiding. 'Better than your husband?'

Her gaze didn't waver. 'Yes.'

None of this can go into any report, he thought; not even to Lisa in the privacy of our bed. 'When you gave Uritzsky the five thousand, what happened then? Did he give you the photos?'

'Yes. I burned them.'

'Did he give you any negatives?'

'I insisted on those. I burned them, too.'

'As far as you know, he hadn't been to see your husband?'

She hesitated, then said, 'He'd been in touch with him. I don't know whether it was on the phone or whether they actually met. My husband brought up the subject when he came back from Melbourne on the Friday night. We had a dreadful row. He moved into another bedroom over that weekend.'

'He knew about John Leeds?'

275

Again she hesitated, as if the memory was painful. 'No, fortunately.'

'What about the gun?'

'I don't know anything about it. I didn't even know it was missing till the ASIO men came here and started poking about.'

'*They* did their own investigating? Not the Commonwealth Police or our own fellers? I came here with Inspector Zanuch –'

'Did you? You must have been very young – I don't remember you.' She smiled apologetically. 'No, it was ASIO who went over everything. I suppose they thought it was their responsibility, with Walter being their boss. They asked me about the gun, but I couldn't tell them anything.' She looked directly at him again. She put her hands on the arms of her chair and leaned forward. 'I'm telling you the truth, Scobie. I didn't murder my husband.'

He didn't move, not shortening the distance between them; he could smell her perfume, could still feel the sexual tension. *I look, but I don't go any further* . . . 'Then Uritzsky must have killed him of his own accord. You may be lucky that he never came back for more money.'

'What for? I'd burned the negatives and the photos.'

'He could've made other copies. Maybe he showed those to your husband, Walter wouldn't come good with any blackmail money and he killed him. He would have had to, otherwise Walter would have given him away to the KGB. Spy organizations work together sometimes, it's a sort of trade union. Unless the KGB was in on the blackmail.' Oh Christ, he thought, I hope not! The hole would only get deeper and deeper.

She sat back, collecting herself and her recollections. 'Nobody has been near me in twenty-one years, not till they found Walter's remains. I thought it was all over and done with. Nobody's been near me since they found his skeleton, nobody but you and Sergeant Clements.'

'And John Leeds.'

'Yes, and John.'

'No one from ASIO?'

'No one at all. One or two of them came to the funeral – they paid their respects to me, but that was all.'

Malone snapped shut his notebook, in which he hadn't made a single note. He stood up and so did she; the coffee-table separated them, but he felt they might have been touching each other. He felt an odd sense of guilt, as if he had betrayed Lisa. Venetia smiled with only her lips, not showing her teeth, a private smile. She knew she had made another conquest, or anyway half a one, but she would never take it any further.

'Will you be talking to Mr Leeds?' he said.

'I may be.'

'You can tell him I'm satisfied with what you've told me today.'

'Thank you.' She put out her hand and he took it. It was a firm handshake and he was glad there was no coquetry in it. 'What about my daughter?'

He blew out a soft sigh. 'There's nothing I can do there. The Crown Prosecutor has it now. I'm sorry, but it doesn't look good for her. You'll just have to wait till the committal proceedings.'

'Do you think she murdered Emma?'

'You really don't expect me to answer that.'

'No, I suppose not.' She took her hand away, but it was not a withdrawal of mood. 'I hated you at one time, Scobie.'

'It's happened to me before. But not now?' It was the closest he could come to going further.

She smiled again, but it was sad this time. 'No, not now.'

5

Christmas came and went. Clements went home to the country, to his parents in Cootamundra. Before he left he wished Malone a Merry Christmas, but sounded as if he

277

himself would be merrier if Malone would confide in him as he once had. Malone, in the spirit of Christmas, almost did. Then he thought of John Leeds, probably spending an agonizing season rather than a festive one, and he held his tongue.

He bought presents for Lisa and the children, spending more than he usually did, grateful that the Lord, whom he acknowledged only seasonally, like a farmer, had given him a family who, so far, had caused him no worries. He bought expensive presents for his mother and father, or at least expensive by his standards, those of a natural-born tightwad. There were ivory and silver rosary beads for Brigid and an Italian panama hat for Con. Brigid at once put the beads away in a bottom drawer, to be used only for births and deaths, afraid that the Lord might strike her down for extravagance if she used them every day. Con, afraid of being taken for a dandy, especially in Erskineville, put the panama hat away in his wardrobe and forgot it. Malone, not surprised at his parents or anything they did, only grinned and wondered ruefully why he had spent the money.

The new year came in, the voters both expectant and apprehensive. This was the nation's two hundredth birthday. The government exhorted the populace to Celebrate in '88. The implication was that one was unpatriotic if one didn't burst into song as soon as one joined a group, even if it was a queue at the dole office. The nation was handicapped in that it slipped out of 1987, when it was only 199 years old, into an immediate celebration of its bicentenary: there was no gradual build-up as the United States had had towards July 4, 1976. The Big Party was held on January 26 and, the day after it, doubts were already expressed that the celebration might turn out to be a case of premature ejaculation. Malone and Clements, however, had little or no time to wave flags or burst into song.

The Police Department was stretched to the limit policing the celebrations. Malone and Clements were switched from the Springfellow cases to the murder by a terrorist of a political refugee; it was a case they wrapped up in five days, though it had many loose ends, like blood-stained streamers left over from the Big Party. The outcome of it did not improve the sour taste in Malone's mouth and he went back to the Springfellow cases pondering what opportunities there might be elsewhere for a 42-year-old disillusioned cop.

The committal proceedings were set down for February 1. They lasted two days. The magistrate, suffering, it seemed, from a Big Party hangover, almost peremptorily committed Justine for trial for the murder of Emma Springfellow. The trial date was announced a day later for May 2. Malone, who in the past had often seen trials held back for nine or twelve months, wondered what strings the Springfellows had pulled for such a quick listing. Justice, it appeared, was being given the hurry-up for Justine.

Chilla Dural abandoned the idea of kidnapping one of the Springfellow women. The arrest of Justine had shocked him; he even felt a certain sympathy for Venetia, the mother; for the first time in a long time he thought long and hard about his own daughters. He continued to pay his fortnightly visit to Les Glizzard, who continued to try and rehabilitate him. He took several casual jobs, but was always glad to leave them. He had an occasional cup of tea and cakes with Jerry Killeen and suffered the old man's ear-bashing; he became more familiar with the city and life in it. But he was still a long way from home.

The nation's stock exchange, against all predictions, recovered from the Crash. Peter Polux disappeared from sight, or anyway from the financial pages of the newspapers; he was glimpsed once on Queensland's Gold Coast, once again wearing white shoes but they were no longer hand-made. Michael Broad sold the Aston-Martin and replaced it with a second-hand Porsche: a dark-green one, so that his slide in status would not be too obvious. Money still made the world go round, though perhaps not as fast as it had last year.

279

The Police Department was reorganized, split into regions. Malone and Clements found themselves in Homicide, South Region, still in the Remington Rand building, still with no more equipment or funding: only the names had been changed to protect the guilty, the State government. Chief Inspector Random was still down for transfer, but all at once there was no place for him elsewhere. Regionalization had produced regional jealousies; the police force had become a collection of tribes. Each tribe had Indians who thought they, and not some outsider, should be the chiefs.

In the last week of April Greg Random, content to remain where he was in South Region, called a conference on the Emma Springfellow case. 'Okay, have we got everything covered in the way of evidence?'

'I think so.'

Malone, with the committal of Justine now a fact, had at last committed himself to the prosecution of the case. He had had one phone conversation with John Leeds since the committal proceedings; the Commissioner had sounded like a man resigned to the possibility of the worst. He had asked no more favours of Malone and the latter had been grateful for that. Sympathy can be more debilitating than a virus.

'We still haven't found the silencer, but maybe she didn't use it. The Fingerprint men and Ballistics say their evidence is watertight. We have the doorkeeper who saw her go up to Emma's flat and we have the doorkeeper from The Wharf apartments who saw her go out at roughly the time the murder was committed. There are Emma's diaries and the entries about Justine threatening her. And there's the motive. With Emma out of the way, there would be no opposition to Justine and her mother taking over the Springfellows' little empire.'

'What about the fact that after the Crash Justine and her mum would have had no financial backing, so that the takeover bid was a dead duck anyway?'

'We can only go on newspaper reports that the Springfellow women knew nothing about Polux's lack of money till after the murder. I've asked the Crown Prosecutor to subpoena Polux

280

for our side, just in case we need him. I don't think he'd be prepared to go into the box and lie for the Springfellows.'

'Where is he?'

'Somewhere up on the Gold Coast amongst all the other white shoe refugees.' Malone suffered from Southern snobbery. He grinned at Clements, acknowledging his own prejudice.

'Who's defending Justine?'

'Albemarle. It figures they'd hire the best.'

'Who's prosecuting?'

'Billy Wellbeck. He's a terrier, he won't let go. He's like Russ, he hates the rich.'

Random looked at Clements. 'Are you a Commo? I didn't know that.'

'No, I'm just a little Aussie battler,' said Clements, fifty kilos overweight as a featherweight battler. 'Don't worry, Greg. I'm not going to let my prejudices get in the way on this one.'

'You just want to nail her to the wall in her mink coat, that's all?' Random grinned. 'Okay, get it all as watertight as you can. Bill Zanuch has suddenly started taking a personal interest in this one. I dunno why. Being promoted Deputy Commissioner has probably gone to his head.'

'I didn't think there'd be any room left in his head,' said Malone. Then he said, 'Do we have to report to him direct?'

'Only through me.'

Malone was determined to stay out of Zanuch's way as much as possible. He was relieved to hear Clements say, 'Keep him away from us, Greg. We've got enough to worry about.'

'What about Walter Springfellow? How are you going on that one?'

Malone said, 'I thought we might tread water for a while, till we get Justine out of the way.'

'I don't think you can. Zanuch is interfering on that one, too. He wants it pursued with all diligence. His phrase.'

'Does he hate the rich, too?' said Clements.

'Maybe only some of them,' said Malone. 'He's the greatest social climber in the Department.'

'Watch yourself,' said Random but grinned.

'My wife's phrase. I'm only quoting her. She's a student of the social columns.'

'Well, anyway, how are you going on it?'

'I want to go easy for a while. I don't think the Department could handle two murder charges against the Springfellow women, not at the same time.'

Random pursed his lips. He never minded rocking the boat, but he was a poor sailor in rough seas. 'Could you conclusively prove anything against her after all these years?'

'I don't know.' Malone hedged, the shadow of John Leeds in his mind. 'I'm beginning to think we could never make a charge stick.'

He was aware of Clements's look at that remark, but he kept looking at Random.

'Well,' said Random, 'do what you can without making waves. Frankly, after all this time I couldn't care less what happened to Sir Walter Springfellow. We've got enough happening today.'

Malone silently agreed. But, as John Leeds and Venetia had both said, the past had a habit of catching up.

6

The first day of Justine's trial was a beautiful day to be free. After the wettest April ever, when half of Sydney seemed to be floating on a lake of water and mud, when houses several miles inland suddenly had waterfrontages, this Monday dawned sunny and warm. Birds, animals and the human elements shook the water from themselves and dug in their pockets and other crevices for some optimism. Only the elements converging on the Criminal Courts at Darlinghurst looked glum: the accused, the witnesses, even the jurors and some of the judges and their associates. The lawyers and the media elements were the only exceptions to the general glumness. They looked at the sky and uttered silent hurrahs. The case in No. 5 court promised to be a remunerative one for the lawyers and a sensational one for the media. Murder has a climate that can be appreciated a hundred ways.

The main building of the Criminal Courts had been built of sandstone over a hundred years before; other sections had been added as the population and concomitant crime increased. No. 5 court had not been built for a murder spectacular; it was an intimate theatre. It had all the trappings of the English courtrooms on which it had been modelled: high ceilings; high windows so that outsiders could not take pot-shots at the judge; dark panelled Bench, boxes and pews. The judge had the highest elevation; high above his head was a wooden canopy and beneath it the coat-of-arms, carved in wood. Immediately to the judge's right and below him was the witness box. Beyond the witness box, coming towards the back of the court, was the jury box and next to it the police box. Facing the judge was the dock; on the accused's right, going back towards the front of the court, was the press box. In the well of the court was the Bar table, the barristers sitting facing the jurors. At the rear of the court were pews for witnesses who had been heard and for the spectators. It was a theatre-in-the-round, legitimate, of course: no television cameras were allowed.

The law men contributed to the theatrical look. The judge wore red robes trimmed with grey silk, the barristers were in black; both judge and lawyers wore short grey wigs that looked like sheep's scalps. Optimism, and certainly not enjoyment, were not encouraged by the atmosphere, though levity, that human cork, was occasionally allowed to bob to the surface. The law, or at least its practitioners, has always prided itself on its wit.

Mr Justice Gilligan was the judge presiding, a tall thin man whose complexion matched the hue of his robe. He was a mixture of mercy and malice, and barristers and veteran court journalists took bets on the daily state of his liver. The

Crown Prosecutor was Ishmael (Billy) Wellbeck, Queen's Counsel, a bantam of a man who pecked at witnesses as in a cock-fight and who spoke so fast the court reporters had difficulty in keeping up with him. Defence Counsel was Joseph Albemarle, QC, reputedly the highest paid barrister in the country, a tall, stout actor manqué whose black silk gown, it was said, had been designed by Giorgio Armani and his wig by the Queen's milliner. The cast, on the legal side, could not have been better for a production.

The swearing-in of the jury took all the first morning. Prosecution and defence were allowed only three challenges each, but at least half of those called for jury duty were looking to be dismissed. It is a natural human instinct to judge one's fellow men and especially fellow women; the backyard fence and the dinner table were invented to encourage such opinions. Yet it is a sad fact that when called upon to give judgement as a civic duty, more than half the voters rush to opt out. Some are influenced by loss of work and income, some put off by the thought of being bored with the law system, some by fear of having to take away another person's freedom: a sense of guilt isn't confined just to the dock. Whatever the reason, there is always a majority of called jurors who want to be excused.

This morning there was a man with a wooden leg who pleaded he couldn't sit still for longer than ten minutes; he was excused by Judge Gilligan. There was a woman who crept up to the Bench and hung by her fingertips to it while she whispered to the judge; he stood up and leaned over to hear her, while the rest of the court almost took their ears off the sides of their heads and held them out like long-range microphones. She, the woman said, was going through the menopause and was subject to hot flushes; the judge sympathized with her, said he occasionally had the same trouble and excused her. A young man candidly confessed he hated women, but said he would lean over forwards to be fair. He, too, was dismissed.

Wellbeck and Albemarle made their challenges. A

punk-haired young man in a black T-shirt and a sleeveless black leather jacket, with brass studs on the back spelling out F—K, was challenged by Albemarle; he did not appear the sort of juror who would find in favour of a rich girl yuppie. A motherly-looking woman, who had brought her knitting and her lunch, was challenged by Wellbeck, who was not looking for a juror to mother the accused. At last, however, there was a full jury: seven women and five men.

Judge Gilligan then adjourned the court for lunch. On resumption he took his place on the Bench, nodded to the court officials and Justine was brought up into the dock from the cells beneath. On her counsel's advice she had dressed as sombrely as possible; she was wearing the black dress she had worn to Walter's funeral. Its price would have bought dresses for all the women in the jury, but only one or two of them recognized that. In the dock the dress only accentuated her pallor.

Malone, sitting in the police box, glanced at her, then looked directly towards the back of the court where Venetia sat between Alice Magee and Michael Broad. Venetia put her hand to her mouth and shut her eyes for just a moment. Edwin and Ruth Springfellow were not exactly conspicuous by their absence, but Malone wondered why they were not here to lend support to their only niece, at least on this first day.

With the trial about to begin, Justine's bail had been revoked yesterday. The Mosman police had taken her out to the remand centre at Mulawa Women's Prison at Silverwater, an industrial suburb in the city's near west. Malone knew what a shock it would have been to her; nothing would have prepared her for it. The prison was being enlarged and rebuilt; at the moment it was overcrowded. She would have been stripped of the expensive clothes she was wearing and put into a green smock that might have fitted her if she were lucky; most of her personal items would have been taken from her and she would have been handed back the bare essentials. She then would have been taken to one of the temporary dormitories and assigned to a cubicle with one or two other women prisoners. The top half of the cubicle walls was glass and privacy was a dormitory joke. Being on remand she might have been fortunate enough not to be quartered with any of the hard cases, but Malone knew that, because of the overcrowding, there was no guarantee of that. From the pale strained look on Justine's face he guessed she had been subjected to the taunts and stand-over attitudes of some of the hard cases, the butch lesbians, the bank robbers and the drug dealers. He suddenly felt glad that John Leeds was not here to see her.

The judge's associate, seated just below the judge, stood up. She was a good-looking woman with a voice that could be heard all over the court, though she didn't shout. She read out the indictment.

'How do you plead, guilty or not guilty?'

For a moment it seemed that Justine didn't realize the question had been addressed to her. The policewoman beside her tapped her on the arm and she straightened up. Her voice was just a whisper: 'Not guilty.'

The judge looked down at Crown Prosecutor Wellbeck. 'Would you care to begin, Mr Crown?'

Wellbeck got to his feet, pulling his shiny, unpressed gown about him; sitting at the Bar table with Albemarle, he looked like an advocate for St Vincent de Paul. He opened with his usual staccato delivery; he sounded as if he wanted everything over and done with by the time the court rose at four o'clock this afternoon. Malone glanced at the jury in the box alongside him and guessed that at least half of them were not getting what Wellbeck was saying. Malone, over numerous cases, had remarked the almost universal habit of local barristers of not raising their voices; they adopted the theatrical trappings of their British models, sometimes went in for dramatic gestures and pauses, but neglected any attempt at voice projection. Wellbeck, one of the worst offenders, rattled on through his teeth, every word shot out like a flattened bullet.

Then Wellbeck finished reading the facts of the case and the first witness was called. It had been agreed that though Malone was the senior officer, Russ Clements would be the one to present the police evidence. Malone knew it was a sort of cowardice on his part: he was trying to remain as distant as possible for as long as possible. Clements didn't mind that it looked like *his* case.

He came in from the back of the court. He had to push his way through spectators standing in the aisle between the public gallery pews. Malone could not remember when he had last seen a courtroom so crowded. A quarter of those in the public gallery, he guessed, were Justine's family and friends; there were a lot of well-dressed young people, Clements's hated yuppies. Half the spectators would have been drawn by the promise of seeing one of the country's richest heiresses on trial for murder. The other quarter, those in the best seats, would be the habitual court watchers, those who turned up every day like audiences to TV shows. They were the ones who knew what real drama was and where it was to be found.

Clements passed Malone, winked and went on up into the witness box. He was sworn in and then, led by Wellbeck, began to give his evidence in his flat drawl. Wellbeck was the sort of prosecutor who believed in the 'water on a stone' technique, the slow deliberate accretion of evidence against the accused; jurors, and even one judge, had been known to fall asleep while the Crown Prosecutor was on his feet. Clements was patient, never once looking irritated by Wellbeck's constant interruptions. He's enjoying this, thought Malone, he's nailing Justine to the wall.

At last Wellbeck sat down and Albemarle rose to his feet like a whale coming up to blow water over the court. He took his time before asking the first question; at four thousand dollars a day he was not interested in quickening the pace. 'Sergeant Clements –' He had a voice, thin and reedy, that didn't suit his build; though he aspired to be theatrical, he was Othello with his balls cut off. 'Sergeant Clements, I under- stand you are a gambling man. Is that correct?'

Clements frowned. 'What's that got to do with this case, sir?'

'Just answer the question, Sergeant.' Albemarle had the usual barrister's talent for looking patiently pained: they learn it at their law professor's skirt.

'That's correct. Yes, I gamble on the horses.'

'SP or with registered bookmakers?'

Clements, still puzzled, grinned. 'The police never have anything to do with SP bookies. It's a well-known fact.'

There was a snigger of laughter in the court, which the judge allowed. At that very moment, in another State, policemen and illegal bookies were following each other into the witness box at a Royal Commission like blood brothers gathering for a family reunion.

'Do you also gamble on the stock market?'

Clements stopped grinning. 'Occasionally. I don't make a habit of it.'

The Crown Prosecutor had been as surprised as Clements at Albemarle's fishing; it took him a minute or two before he grabbed at the line. 'Objection, Your Honour. My learned friend's questions are irrelevant.'

'Indeed they seem to be, Mr Albemarle. This is not an SP bookie's trial.' There was a murmur of mirth and the barristers sat back; this was going to be one of Gilligan J.'s good days. 'Where are you leading us?'

'That's it exactly, Your Honour. I am leading to a point –'

'Well, get on with it, Mr Albemarle. I'll over-rule the objection for the moment, Mr Crown.'

The defence counsel turned back to Clements. 'Sergeant, is it not a fact that you resent those who made more than you out of the recent stock market boom?'

Holy Jesus, thought Malone, where did he get that from? He saw Clements shoot him a hard stare; he gave an almost imperceptible shake of his head, denying the charge. Then he looked at Venetia and saw the chain: she had given that rumour to Albemarle and she had got it from John Leeds. Malone tried to remember what he had told the Commissioner about Clements; he had obviously said more than he should have. In trying to be loyal to Leeds he had somehow been disloyal to Russ Clements.

'Did you not approach this case with prejudice already built up against my client?'

'No, sir.' Clements was splitting hairs; he had had no prejudices against Justine when first called to the case. Albemarle, keen to score an early point, had rushed things. 'We had been on the case some time before we saw the evidence was pointing towards the accused.'

Albemarle saw his mistake. 'We'll come to that evidence in time. But you do admit to subsequent prejudice against my client?'

'Objection!' Wellbeck spat it out through his teeth.

'Sustained,' said the judge. 'I think you have said enough on that subject, Mr Albemarle.'

'As Your Honour wishes.' But the defence counsel had glanced at the jury and seen he had made his point with at least two or three of them.

They were a mixed bunch, eight of them native-born, four of them foreign-born. The forewoman was a dark-haired woman in her forties, well dressed, with an air of command: she might run a charity committee or a ship's company of women sailors on a round-Australia voyage. She would run a tight jury, everything shipshape and no leaky timbers. She was already taking notes and would continue to do so for the rest of the trial. Albemarle gave her a smile, but she froze him with a look: she knew who was at the wheel in this courtroom.

'No more questions at the moment, Your Honour. I may have to seek Your Honour's leave to recall Sergeant Clements at a later date.' Albemarle sat down, tilting his wig like a gambler tipping his hat after picking up some of the cards he wanted.

The government medical officer was then called by Wellbeck. The Crown Prosecutor seemed impatient to get this witness off the stand; this was routine stuff that only

289

established that the victim was indeed dead. Wellbeck kept flicking the tails of his wig, like a schoolgirl annoyed by her pigtails. The doctor finished his evidence and was excused.

Then there was a commotion in the jury box. One of the jurors, a grey-haired Yugoslav woman, had fainted, overcome by a delayed reaction to the photos of the dead Emma Springfellow that had been passed around after the doctor had described the wounds. Malone sat back in his chair, accustomed to such an occasional happening, and instead looked across at Justine.

In the dock she was no more than four or five metres from him. She had been looking at the jury box, but she became aware of his stare and turned and looked directly at him. There was no expression on her beautiful face; her eyes were dark and dull. He felt pity for her, but there was nothing he could do. He hoped John Leeds would not call him tonight for a personal report on today's proceedings.

The woman juror had been carried out. Judge Gilligan looked down at the Bar table. 'Gentlemen, I think we should adjourn for the day. I'm afraid the lady won't feel like giving her full attention when she returns, not this afternoon. Will you take care of her, madame, and let us hope she is well enough to resume in the morning.'

Madame Forewoman gave him a smile that she would repeat at the following sessions: she and he would wrap up this case between them, the captain and the admiral. Justice needs a full fleet if it is to be won; it isn't won by lone sailors in leaky rowing boats. Malone waited for her to salute, but she restrained herself.

Malone lingered in the police box, watching Venetia and Alice Magee say a few soft words to Justine just before she went down through the trapdoor to the cells below and the waiting van that would take her back to Mulawa for yet another depressing, perhaps even frightening night. When she had disappeared, the two older women stood while the rest of the spectators filed out past them. Michael Broad had left just after the lunch adjournment; evidently his had been only a token appearance. Both women looked across at Malone, but he turned away, avoiding their gaze. They would be here every day and he would have to wear their accusing stares. For some reason, neither the prosecution nor the defence were calling them as witnesses; so every day, he expected, they would take their places amongst the watchers. It would not be the first time that he would be made to feel that he, and not the accused in the dock, should be on trial. But he had noticed, before turning away, that Alice Magee's stare was harder than her daughter's.

Clements was waiting for him outside. He came straight to the point: 'Where the bloody hell did Albemarle get that bit about me being prejudiced against the rich?'

Malone hedged. 'Russ, you haven't made any secret of it. I don't know where he got it . . . Anyway, the judge put a stopper on it.'

'Too late.' Clements was sour and angry. 'I saw the jury, especially those two dark-haired blokes, the one with the beard and the guy behind him. They're on Justine's side.'

'They don't look like rich yuppies. They're both in sweaters with no ties. Unless they're cashmere sweaters. I'll try and brush up against them tomorrow, let you know.'

Clements grinned, but it was an effort. 'I have the feeling you're still holding out on me.'

'Maybe I'll tell you when it's all over. Just hang in there till then.'

'If Albemarle keeps at me along the lines he's gone today, you're gunna have to go in the box. He can't accuse you of prejudice.'

He would, if he only knew.

7

Venetia and Alice, having run the gauntlet of the media outside the courthouse, were driven home to Mosman by Leyden in the Bentley. Both women were unnaturally quiet,

291

though Alice looked calmer and more composed that her daughter. She had had no more emotional crises in her life than had Venetia, but she had had them earlier. She was the original flint from which Venetia had been chipped.

'I thought Joe Albemarle did a good job today,' she said after ten minutes of silence.

Venetia had been looking out of the window at the early peak-hour traffic. Crowds stood on street corners waiting impatiently for the lights to change; a young couple stood with their arms round each other, looking sad, absolutely alone in the crowded city. She was not selfish enough to think that none of those out there on the pavements or in the other slowly-moving cars had any problems; but even if they had all worn signs with the nature of their problems round their necks, it would have done nothing to lessen her anguish. One of her secretaries had once put a small sign on her desk in the outer office: it had said, *I complained because I had no shoes till I met a man who had no feet.* She had asked the secretary to remove the sign. One never knew when a footless man might come into the office.

'Joe will do his best. It's the jury I'm worried about. Four of them have already made up their minds, I think. They'll convict Justine.'

'Which four?'

Venetia identified them: two men and two women. 'They're the ones who are making no notes. They'll just go on emotion.'

'I think I might do the same,' said Alice. 'That's why I'd hate jury duty. Can we go and visit Justine out at Mulawa?'

'Only at the weekend.' She looked out of the window again, but this time could see nothing for tears. 'God Almighty, who did kill Emma? Why don't they confess?'

Alice said nothing, just reached for her hand, something she couldn't remember doing in years. They were still mother and daughter, still able to confide in each other up to a point, but the time had long gone when Venetia had needed Alice's support and comfort. Now the need had come back again and Alice recognized it. But she offered no guess as to who had murdered Emma.

The Bentley turned in the big gates, the security guard touching his cap in an unconscious parody of a salute as they went past him. They pulled up in the driveway behind the green Porsche. 'What's Michael doing here?'

'I hope he hasn't come to be sympathetic,' said Venetia. 'He tried to hold my hand in court this morning.'

'He's a smarmy bastard,' said Alice. 'I'll leave you alone with him.'

They went into the house and she went straight upstairs to her bedroom. Venetia paused to speak to Mrs Leyden, who had come into the hallway. The housekeeper looked as if she had spent part of the day crying.

'How did it go?'

Venetia shook her head. 'There's a long way to go yet, Liz. But Justine didn't look well.'

'How could she, out there at that place? I've been reading about it. It's full of –'

'Don't tell me. Is Mr Broad out in the sun-room? Bring us some tea, please.'

She went through to the sun-room. It was far from the biggest and certainly not the grandest room in the house, but it was her favourite, even more so than her bedroom. It was called the sun-room, but it actually did not get the sun till late afternoon. Its view of her own garden and of the harbour beyond gave it its appeal. Here, she always felt relaxed, able to collect her thoughts. She had decided, in one morose moment, that this was where she would like to be when she died.

Broad was standing at the big window looking out at the garden, a glass of Scotch in his hand. 'I helped myself. I needed it. You want one, too?'

'I'm having tea. Why are you here, Michael? I really want to be on my own.'

'I can understand that. But I had to bring some papers you have to sign. Things haven't come to a standstill because

293

Justine is in court.' She looked hard at him at that, a look that slashed his throat. 'I'm sorry, that was too blunt. I'm as upset as you are.'

She sat down, not forgiving him. 'All right, what are the papers?'

He opened his briefcase, a Louis Vuitton item: certain appearances were still being kept up. 'I've taken over Justine's department for the time being. Those girls she collected around her aren't competent enough to run things on their own. They're nothing more than jumped-up secretaries.'

'I always knew you were a male chauvinist. You've managed to hide it up till now.'

'That was out of deference to you.' He tried a tentative smile, but got none in return. 'Anyhow, things have to be tidied up. Justine has let too many things slide.'

'She's had a lot on her mind these past months. A murder charge, for instance. How would you keep your mind on things if you'd been facing the same charge?'

He put down the papers on the coffee-table. 'I would never have got myself into that situation.'

She should have been angry at that remark, but all of a sudden she was too tired for real anger. 'You're probably right. You're too cold-blooded. You'd never murder anyone, Michael. You'd help them commit suicide.'

He picked up the papers, his expression not changing. 'Here's how things stand. The television network is in a hole, a big one.'

'That happened suddenly, didn't it? Thank you, Liz.' Mrs Leyden had come in with the tea-tray. She put it on the table and went out without a word or a glance at Broad. 'What's gone wrong? Is it Justine's fault?'

Justine had run the television and radio division of the corporation.

'Partly. But it's mostly yours. You paid far too much for the Channel 15 network.'

'You advised me on it.'

294

'You ignored my advice, remember? The network isn't taking in nearly enough to service our debt on it. The advertising dollar has dropped off 15 per cent in the last six months. We're bottom of the ratings. *Sydney Beat* has flopped here, after all the money we spent on it, and this week the Fox network cancelled it in the States.'

She took in all the bad news without flinching; it was nothing to the possibility of losing Justine for God knew how many years. *I complained because I had no shoes* . . . She knew she had been losing her grip since the day after Justine's arrest, her fingers slipping almost imperceptibly, like those of a climber on a cliff face. The only one on the rope who could save her was Michael Broad; and looking at him, she knew that he knew it . . . 'What are the papers for?'

'I'm firing Roger Dircks – this is his golden handshake. I'm putting in one of my own men, an accountant. He'll cut the fat out of the network – it's almost as bad as the ABC – and then we'll see what we can do about improving the ratings.'

'Does Roger know he's being fired?'

'I told him this morning before I came to the court. He wilted – all the starch went out of his collar.' He tried another smile, but again there was no return.

She had reached the bottom of the cliff face, it seemed; she was sliding off into the sea. 'You've really taken over, haven't you? Everything, I mean.'

He pushed the papers towards her, offered her his gold pen. 'Someone had to, Venetia. Like Justine, you've had your mind on other things.'

Then she did smile, cold and hard. 'You bastard, Michael.' But she took the pen and signed Roger Dircks out of a job and, probably, out of the television industry. She knew he had lasted far longer than his small talent warranted. 'Anything more to sign? What other divisions are you now running?'

He handed her more papers. 'As you said, *everything*. You can always fire me if I'm not doing things the way you want.'

She knew it was a challenge, but she was too weary to take

it up now. And she knew that he knew that, too. She signed the remaining papers and went to hand back his pen. Then she withdrew it.

'No, I'll keep this for future signings. You can have it back when I take over control again.' It was a token challenge, but it was all she could muster at the moment. 'Don't come to the court tomorrow, Michael. Just stay in the office and run everything.'

He wasn't sure whether she was being sarcastic or not; he played it straight. 'I'll do that tomorrow. But if the trial goes on, I'll drop in occasionally. Just to show you I'm not all bastard.'

When he had gone she sat on in the sun-room. The westering sun struck slantwise across the room, casting shadows that fractured its brightness. She held up her arm and saw its shadow on the back of the chair opposite. She waved her hand limply: she had slipped off the last rock into the sea, it looked like the last desperate appeal of someone drowning.

Then Mrs Leyden came to the door that led into the drawing-room. Behind her was a man standing in the shadows of the other room.

Mrs Leyden was pale, obviously shaken. 'Someone to see you, Lady Springfellow.'

The man stepped forward. He was tall, with steel-rimmed glasses, thinning grey hair and a neatly trimmed white beard.

'Hello, Venetia,' said Walter Springfellow.

ELEVEN

1

'You had better begin at the beginning,' said Alice Magee.

She had come downstairs when she had heard Michael Broad's Porsche drive away and she had been in the kitchen when there had been the ring at the front doorbell and Mrs Leyden had gone to answer it. She had come out to the sun-room only moments after Walter had first spoken to Venetia.

Venetia had stood up when the vaguely familiar man had stepped out into the sunlit room. It was the voice that she recognized before the features; Walter had always had a distinctive voice about which he had been rather vain. It had not lost its timbre, though it did sound softer than she had remembered it.

She could feel herself trembling, though it was not apparent to either Walter or Alice. Mrs Leyden had re-treated to the far door of the drawing-room and stood there, ready to run for the security guard if he were needed. Walter made no move at all after his initial step into the sunlight. He just stood looking at her, an old man who could have been asking for forgiveness or comfort, she wasn't sure which. She took two steps towards him and put her arms round him, was shocked that all she felt beneath the tweed jacket was bones. He held her to him, but there seemed no strength in his arms; she felt him kiss her hair, but he went no further than that. Then she stepped away from him and looked past him at her mother.

'Do you believe it's him?'

'Of course,' said Alice matter-of-factly. She put out her hand. 'Welcome back, Walter. Where the hell have you been?'

He smiled. Venetia, scrutinizing her husband back from the dead, was noticing every small detail about him. She saw that his teeth now were false, that his own, of which he had been so proud, had gone. The more she looked, the more she noticed how much of the old Walter was gone. The years, whatever had occurred during them, had smudged him.

'I've been in Germany ever since I left here. May I sit down? I'm rather tired after the flight. I'm not as young as I used to be.'

Alice looked over her shoulder at Mrs Leyden still standing at the far door of the drawing-room. 'Liz, bring us some fresh tea, please. Do you want something to eat, Walter?'

'Just tea, thank you.' He looked at the two women as they sat down opposite him. Alice was the least awkward of the three of them; but then she was not the deserted wife. Venetia had taken the chair next to Walter's; she was close enough to reach out for his hand, but she didn't. There was a huge gap between them that could not be closed in a hurry with a show of affection. Love, they both knew, had died long ago.

'I read about Justine's arrest. I saw it in *The Times* and the London *Daily Telegraph* – I used to get them every day in the small town in Germany where I lived. English newspapers only run the more sensational Australian news. As soon as I read it, I knew I'd have to come home sooner or later. I've never seen her, you know.'

Venetia, close by Walter, was now seeing beneath the surface of him. He looked ill, drained of substance; he who had once been so strong and healthy looked now as if he could be snapped in half. But then she felt that way herself, and she was not ill. It had taken some time for the reaction to his appearance to hit her; all at once she felt hollow, weightless, as if she were in a dream which neither frightened her nor made her happy. Walter had disappeared from her life all those years ago; months ago she had buried his bones. Now here he was, the bones and the flesh, frail though it was, sitting beside her, giving her a shadow of the once familiar smile that could appear so unexpectedly on that stern, handsome face. She had the bizarre feeling that her whole married life was about to be re-run and she knew she would not have the strength to sit it out.

'I've never seen her,' Walter repeated.

Venetia got up, went into the drawing-room and came back with a photo of Justine. 'That was taken on her twenty-first birthday.'

Walter took off his glasses and replaced them with another steel-rimmed pair. In the moment he was without the glasses Venetia saw something of the Walter of long ago, a hint of the virile handsome man he had once been. He looked at the photo of the smiling Justine and his eyes seemed to mist over.

'She's beautiful. Just like you were.' He looked across at her. 'Still are.'

Venetia ignored the compliment. She was accustomed to compliments from men, but now she felt uncomfortable with one from her husband. 'She looks nothing like that now – I mean, not as happy. She's in trouble, Walter.'

'She didn't murder Emma, of course?'

'Of course not,' snapped Alice. 'Oh, thanks, Liz. Mrs Leyden, this is Sir Walter – we'll explain later. Walter, this is Mrs Dyson's niece. She took over when Mrs Dyson retired.'

'She's still alive? *Danke*.' The German word slipped out, but he didn't seem to notice it, as Alice handed him a cup of tea. He looked up at Mrs Leyden. 'You might give my regards to your aunt, please. But not yet. I'd appreciate it if you said nothing about my being here, at least for the time being.'

'Lady Springfellow will tell you I'm very discreet. It's nice to know you're still –' Then Mrs Leyden stopped.

Walter smiled. 'That I'm still alive? Yes, it is.'

Mrs Leyden went back to the kitchen and Venetia said, 'We'll have to tell someone you're back. Whom do we tell first?'

'I honestly don't know. ASIO? The police? John Leeds perhaps – he's Police Commissioner now, isn't he?'

Venetia said awkwardly, 'I'll call him if you like.'

Walter shook his head. He looked down again at the photo of Justine. 'When can I see her?'

'To speak to her? Not before the weekend. We can visit her in the women's prison. I think I'd better prepare her first. I can usually manage a word with her in court before she leaves the dock.'

'My daughter in the dock –' Again he shook his head. He put down the photo, changed his glasses again. 'But then I'll be there myself soon enough. All the English newspapers will run *that* story.'

'What do you mean?'

'It's a long story.'

'You had better begin at the beginning,' said Alice.

2

Walter Springfellow had never met Alexis Uritzsky till the morning of Monday, March 28, 1966. He had, however, had two phone calls in the previous week, both of them threatening and demanding. The threat was to give to the newspapers incriminating photos of Lady Springfellow with a man; the demand was for ten thousand pounds in cash. The man had not identified himself by name and Walter had not been able to identify the accent. Had the blackmail concerned himself, Walter would have had no hesitation in contacting the Commonwealth Police: he had the arrogant confidence of the totally blameless. If, however, Venetia's affairs were to be exposed, then the blackmail had to be paid and the police kept out of it.

He arranged for ten thousand pounds to be transferred from his Sydney bank account to the account he had opened in Melbourne when he had started work in the southern city. That was on the Wednesday. On the Friday he withdrew the ten thousand, ignoring the restrained curiosity of the bank teller as he paid over the large amount in cash. He had flown back to Sydney on the six p.m. flight, carrying the money with him in his one suitcase.

'I shan't recap that weekend,' he said to Venetia as the afternoon light died in the sun-room and Alice got up and switched on some table lamps. 'That would be too painful for both of us.'

'Let's forget that,' said Alice, the moderator and umpire. 'What happened next?'

On the Monday morning the decision to take the Colt .45 was a last-minute one. He passed the gun-cabinet on his way in from the sun-room where he had had breakfast alone. He paused, looking at the collection of guns, then on the spur of the moment took the Colt and half a dozen rounds from the ammunition drawer below the cabinet. There was no thought of using it unless he had to; it was purely for self-defence. He had loaded the pistol, put it in his briefcase beneath the bundles of bank notes, had paused outside Venetia's door, wondering if he should go in and attempt a reconciliation, decided against it and gone out and got into the Commonwealth car that had called for him as it did every Monday morning.

At Kingsford Smith Airport he had thanked the driver, said he would see him Friday night on his return, gone into the terminal and walked straight through and out another door. He had walked across to the parking lot and found the man standing, as he had promised, beside the Ford Escort with the Australian Capital Territory plates.

'Sir Walter?' The young man was handsome in a broad-faced sort of way, with a pleasant smile. Walter recognized him at once, though he had never met him. ASIO had photos of all the KGB agents in Canberra and the various

301

consulates throughout the capital cities. Walter had a photographic memory and he recognized this smiling young man, though at first he couldn't put a name to him. 'You've brought the money?'

'Yes, Mr –' The name came to him all at once. 'Mr Uritzsky, isn't it?'

The smile was suddenly gone. 'That was a mistake, Sir Walter, letting me know you recognized me.' He put a hand in his pocket and it came out with a pistol. 'Get in the car behind the wheel. You drive.'

Walter carried his suitcase and briefcase round to the driver's side of the car, watching Uritzsky all the time. Other cars were coming into the car-park, but they were at the far end. Uritzsky had chosen a spot where empty cars, their owners already in the terminal or already flying, were banked up on either side of the Ford.

Walter put his suitcase in the back of the car and took his briefcase into the front seat with him. Uritzsky slid in from the other side. He handed Walter the parking ticket and the money.

'Pay the man at the gate. And please – no funny business.'

They drove out of the car-park and Walter instinctively took the road leading out of the airport towards the city. 'No,' said Uritzsky. 'Go west, old man. I'll tell you when to pull up.'

So Walter drove the Ford west, out through the suburbs, out through Parramatta and past the Housing Commission houses beyond. As they climbed into the Blue Mountains, with no word passing between them, Walter realized that Uritzsky intended to kill him.

'This blackmail is your own idea?' he said at last. 'Your masters know nothing about it?'

'Nothing.' Uritzsky studied him for a while. Then: 'When you see who is in the photo with your wife, you are going to be a very sad and angry man.'

'Of course. A husband is always sad and angry if he finds out his wife is unfaithful.' He wondered who the man could be. 'What are you going to do with the money?'

'Disappear. Defect. Call it what you like. Your wife has already paid me five thousand pounds.'

'I know. We discussed you on Friday night.'

'Does she know you were meeting me this morning?' Uritzsky sat up in the seat, his voice grew edgy.

'You'd like to know that, wouldn't you?' Walter was not a recklessly brave man, but he had courage.

Uritzsky raised the gun. Walter recognized it as a Smith & Wesson, standard issue to the NSW police; he wondered where Uritzsky had acquired it. 'I could make you tell me.'

'I don't think so,' said Walter, looking straight ahead up the winding road. His hands were tight on the wheel, but his driving was steady. 'You're going to kill me, anyway, aren't you?'

Uritzsky seemed put off by the accusation. The gun wavered; then he sat back in the corner of the seat. They passed through several towns before he said, 'Turn left here.'

Walter did as he was told, driving through the neat, quiet streets of Blackheath and down into the scrub. At last he could drive no farther and he pulled up, switching off the engine. They were at the end of a long narrow track, at least three-quarters of a mile from the nearest house. Below them lay the deep forest-covered valley, looking as primitive and virgin as if still undiscovered. He'll shoot me, then push me over the cliff, Walter thought, and I'll never be found.

'Get out,' said Uritzsky.

Walter took the briefcase with him as he got out of the Ford. Uritzsky slid across the front seat and followed him out. They stood looking at each other and Walter realized that Uritzsky was having to pluck up the courage to kill him. He belonged to the KGB, but he was not one of their killers, not professionally trained and certainly not licensed to kill.

Walter flipped back the locks on his briefcase. 'You'll want to be sure I've brought the money. There. Ten thousand pounds.'

He held open the case, put his hand under the notes and drew out the Colt .45. He was not a trained killer, but he was far from a novice in the use of guns. He flicked off the safety catch, brought the gun up and fired it at Uritzsky from close range. The Russian, greed making him momentarily unwary, had leaned forward to check the small fortune in the briefcase. Had he been better paid by the KGB, had he been as accustomed to money as Walter was, he would not have been so excited by a mere ten thousand pounds: he died, in a curious way, because he was still a poor farmer's son from outside Smolensk. The bullet hit him in the lower part of his face: his smile died in the blast.

He fell down in an undramatic way. Walter stood over him, for a moment feeling absolutely nothing at all. Then he saw what he had done to Uritzsky's face and was hit suddenly by the larger enormity of what he had done. He turned away and was violently sick.

The sound of the shot had gone cracking across the valley; a faint echo came back from somewhere, or it might have been another gun going off. He leaned against the car, his legs barely holding him up. Then he sat down on the seat behind the wheel, half-in, half-out of the car, the open door shielding the view of the dead Uritzsky, and waited for someone to respond to the sound of the shot and come down from the houses up beyond the scrub. He did not know that all the nearest houses were holiday homes, vacant during the week, and he sat there for twenty minutes, waiting to be found beside the man he had murdered, but nobody came.

At last he stirred, knowing in a dim way that something had been decided but to which he had not yet agreed. He reached into the back of the car and took out the briefcase there; he saw the initials, VS, and recognized it as an old one of Venetia's. He opened it and saw the bundles of fifty-pound notes. Then he took out the brown manila envelope, shook the three ten by eight inch photos from it. He looked at them, saw the man with his hands up under Venetia's raised dress, saw the manic look on her face that he had seen so often right beneath his own: she was in orgasm. Then he saw the man's face: it was almost as if he had tried to avoid looking at him. It was John Leeds.

He dropped the photos and was sick again; but this time nothing came up. He felt sweat break out on him; a sudden wind swept up from the valley, chilling him to the bone. Or perhaps it was not the wind.

He went for a walk back up the track, unconsciously waiting for someone to come down, see what he had done and call the police. Then he thought of the photos lying beside the car: he would never be able to stand anyone's seeing those. He hurried back down the track, stumbling on the uneven ground. He gathered up the three photos, turning them over so that he did not have to look at them again, put them in a hole on the lee side of a large rock and lit them with his cigarette lighter. He watched the photos curl up, turning to brown ash. In a moment the photos were no more than a small pile of ashes. He knew that his life, too, was no more than that.

He looked back up the track once more; but no one was coming. He took out Uritzsky's suitcases from the boot of the car and opened them; he found what he was looking for, a set of negatives different from those from which the burnt photos had been developed. He held them up to the sky: as far as he could tell it was Venetia and John Leeds in another wild embrace. He put a light to the negatives, watched them burn.

He quickly went through Uritzsky's suitcases; there was nothing else incriminating in them. He carried them down the track to the edge of the cliff and flung them far out, one by one, watching them fall, seemingly in slow motion, down to the thick forest of gums far below. He went back to the car and opened Venetia's briefcase again. Tucked into an inner pocket was an airline ticket in the name of Mr A. Skelly, from Broken Hill to Perth; that was why Uritzsky had ordered him to drive west. In a second pocket there were three passports: one British, one Australian, one United States. They were all in the name of Alexander Skelly, who had been born in, respectively, Hove, UK, Melbourne, Australia and Pittsburgh, Pennsylvania, on April 15, 1934.

305

There was only one thing missing from each of the passports: there was no photo. Uritzsky had not yet made up his mind how Alexander Skelly should look.

The passports were forgeries, Walter was sure of that; but they were excellent ones. Uritzsky, somehow, had taken advantage of the KGB's expertise; he may even have forged the passports himself. Walter sat down, again half-in and half-out of the car, and looked at his life, backwards and forwards. Few of us take the time to look both ways at our lives: we have to be strung up high enough on a crisis to get the long view.

There was nothing to go back to but scandal and a murder charge. There was nothing to go forward to but the unknowable. There was really no choice. There was, of course, the child in Venetia's womb; but how could he be sure now that it was his? The question made him sick again, but again there was nothing to come up out of the hollow pit of himself.

('You should have come back,' said Venetia.

'I have,' said Walter, smiling; he had not told her how he had felt at seeing the photos of her and John Leeds. 'Only now.')

He took the signet ring from his finger and put it on one of Uritzsky's fingers. He stripped the clothes from the corpse, turning his gaze away so that he did not look at the mess that had been Uritzsky's face. He took the clothes down to the cliff and flung them out; they floated down much more slowly than the suitcases, ballooning out as the air rushed into them, so that they looked like parts of a sky-diver who had become dismembered in the sky. They drifted down to catch in the tops of the trees on the floor of the valley. No one was likely to climb down the sheer face of the cliff to check the distant scraps of cloth.

He went back to the car, took out his own briefcase and put the ten thousand pounds in his suitcase and the suitcase back in the car. He checked the five thousand pounds in Venetia's briefcase; Uritzsky had spent none of it. He had

306

fifteen thousand pounds, not a fortune but enough for a new start. He would have to lower his standards, but he would learn to penny-pinch.

(Alice laughed. 'You wouldn't have known what being poor was, Walter. How could you pinch a penny? You'd never seen one.'

'I was speaking figuratively,' said Walter, not annoyed at her scepticism. He's become much more tolerant, Venetia thought. 'I don't think I saw myself living in one room in some hill village in Spain or Portugal.')

He dragged Uritzsky's body by the feet deeper into the scrub. He hoped it might not be discovered for a few days, preferably weeks; he hoped for time for the body to decompose, making identification difficult, if not impossible. It never occurred to him that it would be twenty-one years before Uritzsky's skeleton would be found.

He dropped his briefcase beside the body. He picked up the Smith & Wesson and the Colt .45 and put them on the car seat. He took one last look around, walked over and ground the ashes of the photos and the negatives into the ground, then came back and got into the car. He waited a few more minutes for justice to appear at the top of the track; but justice and the world, it seemed, didn't care. An unsuperstitious man, he uncharacteristically took it as an omen.

He started up the Ford, turned it round with some difficulty and drove it back up through the town. He passed the local police station and his foot eased on the accelerator of its own accord; but it was too late now to stop and confess. He turned on to the Great Western Highway, the route of earlier drifters looking for a new life.

He slept that night in the car on the plains just west of Cobar. It was a deliberate stop, a stab in the soul. He sat there in the car in the dark night, looking back at the distant lights of the small town, and wondered how innocent Venetia, or Mary as she then was, had been in her days and nights in the town. When he fell asleep he dreamed of her,

307

but she was looking beyond him, with that wild manic look on her beautiful face, at someone behind him. He tried to turn his head to see who it was, but instead he just woke with a crick in his neck.

Next morning he buried the two hand-guns in the scrub. Murder was behind him, and he was not interested in self-defence. He was still half-hoping to be caught. He was suffering from the conscience of the middle-aged honest man, when conscience itself is halfway between the carelessness of youth and the cynicism of old age.

He drove on to Broken Hill, left the Ford in the small airport car-park after wiping it clean of his fingerprints. He caught an afternoon flight to Adelaide and picked up the last flight to Perth. The western capital in those days had not yet become the entrepreneurs' circus of the later years; the travellers from Sydney and Melbourne who might have recognized Walter had not yet started their pilgrimages to the future tycoons. He was saved from recognition by East Coast snobbery towards the West.

He checked into a small hotel in the city and next morning went out and had some passport photos taken. He had shaved off his grey moustache; he looked younger, though perhaps not young enough to have been born as late as 1934. That was a risk he had to take.

He made certain purchases in a stationery store, then went back to the hotel and put one of the photos in the British passport. He had seen the ASIO experts working on forged passports; he used the right gum, the right finishing off of the photo. Then he went uptown and bought an economy air ticket to Munich via Singapore. He had travelled first class all his life, but this was the first step in the life of Alexander Skelly.

That night he walked down to the river. He ripped up his own passport and the Australian and United States passports he had taken from Uritzsky's briefcase and threw the pieces out into the stream. Then he went back to the hotel and slept his last sleep on Australian soil. He dreamed again of

Venetia, but she was still looking over his shoulder, still with that manic look of lust on her face.

Twenty-four hours after leaving Perth he landed in Munich as Alexander Skelly, British sales representative.

3

'Why did you choose to go to Germany?' said Alice.

'I couldn't go to England, my first choice – I'd have been at home there. But I was afraid of being recognized. I thought of the United States, somewhere in New England, but I don't think I'd have been comfortable there – I'm not American-minded. And the Vietnam War was hotting up – I didn't want to take sides, even in my own mind. I wanted to put all that behind me. It was Germany or France, and I chose Germany. It has a beautiful countryside and I've always been interested in German history and music and literature.'

'I've never read a German book,' said Venetia. She said it only for something to say; she had been quiet all during Walter's story, filling in in her own mind the bits she knew he had left out about herself and John Leeds. 'You've been there all this time?'

'Off and on.' Walter smiled to himself. 'I settled in a small town in the Black Forest, but I made trips.'

'How did you live?' said Alice, practical about day-to-day matters. 'You had that fifteen thousand pounds, but that didn't last you all this time. Germany is expensive, isn't it?'

'Ah, Alice, you haven't changed. Do you still count the pennies?'

Alice nodded, smiling. She's already accepted him back, thought Venetia. She's asking questions, but she's already forgiven him.

'You never lose the habit, Walter, not when you've had to count 'em when you're young.'

'I suppose so.' Perhaps it had something to do with their

common age: he felt more comfortable with Alice than with Venetia. But then he had never been in love with Alice, never lost her to his best friend. 'I invested most of the money on the Frankfurt stock exchange. It didn't take me long to learn which were the good stocks and which were the *zweifelhaft* ones. I may have been a lawyer and a judge, but I came from the oldest stockbroking family in the country. The German economy was booming along then. I did all right,' he said, as matter-of-fact as Alice. Then he added, 'I also got a small stipend I'd rather have forgone.'

'What was that?' said Venetia, sensing that the intervening years had not been as empty as she had thought.

Walter hesitated; but he wanted to rid himself of all his secrets. 'The British, MI6, picked me up after six months. I made the mistake of going to Berlin and an old acquaintance from the SIS recognized me. He'd come out to Melbourne to advise me when I took over ASIO – he was in Berlin as their chief control. You understand what that is?'

'I've read spy stories,' said Alice.

'It was a chance in a million. He sat down opposite me in a pavement café on the Kurfürstendamm, that's Berlin's main street. He was the sort of Englishman who's always playing a part. I remember his first words were, "Sir Walter Springfellow, I presume?" They knew there was some mystery about my disappearance. He told me ASIO and SIS and the CIA –'

'All those initials,' said Alice. 'Isn't there some spy lot that has just a plain simple name?'

'Mossad, the Israelis. The best of them all.' He spoke with a professional's knowledge.

'Go on,' said Venetia, not in the least interested in spy organizations, only interested in this man sitting beside her who had come so unexpectedly (and unwanted? She pushed the thought aside) back into her life. When he had been head of ASIO she had never been able to take seriously, though her intelligence told her she was wrong, that her husband was a spy. She caught a glimpse now that that was what he had

310

become, a professional in espionage. 'What did this English-man want?'

'Further blackmail – in the nicest possible way, of course. They were looking for someone new to control their agents in the Communist bloc, someone who understood how things worked. Their man had just been exposed. He never asked me about what happened to Uritzsky – he was very gentlemanly about that – I told you, he was the sort of Englishman who was always playing a part. But I think they had guessed I'd – *disposed* of him somehow. I think, from remarks he dropped, they also knew about your – your affairs.'

'You mean they spied on me? The British or ASIO or whoever?' She was shocked. Alice looked ready to do battle.

'ASIO, probably. They'd have been investigating my disappearance. Anyhow, the Englishman said he would keep my secret, whatever it was, if I went to work for MI6. My true identity would be kept secret from all but the top men in the SIS. The Secret Intelligence Service,' he explained to Alice, when he saw her exasperation at more initials.

'So that's what you've been doing all this time?' said Venetia. 'Still spying?'

'Up till four years ago, when they allowed me to retire. They paid me a stipend – it wasn't much, but it was enough – and expenses. I moved from the Black Forest to Gebirge, near the East German border. That was frustrating – it was so close to Bayreuth and the Wagner festival, but I could never go, for fear of being recognized by someone from Australia. I'd grown this beard by then, but I didn't feel safe, not after I'd been recognized in Berlin. I used to go over into East Germany and Czechoslovakia and Hungary to check my agents, then go to the opera and concerts there. It is all very good, especially in East Germany,' he added, as if he thought they might think singing and music inevitably suffered because of ideology.

'Did MI6 ever say if they'd told ASIO about you?'

He shook his head. 'They never told me and I never asked. I followed your career. I got the English papers regularly and they ran occasional pieces on you, especially after Mrs Thatcher came to power – the English had never recognized women up till then, except their queens. Somehow, I felt proud of you. It made what I was doing seem mean and small.'

'Spying *is* mean and small,' said Alice, who had read only the sleazier spy novels.

'I didn't think that twenty years ago,' said Walter defensively. 'But mean and small, it's necessary. The world doesn't run according to the Ten Commandments.' He looked at Venetia. 'I'm sure they don't apply in the business world. Not from what I've been reading.'

He was still stiff and proper about certain things; but Venetia could not hold it against him. 'When did you learn about Emma's murder?'

'Last November, when it happened.'

'That was in the English papers?'

'I told you – they're only interested in the sensational stuff from Australia. Sport and scandal and our stupidities. I almost came home then, but I fell ill.' He was silent a moment, covering the pause by sipping the cold tea in his cup. 'I was worried about the scandal, too. Coming back from the dead, turning out to be the murderer and not the victim.'

'Aren't you worried now?'

'Only for Justine's sake. And yours. They can't do much to me now. I'm dying,' he said, his voice dropping. He looked neither for pity nor for love: he knew it was too late for those. 'I have terminal cancer.'

'Oh God!' Venetia suddenly broke. She came out of her chair, almost fell on her knees beside him and grabbed at his hand. 'Oh, my darling!'

He kissed the top of her head. 'I'm resigned to it. I didn't mean to tell you, it slipped out. I've had no one to confide in for so long . . .'

'There's nothing they can do?'

He shook his head. 'I've been to the best specialists. I have three months at the most. I'm sorry – I honestly didn't come home to be nursed. I came home because I wanted to see my daughter before . . .' His voice trailed off.

Venetia knew that what she felt was pity, not love; but it was an aching pity and that was a form of love. 'You'll stay here – we'll look after you. We shan't tell anyone you've come back –'

'We'll have to tell Edwin and Ruth,' said Alice.

'Well, yes, them, of course. But no one else.'

'I have to see Justine,' said Walter, still holding Venetia's hand. 'That was the whole point of coming home. I'll go to the court tomorrow –'

'That would be too dangerous –'

'No, I shan't go with you. I'll sit by myself – no one will recognize me . . . You didn't, did you, not at first?'

'Not at first.' She pressed his hand again, still on her knees in front of him. 'You've changed.'

'We all have, I hope,' he said. 'But too late. Too late.'

4

The reunion with Edwin and Ruth was emotional but restrained. Both of them were shocked to the core: the presumed dead, especially murderers, are not everyday returnees to Mosman. But he was *family*, and it never entered Edwin's and Ruth's heads that they should call the police. Especially when they learned he had come home to die.

Edwin drove him to the Darlinghurst courthouse the next morning, the second day of Justine's trial. 'I'll drop you a block or two from Taylor Square,' said Edwin. 'I shan't come into court with you. I'm afraid, from what I read in this morning's papers, it could turn into a circus. A Roman one.'

'They're throwing her to the lions?'

313

'It looks that way. Venetia has got the best man, Joe Albemarle – you wouldn't know him, he's come along since you went away – but he has a tough task on his hands.'

'Who do *you* think killed Emma?'

'I don't know, Walter. Someone she knew, obviously – she let the murderer in herself to her flat. She made enemies, Walter. She was always difficult, but after you left . . .' He looked sideways at his brother while they were pulled up at traffic lights. 'She had an – an unhealthy regard for you, you know.'

'I know. It always worried me. Did relations between her and Venetia ever improve?'

'They got worse, if anything. And with Justine, too. That's part of the evidence against Justine. I'm afraid you're not going to enjoy today in court.'

Walter took his place in the queue outside Court No. 5 and managed to get a seat in the second row of the public gallery. Venetia and Alice were already in their seats, which one of the court officials had reserved for them. Walter glanced at them and they returned his look, but neither of them nodded or gave any other hint that they knew him.

In the row behind Walter sat Chilla Dural and Jerry Killeen. It had been the latter who had suggested they should come to the court and see what was happening – 'It's only ten minutes' walk, Chilla. We'll go over and see how they treat a silvertail in the dock. How'd they treat you?'

'Fucking terrible,' said Dural without rancour. 'But I was never a silvertail.'

He had never been anti the silvertails. Like most professional crims, he had no interest in class warfare. You stole from the rich only because they were the ones who had it, not because they were silvertails and you had to hate them as a matter of course. Heinie Odets had been rich and he sure as hell had never hated Heinie.

Dural saw the look pass between the grey-haired man in the row in front of him and the two Springfellow women. He could see the man only in profile: the strong straight nose,

314

the short white beard, the steel-rimmed glasses. A vague memory stirred, but it meant nothing. The old bloke was probably a neighbour of the Springfellows, someone he had caught a glimpse of when he had been casing the Mosman lay-out. He turned his gaze back to the business in the court.

Walter Springfellow felt something leap in his chest when Justine came up through the trapdoor into the dock. Despite her wan look, she was more beautiful than he had expected; she had been beautiful enough in her photo, but he knew too well how the camera could lie. She was dressed in a simple dark dress and wore no jewellery: an ex-judge, he knew that would have been the recommendation of her lawyer. She wore make-up, but very little. She glanced at Venetia and Alice, gave them a small smile, then turned towards the Bench and sat down. When the jury filed in she rose politely like a well-trained schoolgirl.

Walter could feel himself fluttering inside. This was his daughter! There was the memory of the fierce row the Friday night before he had disappeared; he had accused Venetia of carrying another man's child. For years he had suffered the cancerous thought that the girl had been John Leeds's child; it had eaten away at him as much as the carcinoma that was now killing him. Yet he looked across at her now and knew she had to be his daughter. He suddenly realized he felt as he had felt when Venetia had first told him she was pregnant: he *wanted* to be a father. He had once been the law, or represented it, and the law recognized blood tests. But now he felt only animal instinct: he knew his own young.

The second day of the trial was given up to forensic evidence. First, there was a video film of the Emma Springfellow flat; it seemed the jury had asked for that. There had been nothing like this in Walter's day on the Bench; he found his interest in the proceedings sharpening. All the old trappings were there: he looked up at Gilligan J. and felt the red robe round his own shoulders. But he was not sitting as the judge in this case; he was a silent defence counsel.

315

Constable Jason James went into the box and Wellbeck led him through the ballistics evidence. The young officer knew his subject and had rehearsed what he had to say; Walter had seen it all before. The police were sure of their charges, they were certain of the accused's guilt.

Wellbeck finished with James and Albemarle rose to begin his questioning. The big man never just *stood up*; he came to his feet in a sort of slow levitation, a series of almost imperceptible pauses. One sensed that if this building collapsed in an earthquake, he would slowly rise, while everyone else fled, and address the roof as it fell in. He would always have the last word.

Walter recognized the type. He was the product of a thousand Law Society dinners and a thousand litres of claret, of after-dinner speeches laced with port and carefully rehearsed ad lib wit. He was a man's man in the social sense, too big and fat for the rugby club, too snobbish for the corner pub; he would have a wife somewhere left to run her own life on a generous allowance.

'Constable James – you have mentioned the weapon, Exhibit B3, the Walther PPK .380, and the ammunition magazine and the bullets found in the body of the deceased. You have mentioned all those, am I right?'

'Yes, sir.'

'You didn't mention a silencer, but I noticed there is threading on the Walther for the fitting of such a device.'

'No silencer was ever found, sir. We don't know if one was used.'

'No, perhaps not.' Albemarle looked down at his papers, though Walter guessed it was only a ploy. The barrister had had all his thoughts and words well sorted out before he had got to his feet. He looked up as if a sudden thought had just struck him. 'Haven't you missed something, Constable?'

James looked puzzled, exactly as Clements had yesterday. 'No, sir, I don't think so.'

'You checked the lands and grooves on the bullets against

those in the pistol and found they matched. You went to all that trouble, but you still don't know what you missed?'

'I'm not sure what you're getting at, sir –'

'Constable James, where are the shells? Doesn't a Walther PPK .380 eject shells when it is fired?'

'Yes, sir.'

'Then where are they?'

'As far as I know, none were found at the scene of the crime.'

'Did you ask if any had been?'

'Yes, sir.'

'If no shells were found, wouldn't that suggest to you that the murderer picked them up and took them with him?'

'Possibly. I'm not sure why he would do that –'

'It is possible, Constable, to find a partial fingerprint on an ejected shell. I once prosecuted a case along those lines –'

'Objection!' gritted Wellbeck, seeing where this was leading.

'Let us confine ourselves to this case, Mr Albemarle. It may be long enough without a recitation of your distinguished career.'

'You under-estimate my modesty, Your Honour. But as you wish . . . Constable, how many instances have you known of a murderer gathering up the shells and taking them with him?'

'I can't recall exactly – I suppose two or three –'

'Would you recall their names?'

'Objection!'

'Mr Albemarle, please –'

Albemarle bowed to the Bench, then turned again to the witness. 'I suggest to you, Constable James, that the murderer in this case did indeed pick up the shells and take them with him, because he was experienced enough to know that he might have put a fingerprint on them when he was loading the magazine. I put it to you, and I will bring evidence for that fact, that my client is an absolute novice in the handling of guns and such attention to detail would never enter her pretty head.'

James kept his own pretty head. 'I don't know about that, sir. My task is to give evidence on technical facts, not on hypotheses.'

'True, Constable, true. But where would justice be without hypothesis?' He glanced up at the judge, who gave him a dry smile. 'All I am saying is –' He had turned to face the jury, though his gaze seemed to be on the window high above their heads. 'All I am saying is that an amateur, an absolute rank amateur like my client, would not know enough about guns to worry, or even think, about collecting the shells after the gun had been fired. This murder, I suggest, was committed by a professional. Would you agree with that hypothesis, Constable?'

Malone, sitting in the police box, looked idly back at the public gallery. He saw the white-bearded man in the steel-rimmed glasses, but took no notice of him. Then he saw Chilla Dural sitting in the row behind; beside him was the little bloke who lived in the same rooming house. Dural was smiling at Malone and shaking his head and Malone got the message. He was a professional, or had been, and he knew the procedure. You didn't pick up bloody hot shells to make sure your fingerprints weren't still on them. You made sure there were no prints *before* you fired the gun.

Walter Springfellow had listened to Albemarle's argument and with every word his heart had sunk further. He recognized a hopeless case. Albemarle didn't believe in what he had been saying; he was clutching at straw ideas. Justine, it seemed, was doomed.

Malone sat up in the police box as Andy Graham pushed his way through the crowded gallery and came towards him. The young detective leaned close to him and whispered, 'There's a Constable Sobers outside. He says he's found the silencer.'

318

TWELVE

1

'It was down in the Gardens, Inspector,' said Gary Sobers. 'We missed it the first time – it hadn't been thrown away near where we found the gun. A gardener found it this morning under a pile of mulch. He called the station and Sergeant Greenup told me to bring it up to you right away.'

Malone looked at the metal cylinder in the narrow plastic envelope. 'Was it in the plastic when you found it?'

'Yes, sir.'

'If she bought that, and it doesn't look like a home-made job, it would be in the plastic bag.' Clements took the envelope and opened it, but did not remove the silencer. 'No, it's not home-made. It's a Gold Spot, the Aussie make. It'd fit the Walther.'

The three policemen were outside the courthouse. Out of the corner of his eye Malone could see the TV cameramen at the gates; one of them had raised his shoulder-borne camera and was aiming it at them. Malone moved round so that what he and the other two were discussing was hidden from the inquisitive eye of the camera.

'Where would she have got it? They're illegal here in New South Wales. I doubt if Justine would have known where to buy it under the counter.'

'You can buy them over the counter in South Australia,' said Clements. 'Evidently the South Australians see no harm in murder, so long as it doesn't wake anyone.'

'Well, first we have to see if there are any prints on it. Then

319

we'll check if it fits the Walther. Don Cheshire is giving evidence today – we'll hold on to it and pass it over to him. Then Ballistics can have a look at it, see if it fits the Walther.'

Sobers looked disappointed. 'You won't be wanting me any further then, Inspector?'

Malone grinned sympathetically. 'Don't worry, Gary, your day will come. If ever you apply to come over to plainclothes, let me know. I'll give you a recommendation.'

Sobers went off, satisfied, and Clements looked after him. 'Were we ever as young and keen as that?'

'Sure,' said Malone. 'In another life.'

He looked at the silencer in the plastic envelope, wondering if it would prove to be another nail to pin Justine to the wall. Then he went looking for Sergeant Cheshire. On the way he passed Chilla Dural and Jerry Killeen coming out of the court, which had risen for the lunch adjournment.

'Hello, Chilla. I thought you'd have had enough of courts.'

'Just looking, Inspector.'

'Seeing how the other half lives,' said Jerry Killeen. 'The public seats are full of silvertails. I never seen so many.'

'Excuse me,' said Walter Springfellow, and Malone and the other two men stood aside to let him pass as he came out of the court entrance.

Dural looked after him. 'He'd be one.'

Malone didn't look after the white-bearded man, just grinned at Dural and Killeen. 'They're everywhere in Sydney now. Everybody's rich but thee and me. Ask Sergeant Clements about them – he's an authority on them.'

'Good luck to 'em,' said Dural.

'Bugger 'em,' said Jerry Killeen.

After lunch on that second day Justine did not have a good day in court. The evidence continued to pile up against her, despite Albemarle's efforts to divert the prosecution's line. Malone went home convinced that Justine had no real hope of being acquitted.

320

The phone rang that evening at Randwick. Lisa went out to answer it and Malone remained in the living-room, sprawled on the couch. The children had gone to bed and he was looking at *LA Law*, wondering at the lifestyles and why he hadn't gone to university and become a lawyer. Lisa came back. 'It's the Commissioner.'

Malone closed his eyes for a moment: Arnie Becker and Michael Kuzak and the others didn't know what trouble was. Then he opened his eyes and looked up at Lisa. 'How did he sound?'

'Quiet. But I don't know him, really. Maybe he's always quiet.'

Malone got up and went out to the hallway. 'Yes, sir?'

'Scobie, I'm sorry to call you at home. I'm ringing from my office. I've just had a session with Deputy Commissioner Zanuch. He tells me things didn't go well today for Miss Springfellow.' The Commissioner's line would never be tapped, but he sounded to Malone as if he feared it might be. 'Does it look bad?'

'I'm afraid so, sir. The Crown start producing Emma's diaries tomorrow. Things will get worse. There are entries about Justine threatening her, all that . . .' He could offer John Leeds no hope for the acquittal of his (possible) daughter. 'What did Mr Zanuch have to say?'

'When it's all over, he wants to announce a commendation for you and Sergeant Clements.'

'Oh Christ,' said Malone softly.

There was silence for a moment, then Leeds said, 'How is Lady Springfellow taking it?'

'It's hard to tell. Bravely, I think would be the word.'

'Yes, I think that would describe her.'

'How are you taking it?'

There was a sound at the other end of the line: it might have been a clearing of the throat or a sour chuckle. 'I can't think of a word. Good-night, Scobie. I'm sorry I called.'

The phone went dead, but Malone continued to hold it in his hand, trying to picture the stricken man at the other end of the line. Then he hung up. There was nothing he could do for the Commissioner or, for that matter, for Justine.

He went back into the living-room. Lisa had turned off the television and was waiting for him. 'He's never done that before.'

'No.'

'Why?'

He sat down beside her on the couch, put his arm round her. 'I shouldn't be telling you this.'

She waited, knowing he wanted to tell it.

'The Commissioner isn't sure he's not Justine Spring-fellow's father.' He went on to tell her everything about John Leeds and Venetia. It would help no one but himself, but telling her seemed to lighten the load. Some of us feed on secrets, hiding them like candy bars in a cupboard, but they only made him sick. He told the nurse everything.

She, with an attempt at Dutch practicality, said, 'There's nothing you can do, so try and forget it.'

'That's the bugger of it – I can't. You couldn't, either.'

'No,' she admitted. 'But I'd be seeing the woman's side. The Commissioner isn't going to suffer as much as Venetia.'

Late next morning Sergeant Cheshire came to the court-house and sent in word that he wanted to see Inspector Malone. The latter came out. 'Come up with anything, Don?'

'G'day, Scobie. We went okay yesterday, don't you reckon? That bastard Albemarle gave me a pain, though. All lawyers do. Yeah, I come up with something.' He held out the silencer in the plastic envelope. 'The plastic protected it. There's a partial print on it, not much, as if he held it by his fingertips.'

'*He?*'

'I couldn't swear to it, but it looks like it could be a male's print. It ain't Justine's, definitely.'

Clements had followed Malone out of the courtroom. He took the silencer, holding it carefully, as if a loaded pistol were attached to it. 'If her prints aren't on it, then I don't think we need to mention this, do we?'

322

Malone could read what was in Clements's mind: he wanted nothing that would weaken the case against Justine, no contradictory evidence. He would not be the first cop who didn't want his convictions discouraged.

'If that's the way you want it,' said Cheshire. 'I'm not gunna say anything. I've never seen the silencer.'

Malone said quietly, 'I don't think that's the way we want it at all. When your fellers went through Emma's flat, how many prints did you come up with?'

'There were six different ones. I give all that information to Russ.' Cheshire was rough and bluff, but he had worked for years in a Department where men rubbed up against each other every day; he was sensitive to friction, if to very little else. He sensed now that Malone and Clements were at odds, and he was surprised: he knew their reputation in the Department as a team.

'What were they? Male or female?'

'Three of them I put down as male. One of them was the doorkeeper's, the one on the bedroom door, so you can cross him off the list. The other two belonged to two different men. One set was on the drinking glass and the other, a single print, was on the bedside table, if I remember right.'

Too late Malone saw his mistake: he had forgotten John Leeds's print on the drinking glass. But he couldn't turn back now. 'Try the one on the bedside table, see if it matches this one on the silencer.'

'I'll call you tomorrow. I gotta give evidence at two other courts today.'

When Cheshire had gone, Malone said to Clements, 'I'm not out to ruin the case against Justine. But . . .'

'I guess you're right,' said Clements reluctantly. 'I'm still sure she did the job. But I've never yet had the wrong person convicted. I don't wanna spoil my record. But unless we get something conclusive from that other print . . .'

'I promise you. Nothing conclusive, we don't mention it.'

'Are you going to ask for the Walther so's we can check the fit of the silencer?'

'Not right away.' Malone knew he had to make some concession to Clements. 'As soon as we start asking for a second look at one of the exhibits, especially the gun, Albemarle is going to be suspicious. He'll start asking awkward questions.'

The third day of the trial was more presentation of evidence; Wellbeck pouring water on the stone. There were minutes of board meetings in which the bitter antagonism between Emma and Justine stood out; there were statements of share sales and purchases by both sides in the takeover battle. The papers were passed round the jury; one woman, a copious note-taker, took fifteen minutes to read her copy, as if she were being paid by the word. The forewoman, as if aware that her ship was slow in the water, whispered to the woman to hurry up, but the latter took no notice of her. Madame Forewoman began to look like Captain Bligh's sister: she was not accustomed to mutiny, she would deal with it once they got back to the jury room.

Boredom settled on the court. The judge began to nod; the spectators shifted restlessly; even Justine looked uninterested. But Billy Wellbeck was leaving nothing to chance: that was not his method.

Just before the lunch adjournment a court officer came in to whisper to Malone that he was wanted on the phone. Malone went out to the sheriff's office to take the call. It was Sergeant Cheshire.

'The print on the bedside table matches the one on the silencer. We got a problem, Scobie.'

'Yeah.' Malone said nothing for a moment; then: 'You'd go into the box and swear they match?'

'If I have to.' Cheshire knew how detectives, having worked to present a watertight case, hated to see cracks in the dam. 'They match, all right, and they ain't Justine's. What are you gunna do? Ask for an adjournment while you follow this up?'

'I can't, Don, not right away. Not till I've got something else to give the Crown Prosecutor besides the prints. If I go in now and say I'm a bit doubtful, Billy Wellbeck's not going to be too bloody happy.'

He thanked Cheshire for his work, hung up and then sent word in for Clements to come out and see him. The big man, as soon as he saw Malone's face, made the correct guess. He bit his lower lip and said, 'The prints match, right?'

Malone nodded. They were alone in the sheriff's office, but he knew the court officer would be back soon. 'Do you have to stay here for the rest of the day?'

'Wellbeck says he may call me again today. I dunno why, but he's not sticking to his usual continuity – he's all over the place in the way he's calling his witnesses. I think he's trying to keep Albemarle off balance.'

'Wellbeck told me this morning he thinks the trial will run another five or six days – he's going to pile on the evidence, the diaries, company papers, Christ knows what. We've got to move fast, if we're to check out those prints. I'll use Andy and get Greg Random to give me a couple of other blokes.'

'Do we tell Billy Wellbeck what's turned up?'

'No,' said Malone firmly. 'Where's the silencer? In your murder box?'

'No, it's in the bottom drawer of my desk. I was keeping it separate.'

'It's not separate any longer, Russ.'

'No, I know that.' Clements was morose; he had worked hard on this case and now it looked as if they might be back at square one. 'I wonder if Justine had a boyfriend who helped her?'

'I'm going to start looking for him now.'

As they went out of the office the sheriff, a middle-aged man, cheerful and hidebound, the only way to survive in a job where the everyday environment was the wreckage of lives, came in. 'G'day, Scobie, how's it going in Number Five? You look as if you've got it cut and dried.'

'Could be,' said Malone.

2

He went back to Homicide, got the silencer from Clements's desk and walked up to Police Centre. Ballistics was on the fifth level of the big new fortress-like complex, which looked as if the architect had been told to design something that would withstand a siege. All it did, Malone thought, was frighten the honest voters.

He checked in, then went up to the fifth level. Constable James met him and grinned as Malone, who had never been up here before, looked around him. 'Spacious, eh, Inspector?'

'I remember when we used to work out of cubby-holes.' But he didn't have time for social conversation; half a mile from here Billy Wellbeck was piling up the case against Justine. 'That's the silencer. Would it fit the Walther?'

'You don't have the piece?'

'No, I can't ask the court to release it, not yet.'

James looked innocent, but Malone remarked the un-spoken question in the young constable's eyes. You're learning, son, he thought. Nothing is as straight and simple as it seems, certainly not police work.

James examined the silencer. 'It'd fit, all right, but I don't know whether it's the one that was used on the murder piece. I'd need that Walther to be absolutely sure.'

'I'm not asking you to go into the box – not yet, anyway. I'm sure the Springfellow Walther and this go together. Could it have been bought here in Sydney?'

'Sure, if you knew where to go. You can buy anything in this town if you know where to go.' James gestured at the stacks of shoulder-high metal cabinets all around them, all of them with deep drawers in them. He pulled out a drawer about five feet wide; it was full of hand-guns, all labelled. 'Everything we have in these cabinets, or the rifles in those racks over there – they're all confiscated weapons, over seven thousand of them. As I say, you can buy anything you

326

want in this town. But you'd have to know where to go. And I don't think Miss Springfellow would know where to go, she didn't look the type. Can you see her in a gun-shop asking where she can buy a silencer, or bailing up someone in a coffee shop up the Cross and trying to buy one?'

'What about South Australia – Adelaide?'

'No problem there.'

'Would they keep a record of the sales?'

'I guess so. I can check – we have a good contact in Ballistics in Adelaide.'

'Check for me. And get a list of all gun-shops in Adelaide. Do you know any of the villains in Sydney who sell guns or silencers under the counter?'

'I don't, but Sergeant Binyan does. He knows *everyone*.' James grinned. 'Let's try him.'

Clarrie Binyan was in his office; he was the sergeant in charge of Ballistics. He was part-Aborigine, a product of the Police Boys' Club, a street fighter who had become a twenty-five-year veteran, who had started on the beat and some-times hankered for the good old days; he was safe from his hankering and so could afford it. He was overweight and had become lazy, but there was nothing he didn't know about guns and the crims of Sydney.

'How soon do you want the info, Scobie?'

'Yesterday,' said Malone. 'It's urgent, Clarrie. Give me the names of the six most likely villains who'd sell a stranger a silencer, and I'll have my blokes visit them.'

Binyan ran his hand through his thick greying curls; his black-brown eyes had a gleam of humour in them. 'Tell your blokes to treat 'em gentle. Some of these crims are mates of mine from the old days. I don't wanna ruin my contact with 'em – they come in handy when we're trying to trace things.'

'I'll have my blokes take them a box of chocolates and some flowers. Now can I have their names?'

'This must be bloody urgent. I thought you had everything wrapped up in the Springfellow case?'

'Just making sure, Clarrie, that's all. Now the names?'

327

Binyan scratched some names and addresses on a slip of paper and Malone grabbed it. As he left Binyan's office James was waiting for him. 'I've just remembered, Inspector. There was a faint scratch on the barrel of that Walther, a burring on the thread as if whoever used it had tried to force the silencer on it. Leave me the silencer. I'll try an endoscope on it and see if there's any corresponding mark inside.'

Malone handed him the silencer. 'Jason, when this is all over, I'll buy you lunch. Are you expensive?'

'I usually eat at McDonald's.'

'We'll go there,' said Malone, careful not to raise the youngster above his station.

He went back to Homicide. He called Andy Graham and two other detectives down to his desk. 'Work singly, take two names each – I want you back here no later than three o'clock. Treat 'em gently, but hint you'll get heavy if you have to. Tell 'em we're not looking for a professional hit man – at least I don't think we are. Just ask them if anyone bought a Gold Spot silencer from them in the month of October or the first week in November last year and if he asked them to do some thread-work on the barrel of a Walther PPK .380.'

'Do we tell 'em Clarrie Binyan sent us?' said Andy Graham.

Malone grinned. 'Why not? That'll probably make it legitimate.'

'Right,' said Graham and led the charge out of the office.

The three of them were back before three o'clock. Malone, in the meantime, had got out his notes and the running sheet on the Emma Springfellow murder, had gone back over everything to see what he and Clements had missed in their investigation. Clements had been particularly thorough: he seemed to have questioned everyone who would have been even remotely connected with Justine. Most of them, unable to believe that Justine would commit murder, had been totally nonplussed by the questioning; one or two, including Michael Broad, had been hostile in their defence of Justine. Several others, who had obviously felt the sting of the Springfellow women, had been slyly malicious in their answers; one of them had been Roger Dircks. Yet as Malone laid down his notes and the running sheet he was convinced they had missed nothing. Then Andy Graham came back, followed a few minutes later by the other two detectives, Truach and Kagal.

'Nothing,' said Graham. Malone was not sure whether he sounded disappointed or not. Then he added, 'If this was meant to save Justine, it isn't going to work.'

'I'm not interested in saving Justine,' Malone snapped; but he knew in his heart that he was. 'I just don't want us out on a limb when the appeal comes up. And you can bet your bottom dollar Albemarle will appeal if the case goes against her.'

Then Truach and Kagal came in. 'I got nothing,' said Kagal, a good-looking young man who had come into plainclothes at the same time as Graham, who had the same enthusiasm but managed to control it more than Graham. 'I think they were playing square. As soon's I mentioned Clarrie Binyan, they opened up. But my two guys knew nothing.'

Truach was older than the other two, a senior constable who would plod his way up the promotion ladder. 'I drew a blank with the first guy. But the second, Joe Koster, he lives up the Cross, he remembers a guy coming to him some time last October, wanting to buy a silencer.'

'Why didn't Koster sell him one?'

'He said he didn't trust the guy. I asked for a description, but all he could remember was that he was tallish and wore dark glasses and a hat. If someone came to me dressed like that, I'd be suspicious, too. Koster was frank, he thought the guy might be an undercover man we'd planted. He seemed hurt we'd stoop to something underhand like that. You remember, we were having a crack-down on guns about then – we had that gun amnesty for anyone with an unlicensed weapon.'

'What did Koster tell him?'

'He said he didn't have any silencers in stock, but if the guy wanted to, he could go to Adelaide and buy one across the counter.'

'Righto,' said Malone, acting swiftly; whatever decisions he made in the next few days, they had to be either totally wrong or totally right. At least, when it was all over, no one would be able to say he hadn't tried. 'Here's a list of gun-shops in Adelaide. When you get there, check in with Police Headquarters and tell 'em what you're after. They may be able to help. I'll get Greg Random to authorize your travel. Go home, pack an overnight bag and be back here to pick up your ticket and catch whatever plane we can get you on tonight.'

Truach went off, followed by Kagal, and Malone looked at the obviously disappointed Graham. 'You wondering why I'm not sending you?'

'Well, I *have* been on the case since the jump –'

'And you're no longer objective about it, Andy. You're convinced Justine did the murder and you don't want all your work wasted. You may be right. But if we've fouled up somewhere and the case goes to appeal, you aren't going to be the one to carry the can. I'll be the bunny. You'd have got the trip to Adelaide if you'd been open-minded that someone else may be involved in this. But you're not.'

But even as he ticked off Andy Graham, he could taste hypocrisy on his tongue. If he himself was open-minded, the entrance was only through a revolving door. Then his phone rang.

It was Constable James. 'I used the endoscope on the silencer. There's a burring on the thread. I can't guarantee it matches that on the Walther barrel, not without having another look at the gun. But I'd like to take a bet on it.'

'Good, Jason. Send over the silencer. I'll be back to you when I need you. You may have to go back into the box.'

'Does this mean Justine mightn't have done it?' It was a hesitant question.

'Have you fallen for a pretty face?'

'Well, no-o . . .'

Malone hung up, smiling sourly. Justine, unknowingly, was gathering backers; but she was a long way from being out of the woods. He looked at Graham, who, so far, seemed to have no doubts about her.

'You wouldn't fall for a pretty face, would you?'

'No,' said Graham doggedly. 'We've worked our guts out on this one. I don't think we've made any mistakes –'

'Our one mistake might be the big one. Sending her to gaol when she didn't commit the murder.'

Truach got back from Adelaide the following afternoon. He rang Malone from Adelaide airport and the latter stayed at Homicide to wait for him. Clements was with him, as morose as yesterday, feeling his case slipping away from him.

Truach came in, unhurried, unexcited, phlegmatic as an old bloodhound familiar with old scents. He sat down opposite Malone and said flatly, 'Bingo.'

'Good,' said Malone, containing his impatience. 'What's the prize?'

'The Adelaide fellers were on our side right from the jump. They sent me to several dealers – the first four, I drew nothing. Then the fifth guy came up with what we wanted.' He paused and lit a cigarette. 'I been dying for a smoke. I couldn't smoke on the plane and then, bugger me, I copped a taxi driver who wouldn't allow smoking in his cab.'

'If you don't get a move on,' said Malone, 'you're going to find *this* is a no-smoking zone.'

Truach grinned, nodded and stubbed out the cigarette on the floor. 'This guy has a small gun-shop. I've got his name if we have to bring him over to give evidence, though he wasn't too happy when I suggested it. You know what they're like, gun dealers.'

'Yes,' said Malone, still patient but only just.

'Anyhow, he said yeah, he'd had a guy come in last October to buy a silencer. He sold him a Gold Spot. Then the guy produced this Walther, a PPK .380, and asked the dealer to fit the silencer to it.'

331

'The dealer asked no questions? No registration of the gun?'

'He was covering up, Scobie. I didn't press him on it, I figured that was something for the Adelaide police. All we wanted was information.'

'Fair enough. Did he ask the cove why he wanted the silencer?'

'Yeah. The guy gave the name of –' Truach looked at his notes. 'Yeah, here it is. Roger Hart. He said the gun and the silencer were needed for a TV fillum they were shooting and they needed it in a hurry, something about the gun not being in the original script.'

'Did the dealer fit the silencer?'

'Yeah. The guy went away while it was done, then come back and paid cash.'

'Any description of him?'

'Tallish, wore a hat and dark glasses, the sort that get darker when you go out in the sunlight. It fits the description of the feller here in Sydney.'

'Did he buy any ammunition?'

'Only a box of blanks – he said that was all they needed for the TV fillum. He could have bought live ammo at another gun-shop.'

Malone looked at Clements. 'At best, it looks like Justine had an accomplice.'

'And at worst?'

'The worst for us? It looks like this cove did it on his own.'

'You got a suspect?'

'Who do you think? Who do we know who'd know something about making TV films?'

'Can I go now?' said Truach. 'I'm dying for a smoke.'

'Go and get lung cancer,' said Malone, but he was smiling. 'Thanks, Phil. Nice work.'

When Truach, already lighting a cigarette, had gone, Malone looked at his watch. 'What time do TV executives knock off?'

'Who cares?' said Clements. 'If he's not at the studio, we'll go to his home.'

'This may mean upsetting the whole bloody apple-cart. You don't mind?'

'I'd be a lying bastard if I said I didn't mind – I thought we had all this sewn up. But like I said, I've never sent the wrong person to gaol yet.'

They drove out to Channel 15 through a clear autumn day, the air sparkling almost as if it were spring. The jacaranda trees were still thick, the green fronds only just streaked with brown needles. As Clements turned the Holden into the parking lot, Malone saw some of the crew and cast of *Sydney Beat* coming out to get into their cars. They were quiet and looked depressed, as if they had just filmed an episode in which the heroes had been beaten to a pulp.

Debby, the assistant floor manager, was about to get into her battered old Honda Civic when Malone got out of the police car right beside her.

'G'day, Debby. How are the dynamics today?'

'Full of shit.' Then she recognized him; he noticed now that her eyes were full of tears. 'Oh, hello, Scobie. We've all just been fired. They're stopping production. The ratings are lousy. But . . .'

'Tough luck.' He couldn't crow, not over someone who had just lost her job. 'Try to get into the soaps. That's what everyone watches. Misery is the recipe.'

'Oh, you got no idea how fucking miserable I am!'

Then he found himself in the parking lot of Channel 15 holding a young foul-mouthed girl while she cried her heart out against his shirt and bawled obscenities for which, in his more strait-laced days, he'd have booked her. Clements stood in the background, grinning with delight. He had hated *Sydney Beat* as much as Malone.

Malone detached himself from Debby. 'Who did the firing? Mr Dircks?'

'No, it came from the fucking Springfellow office – they own us, you know.' She dried her eyes on the sleeve of her

333

bulky sweater, hitched up her jeans. She had dreamed of being another Gillian Armstrong or even a Lina Wertmüller, but some bastard had just removed all the bottom rungs of the ladder. 'What are you doing here, anyway?'

'Getting my own back,' said Malone; then grinned. 'No, it's just public relations.'

He and Clements went on into the administration building, to the receptionist sitting beneath the big pink-and-grey logo.

'Oh, Inspector Malone, you're not back for *Sydney Beat*, are you?'

'I'm told we're a little late for that. Can we see Mr Dircks?'

The girl looked doubtful. 'I gather he's not seeing anyone right now. He's leaving, you know.'

'No, I didn't know. Where's he going?'

The girl shrugged. 'I only work here. Nobody tells me anything.'

'Where's his office? Still on the same floor? Thanks, Sally.'

'Inspector, you can't –!'

But Malone and Clements were already on their way up to the first floor. They strode down the long corridor past the big portraits of stars who were no longer stars; *Sydney Beat* would be off the walls tomorrow, flops had to be erased from memory as quickly as possible. The Singapore Chinese secretary was at her desk, still minding the gates, her sword already half out of its scabbard as soon as she recognized Malone.

'Mr Dircks is not seeing anyone –'

'Wrong, Miss Wong. He's seeing us. Excuse me, please.' She stood up in front of him, but he took her gently by the elbows and lifted her aside. 'I admire your sense of duty, love, but you're in the way.'

All at once she seemed to sense that this intrusion was something serious. 'He'll kill me for letting you go in –'

'I don't think he's going to be around much longer,' said Malone. 'You'll be safe.'

He and Clements stepped round her, opened the door behind her and went into the pink-and-grey executive office. Roger Dircks, looking not at all pink but only grey, was standing at his desk shoving papers into his briefcases. On the floor beside the desk were two large cartons crammed with books, framed prints and a brass desk lamp. It looked as if Dircks, before he fled, was taking looter's privileges. Malone had heard the gossip on the studio floor that it was the custom at top level in the television industry, except at the ABC, where there was nothing to loot.

'Going somewhere, Mr Dircks?'

'Christ Almighty, how did you get in here? Rose, what the hell –?'

'Don't blame her,' said Clements, closing the door. 'She tried to stop us.'

'What the hell do you want? I've got enough to fucking worry about –'

'First,' said Malone, 'I'd better give you the usual warning. You've heard it often enough in *Sydney Beat*, though your actors always seemed to get it wrong. Anything you may say, et cetera . . .'

Dircks's small mouth fell open. 'Anything I may say? Christ, what is this?'

'Mr Dircks, did you go to Adelaide last October?'

'How the fuck do I know? You'd have to ask Rose to look up my diary.' Dircks was in shirt-sleeves, his tie off; he looked unstarched, wilted. With his anger he had regained some colour in his face, he was pink and grey again. 'What is this, for Chrissakes? I got all the bad news I can handle, then you come busting in here –'

'Last October, Mr Dircks – did you go to Adelaide and purchase a silencer for a gun at a dealer's named –' Malone named the Adelaide gun dealer.

Dircks shook his head in wonder. 'Why would I want to do that?'

'You told the dealer you wanted it for a TV film you were shooting.'

'You're crazy, man. We've never shot anything in Adelaide – Christ, *nobody* shoots anything in Adelaide. It's a cemetery.' There was only one city in Australia, right here where he worked and lived; he was not honorary television adviser to the Sydney Chamber of Commerce for nothing. 'The only time I go there is every three months for a board meeting at our network station there. Yeah, I remember – I did go to Adelaide in October, the last week of October. It was a special meeting, it had to do with what was going to happen after the stock market crash and the takeover bid. I spent the whole of my time with the local executives. They were worried about their jobs. I spent all my time reassuring them.' He made a noise that sounded like an attempt at a laugh, but which got caught in his throat. 'Jesus!'

'Have you someone from here who can vouch for that?'

'Not from here, but from head office. Michael Broad. He wasn't with us all the time – he was looking at some of the other Springfellow interests over there. Springfellow owns a couple of vineyards up in the Barossa Valley.'

'Does he usually go with you to the quarterly meetings of the network?'

'Never. He's never concerned himself with the network – not up till now.' There was no mistaking the bitterness in his voice. 'He's just fired me.'

Malone contained his surprise. 'Who usually went with you to Adelaide?'

'Miss Springfellow, Justine. But Michael stepped in for that trip – Justine had that family takeover bid on her hands. Why, are you suggesting *he* bought a silencer?' Dircks was not big enough for this job he had held, but he was not unintelligent. He had got as far as he had on his wits and now, all at once, they came back to full spark. 'Has this got something to do with Justine's trial?'

It had dawned on Malone that they had come to arrest the wrong man. He had been, subconsciously, so intent on getting Justine off the hook that he had lunged for the first alternative suspect. It was sloppy police work and he knew it.

'Can you remember the date you went to Adelaide?'

Dircks was suddenly more helpful. He dipped into one of the briefcases, came up with a diary. 'Yeah, here it is. We flew over on the seven-thirty flight on October 29, a Thursday, and we stayed overnight. Michael was with me.'

Then Clements said, 'Mr Dircks, do you wear a hat?'

'A hat?' Dircks touched his thick grey pelt. It was obvious from the smooth cut of it that he spent money on it, was proud of it, a man in his fifties with not a hint of a bald patch. 'No, never. Well, yes, when I'm out on my boat or playing golf I wear an old terry-towelling job, to keep the sun off. I have to watch out for sun cancers.' He pointed to his pink complexion.

'Does Mr Broad wear a hat?'

'No. I think he likes showing off that bald skull of his – no, wait a minute. He had a hat in Adelaide! I saw him going out of the hotel the second morning wearing one, a tweed one, you know, like the rah-rah boys wear to rugby matches.' Another one with prejudices, Malone thought irrelevantly. 'I thought it a bit peculiar, you know, a winter one, when it was so warm over there –'

'Did you mention it to him?'

'Yeah, I did, but he just ignored me. He's a cold shit, he can cut you dead –' He looked at them shrewdly. 'He's in trouble, isn't he? It couldn't happen to a nicer sonofabitch. You want me to say something against him?' He was once more ready to state the obvious, even if he had to concoct it.

'We may,' said Malone. 'We'll let you know. You're not leaving the country or anything, are you?' He gestured at the briefcases and the cartons.

'Are you kidding? And miss the chance to shaft Michael up the arse? Look, here's my home number, it's unlisted –' He scribbled a number on a slip of paper, shoved it at Malone. He was almost gleeful: he was like a drowning man who, at the moment he felt the rock beneath his feet, had seen a fellow swimmer taken by a shark. *I complained because I had no shoes* . . . He had seen that once on someone's desk. 'Call me any time, any time at all. Oh shit, you don't know how good this makes me feel!'

I'd better get out of here, Malone thought, before I knock him down. On the way out he stopped by the secretary's desk. 'Thanks, Rose. I'm sorry we were so aggressive. Sergeant Clements will send you some flowers.'

'Flowers and dinner,' said Clements, all at once chivalrous, a state of mind that made him giddy. 'How about that?'

'May I bring my husband?' said Rose, but gave them both a charming smile and put away her sword. 'By the way, my name isn't Wong. It's Robinson.'

Out in the car-park Malone leaned on the roof of the Holden and looked across it at Clements. 'Thanks, Russ. We agree who killed Emma?'

Clements nodded. 'Unless he did it in cahoots with Justine. But I don't think so. I dunno what his motive was, but he did it, all right. If that print on the bedside table and on the silencer are his . . .'

They got into the car. Clements put the key in the ignition, but before he turned it he looked at Malone again. 'You still owe me an explanation.'

'I know it, Russ.' He could feel Leeds's secret, like a fish-hook in his mouth. 'But I can't tell you.'

'It's something to do with the Commissioner, isn't it?'

Malone didn't reply.

Clements sighed. 'Okay, you don't need to tell me. I read the diaries, too. *Whose bastard child* . . . He thinks Justine is his daughter, right?'

Malone felt the hook slip free. 'Let's go and pick up Mr Broad.'

3

Walter Springfellow was not exactly jubilant when he came out of the courtroom, but old chemistry was bubbling in him. He had been witness for three days now to the law at work and, though matters were not going as he wanted them to, the professional side of his mind had responded to the atmosphere. He had put himself in the place of Gilligan J. and, as the evidence was presented and the questioning and cross-examination had sliced across the court, he had realized how much he had missed his original profession. The personal side of him had, however, seen what the process was doing to his daughter. Albemarle, QC, was fighting a losing battle for her, and Walter, all the old experience coming back to him, sensed that Albemarle knew it.

He had not yet spoken to Justine. Venetia had decided that she would wait till the weekend before introducing Walter to her; he had agreed with the sense of her suggestion. Thirty seconds, a minute at the most, was not enough for the meeting of a father and daughter who had never met before; he could not come back from the dead and greet her casually . . . 'I'm your father, Justine. Glad we finally met. Now go back to prison and we'll have another thirty-second chat tomorrow.' All that, with the media reporters, rising to leave the press box and stopping, along with everyone else in court, to witness the reunion.

He was impatient for the weekend and the meeting at Mulawa; yet he was afraid of it. He could never tell Justine how and why he had deserted her and her mother; perhaps Venetia could do that when he was dead and buried. Once he had been as confident as any man in dealing with a situation; perhaps too confident, even arrogant. In a couple of days he would be hauled into the court of her affections and he was as depressed and afraid as she had been in the court he had just left.

He walked down Bourke Street, towards Liverpool Street, where Edwin, as on the two previous days, was to pick him up. He felt he had gone unnoticed in the court, had been accepted as no more than a daily spectator. He had not yet decided whether or when he would turn himself in to either the police or ASIO. He would make that decision after he had had his reunion with Justine and after the verdict on her had been brought down. If she was convicted, he would go back to Germany, disappear again. Two convicted murderers in the one family, the *Springfellow* family, would be too much for the name to bear.

'Judge Springfeller?'

Age, sickness and worry had dulled his wits: he responded automatically. 'Yes?'

He looked at the beefy man in the straw hat standing beside him as they waited for the traffic lights. He remembered the man had been sitting behind him for the past three days in court, but they hadn't exchanged so much as a nod, even though they had become regulars. He had no idea who the man was.

'I been looking at you for three days now,' said Chilla Dural. 'I knew I'd seen you before, but I couldn't place you. No, don't cross. We're going up this way.'

He nodded up the steep hill of Liverpool Street. Edwin, Walter knew, would be waiting two blocks down the other way. 'I'm afraid you have the wrong man –'

'Don't argue, Judge.' Dural had his hand in his jacket pocket. 'I got a gun in here. Now let's go nice and quiet up this way. You don't recognize me, do you? I'm Chilla Dural. You gimme life, your last time on the Bench before you went to join them spooks, ASIO, whatever it is.'

Throughout his adult life Walter had become accustomed to the bizarre. The years in the courts, as barrister and then as judge, the year as ASIO chief, the long years since his disappearance, had taught him that beneath the surface of the mundane the grotesque was always ready to erupt. He stood now in a street busy with motor traffic, though there were no pedestrians but Dural and himself; life flowed by in the cars and trucks, but it was as remote as a newsreel on a screen. He was being kidnapped by a man with a gun, but the peak-hour traffic couldn't be stopped, everyone was rushing to get home to the mundane or the bizarre, whatever their luck was.

340

Halfway up the steep incline Walter paused to catch his breath. 'You will have to give me a moment. I'm not well.'

'Take your time. Once we get to the top, it's flat all the rest of the way.'

Dural stood looking patiently at this man whom he had once hated so fiercely. It had taken him two full days to recognize Walter Springfellow at last; memory plays games, it hinders us as we try to remove the layers of age from a once-familiar face. He had become obsessed with identifying the white-bearded man in front of him as, in less serious circumstances, we lie in bed and try to remember the name of an old actor we have just seen in a late-night movie.

Jerry Killeen had not come with him to the trial after the first day; the little man had had to go into hospital for removal of a poisoned cyst. Dural, no lover of hospitals, had not visited the garrulous Killeen; the little man would give him all the details when he came home. Dural had gone to the court today, but left when the afternoon session began, after satisfying himself that Springfellow would be there till the court rose at four o'clock. He had gone back to the rooming-house, got the Walther and come back to wait for Springfellow in the grounds of the courthouse. He had no plan in mind. His mind, in fact, was still getting over the shock of his recognition of the ex-judge. What did you do with a man who was supposed to be dead? Heinie Odets might have advised him, but Heinie was genuinely dead.

'What are you going to do with me?' Walter was taking deep breaths.

'I dunno, exactly. We'll see when we get to my place.'

'You're kidnapping me and taking me to your own house or flat? That's not the way it's usually done, is it?' He had got his breath back.

Dural smiled. 'No, I guess not. But you and me ain't a usual pair, are we? You okay now?'

The short halt seemed to have put them on an amiable basis; stiff perhaps, but agreeable. Walter had twice been in close danger when he had crossed into East Germany; each time he had kept his head and escaped. He would try to do the same this time, but he was weakened by resignation. It was as if the cancer had suddenly begun to race inside him.

It took them ten minutes, at a slow pace, to walk to Dural's rooming-house. As they entered the front door the two Vietnamese from upstairs came down the hallway. They smiled at Dural, said, 'G'day, mate,' passed him, one of them munching a meat pie as they went, and were gone. They were halfway to becoming Aussies, a prospect that would poison Jerry Killeen even more.

Dural looked at Walter. 'Why didn't you grab one of them, tell him what I'm doing?'

'I – I really don't know. I wasn't sure they'd understand. I'm not used to Asians.'

'It's another country now, Judge. Even the gaols, they're full of Wogs and darkies.'

He opened his door and stood back to let the other conservative enter. They were birds of a feather, Anglo-Saxon birds: the jungle was becoming too exotic for them.

In Dural's room Walter looked at the impersonal bareness, except for the single photo of a young woman and two small girls. 'This is your home?' The old upper-middle-class attitude still lingered; he was still continually surprised at how the other 90 per cent lived. 'You live here permanently?'

Chilla Dural missed the unintended snobbery. 'It's only temporary. I don't think of it as home.' He took the gun out of his pocket; he still had no ammunition for it, but Springfellow wouldn't know that. 'You see, a Walther? Just like your daughter used.'

'I don't believe she used any gun at all. Is that why I'm here, to discuss the trial?'

'Siddown, Judge. You want some tea or coffee?' Dural switched on an electric kettle, got some cups and saucers out of a small corner cupboard. He had put the gun down on the bench beside the electric-plate, but Walter was on the opposite side of the room and too far away to grab it. 'I

342

dunno what I'm gunna do with you, but I hadda get you here and let you know I hadn't forgotten you. I had a sort of –' He fumbled for the word.

'Compulsion? No milk, thanks. I like it black.'

'Compulsion, yeah. I got some biscuits here, Iced Vo-Vo's. I'm old-fashioned in me taste.'

'So am I.' Keep them talking, let them ramble on; he remembered the intelligence lessons. 'Mr Dural, you may not know what you are going to do with me – neither do I. But I don't think you're going to make any profit out of it.'

Dural picked up the gun again. He looked at this thin, sick-looking man and suddenly had a resurgence of the old hatred for him. He had thought he had long forgotten it, but it came surging back. He felt himself trembling and his grip tightened on the gun; there were no bullets in it, but he could use it to smash in the old man's thin skull. This bastard had put him away for life: everything he had once had, the easy living, the working for Heinie Odets, the available women, had been taken away from him by this cold, soft-spoken bastard. His vision blurred and for a moment he was on the point of yet another murder.

Walter Springfellow said, 'Are you going to kill me, Mr Dural?'

Then the trembling stopped, his vision cleared. He looked down at the gun in his hand and was surprised to see how tightly he was grasping it. He put it down again on the bench, was all at once, and with relief, sane again. If he killed the judge, he might just as well go out and buy some bullets and kill himself. The screws at Parramatta wouldn't welcome him back.

'I was gunna ask for a ransom for you. I thought I might ask you to set the price.' He grinned, but it was lopsided on his face, as if he had no control over it.

'There'd be no point,' said Walter, dying gradually and not afraid.

'You mean your missus won't pay cash to get you back?' Dural made the instant coffee, handed Walter his cup and saucer and a small plate of sweet biscuits. He sat down opposite Walter, the gun on the bench beside him. 'I dunno I'm even interested in the money any more. You're just a means to an end.' He was pleased with the phrase and hoped the educated joker opposite him appreciated it. He had always respected education: Heinie Odets had had it.

'What end is that?' Walter ate an Iced Vo-Vo: it was another step nearer home, a retreat from *apfel strudel* or *schnecken*.

Dural took his time about answering that. Would this man, an ex-judge, understand his obsession? He took a risk, a small one; after all, his aim was to be caught eventually. 'I done time in Parramatta, a long time – you helped with that. I got *used* to it, you know what I mean?'

Walter took his own time, sipping his coffee. After years of the best German coffee, the instant muck had nothing to recommend it; but he had always been well-mannered, at least in the smaller customs. At last he said, 'Yes, I think I do know what you mean, Mr Dural. I was in a sort of gaol for many years, though not in your sense. I grew accustomed to it. There was a sort of safety to it, is that what you mean?'

'You put your finger on it, Judge!' Chilla Dural leaned forward. 'Now I could shoot you and give meself up and they'd chuck me back in quick as you like. But it wouldn't work. Villains who kill cops and judges don't have a good time of it in gaol. I wanna go back to what I was used to, comfort and security.'

Walter began to feel safe; he was not going to be murdered. 'Well, we'll have to work something out, won't we? I think we both have a problem, Mr Dural.'

'You, too? Yeah, of course, your daughter. More coffee?'

'No, thanks. Yes, I too. Perhaps we can help each other.' But he could think of nothing that would help either of them. Depression settled on him again, as it had while he had listened to the prosecution of his daughter. 'You see, Mr Dural, I'm dying.'

344

'I can't help you there,' said Chilla Dural, rearing back in shock. 'I'm sorry to hear it. But don't ask me to kill you. I never done a mercy killing.'

4

Malone and Clements drove straight from Channel 15 to Springfellow House at Circular Quay. It was dark now, light reflections trembling on the harbour waters like fish scales, the floodlit bridge looming like the grey-green skeleton of a monster wombat. Homeward-bound workers streamed towards the wharves and the ferries, cars crawled along the expressway above their heads, trains rumbled along the elevated tracks. Working Sydney was closing down till another day, its blood was draining out of it towards the suburbs.

The two detectives, still working, went up to the twenty-ninth floor, where they had interviewed Michael Broad at the beginning of their investigations into the murder of Emma Springfellow. It was the sort of floor that had become standard environment for top executives during the boom: spacious, thickly carpeted, expensively furnished, enough art on the walls to start a small gallery; it was commercial pomp. The colour scheme, of course, was pink and grey.

Broad's secretary, pink and blonde, was behind her grey word processor on her grey desk. She looked up with some disdain at the two detectives spoiling the colour scheme in their polyester blue. Reception desks have created a new class of snobbery.

'Mr Broad is not in. He is upstairs with the chairwoman.'

'Good,' said Malone, thinking quickly. 'Then I'll have a look in his office.'

'You will not!'

Malone looked at Clements. 'Read the Riot Act to her, Russ. The bit about obstructing the police in the course of their duty.'

He opened the door to Broad's office and went in, closing it behind him. It was an office in which the word *success* was all but inscribed on the walls. Some shareholders had contributed, unwittingly, all their lifetime dividends to the furnishing of this room. Broad, with or without the chairwoman's consent, had surrounded himself with the trappings: appearances were everywhere, even when he was alone. The framed scrolls on the walls, between the paintings, told him what he already knew: Businessman of the Year, Corporation Man of the Year, Et Cetera of the Year . . . It would send him into a nervous breakdown to give up all this.

Malone went behind the big desk, remarking its neatness as he looked for what he wanted. He saw the gold pen and pencil set; the pen was missing, probably upstairs with Broad. Malone carefully took the pencil out of its holder, laid it on the leather top of the desk. Just as carefully he picked up the gold-embossed blotter, taking it by the blotter half-cylinder and not by the handle. He laid it beside the pencil, then added a leather spectacles case to the other two items. A large envelope full of papers was in the In basket; he emptied the papers from it and put the pencil, the blotter and the spectacles case in the envelope. Then he went back to the outer office.

He handed the envelope to Clements. 'Ring Don Cheshire, tell him to stay at his office and you're on your way out there now. If he's already gone home, get him there and tell him to meet you at his office. I want a check on those prints within two hours. I'll be back at Homicide by then with you-know-who.'

'Have you been doing what I think you've been doing?'

Malone winked. 'You've only got yourself to blame. You taught me.' Then he looked at the secretary. 'Sorry, miss, for barging in like that.'

'Shouldn't you have a warrant or something?'

Malone clicked his fingers. 'Damn! I left it back on my desk. I knew I'd forgotten something. It's been one of those days.'

The secretary's look told him she knew a liar when she heard one. 'Shall I tell Mr Broad you want to see him?'

She reached for her phone, but Clements already had his hand on it. 'No, love, Inspector Malone will announce himself. He's good at that. Good luck, Scobie. I'll see you back at the office.'

Malone didn't bother to wait for the lifts, which had been commandeered by the workers on the lower floors on their way home. He went up the fire stairs two at a time. On the thirtieth floor the secretaries were still at their desks; up here you went home, if you were lucky, when the boss went home. There were two secretaries and they both stood up as Malone, a little abruptly, demanded to see Lady Spring-fellow.

'She's in conference –'

'Tell her I've got something to add to the conference. Come on, girls, don't muck around!' He was losing patience, one of his best assets. 'I want to see her *now*!'

The secretaries looked at each other, then one of them went into the inner office. She was gone a full minute before she emerged; she came out just as Malone was on the point of bursting in. 'Lady Springfellow says you may go in. But I warn you, she's not happy –'

'I'll make her happy,' said Malone.

He went into the chairwoman's office, closing the door behind him. He had not been in this room before; he was not surprised to find that it suited Venetia exactly. She sat behind her big desk and looked at him with all the hospitality of Elizabeth I greeting a Spanish messenger boy. Beside her desk Michael Broad sat like a chancellor, his chair pulled round to face the intruder.

'This had better be important, Inspector –'

'It is, Lady Springfellow. I've really come to see Mr Broad, but I think you'll be interested in what I have to say.'

Broad had stiffened almost imperceptibly, but Malone had caught the clawing of the hand on the knee. 'I think you'd better explain all that, Inspector.'

'I'd like you to come up to Homicide with me, Mr Broad. I think you can help us with our enquiries into the murder of Emma Springfellow.'

'What enquiries? They're all finished! Dammit, is this some police joke?' Broad now had both hands on the arms of his chair; he seemed to be holding himself in. 'Lady Springfellow doesn't want this sort of sick joke played on her –'

'Just a minute, Michael,' said Venetia. 'It's not a joke, is it, Mr Malone?'

'No, it isn't. I have to warn you, Mr Broad, don't say anything till you have your lawyer with you. In the meantime it will save a lot of fuss and bother if you come quietly.'

Broad still sat tensed in his chair, but he said nothing. His face had become a mask; almost, with his bald skull, a death-mask. Venetia turned towards him; for a moment she looked ugly. Then the expression was gone as quickly as it had come and she looked back at Malone. 'Is this going to help Justine?'

'I don't know,' said Malone. 'I hope so. But it will depend on how much we get out of Mr Broad. Coming?'

For a moment it looked as if Broad was going to refuse; then he stood up, his legs unlocking like those of a mechanical man. 'I'll be back, Venetia. This is all some stupid mistake –'

Then the phone rang. Venetia picked it up. 'Yes, Edwin? Oh no – where can he –?' Then she collected herself, put her hand over the mouthpiece and looked at Malone. 'I'm sorry, there's an emergency at home. Will you excuse me?'

Broad said, 'Venetia, will you ring Brownlow and tell him I want him up at Homicide, wherever it is?'

Venetia looked directly at Broad with a stare that chilled even Malone: Christ, he thought, she's tough.

'No, Michael,' she said. 'Get your own lawyer. Mr Brownlow works for me and Justine.'

Malone saw the sudden look of hatred in Broad's face; or was it fear? He stared at Venetia, then abruptly he turned and went ahead of Malone out of the room. Malone paused a moment.

'I'll let you know how it goes. But don't build your hopes too high.'

'Thank you, Scobie.'

She waited till the door closed behind him, then she took her hand away from the phone's mouthpiece. 'Edwin?'

'I'm sorry – I've interrupted you at something –'

'No, no. Something's happening, but I'll tell you when I come home . . . I'm worried about Walter. How could he disappear in a couple of blocks? I saw him leave the court. I hope, oh God, I hope he hasn't gone off again!'

'Don't let's think the worst, not yet.' But Edwin sounded as if he had already begun to feel that way. 'He may have just decided he wanted to be on his own to think. How was he at court today?'

'He *looked* all right. But how can I tell? Alice and I never speak to him there – we play at being strangers. Is Alice at the house?'

'Yes, I've spoken to her – I thought he might have called and left a message. But she hasn't heard from him. I'm stumped as to what we should do. If he doesn't turn up in the next hour or so, do we go to the police? Or to ASIO?'

'Edwin, we can't! Let's wait a while. I'll be home in an hour or so – I have things to tidy up here. You and Ruth go over to the house, stay with Alice, just in case he rings.'

'We'll do that.' Then he said solicitously, 'Are you all right? You sound as if something had happened *before* I called . . .'

'I'll tell you when I come home.'

She hung up the phone. Though she had sounded reasonably calm, she was in absolute turmoil. She was still in shock from the revelation that Michael Broad might have murdered Emma, when Edwin hit her with the news that Walter had once more disappeared. She was accustomed to coping with crises; but the last five minutes had been too much. She began to shiver, then she burst into tears. She was weeping, crumpled in her chair, when one of her secretaries knocked on the door and came in.

Miss Misson was a practical, commonsensical girl. She had never seen her boss like this before, but she knew that everyone had some tears in them. She didn't ask what had brought on the tears, just said, 'Tea or a drink?'

Venetia dried her eyes, sighed deeply to move the weight in her chest. 'I think tea would be best, Kate. My mind's in a fog enough as it is.'

'A bad day at court?'

'Tomorrow may be better. But if it's not one thing, it's another.'

But already her spirit was reviving, even before the tea arrived. There is nothing to be done but to make the best of what cannot be helped: she had read that somewhere. She placed her faith in God, a partner she had never previously considered. God, somewhere, smiled in satisfaction, if a little surprised.

'I think I'll learn to pray again,' she said and Miss Misson, on her way out, stumbled on an invisible hump in the carpet.

5

Clements and Sergeant Cheshire arrived at Homicide an hour and a half after Malone had brought Michael Broad back there. When they had gone down in the lift at Springfellow House Malone had said, 'I don't have a car. We've got the choice of yours or a taxi.'

There was no one else in the lift; the last of the workers had gone. 'You mean I have to drive myself to my own arrest?'

'I thought that would appeal to your sense of style.'

As they drove up Macquarie Street in the Porsche, past The Vanderbilt looking solid and impregnable, the murder inside it those six months ago now swept into a cupboard and never mentioned, despite the current trial, Broad said, 'You're making a great mistake.'

'Maybe. Our game is a bit like yours, I think. You make your assessments, then you make your investment. We do the same. You win a few, you lose a few. The difference is, when we lose we can't write it off as a tax loss.'

'You're going to lose this one. I had nothing to do with Emma's murder.'

Malone glanced back at the tweed hat lying on the back bench of the car. 'Bring that hat with you when we go up to my office.'

Broad didn't ask why: which was the first of his mistakes. He had evidently decided indignation was no defence; he had gone to the other extreme, he had decided to remain silent. But there was a growing tension in him that Malone noted: Broad was more highly strung than he had suspected. The cold exterior was an armour.

Broad said nothing further till he reached the sixth floor of the Remington Rand building and asked Malone if he could call a lawyer.

'Go ahead. But don't try Brownlow – I wouldn't mind betting Lady Springfellow has already been on to him.'

'The bitch,' said Broad, but he was talking to himself and not to Malone.

He called a lawyer named Langer, who arrived within twenty minutes. He was Jewish, a refugee like Broad but an earlier arrival. He had come out of an Austrian Displaced Persons camp as a boy after the Second World War and had taken to Australia like a native. He had played rugby and now played golf; he preferred beer to wine and he couldn't stand Strauss or Schubert; his tales from the Vienna Woods were usually dirty. He was short, fat and knew as much about the law as a whole Bench of judges.

'Hello, Scobie, what have we got here?'

'Nothing so far, Freddie, just some questions.'

Broad was shocked that Malone and Langer were so friendly. 'Relax,' said Langer. 'The police don't pay me, you do. You'll get your money's worth. Can we go somewhere, Scobie, while I talk to my client?'

Most of Homicide had gone home; only a few detectives remained at their desks. Malone gestured to an empty corner at the far end of the room. 'Take your time. I don't want to start questioning Mr Broad till some evidence I'm expecting arrives.'

When Clements and Cheshire did arrive, Broad and Langer were still down at the far end of the room, though they seemed now to have nothing to say to each other. They half-rose as the two newcomers arrived, but Malone waved to them to stay where they were.

'Well, do we have anything?'

'Bloody oath we do,' said Cheshire and laid out some magnified prints on Malone's desk. 'This is the print from the silencer. This is the one from the bedside table in Emma's flat. These I took from the gold pencil, the blotter handle and the glasses case. He goes in for the best, don't he?' Cheshire paused to admire the taste of someone who could afford the best. Then he said, 'They all match perfectly. They're his index finger.'

'We've got him!' said Clements.

'Have we got him on his own? That's the point.' Malone looked down the long room. 'Did he do the job for Justine? Or with her? Or on his own?'

Cheshire was gathering up the prints. 'I'll leave you blokes to work that out. I better make myself scarce with these, except the ones on the silencer and the table. We don't want his legal eagle to know how you got the other prints. You want me to throw 'em away?'

'Don, you know better than that – we never throw anything away. Sometimes we can't find things, like illegal tapes, but we never throw anything away. Keep 'em. I'll question him, then I'll take him over to the Centre and charge him and take his prints officially. I'll let you know when we need you. And thanks, Don.'

'Any time,' said Cheshire and departed, a tradesman to his fingertips and anyone else's.

Malone got out his running sheets and waved to Broad and

Langer to join him and Clements. The few remaining detectives in the big room looked up curiously as the two men passed them, but once Malone got down to his questioning they studiously avoided looking towards him and Clements. It was the old territorial imperative at work: stay out of my case till you're invited in.

'According to our earlier investigation, Mr Broad, on the night of Emma Springfellow's murder you went to dinner with a Miss Donatelli, you took her home, left her at her door and went home to your own flat at Double Bay. Miss Donatelli corroborated all that, at least her part. You reached home at approximately ten-fifteen. Correct?'

'As far as I can remember. That was six months ago.'

'Sure, but it wasn't just an ordinary night when nothing happened. Let's try another date.' He was looking at his notes now, which had nothing to do with the running sheet. 'Thursday, October twenty-ninth, you went over to Adelaide with Mr Dircks from Channel Fifteen.'

'Did I?'

Malone, tired now but trying not to show it, glanced at Langer. 'Tell your client not to be a smart-arse, Freddie. It will be quicker and easier all round.'

'I'd advise you to just answer the questions, Michael,' said Langer. 'At this stage these are just questions of fact.'

Broad stared at him as if deciding whether to sack him or not; then he looked back at Malone. 'Yes, I went to Adelaide. It was business.'

'I'm sure it was. Business business and personal business.'

'This is where I have to advise my client to be careful, Inspector. We're getting into conjecture now.'

Malone acknowledged that with a nod. He picked up the tweed hat which was lying on his desk. 'Did you wear this while in Adelaide?'

'Not that I remember.'

Malone tried another tack. 'What were your relations with Emma?'

353

'Cool but correct.' Broad had become stiff, in posture and voice. A vein throbbed just once in his temple.

'She wasn't threatening you?'

There was just a flicker of apprehension in the eyes; it could have been a trick of light. 'Why me? Her fight was with the Springfellow women.'

'You worked for – the Springfellow women. She wasn't threatening you with the Companies and Securities Commission?' He had remembered the entry in Emma's diary: *Someone should be reported to the NCSC. How do these people get away with these swindles?*

Again there was the flicker in the eyes: Broad was beginning to crack inside. But he was still ceramic-hard on the outside.

'Don't answer that,' said Langer.

Broad waved him to be silent; he didn't take his gaze away from Malone. 'If she was threatening me, and I can't remember that she was, it was only part of the larger threat to the Springfellow women.' The Springfellow women sounded like a tribe, one with whom he had only the slightest connection. He gestured at the running sheets. 'I'm sure you have all that in there.'

'You didn't visit Emma on the night of her murder, after you had gone home to your flat?'

'No.'

Malone opened a drawer in his desk and took out the silencer in its plastic envelope. 'Have you seen that before?'

'No.'

Malone stared at him for a while, till he saw the vein throb again in the temple. Broad was clutching at himself from the inside.

'Mr Broad, you didn't ask what it was. Most law-abiding people have never seen a silencer – they would just take that for some sort of metal pipe. Did you know it was a silencer?'

Broad looked at Langer, though he didn't seem to see him. The latter said to Malone, 'I'd advise him not to answer that.'

'It's a Gold Spot silencer, made here in Australia,' Malone

told Broad, not taking his eyes off him. 'Did you go to a gun dealer in Adelaide named –' he named the dealer '– and purchase this silencer and have him fit it to a Walther PPK .380? The same gun that's been presented in evidence in Justine's trial?'

'Again, Inspector, I have to advise my client not to answer. You're asking him to incriminate himself.'

Malone nodded again, but hadn't stopped looking at Broad. 'Did you remove the Walther from the gun cabinet at the Springfellow home? You were a frequent visitor there, weren't you?'

'Not that frequent.' Broad now was almost robot-like.

'I don't think these questions should be allowed,' said Langer. 'I don't mean to be rude, Inspector, but I think it's reached a stage of put up or shut up.'

Malone grinned, though he had no real humour left. 'Now *you're* sounding like a smart-arse, Freddie. But one last question for Mr Broad. Do you know a man named Koster?'

'No.' Broad was holding himself rigid, the rein at breaking point.

'He's a gun dealer, mostly illegal. You approached him here in Sydney about buying a silencer.'

'My client has already answered your question,' said Langer. 'He's said he doesn't know this man Koster. So are you going to put up?'

Malone looked at Clements, who nodded. Both knew that at the moment they had very little that would stand up in court; they could start nothing official till they had Broad's fingerprints on the record. Then they would have to produce Koster and the gun dealer from Adelaide to identify him.

Malone took the jump: 'We're arresting Mr Broad on being an accessory before the fact of the murder of Emma Springfellow. There may be other charges to follow. We'll take him up to Police Centre and charge him. We'll ask that bail be denied tonight, but you can apply for it tomorrow morning when we take him before the magistrate. On your feet, Mr Broad.'

Broad sat as if refusing to move. Then he slowly stood up. None of the others recognized it, but the madness that had gripped his mother was taking hold of him. It had happened before, when Emma had threatened him with exposure to the NCSC. Everything that he had built in the last twenty years had been cracked at the base when he had lost so much in the Crash; Emma, with her malicious threat, had been ready to topple the whole edifice of his life to the ground. Then she was dead, out of the way, and Justine, his unlucky, unsuspecting saviour, had been laid with the blame. He had taken control of the Springfellow Corporation, and begun to rebuild his life and his fortune, had begun to enlarge his ambitions. And now this policeman, this Malone, this dull plodding nobody, was threatening the whole edifice again.

'You'll regret this, Mr Malone. You'll regret it to your dying day.' He said it quietly, like the sanest of men.

THIRTEEN

1

Malone was having breakfast next morning when the phone rang. Claire, house telephonist in case all calls were for her, answered it. 'Dad, it's for you!'

Malone didn't know why, but his first thought was that Broad had committed suicide in the cells at Police Centre. 'Who is it?'

'It's the Commissioner.' Claire lowered her voice, put on her best elocution tones, a hundred dollars a term extra: 'Just a moment, sir. My father is coming. Thank you, sir. One tries.' She put her hand over the mouthpiece as Malone came out into the hallway. 'He said I had a nice phone voice.'

'*One tries?*' said Malone. 'You sound like a female stuffed shirt.'

She made a face at him, gave him the phone and went back to her bedroom to finish getting ready for school. It was an ordinary day, just like any other weekday morning. Except, of course, that the Police Commissioner did not call every morning.

'Scobie? Something's come up. I'm at my office.' Malone looked at his watch: 7.50. The Commissioner was known to be an early starter, but he was not usually in his office before 8.30. 'Come and see me at once.'

Malone was on the point of refusing, of finding some excuse. He was exhausted; he had slept only fitfully last night. He knew instinctively that this wasn't official business, it could have nothing to do with Broad's arrest last night; or

357

could it? He had already done far too much for the Commissioner. Yet even as he thought of trying to find an excuse, he knew that he couldn't. It had nothing to do with rank; he bowed to that other badge, respect. 'I'll be there as soon as I can, sir.'

He hung up the phone, went back to the kitchen. 'I have to go.'

'The Commissioner?' said Lisa. 'Let him wait. Finish your breakfast. The bacon and eggs are ready.'

'I can't –'

'Have your breakfast,' said Lisa firmly, as if she were speaking to one of the children. 'Tell him you were held up in the traffic. Someone around here had better start arranging your priorities. You tossed and turned all night and now you want to rush off on an empty stomach.'

'I've had my porridge –' Lisa still believed in a hearty Dutch breakfast for cold mornings.

'There, eat that and no argument!' She thumped a plate of bacon and eggs in front of him. Then she kissed the top of his head. 'You're ours more than you're his.'

'If Dad takes the car,' said Tom, 'who's gunna drive us to school?'

'You're going to walk,' said Lisa. 'Dutch children always walk to school or go on their bikes. It's why they're always so healthy.'

'Stuff the Dutch,' said Maureen, who had been listening to rock stars being interviewed on 2JJJ, and got a heavy Dutch clip under the ear from her mother.

Malone, having had his priorities arranged for him by his loving wife, ate his breakfast, had a second cup of coffee, then went out and got into the Commodore and drove with the peak-hour traffic into Homicide. He parked in the garage and got out of the car as Clements drove in beside him.

'I've got to go and see the Commissioner.' Clements looked enquiringly at him. 'I'll tell you about it later. In the meantime, you handle Broad at the magistrate's court. He'll ask for bail. I'd rather object to it, but at this stage I don't think we can, not till we get all the evidence in. Ask for as high a bail as you can get.'

'How would a million do?' Clements had another rich yuppie he could turn his attention to.

Malone grinned. 'Try it. Then bring in Koster to identify Broad from those pictures we took of him last night. Fax a copy to Adelaide and get the fellers there to bring in the gun dealer and have him identify Broad. Have them get a statement from him.'

'He's a dangerous bugger, I think. We oughtn't to let him go at all.'

'We can't hold him, not if he puts up the bail. You'd better warn the Crown Prosecutor, too, that the case against Justine may be going under.'

'They're gunna love that. Billy Wellbeck will tear his hair out, what's left of it.'

Malone left him and walked over to Police Headquarters. Commissioner Leeds was impatiently waiting for him.

'You took your time!'

'I'm sorry, sir. The traffic's pretty heavy . . . I was going to call you first thing this morning –'

'Scobie,' Leeds interrupted without preliminary, 'Walter Springfellow is alive and back in Sydney. Or he was, up till yesterday afternoon.'

Malone sat down without asking if he might. He squinted at Leeds as if the latter had told him something in a foreign language. 'Alive?'

'Lady Springfellow called me about seven o'clock last night. I went down to her office – I took a risk, I know, but I had to go, she sounded desperate. I thought it had something to do with Justine . . . Walter turned up out of the blue four days ago. He's been living in Germany for the past twenty-odd years, working for British Intelligence. Venetia doesn't know whether ASIO knew about it – maybe they did, maybe they didn't. They could have been stringing you along all this time.'

'I don't think so. I think Fortague was fair dinkum with me. Whose was the skeleton we found – the Russian's?'

Leeds nodded. 'Venetia told me everything. Walter shot him. He was blackmailing both Walter and her.'

'Oh Christ.'

'Exactly,' said Leeds, who had never been known to be profane. 'He came back when he read that Justine was going on trial. He's been in court these past three days – on his own, not with Venetia. His brother Edwin has been bringing him in each day, dropping him some distance away and picking him up again in the afternoon. He was to pick up Walter yesterday afternoon, but Walter didn't turn up. I called Venetia first thing this morning. They've had no phone calls from him, nothing. He's disappeared again.'

'What do you want me to do?' He wanted to ask if John Leeds's wife knew anything of this, but that was none of his business. He wished that none of it was his business, but it was too late now.

'Find him.'

Malone tried to laugh, but it was just a dry cough of disbelief. 'Just like that? What do I do with him when I find him? What if ASIO has got him? Christ Almighty, I came over here to give you some good news –'

'What good news?' Leeds looked as if he didn't believe such a possibility existed.

'We're charging Michael Broad with the murder of Emma.'

It was Leeds's turn to look as if he didn't understand what had been said. 'Broad? The fellow who works for Venetia?'

'I think we have enough on him to make it stick. He's not going to offer any confession, not yet anyway. I tried for a verbal last night, but his lawyer was there. Still, I'm sure we can pin it on him.' He told Leeds what evidence they had.

'Why didn't you come up with all this before?' Leeds was angry.

'Because all the evidence against him has only come up in the past couple of days.'

'You were certain you had all the evidence you needed against Justine!' He was an angry father; or might-be father. 'You've put us all through this –'

Malone, too, was suddenly angry; but he contained himself. 'We did have evidence against her. The Crown Prosecutor thought it was enough, they were the ones who decided to go ahead. You've read the evidence so far – Jesus, you're a cop, the same as I am! You'd have gone on it, too –'

'You had your doubts – you blamed Russ Clements for pushing it –'

'In the end it was my decision and I went with it. Righto, I was wrong, but don't blame me for not doing my best –' Abruptly he shut up, tried to cool down. 'I'm sorry, sir. I shouldn't have blown my top like that.'

Leeds, too, cooled down. 'I apologize, Scobie. I think we've both been stretched too far. So you think they'll dismiss Justine?'

'Once we've got the identification of Broad from the gun dealers, we'll put the case to the Crown Prosecutor. Russ Clements is warning them this morning. They'll probably ask for an adjournment today. She may even be free by this evening.'

'One Springfellow goes free and you bring in another one. If you can find him.'

'What frame of mind was he in? Was he likely to commit suicide?'

'I don't know. I didn't ask Venetia that – how could I? He is dying, though – he has terminal cancer. That was probably what prompted him to come home, to see Justine before he died. He certainly hasn't helped her by coming back from the dead.'

'If I find him, this is going to create a bigger sensation than Justine's case.'

'We know that. Venetia told me she thought long and hard before she called me. But she said she couldn't just let him disappear again –'

'Is she still in love with him?' What a question to ask your Commissioner, the man who himself had once been in love with the lady. *How did I get myself into this?* Tibooburra all at once began to look like Utopia.

361

'She told me no. I believe her. I think she feels – *sorry* for him. And guilty.'

So she should. 'What does he look like now?'

'He's aged, she says. He has a white beard, he wears steel-rimmed glasses –'

Malone had a sudden clear picture of the regulars in the spectators' gallery. 'I saw him! But I didn't recognize him – I don't think anyone would, not unless they knew who he was –'

'The question is, do you go to ASIO and ask them if they know anything about him being back here?'

'That's your decision, not mine. I've had enough.'

For a moment Leeds reverted to being the Commissioner; there was a flash of outrage in his face. Then he came back to the reality of the situation: there was no rank in this. He nodded reluctantly. 'Yes, it is. I suppose we have to go to them – it's the obvious place to start.'

Malone stood up. 'I'd prefer it if you came with me – sir.'

Leeds remarked the note of respect; and respected Malone for it. The junior man had restored the equilibrium of their relationship. 'Yes, I should. As you say, you've had enough. More than enough. But you'll stay with it?' It was a plea, not an order.

'I'll stay with it,' said Malone, but prayed for a quick and merciful end to it all. Though he had no real hope that there would be any mercy at all in the end. 'We'll go in my car, it's over at Homicide. Do you want me to pick you up?'

Leeds had come to the office in mufti, almost as if he had expected this to be a day of clandestine meetings. He hated anything underhand, but the need for secrecy had trapped him. 'I'll walk through the park to Elizabeth Street. Pick me up at the corner of Bathurst.'

Malone hesitated, then said, 'Does Mr Zanuch know anything about this?'

'Nothing. If it should ever get out how I've been involved in this, he'll be the next Commissioner. I'd have to recommend him.'

Malone dragged up a sour grin. 'Then I think I might ask for an early retirement.'

He picked up Leeds on the other side of Hyde Park and they drove over to Kirribilli. 'Should we have phoned ASIO and told them we were coming?' Leeds was a stickler for protocol.

'No. I think Fortague is on our side, but I don't want to give him the chance to put Springfellow away and hide him somewhere.'

'Maybe they've done that already. You never know what the spooks are going to do.'

Malone's ear, like the rest of him, was tired, but it sounded to him as if Leeds was hoping that ASIO would have solved the problem of Walter Springfellow. He glanced at the Commissioner and saw that he looked just as weary, though in a different way. There was a weariness of spirit there in the stern face.

When they were ushered into his office Fortague showed no surprise, not even at the presence of the Police Commissioner. 'Hello, John. I didn't expect to see you. But in the circumstances . . .'

'You know why we're here?' said Leeds.

'I guessed it as soon as they told me who wanted to see me.'

'Were you going to get in touch with us?' said Malone.

'No.' Fortague glanced at Malone, then back at Leeds. 'John, I think Inspector Malone has some difficulty appreciating how restricted we are. I hope you appreciate it. Our work can't be as open as yours.'

Leeds said, 'On this one, Guy, we've been as restricted as you.'

'Is your interest in this personal or official? Forgive me for asking that . . . I mean, we've known all along that you were Walter Springfellow's closest friend.'

'It's personal,' said Leeds and looked uncomfortable. 'I take it you know he's back in Sydney?'

'Yes.' Fortague turned to Malone. 'I haven't been leading you up the garden path, Scobie. Up till four days ago I

363

didn't know he was still alive. Only the Director-General knew that.'

'Nobody else? The PM, for instance?'

'No, nobody, at least nobody in this country. When Harold Holt drowned, he was the last PM to know anything about Springfellow's disappearance. It was decided there was nobody with the need to know, outside of the Director-General. No succeeding PM was ever told and nothing had ever been put on paper to the PM's office while Harold Holt was there. I wasn't told anything up till four days ago. He's been working for the Brits in Germany the last twenty years. Or anyway up till they retired him four years ago.'

'We know all that,' said Leeds. 'Do you know where he is now?'

'Yes. We've had him under surveillance since he got off the plane. He's been kidnapped, we think, and he's being held in a house in King's Cross.'

'*Kidnapped?* And you've done nothing about it?'

'We're not sure whether it's an actual kidnapping or not. He seemed to go willingly enough with the man who's holding him. If he *is* holding him . . . While he's there, he's out of mischief, he can't get away from us. We thought we'd let him sit out his daughter's trial, that should be over early next week –'

'It'll be over today,' said Malone. 'We're charging someone else with that murder.'

Fortague raised a thick eyebrow. 'That was unexpected, wasn't it?'

'So was Walter Springfellow coming back from the dead. Now I've got to pick him up for the murder of that Russian, Uritzsky.'

Fortague looked at Leeds, then both men looked at Malone. He waited, was not at all surprised when Fortague said, 'We don't think that's necessary.'

'No, I had the feeling you wouldn't. Who's the man holding him? One of your ex-agents? Another Russian?'

364

'None of those. His name is Charles Dural, he's known as Chilla. We only got his name last night from one of his fellow-roomers, a Vietnamese. We're checking on him now.'

Malone was surprised this time; the unexpected was going off like firecrackers. 'Chilla ·Dural! Christ, he's probably already done him in! He's an ex-con, Springfellow sent him up for life!'

At last the unexpected got some reaction from Fortague: he sat up straight, as did Leeds. 'We'd better get him out of there at once! We'd even thought that Dural might be his old court tipstaff –'

Malone would have laughed at that, but he had no laughter left in him; but he would remember to tell it to Dural and then he might laugh. He stood up, not waiting for any order from his Commissioner.

'How do you want this done, sir? Do you want the works, the Tac Response team and all the rest of it? Or do we do it on the quiet?'

'On the quiet,' said Leeds, getting to his feet, almost painfully, it seemed. 'You and I. And Mr Fortague's men as back-up, if we need them.'

2

'They say that the end of man is knowledge,' said Walter Springfellow, 'but we'll never really know, will we?'

It is possible to have a philosophical discussion with an uneducated, not-too-bright man. Long hours together and heightened circumstances meld minds if they are sympathetic to each other. Walter and Dural had been together for almost eighteen hours and the circumstances, though quiet, were certainly heightened.

When it had come time for them to sleep last night, Dural had still not made up his mind what he was going to do with Walter. The news that Walter was dying had unsettled him; he was accustomed to death, but he had never had to deal with it directly, except in murder. Dying from an illness was a different death. They had discussed that last night and it had left him depressed, abruptly aware of his own mortality.

He had given Walter his bed – 'You're the sick one, mate,' – and had, apologetically, tied him to it with the cord of his dressing-gown. He had recognized that Walter had no strength to break the cord and he had not been disturbed by any fears that the older man might try to escape. He himself had gone to sleep in the room's one armchair and had slept fitfully, his mind more uncomfortable than his body. He had woken early, gone along to the bathroom at the end of the hallway while Walter still slept, showered and come back and dressed. He had just finished putting on a clean shirt when Walter woke. It was then that Walter, having dreamed of his own death, had made his remark.

'I wouldn't know, Wal.' He untied the cord. Walter sat up and began to massage his wrists. 'The day they bury me, that'll be it. I don't believe in the hereafter. I just hope I die quick, I don't want time to regret nothing.'

'I think we all regret something, Chilla. What's for breakfast?'

'Cornflakes and some scrambled eggs. I wasn't expecting you to stay all night.'

Walter smiled. 'I didn't invite myself. You asked me to stay.'

Dural smiled, began setting up the small table for breakfast. 'Yeah, that's right.'

'What are you going to do with me? Have you decided?'

'I still dunno what you been doing, where you been all these years. I don't even know why you pissed off. You gunna tell me any of that?'

'I can't, Chilla. There are too many other people involved.'

'Your missus?'

'Yes, her. And others.'

'Your daughter?'

'Only in an indirect way.'

366

For almost twenty years he had talked with men he had controlled, had discussed secrets of state, the proximity of danger, had brought them back in from the cold; yet his natural arrogance, his inborn sense of superiority, had always prevented him from any relaxed intimacy with them. Yet now, though he could not release his secrets, he was talking to this rough, crude ex-murderer as to an old friend. The realization of it amazed him, but also warmed him. He was discovering his own humanity, that specific gravity that binds us all together, but which some owners of it sometimes fail to recognize.

Over the scrambled eggs, perfectly cooked, Dural said, 'I think I'll let you go. You can't help me go back to Parramatta, not unless I dob you in for a lotta publicity and I don't wanna do that.'

Walter was grateful for the other's consideration. 'You have that gun. What if I made an anonymous phone call to the police? If you're on licence, having a gun is an offence.'

'I still got my bleeding-heart to worry about. I told you, he'd find some excuse for me. No, you go back to your missus and daughter and I'll think of something else.'

'I wish I could help you, Chilla, I really do.'

'I wish I could help you. I mean, about the cancer.' He picked up the Walther. He still hadn't told his captive that it wasn't loaded, but now he felt it was time. The kidnapping, if that was what you could call it, was over. 'There's no bullets in this, y'know. I never had any intention of shooting you.'

Walter was not surprised by the information; it no longer mattered. What did surprise him was that he was concerned about Chilla Dural's future as much as he was about his own. Perhaps more so: he knew that he himself had very little future.

'I once had to make up my mind whether to take a Walther or another pistol, a Colt .45. I expected problems with someone . . . I often wonder what would have happened if I'd chosen the Walther. It does less damage.'

Then there was a knock at the door.

3

'What do we do if Dural has a gun?' said the younger of the two ASIO men who had been watching the rooming-house. 'Neither of us is carrying one.'

Malone looked at Fortague, who said, 'It's not standard practice with us. We don't have a licence to kill.'

'Do you have yours, sir?' Malone said to Leeds.

The Commissioner shook his head. 'I never carry one.'

Malone swore. 'So I'm the only one? I really am the bunny in all this, aren't I?'

Leeds flushed, but said nothing. Fortague looked at this clash between the Commissioner and his junior officer, but he, too, said nothing. He, too, was a bunny in a way, placed there by *his* senior officer, the Director-General, who had told him nothing up until he had needed help.

'I think we should get the Tactical Response fellers,' said Malone.

'No,' said Leeds. 'Give me your gun and I'll go in myself.'

Broughton Street was a one-way street and Malone and Leeds had had to come the long way round, coming up from the bottom end. Fortague had followed in his own car, driving himself; even at Kirribilli, it seemed, the need to know was being kept to the minimum. Both cars had been parked in a No Parking zone, the only clear space left in the narrow street, and the three men had got out and waited to be joined by the two observers.

Malone made no attempt to offer his gun. 'If they're in Dural's own room, he won't be able to see us – it's a back room. We'll have to approach him down a hallway, but first we've got to get in the front door.'

'I'll go in and see if Dural will talk with us. Give me your gun.'

'No,' said Malone. 'I'll go with you.'

368

Fortague broke away from them. 'Paxter, where are you going?'

The younger ASIO man had suddenly spun away and dashed across the street. Two Vietnamese had come out of the front door, were about to pull it to behind them when he reached them and put his foot in the doorway. Malone, reacting more quickly than the others, was only a few yards behind him. He pulled up sharply, almost knocking down the small thin Asians.

'It's all right, gentlemen. We're just going in to see our friend Mr Dural.'

The two Vietnamese looked at each other, across the street at Leeds, Fortague and the other ASIO man, then back at Malone and Paxter. They knew the signs; they had come out of the streets of Saigon, not from some up-country village. These five men, all bigger than themselves, were either the law or criminals outside it: in either event, it was none of their business. It was a typical Australian, or anyway King's Cross, reaction.

They both smiled, pushed the door further ajar and smiled. 'You're very welcome. G'day, mate.'

And off they went, not looking back, which their first immigration officer, in welcoming them to their new life, had told them never to do.

Leeds, Fortague and the other ASIO man had now crossed the street. Malone took out his gun. 'The Commissioner and I will go in. If he starts shooting, find a phone and call Police Centre. They'll have the Tac Response men here within five minutes.'

'Can he get out a back way?' said Fortague, who looked as if he would rather have stayed at Kirribilli. Shoot-outs were not part of spy programmes, it wasn't the way the game was played.

'I don't know.' Malone looked at Leeds. 'Ready, sir?'

Leeds nodded at the Smith & Wesson in Malone's hand. 'Don't use it unless you absolutely have to. We want the quiet approach.'

'It may be a bit late for that,' said Malone and led the way down the narrow hallway. There was a lingering smell of cooking; upstairs a radio was playing an old Springsteen number. Malone reached Dural's door, paused, then knocked.

The door was opened almost immediately. Dural stood there, the Walther in his hand, half-raised as if ready to fire it. Malone brought up his own gun, his finger tightening on the trigger. Then behind Dural there was a feeble shout: 'No! Don't shoot!'

Malone would never know what stopped the pressure on his finger, what quirk of fate held him from putting a bullet right through Dural. His hand stiffened till it hurt; his vision blurred for a split second. Then behind him Leeds said, 'Put down your gun, Dural.'

He reached out past Malone, and Chilla Dural, looking a little bemused, gave him the Walther without protest. Malone lowered his own gun and let out a gasp of air.

'Christ, Chilla, you were lucky then!'

'Mine's not loaded, Mr Malone. I was never gunna do anyone with it. Ask the Judge.'

He stepped aside, like someone inviting visitors into his room for a cuppa. Malone nodded for Leeds to go in first, then he stood in the doorway, blocking Fortague and the two ASIO men as they came hurrying down the hallway. He jerked his head at Dural.

'Out here, Chilla.'

Dural looked at him in puzzlement, then he stepped out into the hallway and Malone closed the door. 'They're old friends,' he said. 'Give them a minute or two on their own.'

Fortague hesitated, then he nodded to his two men. 'Let's wait outside. You won't take him away, Scobie, before we can talk to him?'

'He's your pigeon as much as ours,' said Malone, though he only half-believed that. Murder, even of a Russian blackmailing defector, was still a police matter. 'But it's up to what the Commissioner says.'

Inside the room John Leeds and Walter Springfellow stood facing each other like duellists, not friends but strangers. There was twenty-two years' silence between them and neither was sure how to break it. Walter had long forgotten his anger and disappointment; but Leeds still had his guilt, which, with an honest man, is never forgettable. At last Leeds, playing policeman, said, 'Was he going to kill you?'

'Good God, no!' The question somehow seemed melo-dramatic; his relations with Dural had become almost domestic. 'The man's harmless –'

'Walter, he's a two-time murderer –'

'John, that was years ago – he's changed!' The use of their given names broke the ice. 'All he wants . . . Never mind, let him tell you himself. What are you going to do with me, that's what concerns us, isn't it?'

'I'm not the only one. Some ASIO men are outside. And one of my inspectors from Homicide.'

'There's no statute of limitations on murder, is there? You know what happened?'

'Not all of it, but most of it. Venetia called me in last night, when you didn't go home.'

'Have you been seeing her over the years, while I've been gone? I couldn't bring myself to ask her.'

'No, I'm married, Walter, with three children – I'm happily married.' He was silent for a moment, then he said quietly, 'I'm sorry, Walter. I've never forgiven myself for what happened.'

'If it hadn't been for you, I'd never have been in this situation.' He couldn't help the momentary bitterness, a residue was still there; but there was no rage, he hadn't the will for that. He picked up his jacket from the bed and began to put it on. 'I came home because of my daughter – did Venetia tell you that?'

'Yes.'

'She *is* my daughter, you know that?'

'Yes,' said Leeds and, perversely, felt relieved of a

371

burden. Men are fortunate having no womb; all they expend is their seed and they never miss that. 'Yes, she is.'

Walter was putting on his tie, one that looked like a club tie; but what club, Leeds wondered, could he have belonged to in the intervening years? But he didn't ask: he knew that he and Walter would never again be friends, would never again be a club of two as they had once been.

'So what will happen to me?' said Walter, dressed now, a pillar of conservative respectability, just as he had been when he had left his Mosman home twenty-two years before.

Leeds hesitated, then, out of guilt, said, 'I think we'll let ASIO decide that.'

It was the only recompense he could make.

4

Malone said, 'If you really want to go back to Parramatta, Chilla, I think we can arrange it.'

'You dunno my do-gooder,' said Dural morosely.

'We can over-ride him. You had the gun, you threatened me with it –'

'I never done that!'

'Chilla, who's making up this case? I'll write you out a verbal and you'll sign it, okay? You threatened me with the gun –'

'What about it not being loaded?'

'Do you want to go back to Parramatta or not?'

'Christ, do I! Yeah, of course. Okay, you make up the verbal for me and I'll sign it. I just hope the screws won't have it in for me when I get back, but. Threatening a cop.'

'They know you, don't they? You'll be all right. Leave it to me, Chilla. You're on your way home. One thing, though – you keep your mouth shut for ever about Judge Spring-fellow. Understand?'

'I was never a grass. I got me principles.'

'I hope so, Chilla. This is big stuff, don't ever try to sell it to the media. He's dying –'

'I know that. I dunno what he done, but it's none of my business. Live and let live. Or live and let die, I guess it is. There was a fillum called that, wasn't there?'

'Yeah. Be a hero – live and let die.'

'You'll never have to worry about me, Mr Malone. I liked him, I really felt sorry for him. I thought I'd hate his guts, but I didn't. I guess I'm getting old and – mellowed, is that the word?'

'That's it, Chilla. Old and mellowed, and your trap shut.'

He pulled the Commodore in in front of the Police Centre. He had seen Russ Clements come out of the main door and down the steps and he wanted to catch him before he went back to Homicide. He jumped out of the car and Dural followed him, like a well-trained villain.

'Russ!'

Clements turned, then came across to Malone and Dural. He nodded at the ex-con, then looked enquiringly at Malone. 'What happened?'

'We're charging Chilla with having an unlicensed gun and threatening me with it.' Clements looked threateningly at Dural, and Malone grinned. 'Relax. It's between me and Chilla. No harm's been done.'

Clements, puzzlement creasing his big face, said, 'Then where the hell have you been?'

It was not something Malone wanted to discuss in front of Chilla Dural. He, Leeds and Dural had gone back to Kirribilli. Fortague had followed, Walter Springfellow riding with him, and the two ASIO men who had been on the stake-out had brought up the rear. Malone and Dural had sat outside in the Commodore and it had been almost an hour before the Commissioner had emerged.

He had paused some distance from the car and called Malone over to him. 'Sorry we've been so long. Fortague had to talk to all of those with the need to know.' He twisted his mouth, as if he found the phrase and the process behind it distasteful. 'The Director-General down in Canberra and then they had to get someone from SIS in London out of bed.'

'Did they tell the PM?'

'An ex-TV chat star? He'd never be able to resist making an anecdote out of it. No, there's only the D-G of ASIO, Fortague, those two men who were with us this morning and whoever it is at SIS in London.'

'And you and me.' Then he looked across at his car. 'And Chilla Dural.'

'Yes,' said Leeds. 'He's the real risk.'

Malone wasn't certain, now, that Dural would be a risk. But, of course, no one could be certain of what confidences were kept or exchanged in the loneliness of a prison.

'I'll tell you about it later,' he told Clements. 'What happened to Broad?'

'The beak gave him bail, a hundred thousand and his passport surrendered. You wouldn't believe it, he had the hide to ring Venetia and ask her to stand surety for him – I think he's around the bend, in a cold-blooded sorta way. She must have told him to get stuffed, because he got off the phone looking ready for another murder. He threatened me and you.' He looked at Dural at that.

'I dunno the guy,' said Dural, all true innocence. He was going home and he wanted no more fights with the police.

'Who put up the bail?'

'In the end he raised it himself. He got the magistrate to accept his car and his flat as surety and his bank lent him the money on the strength of those. He left the court about an hour ago.'

'Has he still got it in for you and me?'

'He's got it in for everyone –'

Then the shot rang out and the bullet bounced off the roof of the Commodore. It hit Chilla Dural right between the eyes and he died without time to regret anything. He fell against Malone, who went down under his weight. Clements dropped behind the car, looking wildly around for the gunman.

'Where the hell is he?'

Malone rolled out from under the dead Dural and got his gun awkwardly out of his holster. He looked back over his shoulder and saw that two uniformed officers had come out of the Centre and were crouched behind two pillars.

'Can you see him?' he yelled.

'He's up there behind the green Porsche!'

'It's him!' said Clements. 'What the hell's he trying to do? Take on the whole force? What a place to choose!'

If he's after me, thought Malone, better here than out in a quiet street in Randwick, with Lisa and the kids cowering inside the house and him outside trying to battle Broad on his own.

Another bullet hit the car, this time slamming into a tyre which went down with a loud hiss. Broad was evidently trying to fire *under* the Commodore, but Malone and Clements were lying flat on the pavement, protected by the height of the kerb. A car came up the street and drove directly between the gunman and the police officers, its driver unaware that he was crossing a battlefield. Broad waited till he had gone, then he fired again, this time at the two officers crouched behind the pillars. Malone, glancing back, saw figures behind the glass doors of the lobby; even as he looked at them, a splintered star suddenly appeared in one of the doors and two people in the lobby dropped to the floor and crawled away. He glanced down to his left and saw the Tactical Response team in their protective vests coming on the run up from the underground garage.

'He's a goner now!' Clements got up on one knee, held his gun with both hands and fired in the direction of the Porsche. 'They'll fix him!'

Malone raised himself cautiously, looked over the bonnet of his car and up the street. He saw the barrel of a rifle come up over the roof of the Porsche and he ducked as a bullet smashed the windscreen of the Commodore. 'He's got a bloody rifle! Where did he get that?'

A marked car screeched its way up the ramp of the garage,

swung left and went down to the end of the street, where it slewed to a stop, blocking two cars and a truck as they came up from Wentworth Avenue. They slammed on their brakes, but the two cars still managed to crash into the truck. A car turned in at the top end of the street and cruised slowly down as its driver looked for a parking spot. Broad fired at it, smashing a rear side-window; the driver slammed on his brakes, as if he were going to get out and start a fight with whoever had damaged his car. Then he saw Broad aiming his rifle at him again and he abruptly changed his mind. He stepped on the accelerator and he went down the slight hill and swung into a side-street in a tyre-screeching turn that almost put his car on its side.

People were hanging out of windows in the buildings opposite the Police Centre; someone, through a bullhorn, advised them to pull their heads in and the spectators suddenly disappeared. The Tactical Response men were working their way up the line of parked cars on the opposite side of the street from Malone's Commodore. Broad would be totally exposed to their fire in another moment or two.

All at once he stood up, in full view of everyone, put the end of the rifle barrel in his mouth and pulled the trigger. Malone shut his eyes, not wanting to see the terrible sight, even at a distance; then he opened them and Broad was still standing there, looking frighteningly ridiculous, the gun barrel still in his mouth while he kept jerking at the trigger. Then he threw the gun away, screaming at it, walked out into the middle of the roadway, sat down and put his face in his hands and began to weep.

'The bugger's mad!' said Clements.

Malone stood up; he felt he had been crouched down for hours. He looked down at poor, dead Chilla Dural; then he took out his handkerchief and spread it over the bloody face. He wondered who, if anyone, would grieve for the ex-con and made up his mind that he would be there when Dural was buried.

Then he walked up the street, his legs unsteady, towards

where the Tactical Response men were hauling Michael Broad to his feet.

'Where did you get the gun?' he said.

But Michael Broad was past giving a sane answer to any question.

FOURTEEN

1

'He came here looking for me,' said Venetia. 'But my mother and I had gone out to Mulawa early, to the prison. We had to see Justine before she heard the news about her father. We expected the worst, that something terrible had happened to him and she would hear it on the radio before we'd even told her that he was alive.'

'How did Broad get into the house?' said Malone.

'Why wouldn't the security guard let him in? Or Mrs Leyden? They didn't know he'd been arrested and charged. There was a news flash on the radio after he'd been charged at the magistrate's court, but neither the guard nor Mrs Leyden heard it. You kept it out of the news last night that you'd charged him.'

'We had to,' said Malone. 'We wanted all the evidence in first. We've got it all now, the Crown Prosecutor has it. That's how your daughter was freed this afternoon. What did he do when he got in here?'

'He smashed the gun cabinet, as you saw. Mrs Leyden had left him alone, to go and get him some coffee. When she came back he'd gone with the gun – was it a Winchester? Something like that – and he'd taken ammunition from the bottom drawer.'

They were in the big drawing-room: Malone, Clements, Venetia and Alice Magee. It was early evening and the lights were on; beyond the darkened sun-room and the black garden there were moving lights on the harbour. Malone could not remember having lived a longer day, yet his watch told him it was only 6.30. The day had better be finished or he was going to give up.

'Did you know there was still all that ammunition in that drawer?'

'Inspector, we never opened it,' said Alice, taking over. Venetia was pale and drawn, looking her age and even beyond it; her day, Malone guessed, had been even longer than his own. 'Why would we? The security guards checked it once a month, but we left it there. The drawer is sealed tight, Walter had it made that way . . . Michael knew it was there, he arranged all the insurance. I don't think he came here *looking* for a gun, but when he saw the cabinet with all the guns in it . . .' She looked at Venetia almost accusingly. 'We should have got rid of it, all the guns, everything, years ago. Then maybe none of this would have happened.'

Malone said gently, 'You would have had to have got rid of it before Sir Walter took the Colt from it. It's no use talking about ifs and maybes . . .'

Then Walter and Justine came into the room. They were holding hands, and Malone noticed the constraint that still gripped each of them. They were not yet father and daughter, not as Malone and Claire or Maureen were. That might take months, but Walter Springfellow had left it too late.

'I want to thank you, Inspector. And you, too, Sergeant.' Justine took her hand out of her father's and put it out to Malone and then to Clements. 'I hated you both for a while, you were so determined to . . . But you've both been fair. You could have stopped looking for the real murderer.'

Malone didn't look at Clements, but he could feel the other's discomfort. 'There were certain things that nagged at us. We just followed them up. That's all police work is – following up things.'

'Well, I'm grateful, anyway. So is my – my father.'

'Yes,' said Walter. 'We're grateful for certain other things, too.' He looked at Clements. 'Inspector Malone has explained the situation to you, Sergeant?'

'In the car coming over here,' said Clements. 'Scobie and I have no secrets from each other. Otherwise we couldn't work together.'

Get the knife out of my ribs, Russ.

'The Commissioner has had a word with me, too,' said Clements. 'If ever I open my mouth, I'm to be shot.'

Walter shut his eyes for a moment and Malone shook his mind, if not his head. 'You shouldn't have put it that way, Sergeant. Enough people have been shot. Poor Chilla Dural –'

'I'm sorry, sir.' Clements bit his lip, looked as if he also wanted to bite his tongue.

Venetia said, 'Will Justine or I have to give evidence against Michael Broad?'

'I'm afraid so,' Malone told her. 'We'll probably never know why he shot your sister-in-law – she must have had something on him, something to do with the takeover. Losing everything in the Crash could have tipped him over the edge – maybe there was a history of family madness or instability, but I don't know if the Czechs will ever give us any help on that. They'll just put it down as another symptom of capitalist greed.' He saw the sudden amused look on Venetia's face and he realized that, like Clements, he had just put his foot in his mouth.

'Well, Inspector, it might just be the truth.'

She doesn't believe that, he thought. He went on, 'He won't be allowed to plead, not the way he is at present. The trial won't be for another six months at least. By then . . .'

'We leave on Monday,' said Venetia. 'Justine and I will be going in our company plane, but my husband –' She hadn't hesitated, as Justine had in claiming her father, '– he'll be going by Lufthansa. We don't want our own crew suspecting who he might be.'

'You'll have to tell us where you'll be,' said Malone. 'Just in case.'

'We've already told that to ASIO and Commissioner Leeds,' said Walter. 'We're going to a village in the Black

380

Forest in Germany. I lived there years ago, when I first – disappeared. But nobody will remember me. At least not enough to be suspicious of me. I'll just be Mr Skelly, who's come back for a long holiday with his wife and daughter.' With him, too, there was no hesitation in the claim.

A short holiday, thought Malone; and saw the look of pain in the faces of the three women. 'Well, if we need you, Lady Springfellow, though I don't think we shall –'

'I'll be here,' said Alice Magee. 'Keeping an eye on things.' And you knew she would be, too. 'Getting rid of a few things, too. I'm going to sell your gun collection, Walter.'

'Whatever you say, Alice.' Walter smiled: he was at peace with everyone, with whatever they wanted to do.

'If we have to go to your company, Lady Springfellow, I mean to look at Broad's papers –'

'Edwin is coming out of retirement,' said Venetia. 'He's going to run everything till – till I come back. He'll be co-operative.'

There was nothing more to say. Malone and Clements shook hands all round, then went out to the front door. Venetia followed them. Malone had noticed that this evening she was not wearing her trademark colours; the pink and grey had given way to a pale blue. She noticed his look.

'It used to be Walter's favourite colour. I've had it for years – it's a little tight –'

He wondered how many other women kept a garment in a closet as a memento (or a reminder of guilt?) of a missing husband. He also wondered how many women could fit into a dress they had last worn twenty-two years ago. It would be something to discuss with Lisa. John Leeds and Guy Fortague had decided the list of those with the need to know about Walter Springfellow; Malone had added Lisa's name to the list, though the Commissioner and the ASIO chief would never need to know that. There were certain debts that had to be paid to a policeman's wife.

'We'll never be able to repay you,' said Venetia.

There was nothing to say to that. Truly charitable men don't add up what debts are owed to them; and Malone and Clements, each in his own way, were charitable men. Clements smiled and said, 'Just let me know when the next stock market boom is going to start.'

'You're an investor?'

'Through and through,' said Malone. 'He's a little long in the tooth, a late starter, but he wants to be a rich yuppie.'

2

Three months later, almost to a day, Commissioner Leeds rang Malone at Homicide. 'Walter Springfellow died yesterday. Venetia and Justine are going to bury him in Germany, then they'll be coming home.'

'So it's all over.'

There was silence at the other end of the line, then Leeds said, 'Yes, I suppose as much as anything is ever over. Some day someone will discover the secret of it all. I just hope we are all gone by then.'

A couple of days later Jack Montgomery rang from the *Herald*. 'Scobie, you never got back to me about that Russian, Uritzsky, and the disappearance of Walter Springfellow.'

He's heard something, Malone thought; but all he said was, 'Nothing ever came of it, Jack.'

'We-e-ell –' The slow drawl seemed stretched out even more than usual. 'If it ever does, you owe me, Scobie.'

'You'll be the first to know, Jack.'

But not from me. He was working on another homicide. The Springfellow files, both sets of them, had been taken away. Russ Clements had a new murder box and the running sheets had a new name at the top, a new reference number. Life, and death, goes on.